HEIR LINE FRACTURE

Marc freden

heir line fracture

UNCOVERING THE DARK SIDE OF THE BRIGHT LIGHTS

SUNSTONE PRESS

SANTA FE

© 2015 by Marc Freden
All Rights Reserved.

No part of this book may be reproduced in any form or by any electronic or
mechanical means including information storage and retrieval systems
without permission in writing from the publisher, except by a reviewer
who may quote brief passages in a review.

Sunstone books may be purchased for educational, business, or sales promotional use.
For information please write: Special Markets Department, Sunstone Press,
P.O. Box 2321, Santa Fe, New Mexico 87504-2321.
Cover design by James Messer
Book design › Vicki Ahl
Body typeface › Cambria
Printed on acid-free paper
∞
eBook 978-1-61139-391-0

Library of Congress Cataloging-in-Publication Data

Freden, Marc, 1962-
Heir line fracture : uncovering more from the dark side of the bright lights :
novel / by Marc Freden.
    pages ; cm
ISBN 978-1-63293-075-0 (softcover : alk. paper)
I. Title.
PS3606.R42958H45 2015
813'.6--dc23

                    2015022938

WWW.SUNSTONEPRESS.COM
SUNSTONE PRESS / POST OFFICE BOX 2321 / SANTA FE, NM 87504-2321 /USA
(505) 988-4418 / ORDERS ONLY (800) 243-5644 / FAX (505) 988-1025

Dedication

I can't thank the following people enough. . .but here is at the very least
an acknowledgment of their support:

Chris Harris and Bradyn Podhajsky for their keen eyes.
James Messer for his clever artistry.
Toula Mavridou Messer and Barbara de Georgiou for their constant support.

The glow off the computer screen cast just enough light to illuminate the chiseled facial features of the man simply known as "G"—a tall, forty something, handsome but undistinguished every man. He lives, he breathes, but in all other public aspects of his life he is nothing more than a walking shadow. He would be best described as illusive, if one were prone to describe him at all. But you wouldn't bother; you wouldn't even notice him. No friends, no family, no girlfriend—or boyfriend for that matter. With no apparent social life, he is a loner by design rather than affliction, affectation or impairment. He spends his time routinely and judiciously—working out, following the twenty-four hour news cycle or staring at the computer screen—all of which is done inside the dank loft he calls home.

There is no sound except the ticking of an old-fashioned wall clock, the precision of which has gone unchallenged as if it were Big Ben itself. The moon is full and casts an eerie glow from the oversized windows that line the far wall and from these you can see the lights of the O2 Center where some concert or other is in mid-performance. But he doesn't notice the spectacle of color or even the amazing view. He never notices.

The loft is in a building along the Thames in the industrial waterfront enclave of Wapping. Bought for pennies two decades ago. Two decades ago, the cry would have been, "Wapping? Why on earth would anyone want to live out in Wapping?" Back then it was nothing but factories with little infrastructure such as public transportation, grocery stores—or, God forbid—a Starbucks. There was the occasional pub—so civilization had survived—but that was it. But all that was before the gentrification of the East End, with its view of the river, the Docklands and Greenwich beyond.

This loft, too, is in a requisite converted warehouse with its wood plank floors, high beamed ceilings and exposed brick walls that is now what is considered 'industrial chic' and worth a fortune on the open market. But it is not for sale. Some would say, in its present state, it is barely livable.

Unlike the unit two doors down which was featured in not one but two separate design magazines, this loft is what would be called a fixer-upper, a blank canvas for any 'stylista' with a vision. The fifteen hundred square foot single room with separate bath consists of what could pass for a kitchenette—a small oven and stove top, squat refrigerator, free standing sink and a couple of above the counter cabinets, an industrial stainless steel workbench which doubles as a dining table/catch all, a mattress on the floor, a clothes rack, a battered sofa, one chair, a set of weights, a bench press and a selection of mismatched bookshelves. The only luxuries are a large desk with a state of the art computer system and a large flat screen television on the wall. If it weren't for the chic address, his unit could easily pass for a Bohemian squat. This blank slate is an interior designer's wet dream for sure.

A slam of a door down the hall startles him from an intense stare into the vast recesses of the internet. His honed cat-like reflexes conditioned him to reach for his favorite gun—the Glock 19—conveniently sitting next to the keyboard on the desk and point it around the dimly lit room encircling him. He stands and glides to the front door, peers through the fisheye peephole and sees the coast is clear. He lowers the gun but not his senses.

When the phone rings he is not surprised. He has been waiting for a call. "Yeah?" His voice is glottal and deep. "Got it."

With that he hangs up the call, turns off the computer, opens the door, checks the hallway and with stealthily quiet he makes his way down the hall and out into the night.

Λ Λ Λ

The number of deaths by firearms in Great Britain was significantly less than one hundred, at least in 2011. In the United States the number of gun deaths came precariously close to ten thousand. It is not uncommon to find a gun, or guns for that matter, in the average American household. The same can't be said for a British home. So it is surprising to see not just one, but rather an array of firearms hidden behind a bookcase inside a loft flat in Wapping, East London.

Among the stash are a couple of high powered rifles, a Bond-style Walther PPK, and the American favorite concealed carry German import, the fifteen round Glock 19, all of which are readily available at gun shows in the United States and on the internet but not in Great Britain. So how did they end up in Wapping owned by the man who only goes by the name "G"?

1

"Your tea, m'Lord," announced the valet as he walked into the sitting area where he would inevitably find Fredrick Charles Arthur Henry—a.k.a. Freddy—Duke of Clarence just about everyday at 4:30.

Tea, for the record, is never just tea. Served on the solid sterling silver tray, with the Limoges service—a 'family' heirloom dating back to Louis XVI—consisting of an ornate teapot, cup, saucer, milk and sugar containers; is a selection of traditional cucumber finger sandwiches and scones, jam not jelly and Devon clotted cream. Along with the traditional spread, the tray also held a decanted bottle of vodka, one of gin, a crystal martini glass and double old fashion tumbler along with a requisite seltzer bottle and tonic. Choices.

"Thank you Ben," Freddy said as the small-framed valet delicately lowered the heavy spread of china and crystal to the coffee table in front of the fireplace.

"Will that be all, m'Lord?"

"Oh no," Freddy said with a smirk. "I think I can find something for you to do."

Ben, just twenty two and from a small village just outside of the city of Plymouth in Southern England, has only been with the Palace staff and Freddy in particular for less than a year. It was a particularly high honor for his working class family to see Ben in his liveried uniform walk through the gates at St. James's Palace and start his new life in service.

"You look grand my son, simply grand," was all his teary-eyed mother Thelma could utter as she brushed the last of the imagined lint off Ben's lapels.

His father, in turn, held fast with his British stiff upper lip comportment. "You've done us proud."

Ben wasn't the type of child you would think would take to public life. This would be as lofty as it got. He was quiet as a child, an only child at that. He was lanky, not great at sports, socially awkward and found himself on the wrong end of a fist more times than not as a favorite of the local bully. His parents never believed he would aspire past a farmer, or a stock boy in a shop or, perhaps, maybe, a profession as high as mid-level factory worker. He was just that shy growing up. And they never pushed him to be more than he would ever be comfortable in wanting to be. It would never have occurred to either mother or father that he would end up in London and at the Palace no less—even if the job was that of valet rather than something more prestigious like secretary. Nonetheless, they could not be more proud. He was, in fact, growing into the world around him.

Both parents insisted in coming up on the train to see their son walk his first steps through the gate and into service. Dressed in her Sunday best dress and hat, dad in his only suit, they'd packed sandwiches for the journey but were too nervous to eat. London is a place to both fear and marvel, they thought and were afraid it would overwhelm their sheltered boy. But Ben had taken to the city quickly and confidently—not that a life in service provides much time to take advantage of what the city has to offer. His time would not be his own and both parents were comfortable in knowing that structure would protect their newly minted man.

"Sir?" Ben stood erect ready to pour, serve or shake depending on the needs of the publically petulant and always entitled Duke.

For his part, Freddy likes to keep Ben around as often and as long as possible but in spurts short enough to keep the other staff from wondering about their goings-on. They have, in fact, been an 'item' for almost as long as Ben has been in service. Freddy has a thing for the younger Aryan types with boyish faces and smooth bodies—'twinks' as they would be called in gay common-speak. Although it is not as if Freddy can cruise the saunas of London's gay underbelly—or even the bar scene as it is. So when Ben was hired, Freddy redefined what it meant to be in service and in Ben, he found a willing if slightly naïve participant. Just out of his own closet, Ben is old enough to fuck but not mature enough to demand better.

Freddy can get a hard-on just looking at Ben in his uniform. On many occasions, this not being one of them, Freddy has instructed Ben to walk in to his apartment with his dick out of his pants and then proceeds to ignore the phallic friend as Ben goes along with his duties. Its just part of the erotic power play Freddy lauds over Ben. Ben is just too new to the world around him and not worldly or sophisticated enough to know this is highly inappropriate behavior.

The one thing Ben has caught on to is that the size of his cock is bigger than most. It is six and half inches flaccid and grows to an enviable twelve inches hard. Freddy's cock, while handsome and profound, doesn't fully compare. That's Ben's only power over his Lord and master—a big cock. But he has yet to figure out there is magic in that wand. He will. As like most Brits, Ben is uncut and Freddy is obsessed with his foreskin as he, like most British Royals, is circumcised. And Freddy finds any excuse to play with the valet's flap.

"Sir?" Ben asks again.

"I think no tea, but a strong G and T," Freddy finally responds.

"Certainly Sir."

"Oh for heaven's sake. When we are alone, you don't have to be so formal. Freddy will do."

While Ben turned towards the tray and bends over slightly to mix the Hendricks, Freddy's gin of choice, and tonic, Freddy walks up from behind and begins to rub Ben's slightly protruding ass. He doesn't flinch as Freddy's hand moves its way through Ben's legs and cups his package.

"Are you wearing anything under your uniform?" Freddy asked, feeling the freedom of movement with Ben's balls and cock.

Ben had learned from the cumbersome way of releasing his cock from his pants on demand, it was easier to wear nothing underneath and be able to unfurl with little restraint. "No...Freddy." He handed his Lordship his drink.

"Will you join me?"

"That would not be prudent, to have the smell of alcohol on one's breath below stairs."

"Have a martini. You know you like your vodka."

"Not during duties, sir," Ben obediently answers back.

"I have a breath mint somewhere around here for when you leave. Besides I make the rules around here."

Unlike Ben, Freddy was a precocious child. Like Ben, he too is an only child. And both grew up rather humbly. His single mother understood that Freddy might have been born into greatness, even though that was never recognized, but that he had to be ready for it. Her favorite expression was always, "Ready Freddy?" And he was ready for anything. But being ready for the truth doesn't always mean the truth was ready for him.

Freddy became the Duke of Clarence—a long since unused and virtually extinct title—by decree and not birth. Born of a single common mother, Anna, during a much speculated, then quietly verified, affair with an unnamed but understood Royal father, Freddy has long believed he is the rightful heir to the throne.

"Forget about it Freddy," his mother would say, never completely denying the affair but recognizing the consequences of the circumstances as never being favorable to either her or Freddy.

Freddy, for his part, couldn't or wouldn't ignore the historic significance of a recognized birthright and when he got old enough to be loud enough about his suspicions, he threatened to go public. As a result, Anna signed the proper papers to never speak publically and received a respectable cash payout. To shut Freddy up, he was granted a dusted off title, peerage, a financial stipend and a handout grace and favor apartment in St. James's Palace.

He may have been shut up but has hardly remained silent. In recent years he has made a name for himself as "Fast Freddy"—one of those pesky nobles who fall out of private clubs and on to the pages of the tabloids running with an obnoxious crowd of entitled rich public school kids and Sloane Ranger 'IT' girls.

As far as what he calls home, the "rooms" as Freddy refers to his spacious gilded cage of a royal apartment, sit in the former stables section of the Palace. The apartment consists of a formal reception room, a separate sitting room, a dining room, a small office, two bedrooms with en suite baths, a separate powder room and, of course, the kitchen. Everything about the "rooms" has a formality—every bit a Palace enclave with its ornate moldings and antique furnishings, portraiture and accouterment. It is not Freddy's taste, per se, but he does fit comfortably into the grandeur of it all. Although he loves the privilege, Freddy very rarely uses the formal reception room, rather choosing the more comfortable sitting room for his day-to-day living. To that end, he rarely has guests, preferring to meet 'off campus'—as he puts it—at some en vogue restaurant or hip club. As far as Ben is concerned, he could never be seen out socially with one of 'the staff' nor would he ever venture to Ben's room—a literal singular room in the staff quarters. So unless Freddy is feeling exceedingly high and mighty—a time during which he likes to fuck Ben in the middle of the reception room as if to say, "fuck you" to the royal establishment—the sitting room has become their spot.

Ben has never been comfortable with pouring himself a cocktail in the presence of Freddy and Freddy finds that endearing. So Freddy takes it upon himself to pour a healthy amount of vodka into the Waterford martini glass, squeezes a lemon meant for tea over the glass and hands it to Ben.

"Thank you, sir."

"You mean..."

"Freddy."

Freddy raised his glass and Ben followed suit. The clink of fine crystal makes a sound so pure and tonal, like no other. Freddy leaned in and gave Ben the most delicate of kisses.

"Thank you, sir."

Freddy rolled his eyes as Ben blushed, put down his drink and walked over to the antique writing table in the corner in front of a wall of books. "I have something for you."

"Oh?" With that, Ben, too, put down his drink.

Pulling a burgundy colored box from the center drawer of the table, he walks over and hands the box to Ben.

"Sir...Freddy...what is this for?"

"Oh you will see."

Even Ben could tell from the distinctive box that whatever is inside comes from the prestigious jeweler Asprey. Ben immediately hands the box back to Freddy. "I couldn't possibly..."

"You'd better," Freddy clarified. "It was made especially for you." Ben started to undo the ribbon and open the box. "I have a friend who is one of the craftsmen at Asprey and I asked him to indulge me in this little creation."

Inside, sitting upright, larger than a wedding band and smaller than a wrist bangle is a solid gold ring, three inches in diameter, with a center channel setting of baguette diamonds around the circumference. Ben looked slightly confused.

"It is a cock ring," Freddy blurted out excitedly. "I do hope it fits."

"Freddy?" Ben gasped with shock and bemusement.

"I simply gathered some bits and bobs from family pieces given to my mother from *him* over the years and had them melted down."

"You shouldn't have," Ben mumbled, embarrassed by the gesture.

"So that now you can say you have your own royal jewels or, as I like to put it: family jewels for your family jewels." Freddy chuckled, "I do love the common sensibility of a pun."

"Again, Freddy, I can't possibly."

"You can and you will. It is not like I can return the damn thing. Besides I simply adore toys. Let's play. Put it on." It is true, Freddy has quite the collection of fetish and erotic playthings—none of which has he tried to use with Ben...yet.

Ben took a large swig of his cocktail, grimaced as he swallowed and then reached for his belt buckle. He dropped his pants and, as foretold, is wearing nothing underneath. Again, the sight of Ben's impressive cock took Freddy aback. Ben fumbled with the ring, sliding it over his shaft and then pulling his scrotum through, pulling one testicle through the ring after the other. It fit perfectly and is just tight enough to do the job it is meant for.

"Take it all off, so I can so you in your new regal splendor," Freddy instructed, unzipping his own fly and pulling out his own semi-erection.

Somewhat embarrassed, Ben turned his back on Freddy, removed his jacket, tie and unbuttoned his shirt. Again, Freddy began to slide his hands all over Ben's naked smooth ass. Ben is naturally smooth—no hair on his chest, a light dusting on his legs and a cropped blond tuft which is almost unnoticeable in the pubic area. Ben turned to face Freddy who stood back to take in his creation and the model wearing it. "I love it! Do you love it? How does it feel?"

"It feels heavy," Ben said, not sure how it should feel as he's never worn one.

"Now, let's see if it does the trick," Freddy began.

"What is it supposed to do?" asked Ben.

"Prolong an erection and intensify an orgasm," Freddy said not even realizing the ludicrous nature of what he was saying. No twenty two year old has trouble keeping it up nor having intense orgasms. It is just a toy and toys are fun.

They both sipped their drinks while Freddy intermittently nuzzled Ben's neck and flicked his tongue into Ben's open mouth. Freddy's free hand slid down Ben's tight torso and headed to his cock. Ben's cock twitched with anticipation. Freddy followed his hand with his tongue, stopping to suck and tease Ben's nipples, which grew hard as Freddy worked on them. His hand cupped Ben's balls as Freddy stood and gave Ben a hard lustful kiss. Ben moaned his pleasure.

Freddy took his drink, placed Ben's hardening cock into it and swirled it around.

"I much prefer a swizzle prick to a swizzle stick," Freddy punned again and chuckled with self-satisfaction.

The cold sensation caused Ben to flinch but Freddy held firm. He knelt down in front of Ben's cock, admired the cock ring as it glistened against his soft skin and blond hairs and placed the dripping foreskin, now marinated in gin, into his mouth and he slid his tongue under the foreskin and against the head. His tongue circled the head and Freddy got a whiff of a combination of lavender soap and gin from Ben's clean but liquored cock. Freddy stood as Ben's cock grew to its enormity.

As Freddy slipped out of his own clothes, his own cock growing, he could see the cock ring's effect on Ben's cock. The ever so perfect squeeze of the ring against the swelling cock forced the blood to surge and stay, making the veins and head swell as if straining to explode. This blood rush only heightened the sensitivity of Ben's engorged cock. As Freddy sucked, Ben moaned—feeling what he is supposed to feel. Not wanting to cum from over stimulation, Ben pulled out of Freddy's mouth, dropped to his knees and gave as good as he's gotten.

"That's right. Kneel before your Lord."

As he stood there, Freddy moaned between sips of his own drink. There is nothing like a cocktail when you are enjoying cock and tail. Freddy arched back just slightly to watch Ben bob along the shaft of his cock. He took a swig from his glass and let the fluid dribble out of his mouth, over his chin, down his arched body and to his spit-lubricated cock. Ben looked up when he tasted the gin and sucked harder and faster to lap up the spit and alcohol mixture.

Freddy inched his way back to the chintz-covered sofa next to the coffee table and reclined. Ben moved along accordingly and, once Freddy was situated, found himself with his own cock dangling above Freddy's face. He bent his knee and lowered himself on to Freddy's waiting face.

Freddy licked Ben's swollen balls one at a time and then, again one at a time, sucked each into his mouth and massaged them with his tongue while he reached up and stroked Ben's cock. He couldn't believe how hard it was—thanks to his golden gift. Ben sat upward and pulled his balls from Freddy's mouth. Freddy instinctually slid his tongue back up the crack of Ben's ass and began to lick. Ben's ass, a virgin before Freddy, is very tight and even more sensitive. Ben loves Freddy's long tongue darting in and out, softening and relaxing his hole. Alternatively, Freddy loves Ben's hairless button of an asshole and could lap on it for hours on end. But, Freddy had other things in mind.

"I want your scepter in me this time," Freddy said, between licks, his voice muffled in Ben's ass cheeks. "Your cock has never felt so hard. I want to know if I will feel this incredible hardness in me. Maybe I, too, can benefit from that cock ring." Ben would have no problem fulfilling his Lord's request.

Being unusually aggressive, Ben rolled Freddy over doggy style, scooped up a dollop of butter from next to the scones on the tea tray and smeared it in and around Freddy's puckered hole. Freddy's ass isn't as smooth as Ben's is and has just a dusting of fuzz around the crack. Quietly, Ben finds it a turn on. Ben smeared the butter over the hair and, as a result, plastered it on each side of his ass crack. Ben slid one, then a second, finger into Freddy's eager hole. Freddy moaned and spread his knees to accommodate what would be coming next.

With one thrust, Ben pushed his cock into Freddy's ass but, luckily for Freddy, it missed the target and slid up the length of his crack.

"Gently, you're bigger than ever," Freddy pleaded and Ben reached for more butter to grease his wanting pole.

Again with a slower but singular thrust, Ben forced the head of his cock into Freddy's ass and paused. Freddy buried his scream into a sofa pillow. After a moment or so Ben pushed on and in. Who is the bully now? And without letting Freddy relax began thrusting. Freddy twisted and bucked with pain and pleasure but let Ben continue. As he clenched his muscles around the thick stick, Freddy could feel the veins rubbing his sensitive inner chamber and the head pushing deeper and deeper. Pure ecstasy.

It didn't take long for Ben to explode, shooting his load deep into Freddy.

That wasn't the plan but neither participant was willing to stop the action to be careful. Ben pushed harder and harder, draining that engorged dick. He had never felt an orgasm as explosive as this.

Within moments, Freddy pulled away, flipped over and started stroking his own dick, which, too, was ready to explode. He pushed Ben's face down into his crotch and Ben began to dutifully suck. Ben gagged as Freddy pushed his head down lower and lower on to Freddy's shaft but despite the gagging, Freddy had reached the point of no return. He pumped his load deep into Ben's mouth.

Ben sucked several strokes beyond the draining of Freddy's cock and without saying a word, climbed up and kissed Freddy deep and hard, shifting Freddy's slimy load from his own mouth to the Duke's. Freddy took it and swallowed and, then reaching for his cocktail, took a big gulp.

"I suppose that's what one would call a Royal flush," Freddy joked as Ben collapsed on him in exhaustion.

After several moments, Ben pulled himself to his feet and too reached for his drink. Standing naked in front of Freddy, Ben blushed his usual post-coital blush and Freddy pointed to the diamond studded ornamentation encircling Ben's shaft. "I never want to see you out of uniform again." Freddy winked and leaned over to lick the last droplet of wet from the end of Ben's foreskin. "Now, don't you have duties to attend to young man?" Freddy can never end one of their 'sessions' without a subtle—and often not too subtle—reminder that it is always classism over romanticism. 'For Queen and country' is Freddy's motto. And when it comes to Queens, there is none more important than Freddy.

2

ithin the months between being unfairly let go from his reporter job on the hit syndicated America entertainment news series *Drop Zone* and being picked up and featured as the entertainment anchor for the British morning news magazine program *Rise 'N Shine,* Mica Daly has become quite an international celebrity. Although for a while it was safe to say that Mica was more infamous than famous. His firing from *Drop Zone* was the result of his well-speculated affair with Hollywood superstar Chad Martin, an affair that was the stuff of tabloid headlines, salacious pictures and plenty of gossip. Truth be told, he was having that affair.

Chad and he met at one of Roger Keenan's infamous Hollywood parties where the young meet the established and anything goes. Of course, these are dinner parties. So there is plenty to eat, drink and discuss along with the clear debauchery going on around a guest list that always ranges from A-listers to wannabes. Nevertheless, Chad, the wannabe, and Mica, the syndicated television reporter, hit it off. Chad was a nobody at the time who had very little work to his credit except a movie that had been mercifully shelved. The only thing it had going for it was Chad's nude scenes. But at the time, who the hell was Chad Martin? Then came *Divas,* the sleeper hit television series that made Chad a star. When the previously shelved movie was released and revealed Chad in all his splendor—naked and well hung—he became an international sensation. Mica was charmed by Chad's success. He was sleeping with the very man everyone wanted or wanted to be.

Everything would have been fine, their tawdry secret safe, except for those damned pictures. Chad by the pool naked with another man next to him. The tabloids demanded names. Mica was given the assignment by his show, *Drop Zone,* to out the man fast becoming the biggest male star in the world. To his credit, Mica never confirmed or denied the affair. Instead, he chose not to discuss it rather than ruin his relationship and Chad's skyrocketing career. But the truth always bubbles to the surface.

When Chad Martin married Aussie actress Ashley Beckwith—certainly more strategy than storybook—in what was called the wedding of the decade, which elevated them to 'IT' couple status, Mica's affair seemed the stuff of lies and innuendo. It was not. Mica could have spoken out in his own defense but Chad's penchant for suing for defamation to the tune of one hundred million dollars if anyone even questioned Chad's sexuality was a strong deterrent. But, moreover, Mica simply believed in taking the high road. Nevertheless, there was a high cost to the high road. By not speaking up, when the tabloids were blowing up, Mica found himself fired from *Drop Zone*. In fact it was more than not speaking up. By not outing himself as the other man in Chad's life—which would have outed one of the biggest stars in Hollywood—Mica was accused of lying by omission.

The upside in this dark period of his career was that Mica was seen as a curiosity, a man who knew more than he was willing to say and therefore, a true Hollywood insider. And thanks to the aggressive marketing of Mica's agent, Anthony Wright—who, ironically discovered Chad Martin sitting on a West Hollywood barstool when Anthony was a young upstart agent working for former child star turned C-list agent, Albert Switzer—Mica caught the attention of the executive producer at *Rise 'N Shine,* Stuart Brewster. It was Brewster who set up a guest appearance interview on the show during the height of the Chad Martin scandal with his bubbly, Scottish, everywoman, anchor Corrine McGraw. They got on famously—his wink and a nod innuendo and ability to say nothing while making the audience feel completely in the know, combined with Corrine's star-struck fanaticism for all things Hollywood, was the stuff of television magic.

All that was months ago, and these days Mica is a regular fixture on British morning television, reporting regularly from Hollywood on the comings and goings of the rich and famous. And according to the ratings reports, the audiences are eating it up. As such it was time for Mica to spend some time on the sofa, in the studio, live in London.

"I can't believe you're here," Corrine squeals from her seat in the makeup room as Mica walks in.

"I must say it is a little surreal to be here and meeting everyone face to face. I don't have the advantage of seeing any of you people when I look down the lens in the studio in Los Angeles. So I feel you all know who I am and what I look like and I, in turn, only know you as faceless voices in my ear."

"I hadn't thought of that," Corrine says to Annie, the makeup gal, who is busily powdering her down. Corrine has the ability to dismiss anything that puzzles her. That is part of her charm. "Well welcome."

It had been a strange forty-eight hours for Mica—a whirlwind for sure. He had arrived two days before on Saturday, allowing for jet lag, before his Monday debut on the sofa. Besides a car and driver to meet him at Heathrow Airport, he has had no contact with anyone from the show—not a gift basket in the hotel room or even a note to say: welcome. He was simply expected to turn up on Monday morning at the studio complex south of the Thames—a place he had never been before—and start his workweek.

He had spent his two days acclimating to London, walking the streets and getting his bearings. Come Monday morning, this morning, he climbed in to an early taxi, in which the driver recognized him as the whacky American guy on *Rise 'N Shine,* and drove him past Parliament, over the bridge, around Waterloo station and to the network studios. Ironically, the cabbie knew Mica, even if he couldn't remember Mica's name. But the security lady at the front desk of the studio had no idea who Mica is and the name Mica Daly simply drew a blank stare. No one had left notification that Mica would be coming.

"You need an I.D. to get in or a name for us to call," the pudgy uniformed woman said from behind the oversized reception desk. Mica found it funny and frustrating that there are televisions on all over the reception area. Therefore, she surely must have seen his face sometime over the past few months and yet had no idea who he is. Moreover, he has no idea who to call upstairs to tell them that he is here. This went on for several minutes and Mica began to believe he was going to miss his live slot on the show if someone didn't let him in soon. "Could you be on the guest list? Guests of the show enter through the side door."

Mica gathered up his stuff and was just about to try his luck at the side entrance when a big gust of personality blew in the front door.

"Mica! Mica Daly!" a woman shouted from behind him just as Mica had run out of options. "Mica, I am Andrea Lyttle the news anchor on the show. I appear just before you do in the running order." Mica had heard her voice just before they introduce him, so he is aware who she is.

"So good to put a face to the name," Mica said, shaking her hand.

"What are you doing down here?"

"They won't let me up without an I.D. and, of course, I can't get an I.D. until I get upstairs."

Andrea rolled her eyes. "I will sign you in. Where are you supposed to go first?"

"Haven't a clue. Ironically, I am gathering communications are not a strong suit around here."

"Say no more. Come with me. We'll go straight to the studio." He followed her aggressive gait as she trotted forward through the glass doors and down the hallway. She is a woman on a mission.

Andrea Lyttle is an institution in her own right. She is older than Mica and the other on-air staff by a decade or so. And in that decade she's earned her stripes: first as an international correspondent, covering the world's war torn hotspots, and then as BBC anchorwoman for the nightly news. Along the way she has won a BAFTA award, been voted 'the most trusted woman on television' and been on the international 'best dressed' list more years than not. People all said it would be a step down in her career for Andrea to do morning television. But as Andrea put it, "I have reported from some of the world's shithole locations and no one thought that was hurting my career. I can read the news from anywhere, at any time of the day and it is still news." She doesn't bother to tell people about the two hundred thousand pound bump in salary she got when she 'stepped down'.

"We will have to get together while you're in town," she warbled. She is no stranger to a night out and is mentioned in the tabloid pages as a result.

Andrea pushed through two double doors on the studio floor, landing the both of them into a hallway that leads to the dressing rooms and the makeup room. "If you take this left," Andrea pointed out, "There is the green room, the control room beyond that and then the doors to the studio. I am going to have to love you and leave you as I have to check in with the news desk to see what has been happening over night." She gave him a peck on both cheeks and as she darted off she shouted back to Mica, "Great to have you here!"

Once ensconced in the makeup chair, Mica had a steady stream of welcomes and well wishes from various members of the staff—some surely more important than others and some simply production assistants. Their names are going in one ear and out the other but Mica is determined to make each feel important to his success. One rather perky young lady, seemingly straight out of college, brought him a coffee—instant, but coffee nonetheless—and he is determined to remember her as the godsend on day one.

"Mica Daly," a familiar voice bellowed from just beyond Mica's eye line. "It's about time we got your ass over here."

"I'd know that voice anywhere," Mica returned excitedly. "I literally can't get you out of my head." Show director Nate Griffin and Mica hugged like old friends. "I want to thank you for being so helpful and patient with me."

"Patient? It is nice to work with someone who is such a professional," Nate said. "So you got here alright? Did they put you up in somewhere decent?"

"The Coliseum on Piccadilly."

"Posh," Corrine said as she passed from her seat to the door. "I will see you on the set."

Mica smiled and turned back to Nate. "Should I not tell people where I am staying?"

"No," Nate shrugged. "Corrine has this reputation to be shocked by the price of everything as if she cuts coupons before she heads to the grocery store. She is one of the highest paid personalities on television. So don't let her frugality fool you. It's all her act to be one of the people. But, The Coliseum…good for you."

"I got a deal. A friend of mine in Los Angeles, Marilyn Lassiter, stays there when she is in town and arranged for the proprietress, if that is what you call her, Hillary Stewart, to give me a good rate. Hillary, as I have come to learn, is quite the society maven in her own right and is a hoot to have a drink with. You should come over and meet her while I am here."

"There will be plenty of time for that. What there isn't time for is chitchat. I have to get you on the sofa."

Mica follows Nate past the green room full of interviewees for various segments of the show. "That's Mica Daly," he hears them whisper. They pass the control room, which is a buzz of activity, through the doors and on to the set. Andrea had just finished the national news and the show is in a newsbreak for local affiliates.

"Is this him?" a heavy-set man said from the sofa.

"Euan this is Mica," Nate said by way of introduction as they raced back to the control room.

The stage manager interrupted Euan, "Five minutes back."

"Hello," Mica said and stretched out his hand to shake Euan's.

Euan ignored the hand. "How old are you?"

"I beg your pardon?"

"Don't mind him," Corrine harrumphed. "He just turned forty and thinks everyone's a career threat if they are younger then he is."

Euan Thatcher is just that insecure. He didn't enter his forties willingly. Slightly over weight and with the clock ticking, he knows television has become the domain of the young and pretty. A smart, attractive and unique flavor of the month like Mica Daly could easily take his place on the sofa at the whim of the management. As if that is going to happen, he thought. Euan's quick wit and surprising intelligence, has made him a beloved figure on British television—having come to *Rise 'N Shine* from a career as a game show host, first on the popular *Double Trouble* and then the afternoon favorite word quiz, *Letter Perfect.* But a game show background rather than a national news background, such as Andrea has, or even a local news background such as Corrine's, he feels is a handicap. All of which is an irrational notion but there it sits, in the back of his mind, gnawing at him. So he is quick to mask his insecurities with a bravado that borders on obnoxious. And that bravado isn't lost on Mica. But Mica is from Hollywood where he has faced plenty of bigger egos than that of Euan Thatcher. They would be fine together.

Before Euan could say a word, the stage manager sits Mica on the sofa, places a microphone on his lapel and feeds the wire down the back of his jacket and provides him with an earpiece in order to hear Nate in the booth. "One minute back."

"He's staying at The Coliseum," Corrine whispered to Euan, just to get him wound up. "Posh. Don't you think?"

Again, before Euan could react, Nate counted the three of them down from ten to one and they are live.

"Well isn't this a pleasure," Euan began. "Our own Mica Daly has made it off the red carpet, across the pond and on to the sofa."

"We couldn't be more happy to have you here," Corrine interjected.

"Well thank you both. It is so nice to be here with you and finally meet face to face," Mica began cordially.

"And how long are we going to have you here in the homeland?" Euan asked.

"Well...I intend to stay here, right here, on the sofa for as long as I can. I have gone from being infamous in Hollywood to an illegal immigrant on the sofa. How do you like that career trajectory?"

Even Euan forced a chuckle.

∧ ∧ ∧

"So I am assuming you are gay but I guess I should officially ask," Stuart Brewster said between the slurp of wine and the nod to the waiter that it would be fine and to begin pouring.

Mica is taken aback. He assumed his being gay is at the very least an open secret, if not having been stated openly. The Chad Martin incident initially put him on the air on *Rise 'N Shine*. So a formal declaration to the boss is hardly necessary—unless, of course, he is digging for something.

"You know, in the States you could be sued for simply asking that question," Mica shot back a little more brazenly than is probably appropriate for a first meeting with his new boss.

Stuart Brewster is the new executive producer and managing editor of *Rise 'N Shine*. He, like Mica, has been brought in to shake things up a bit. Mica's hiring, it turns out, was Stuart's idea. Never had a British news show had a foreign reporter under contract in British television history. Mica is officially a piece of television trivia. But Mica's place in history was almost not to be. After the first segment aired, nearly the entire staff was brought into a meeting to discuss what they had seen. Euan was the first to suggest the Hollywood guy might be *too* 'Hollywood!' "He is as camp as Christmas," was Euan's assessment—meaning too over the top, thus meaning too gay. More buzz and more debate only secured in Stuart's mind that love him or hate him, Mica Daly would get people talking.

"Fear not, you're being gay is an asset. You're camp and the audience loves it."

Mica isn't sure how to take that either. "I know there is a compliment in there somewhere." They both laugh and shake hands to new beginnings.

Lunch is at The Ivy, the chicest of restaurants to the industry power lunch crowd, located just behind the theater district, is quite the place to see and be seen. When Mica stepped out of the cab with Stuart, the paparazzi snapped away, making Stuart all the more confident in his new investment.

"Do they really know who I am or are they assuming I am somebody because I am here with you," Mica asked once inside the lobby.

"They didn't take my picture," Stuart pointed out. And Mica got it.

Reservations had been booked in the name of the show but once Stuart and Mica walked in, the maître d' greeted Mica by name. Now, that is impressive.

"Great to have you with us Mr. Daly," he says as he escorts them to the perfect center table.

"And for the record," Stuart said, "I don't get a table this good on my own." Mica duly noted. Stuart waved to a couple of executives and celebrities all unfamiliar to Mica and he suddenly, for the first time, felt like a fish out of water. "We'll have to do the circuit after lunch...show you off."

Mica simply nodded.

"Is Mica your real name?" Stuart quizzed.

"You're just full of blunt one liners," Mica shot back.

"It is the journalist in me," Stuart returned somewhat apologetically.

"For the record, Mica is short for Michael and Daly is my mother's maiden name. I made the change on a whim and it just sort of stuck."

"Well let me tell you Michael, last name unknown, your life is going to be a bit of a roller coaster from here on in," Stuart said, topping up Mica's wine. Lunch had been delicious—shepard's pie and bubble & squeak, two of the house specialties, for Mica and the salmon for Stuart. Their 'getting to know you' conversation was upbeat and courteous. Stuart is a radical thinker and clearly colors outside of the lines when it comes to his television creativity. For his part, Mica told Stuart about his background and how he had come to where he is today. Stuart hadn't pushed the Chad Martin affair and Mica didn't offer.

"A roller coaster?"

"Let's put it this way. I hope you aren't in a relationship or you don't have a dog at home. Because I would like to see you here more often, looking at our entertainment world and pop culture as well as back in Hollywood. If something big is happening here, I would like you to cover it."

"That sounds great. And for the record…no dog and no significant other," Mica said. "As most people know by now!"

"Great because it all begins tomorrow. There is a royal premiere in Leicester Square. Hope you brought a dinner jacket."

"A tuxedo? No, I didn't," Mica said.

"I will call our wardrobe people and they can get you set up. They will have something sent to your hotel."

"Thanks," Mica sighed.

"And remember we didn't hire you to report on the premiere. Any Brit or anyone on our staff could do that. We want you to take us to the premiere as only you can," Stuart said. "You are a unique personality and our audience is living vicariously through you. Remember that."

"Will do. But of course I am not going to readily recognize your local British stars," Mica cautioned.

"We'll send a producer who can help you with that. But there will be plenty of big names like your friend Chad Martin. I trust that is not going to be a problem."

"Not from me."

"We haven't talked about Chad," Stuart prodded, teasingly.

"And we aren't going to, are we?" Mica questioned and somehow stipulated.

"That's fine," Stuart smiled. "But off the record and over too many cocktails, I would love to have that conversation sometime."

"You are not alone."

Just then a bottle of Dom Perignon arrived at the table. The waiter indicated it was from the table across the room and handed a note to Mica, which read: Welcome to this side of the pond. We look forward to the competition. Your friends at the BBC.

"That was very nice," Mica acknowledged and politely waved. "Who is that?"

"Just like it says," Stuart spit through a clenched smile, "the competition. We'll send a bottle back when the ratings are in and can prove that we are winning."

The waiter uncorked the bottle with the most delicate of a pop and poured each a glass. Mica raised his to the mystery executive across the room. Stuart simply swallowed a big gulp.

"I never could understand why this shit is so expensive," Stuart said with a shrug. "Now, you must try the frozen berries. They serve them with a warm white chocolate sauce."

"Sounds great," Mica responded while still giving a cursory glance at the other selections on the dessert menu. Mica is feeling a little heady at the moment, thanks to the gift of the champagne on top of the previously imbibed wine.

"You should not get used to this. It's not everyday we eat at The Ivy and remember there is no such thing as a free lunch. You're going to work this off." Stuart can always bring people down to earth—it's one of his gifts that got him the job.

"Oh I know," Mica returned and they both raised their glasses to toast.

∧ ∧ ∧

"What do you think?" Euan asked behind his forced smile as he waited for the flash.

"About?" Corrine asked as soon as the flash went off.

"Our American import."

Euan, Corrine and Andrea had stayed late in the studio to take some promotional photos for the show. Euan never likes to do anything extracurricular which leads to him staying in the office longer than is absolutely necessary. But today, while Mica is being wined and dined by Stuart, Euan didn't mind the chance to take the temperature of his fellow compatriots.

"Euan, he has been with the show sometime now," Corrine dismissed sensing Euan's obvious insecurity and not wanting to get in the middle of anything brewing. "I think if he wasn't liked, we would all know it by now."

"I mean in person, not on the air," Euan pushed.

"I think he is charming," Corrine answered.

"I think he is a fucking breath of fresh air around here," Andrea barked as she pushed past Corrine and Euan to get in front of the camera. "There is a lot of the same old, same old around here and I think Mica Daly brings a certain uncertainty to what he might say or know. It keeps the audience, and the producers I might add, on their toes. I have already suggested that he come back to sit on the set as often as possible."

That is just what Euan didn't want to hear. Flash!

∧ ∧ ∧

Leicester Square has never looked better. Renovated as more of a park-like setting and more pedestrian friendly for the Olympics, it was and still remains the epicenter for London's top and most prestigious premieres. And for this night, the square had been done up like a mini Las Vegas strip for the opening of *Scratch—*

25

the psychological thriller set in the world of gambling starring Welsh sensation Sean Jones. It is promising to be all black tie and bawdiness—the glamour of a royal premiere set against glitz of Las Vegas.

A tuxedoed Mica and crew from *Rise 'N Shine* were situated at the front of the media line-up, a spot befitting the high profile position Mica holds in entertainment reportage—a position he has yet to wrap his head around as he actually lives in Los Angeles, nearly six thousand miles away from his fame. One after the other, publicists stepped forward to introduce themselves and then the P.R. representative from the Palace stepped forward to point out to the clearly uninitiated American that the top royals—meaning anyone with an HRH in front of their name—will not be walking the gauntlet of media and that it is déclassé to shout questions to them as they enter the theater. Of course this being a royal premiere they all promised an A-list star turnout Mica is used to—plenty of faces, plenty of names.

Mica signaled to the studio publicist and his crew that he was ready to tape his stand-up bridge—a piece to camera which, in the finished on-air segment, puts Mica at the scene of the premiere and bridges the part of the segment between the introductory interviews with his patented playful question of the night. Mica chose to stand on the red carpet situated close to the oversized craps table. He rolled the dice toward the camera and spoke, "When it comes to a movie in which the psychological tension centers around gambling, I couldn't help but to ask those on the red carpet: just what was the biggest gamble of your life?" With that, he wrapped the crew and all retreated back to the coveted first space on the carpet.

By the time they got back in to place, Michelle Bianco from Regis & Canning—the haute Los Angeles based public relations firm—stepped up to the *Rise 'N Shine* crew. Without looking up from her handful of notes, she barked, "And who is your reporter or talent?

"That would be me, Michelle," Mica said.

"Mica?" She was so thrown by seeing Mica Daly on the red carpet in London; she instinctually, but awkwardly, leaned in to give his familiar face a kiss on the cheek. He, in return, reluctantly gave her a peck back.

Michelle and Mica have had nothing short of a tumultuous professional relationship. When Mica was the respected correspondent known for putting 'entertainment' into 'entertainment reporting' for *Drop Zone*, Michelle couldn't have been friendlier to Mica. She became beholden to Mica when he introduced her to the upstart Chad Martin—now the highest paid star in Hollywood and her number one client.

But it all went terribly wrong, when the innuendo and gossip surrounding Chad Martin's sexuality revealed a much-exploited 'relationship' between Chad and Mica. Michelle felt betrayed, both professionally and personally, and sought a vendetta against Mica, leading to her metaphorically cocking a gun to the head of *Drop Zone* executive producer, Lydia Gray, with the ultimatum: fire Mica Daly or you will have no access to Chad Martin or any other Regis & Canning events or stars. Mica was out on his ass. Although it is a necessity to play nice at events such as this, the professional relationship between Mica and Michelle is, to say the least, frosty. "I wouldn't have expected to see you here in London," Mica said, breaking from their fake hug.

"Regis & Canning has opened a satellite office. There is so much work here for our clients."

"Obviously, you have Sean Jones walking the carpet tonight," Mica began rather professionally. "I trust you will let the show have a moment with him as he is the star of the film."

"Of course, Mica," she returned in that cool detached way she has when she if forced to do something she doesn't want to do. She would love to snub Mica but knew that *Rise 'N Shine* is too important a program to ignore, professionally, for her clients exposure. In fact, if memory serves her correctly, Sean Jones is booked to sit on the sofa this week.

"Besides Sean, is there anyone else we should pay attention to?" Mica questioned.

"Ashley Beckwith will be here," she mumbled.

"Along with Chad?"

Since their storybook, over the top, marriage and the provocative nude wedding photos taken by famed celebrity photographer Chuck Corman, Ashley Beckwith and Chad Martin have eclipsed Brangelina as the international 'IT' couple and a shot of them on a red carpet together has become what is known in the business as 'the money shot' at event coverage. Mica knew he had to play nicely with Michelle if he expected her to offer her prized clients up for a word with *Rise 'N Shine.* Moreover, this is his first assignment in London and he did not want to go back to the office without a sound bite from the most celebrated couple in entertainment. What kind of entertainment reporter would that make him?

"Yes, but Mica I am warning you she is the focus. She is working on a project here and Chad has just flown in to be by her side, not the other way around. I don't want any of the bullshit that happened back at the Beverly Hilton. You know what you eventually got for that moment. FIRED!"

Jeez that bitch Bianco never forgets anything and can she hold on to a grudge, Mica thought. Michelle was, of course, referring to a night many months ago when Mica, under pressure from his boss at *Drop Zone*, confronted Chad at a charity event and asked him about the infamous photos that appeared on the cover of a tabloid magazine showing a naked Chad Martin and an unrecognizable naked friend poolside—which began the rumors of Chad being closeted and gay. As it turned out, the 'friend' was Mica.

"No problem, Michelle," Mica said. "Perhaps we should talk about a set visit with Ashley."

"Let's see how tonight goes."

As it turned out, it went perfectly. Ashley couldn't have been sweeter to Mica and Chad not only shook Mica's hand but also pulled him close for one of those bro-hugs, which nearly brought a tear to Mica's eye. "Miss you," he whispered in Chad's ear but wasn't sure he heard him over the cacophony of the roaring crowd. Chad pulled back and waved to the adoring crowd. It still stuns Mica to see how the wannabe actor he met at his friend and marketing guru, Roger Keenan's house for what seems like a lifetime ago, grew into this international superstar. He missed being a part of Chad's ambition. And he missed Chad—that taught body, his penchant for wanting to be naked, the 'Chamtini' cocktails they created and shared in bed...and *that* cock.

"I have to ask," Mica began and Michelle instinctively leaned in to see where he was going with this. "It wouldn't be the premiere of *Scratch*, a movie set in the world of gambling, without asking what is the biggest thing you have ever gambled on?" Without a moment's thought, both Ashley and Chad pointed at each other and shared a laugh. It will be a good moment to end the segment on when it comes out of the editing room tomorrow morning.

Mica had no sooner finished with Ashley and Chad than the first of the HRH contingent wheeled up. The Princess Royal stepped out of her Jaguar sedan and walked into the theater without so much as a wave or acknowledgement of the shouting crowd. It all happened so quickly, Mica wasn't sure the cameraman had the chance to redirect his focus in time to capture the moment. "Did you get that?" The cameraman, whom Mica had forgotten his name, gave him the thumb's up and then pointed over Mica's shoulder.

Mica turned just in time to be temporarily blinded by the peripheral flashing from the paparazzi's cameras. Pamela Smythe-Lyons had arrived—committing a faux pas having arrived after any of the Royals.

Not since the arrivals of Chad and Ashley or the villain of the movie, former rugby star turned actor Daniel Thomas, had the crowd erupted so feverishly. Pamela Smythe-Lyons is quite literally famous for proximity and nothing else. Her father is an old school chum of the Prince of Wales and as a peripheral she has grown up in the spotlight on the slopes of Gstaad and the Highlands of Scotland and remains a darling of the media. Waifish with long legs and higher cheekbones, there isn't a bad picture of Pamela despite several unsavory circumstances under which her picture has been taken. There was the nasty drug allegation and that tussle with one of the rock star twins from that brother band and the occasional trashing of a hotel room here and there for which her memorable statement to the media was, "It's fun to have fun." All of which, have garnered her a reputation of 'poor little rich girl' rather than 'spoiled brat' which would be more the case. Her life, even her legitimate attempts at business—a clothing line which reputedly started with a dress doodle on a cocktail napkin—have been heavily subsidized by her father, the Prince's pal.

"Mica Daly! I love your segments," Pamela squealed as she broke from the intoxication of the paparazzi and darted toward the *Rise 'N Shine* crew. "You make my morning. I am so jealous. You have the best job in the world," she nattered on, not really knowing what it means to work.

For a woman with not much to think about, Pamela Smythe-Lyons had plenty to say. She went on about her favorite star of the moment, Sean Jones; how envious she is of Ashley Beckwith being married to the hunky Chad Martin; snuck in a plug for her clothing line, which she would be modeling during the next London Fashion Week and about her recent spread in *Gotcha!* magazine. Mica was exhausted by the time he managed to shut her up and send her down the carpet to the next unsuspecting victim. And as he said his last good byes to Pamela, a rather dashing man walked by with a rather steady but quickening gait to his walk. Their eyes met and he politely nodded in Mica's direction. Mica blushed like a school kid and it seemed fated that they should meet. But by the time Pamela had planted a kiss on his cheek, slipping her card into his jacket pocket at the same time, the mystery man with the reddish blond hair and piercing blue eyes was gone.

Michelle Bianco made her way back down the red carpet, having ensconced her Hollywood royalty in among actual royalty. She had that frantic look on her face Mica has seen so many times before at past events and on plenty of publicists. Something isn't right.

"Sean is running late. And it is against protocol to hold the movie when the royals are here," Michelle spit out in Mica's general direction.

"Oh?" Mica knew exactly where she was going with this but wanted her to say it, out loud, that her perfectly laid plans were going awry.

"So what I am trying to say is that he won't be doing interviews. I suggest your camera be ready for the photo-op and then we have to get him into the theater."

"No problem," Mica assured her but was then interrupted by yet another unfamiliar face.

The Duke of Clarence, Freddy to his friends and the media alike, is quite the man about town. Of course he would want to be here. This is his kind of night. Although it is unusual for anyone with an HRH to be seen publicly with the wayward playboy. His wicked ways annoy the 'family' and his big mouth embarrasses them even more. Somehow, someway, someone wasn't diligent with the invitation list. Freddy should not be here, in the presence of the Princess Royal or any of the next generation who have made their way in over the course of the arrivals.

"Mica Daly!" Freddy said as he stepped from the flashing photographers as they shifted their focus from Duke to the star. Sean Jones has finally arrived. Smartly the *Rise 'N Shine* cameraman stayed with the action of the star and not on the antics of Fearless Freddy and his attempt to commandeer Mica and the spotlight. Mica could see the cameraman had the right intentions, so he turned his attention to the man standing in front of him.

"I am so glad to meet you," Freddy said aggressively shaking Mica's hand. "I think we could be the best of friends"

"Oh really?" Mica questioned somewhat shell shocked by the onslaught.

"You're a reporter and I have plenty to say, as you will eventually begin to understand," he teased. "Now, I know you are working right at the moment. So I won't take up your time. Can't keep the stars waiting. Are you coming to the Palace afterward? We can talk there."

St. James's Palace is the setting for a late night post premiere gathering—an intimate grouping made up of the cast, the more important stars and the 'family'. This was not and never is a media invitation. But Mica is intrigued nonetheless.

"The Palace?"

Right then, Freddy knew he had put Mica on the spot. Of course the palace would not have invited the media or even media personalities as guests. "Here is my card. Perhaps a smart lunch?"

Mica, still not knowing who this man is or why he was being courted, took his card and smiled. "Perhaps."

With that the crowd shouted for Sean Jones as he passed and waved directly at the *Rise 'N Shine* camera, which was as close to an interview as anyone was going to get this night. Michelle looked over her shoulder as she scurried to keep up with the trotting star and mouthed "Thank you" to Mica. Perhaps, finally, all is forgiven between them. That is until Mica pisses her off in some other way. But for now it is a truce and for Mica the night is a wrap.

⋀ ⋀ ⋀

Through the gate, up the grandiose split staircase and into one of several ornate reception rooms at St. James's Palace, walked Ashley Beckwith and Chad Martin, Pamela Smythe-Lyons, Sean Jones—who received a rousing applause at the reception as the movie was fantastic—and various V.I.P.s from the worlds of entertainment, politics and business. Ironically, Michelle Bianco, the P.R. maven from Regis & Canning International, as it is now known, was stopped at the gate. You just don't walk into a royal palace without credentials and being a star's publicist, even if your clients consist of the highest paid actor and the star of the film, when there is no media to control, does not necessitate an invitation. She is grateful no media caught her clear and present humiliation.

"Isn't that Dame Shirley Bassey?" Ashley nearly giggled into Chad's ear.

Thanks to Mica and their time as 'friends' Chad knows exactly who Dame Shirley Bassey is. What he didn't know was her connection to the Prince of Wales and the work she has done for his charities over the years. So, although she wasn't at the screening, she's at the Palace. "Yes it is. Let's go and say hello."

Chad and Ashley were not accustomed to these kinds of events and the protocol that surrounds it. The reception line, which thankfully ended with the Princess Royal and not Her Majesty, was a blessing. Everything was just a little, but not completely, relaxed. There are some one hundred and twenty people here, small by palace standards, but substantial just the same.

Two men used to the protocol and, in fact, parties at the Palace are Sir David Mackenzie and Edward "Ted" Harrelson—'businessmen'. Sir David—Mac to his friends—trained with the Prince of Wales during their military days and Ted works for Mac. It wasn't long before Ted spotted what he had come for, a rather distinguished gentleman in the far side of the hall talking with a Member of Parliament.

Without introduction, Ted stuck his hand between the honorable representative and his target, grabbed the man by the hand firmly and grasped his lower arm with the other hand. With no regard for the conversation between the M.P. and the gentleman, Ted gently pulled the man forward and in front of Mac. "May I introduce you to Sir David Mackenzie. I believe you two have something in common." With that, Mac and the unknown gentlemen stepped out into the maze of corridors and into the abyss.

Ted had done what he'd come for and headed for the bar for a well-deserved nightcap—G & T.

"Do I know you?" the Duke of Clarence asked the tall reddish blond, blue eyed, 'businessman'.

"No," he said, nonplussed and unimpressed and then started to walk away.

"I'm Freddy. You've been here before?" Freddy questioned in a tone that demanded an answer. Ted had, in fact, been to the Palace many times for many such occasions and others more clandestine.

Coyly, Ted turned back to the Duke, "Have I?" With that non-answer, Ted made his exit.

No one walks away from Fredrick Charles Arthur Henry, Duke of Clarence—not when Freddy finds him interesting. But before Freddy could do anything that would normally lead to embarrassing himself, a tray slid between the Duke and the escaping 'businessman'.

"Canapé?" the valet asked politely and professionally.

"Is that all you have to put in my mouth?" Freddy returned.

Ben blushed.

"It is 12:15. At 1:00 a.m. you have business to take care of."

"At your service, m'Lord." Ben said and walked away, tray in hand and a slight hard on from his golden cock ring.

∧ ∧ ∧

Back at The Coliseum, Mica had sidled up to the bar in the oak walled lounge now known as Fluid. And it wasn't long before the hotel hostess, Hillary Stewart, swanned in, greeting the entire room table by table, offering a round of drinks to the regulars and shaking the hands of the newcomers and then took the seat next to Mica. She waved her hand and with an unspoken signal ordered a bottle of champagne, ignoring Mica's still full martini.

"I have a show to pitch to you," Hillary said as she poured for both of them. The rasp in her voice seems to compliment her ruddy complexion. She is a woman of questionable, but advanced age, who has seen plenty of life. But she is what one would say is 'put together'. A cream-colored turtleneck sweater complimented her monochromatic cream-colored pants. A sensible heeled boot and Hermes scarf and it is a look that could have been carried off by a woman half her age and been considered chic. "I know you get that all the time in L.A. and probably never thought you'd hear that from me."

"Oh you would be surprised who has pitched me a show idea over the years."

"My brother is in Hollywood. Does film though. Did you see *Hell's Chariot?* He directed that. Well, that and a shit-load of others. I spend a significant amount of time in L.A. That is where I met Marilyn Lassiter. At one of her parties."

Hollywood somewhat socialite Marilyn Lassiter, the last of the great hangers-on, throws some of Mica's favorite parties in Los Angeles. Hers are always a mix of headliners, artists and stars, most of whom are from decades past and whose careers, if not themselves, had been decomposing for years. But Mica likes mingling with Hollywood history. They have such great stories about when stars were royalty and debauchery was the rite and privilege of the rich and famous. Most of those party guests, it turns out, are usual guests of The Coliseum. So it is no wonder Hillary and Marilyn would meet.

Hillary Stewart is a 'broad' in the best of meanings—tough a nails, socially relevant and aware, charming and unapologetic. She is a latter day Perle Mesta—the infamous Washington hostess and the inspiration for the Broadway musical *Call Me Madam*—who has turned being a social doyenne into a career. Hillary came to The Coliseum on a whim some years ago. The hotel then was a stylish, unpretentious, if not unremarkable place known more for its convenient location than its panache. Hillary's brother introduced her to the owner of the hotel after having dropped a large amount of money putting up his cast and crew during a location shoot. Hillary, not one to mince words, began the conversation with, "You know what I would do with this place…" and the rest is history. Her smart eye for design freshened up the rooms, her culinary tastes revamped the restaurant to a rechristened 'Stewarts', her penchant for the naughty turned the dark oak bar in to a clubby insiders place for cocktails and gossip and her power-packed rolodex brought in the V.I.P.s. Mica liked her instantly and could see how Marilyn would have gravitated to her as well. Marilyn Lassiter is a climber and Hillary Stewart gives her international entree.

"So what is this show idea?" Mica asked, already trapped into her charmed web.

"It is called *Live From the Lobby* and it happens right here in different parts of the hotel. The idea is that so many stars stay here and we get the theater folk from just down the Lane dropping in for a drink after a show, I see a live chat show, late night, for the after theater crowd. I have already talked to some of my friends who have said they are more than excited to be guests on the show."

"Oh?"

"Well we have Joan here all the time…"

"Joan?" Mica questioned.

"Collins, darling. She stays when she is in town. The Stephanies, Beecham and Powers. Linda, as in Gray. Michael and Catherine, together and alone. We get them all."

Contemporaries of a certain age, Mica thought. 'No wonder Marilyn Lassiter likes it here. It's like one of her parties. Where are the people under forty, under thirty?'

"We've even got Chad Martin and Ashley Beckwith booked." Funny, Mica hasn't run into them.

"Perfect," Mica mumbled. "The under thirties at least."

"Oh, I didn't mean to bring up a touchy subject," Hillary said, touching his arm as if the comment required sympathy.

"No problem," Mica returned with a smile, somewhat surprised that Hillary would have even made the connection. "In fact, I was expecting all kinds of questions about it since I have been here and either people are being kind or finally it is a story that is past its 'sell by' date."

"Between you and I," Hillary leaned in to whisper. This close to Hillary, Mica could see the lines of age. Drinking and smoking haven't been kind and for the first time he noticed her bobbed blonde hair and bangs may not be the most flattering of choices on her. She is a character, if not a caricature. That is for sure. "I think you handled the whole affair with dignity. By not speaking, you speak volumes."

"It's not as if it is painful to talk about. I just choose not to talk about it. Because there is no upside. There is nothing in it for me to tell my side of the story other than a he said/he said bitch fight and being slapped with a one hundred million dollar baseless lawsuit that will cost me a fortune to vindicate," Mica explained.

"Well if you ever want to talk, I am a good listener," she said taking his hand sincerely. "You would be shocked to know what people unload in this bar." With that, she roars a whiskey soaked laugh that invites the room to laugh with her.

"I would love you to be my co-host on *Live From the Lobby*," Hillary declared. "Your high-ground morality is admirable and I would be honored to work with you." Normally Mica would have politely scoffed at the notion of a 'nobody' thinking she could host a live television show. But, in fact, Mica thought Hillary could actually do it.

"Interesting," Mica said.

Hillary signaled for another bottle. "You sit here and start on this. I have to nip out for a cigarette. But don't go anywhere. We have so much to talk about. I have so many people to introduce you to. I just know we are going to be the best of friends."

Somehow, Mica thought the same thing.

3

I t didn't take long before Mica assessed his relationships with his other *Rise 'N Shine* cronies. As welcoming as most of them are, they are hardly the social fraternity Mica had hoped for. Stuart Brewster, the news director, it turns out is a workaholic, getting into the office at the crack of dawn and not leaving until well past eight at night. Euan Thatcher is too intimidated by Mica to be seen publically with him. As far as Corrine McGraw, she is out the door by ten in the morning—eleven at the latest—and off to home and family which keeps her 'mumsy' every woman reputation in tact. Not that you couldn't coerce her in to a cup of a tea or a rare glass of wine of an afternoon, but that was hardly the social life Mica had envisioned. The director, Nate Griffin, has shown more than a passing interest in Mica's well being while in town and has promised to hit the town with him as soon as his schedule allows. Nate looks as promising as a long-term friend in Mica's mind as anyone. And that leaves the older, wiser and certainly more seasoned, Andrea Lyttle. Mica is drawn to her smarts from day one and he could tell that under the professional demeanor, is a sarcastic eye and a sharp sense of humor—two qualities he likes in a potential friend. She doesn't gossip as much as she informs.

Mica doesn't have an office at *Rise 'N Shine*, per se. He can, if need be, use one of the desks in the entertainment bullpen section of the open plan office space that occupies two floors above the studio. The first of those floors is for the talent, management, conference rooms and the video library, which is where he should be stationed. The second floor is the work center—the hub of the activity. Those with offices are ensconced in glass cubicles, the rest of the work force are positioned at low-walled work stations grouped into pods according to the expertise of the department—such as entertainment versus breaking news, sports and weather. There are a myriad of reporters, producers and production assistants scurrying around at all times making for a feeling of a beehive of activity. Although she is high ranking talent, Andrea likes to be up on the second floor, close to the activity, where the news comes in and is disseminated. Too often talent isn't respected for their intelligence, just their presence. Andrea does not want the staff to ever feel she is just a 'spokesmouth' for the news and only reading the printed copy and not contributing to the analysis and shaping of the stories as they break. Because of that, she has been granted one of the coveted glass cubicles on the second floor.

There is just enough room in these glass cubicles for a desk, a file cabinet and two chairs. What more do you need? Mica is in one of the chairs and is intrigued by Andrea's ability to multi-task. She is currently on hold with one of the editors who has a pressing question regarding shot selection, all the while writing a script for the next week's feature package and is holding her own conversationally with Mica. All of which is interrupted by a sudden thought.

"I should make a reservation. The pub across the street is fine for you isn't it?" Mica nodded. He loved the idea of a pub lunch, as that is hardly the norm in Los Angeles. "I usually don't go to the place across the street as it filled with people from the office. I like to get away from the masses over lunch but unfortunately, I have to be back to finish the edit session in the afternoon. And I am determined to get this piece edited today, come hell or high heels!"

Mica blurted out a chuckle. "Now that is a line I am going to borrow."

"I hope you don't mind a quick lunch?"

The question is rhetorical as there really isn't an option. But lunch is never quick in London, as Mica has come to learn—not with this group anyway. It's at least two bottles of the house wine long. Mica nodded again as she punched the second line button on her phone and speed dialed the pub across the way. "Two… fifteen minutes…the name is Lyttle."

As they walked out of the building and Andrea pointed directly across the street to the promised pub, Mica fumbled with his umbrella. Living in Los Angeles, it is rare for Mica to need or even think about an umbrella. So even one of these ultra small, collapsible umbrellas is a distraction.

"Can you hold this in your bag?" Mica asked innocently enough as he is prone to leave something as unfamiliar as an umbrella in the seat next to him after lunch.

"Of course I can," Andrea returned with a huff. "Because we are the sex that schleps."

"I beg your pardon."

"Women are the sex that schleps. All you men see us with handbags and it's: can you carry this for me…can you carry that for me? Hence, we have become the sex that schleps. And fuck you very much for that." Right there, Mica's friendly feelings for Andrea turned from like to love.

They settled into a corner table and a bottle of white wine arrived without having seemingly been asked for. "Again, I hope you don't mind?" Andrea asked. "It's the usual."

"I love this city. No one drinks at lunch in Los Angeles."

"No one actually swallows their food in Los Angeles," she quipped as she poured.

"I think we are going to be the best of friends," Mica returned.

"I hope so," Andrea said with genuine sincerity. "I like your work. I think you add a real individuality to the art of reportage."

"Thank you. I'd like to be considered a journalist rather than the often assumed P.R. flack."

"And I really think you need to capitalize on your popularity. We will have to hit the town. I am always looking for people to accompany me to the theater, dinners, and openings...that sort of thing. Who represents you?"

"Anthony White in L.A."

"No here?"

"No one."

"Let me set you up with a meeting with my agents, Angela and Elizabeth Owens."

"Are they sisters, lesbian wives?"

Andrea had to think a minute to understand what Mica was asking. "No, it is a coincidence that they both have the same last name. But they are the best."

"Well I'd appreciate the introduction. I would like to capitalize on whatever is happening here. Speaking of here, how did you get here to *Rise 'N Shine*? You have quite the impressive reputation."

"Well it was the Owens duo and the vision of Stuart Brewster. Stuart is really a maverick which, of course, is why we have you with us now." Mica smiled. "But I was doing the evening news and was assigned to Somalia. I was doing my report to camera when gunfire erupted. We all took cover, as you do, and we found ourselves in a school. Long story short, the gunfire continued and a stray bullet hit and killed one of the school children. And I decided right then and there that the stories had to be told, I just didn't need to be part of the making of them. I asked for a desk job and that wasn't acceptable to my then bosses. So I was out. As luck would have it, Stuart had come to *Rise 'N Shine* and he was looking to make the news segment more credible, if that is what I bring to it. And so a deal was done."

"Wow," Mica sighed. "And all I do is interview spoiled celebrities."

"Now, now, there is room for...no, I take that back. There is a need for both forms of journalism. Hard news and what I call escapism, vicarious news. They are both important."

"That is very nice of you to say," Mica thanked. "Most people think of what I do as fluff. I mean I have heard people talk about you, with both fear and respect.

People laugh at what I do. But there are juicy stories out there, even in the world of entertainment."

"Like Chad Martin?"

"Heard about that have you?" Mica began, filling his glass as he spoke. "Well, the point of the Chad Martin story is not whether he is or he isn't. It is about the prevailing belief that you still can't be and reach your full potential. There is still an institution of homophobia in Hollywood and that was what I was trying to point out. That is why I have never tried to publically 'out' Chad but to tell the tale of 'what if he was out?' Unfortunately people just wanted the scandal and not the morality tale. Let's just say I wish Chad well in his career and his personal life...of which, it seems the two are not mutually exclusive."

"See? That is what I am talking about," she said, "Just the way you explained a messy situation like that shows that you are more than just an 'entertainment gossip' but rather a true journalist. That is why I think you can and will be heard here. You need to meet with the Owens ladies and they can surely set some opportunities up for you. You, my friend, are going to be a star."

Heady talk for Mica. They ordered a second bottle of wine and decided food might also be a smart idea.

∧ ∧ ∧

Owens & Owens is, as it turns out, the hottest boutique agency in British entertainment. Two women, Angela and Elizabeth, who coincidentally have the same last name of Owens, came together some fifteen years ago. Angela came to the partnership with theater experience having been the managing director serving under one of Britain's top theatrical impresarios, Sir Richard Long. And Elizabeth came from broadcast news, working her way up from a production assistant to producer along side rising on-camera star, Andrea Lyttle. On the side, Elizabeth was booking speaking engagements for Andrea—who, at the time, thought representation was déclassé. Eventually, when Elizabeth broke free, Andrea was her first client and Elizabeth, with her bawdy, in-your-face attitude, was able to secure Andrea a top anchor slot on the evening news within a very short amount of time. Elizabeth's reputation caught on and when she decided to merge with Angela, who by now had a cadre of several entertainers she was pushing, the two had amassed an impressive stable of talent. And Owens & Owens became *the* management company.

Before his meeting with the Owens à deux, Mica had a long conversation with Anthony White, his Los Angeles based agent. Anthony and Mica's professional relationship grew out of the confluence of 'circumstance' meeting 'opportunity'. Anthony, whose claim to fame was having discovered an unknown Chad Martin while Anthony was working as an assistant to the now retired veteran talent agent Albert Switzer, saw Mica as a potential client when Mica's purported affair with the 'publically declared heterosexual' Chad Martin led to international scandal, a marriage of convenience between Martin and Aussie actress Ashley Beckwith and the ending of Mica's career on *Drop Zone.* It was Anthony who realized there was gold in Mica's newfound infamy and negotiated Mica's audition with *Rise 'N Shine.* And because of that, Mica Daly became the first official client of Anthony's new Los Angeles based talent agency, White Hot. But even Anthony understands that he can't reasonably find opportunities for Mica in Great Britain the way the Owens gals will be able to. Mica and Anthony came to an understanding that the Owens will represent Mica's interests abroad.

For all the Owens's prestige, one would never know it from their office. The client enters into a cramped anti-office of worker bee assistants who share four desks pushed together in the center of the room. The walls are lined with mismatched file cabinets. Above the file cabinets are posters advertising clients' past work, a smattering of outdated 8 x10s and a collection of books written by those same clients. Through a glass door is the Owens' office—a shared space that looks over the hustle and bustle of St. Martin's Lane. Their office is, to say the least, unglamorous, with mismatched desks pushed together in the center in order to overlook the street, piles of files on either side and paperwork in neat stacks covering each flat surface.

Mica sat in one of the two, again mismatched, love seats in the Owens's office—one on each side of each desk respectively.

"Well, I must say it is impressive the impact you have already had on *Rise 'N Shine,*" Elizabeth began.

"Ratings are up and people are talking about you," Angela added.

"Thank you," Mica returned.

"We think you can be a real star," Elizabeth punctuated. And already Mica felt he was watching a verbal tennis match, back and forth, back and forth.

"Let me tell you how we work," Elizabeth said.

"Oh how rude of us," Angela interrupted. "Would you like tea or coffee or something?"

"No thank you," Mica answered politely.

"I work with clients in news, current affairs, radio and documentary work, that sort of thing," Elizabeth explained.

"And I work with the entertainment side of things…guest spots on variety shows, game shows, talk shows and anything outside of broadcast, such as magazine spreads." Angela followed up.

"Bottom line is," Elizabeth said, "I will be your primary caregiver." They both laughed at the term. "Caregivers, that's what we call ourselves." She paused and brought herself back to the business at hand. "Having said that, I am already in talks for you to write a Hollywood Diary for *Gotcha!* magazine...But that may be down the line."

"And there is talk about you appearing on the comedian Angus McFarland's late night show," Angela countered.

"Great!" Mica said, careful not to get into the verbal strafing occurring as the two Owens got more and more excited by their new prospect.

"Now, there is something we need to talk to you about," Elizabeth said as she got up and walked from behind her desk to join Mica on the loveseat. For the first time, Mica was able to take a good look at his 'caregiver'. She is squat in stature, maybe five feet tall, and plump in girth. Her blond bobbed hair and English rose skin complexion defied her years—something close to, if not over, fifty. By comparison, Angela is tall, five foot eight or so, thin as a greyhound and with stringy hair grown too long to flatter her face. They're characters for sure and far from the stereotypical hard assed, designer chic, power broad agents of Los Angeles.

"You may have had a career in Los Angeles but here you are a genuine celebrity in your own right. You have to respect that," Elizabeth said with the nodding affirmation of Angela. "You are also a novelty. The tabloid press will go after you to knock you down. That is what they do. So be cautious about coming out of a club at three in the morning or being loud or obnoxious in a restaurant. Because your celebrity is tied to journalism, you are held to a higher standard."

"Understood," was all Mica could say. He'd yet to be ambushed by the press and frankly assumed he could hold his own if he were.

∧ ∧ ∧

They had had drinks in several places already, the bar at the Ivy and two of London's exclusive entertainment industry clubs—one of which has an annex on Sunset Boulevard in Los Angeles to which Mica has been but has yet, until now, been a member. But once inside the converted townhouse in Soho and after a meet and greet with the membership team, he was officially put up for nomination and then seconded. After handing over a healthy membership fee, the deed was done. He had an official card to all locations world wide, including clubs in New York, Miami and Los Angeles.

Nate Griffin had been promising to take Mica on an old-fashioned pub crawl since he'd been in London. By the time the Friday of a busy week had rolled around, they were both ready to tie one on. Though their jaunt had hardly been a round of traditional English pubs, but rather some of the more chic establishments London had to offer, Mica was grateful for the choices, as he is more of a martini drinker than a pint of beer man. And to Mica's amazement, each of these places was within walking distance of each other making the migration from one to the next all the more easier. Mica had been pacing himself. Still, with three stops behind them, even nibbling on mixed nuts, potato crisps and marinated olives along the way, it was not enough to stem the tipsy tide that began to wash over Mica. By the time they hit the fourth stop, Nate promised there would be a dinner break next.

This fourth stop came a bit of a surprise to Mica. It is a simple bar; a corner unit with three sides of glass tucked away around the corner from the end of Old Compton Street in the West End. Mica, even in a tipsy state, still had a few powers of observation going for him. He not only figured out they were in the middle of the gay neighborhood of London but also now in a gay bar. Mica, up until now, had yet to figure out that Nate, too, is gay.

As the program director of *Rise 'N Shine* and the first and last voice Mica hears in his ear during his in-studio segments in Los Angeles, Nate Griffin and Mica have struck up what is as close to a professional friendship as possible from six thousand-odd miles away. Although there is an entertainment department in London who are responsible for the content, Nate is responsible for how Mica appears live on the show. As far as Mica is concerned, the content takes care of itself—he can control the content. What he can't control are the foibles of live television, certainly not from his studio in Los Angeles. Nate tells him when the lighting is off, or his makeup is too harsh, or when to hold back or liven it up. He has to trust in Nate more than the entertainment department and as such they have a special bond.

"I thought you might like this place," Nate said.

Mica smiled. "And you? Do you like this place?"

"Very much. You could say I am a regular here."

"I see," Mica returned. "I suppose now everything is out in the open. It's good to have an ally in town."

"I will drink to that," Nate said as he signaled for a bartender. "What will you have?"

"Nothing at the moment. I need to slow down."

"Light weight yank," Nate chuckled and ordered a gin and tonic, no ice.

Nate wasn't your typical gay man. But then again, looking around the room, Mica knew he was far from the gym perfect Los Angeles scene. There was a hodge-podge of shapes and sizes—from t-shirted gym bunnies to the woolen suited financial types all with that slightly pasty but smooth British skin. Nate fell into the category of those slightly pudgy but casually stylish.

"I must say, you had me fooled," Mica said as they made their way from the bar to the window.

"How so?"

"I thought you were married."

"I was, to Madeline. She's passed away. We met when we were the outcasts in our little town in the North. We thought we were the only two like ourselves. She wasn't a lesbian, just marched to a different drummer. When we were 18 we ran off and got married, promising to be each other's best friends for life. And we were. She knew about me, and my needs, and accepted it. But I never threw it in her face and we had a great life. We threw the most enviable parties and had a voluminous amount of friends. She would have adored you. And I think you her."

"Do you mind if I ask how she passed?" Mica questioned tentatively.

"Madeline could always hold her liquor until one day she couldn't. She died of cirrhosis of the liver."

"I am sorry. I didn't mean to pry."

"You didn't and you haven't."

After an awkward pause and the desperate need to change the subject a rather loud gay man screeched loudly for the entire bar to hear, "MICA DALY, I LOVE YOU!" The man pushed his way through the crowd and over to Mica, gave him a big hug and an obvious kiss on the cheek. "Will you marry me?"

Nate nearly spit his drink out trying to suppress a mighty laugh. And Mica simply blushed as other people in the bar began to recognize the morning television star.

"You haven't answered my question," the man insisted still clinging to Mica.

Those around them started to chant, "Marry him! Marry him!"

"That might be a little premature as I don't even know your name," Mica returned.

"Jonny…no 'h'."

"Nice to meet you Jonny…no 'h'. This is my friend Nate."

Jonny pulled away rather indignantly. "I see. Are you two a couple?"

Nate, who had finally regained his composure and could see that Mica was getting just a bit uneasy, jumped in. "We are work colleagues."

"So you're available," the persistent Jonny began again about to clasp his arms around Mica.

"No, he's with me." A familiar looking, well tailored, distinguished thirty something gentleman stepped between the offending fan and Mica, took Mica by the arm and lead him and Nate to the corner where a table and three low slung chairs had opened up.

"Thank you for the rescue. I am Mica Daly."

"I know..."

"And I am Nate Griffin, Mica's co-worker," Nate stammered slightly taken aback by how classically handsome this stranger is.

"I am Ted." Handshakes all around. "Did you enjoy the premiere the other evening?"

Mica thought for a second and then connected the dots. "That is where I saw you. But for just a second." The reddish blonde hair and blue—very blue—eyes had stuck in Mica's memory. "Nice to meet you." Mica blushed.

They, Nate and Ted, both noticed the blush and there was a clear pause in the conversation.

"I am sorry," Mica fumbled. "But I just have to say that you are very hand-some."

"How American of you to speak your mind," Ted returned. It was his turn to blush. "I see you don't have a drink. Can I get you something?"

"Vodka...on the rocks," Mica shot back. Nate waved him off when Ted turned to him with the same offer, holding his half emptied glass as proof he did not need another.

As Ted got up to make his way to the bar, Nate leaned into Mica, "Well...?"

"Well nothing. I don't know who he is. I just remember him walking the red carpet the other evening. And, as proven in the bar already, more people know me than I am likely to know in return." To prove his point, Mica waved at a couple of young kids pointing from across the room.

Within what seemed like just moments, Ted returned with not only Mica's vodka rocks but also with a waiter following with three glasses of champagne.

"I think a toast is in order." They all reached for a glass. "To new friendships." The clinked and sipped and Ted winked at Mica—a gesture not lost on Nate.

"Did you like the movie the other night?" Mica asked by way of making conversation.

"Yes in a superficial sort of way," Ted critiqued. "I thought I would have seen you at the Palace afterwards."

"Us lowly journalists and media types aren't invited to such affairs," Mica returned with a slight joking sarcasm. "And you? How did you warrant such an invite?"

Ted paused for just a moment as if to measure his answer. "I was there with my boss."

"What do you do?" Nate interjected. "If you don't mind me asking."

"I am an undertaker," Ted returned as matter of fact.

"An undertaker? At a Royal Premiere?" Nate queried.

"With an invitation to the palace afterwards?" Mica added.

"That's correct. I am an undertaker. Whatever you need I undertake it." They all laugh.

"No, seriously, I am curious. What do you do?"

"Boring business stuff," Ted began as he stood and turned deliberately to Mica. "But I would like to take you to dinner while you are in town."

"We're heading to dinner now," Nate jumped in not letting Mica answer. "Would you like to join us?"

"As much as I appreciate the offer, I can't. I have work early tomorrow."

"On a Saturday?" Mica prodded.

"I have a project I have to undertake," Ted returned. The three chuckled at his quick wit. "So dinner?"

"Sure. But how do I reach you?"

"Don't worry. I will find you." With that Ted nodded politely in both directions, Mica then Nate, and headed out.

After a noticeable amount of time while neither Mica nor Nate seemed to be able to speak, Mica spoke first. "That shit never happens to me in Los Angeles!"

"I must say," Nate returned sipping the last of his gin and tonic and then reaching for his champagne, "It did seem like something out of a movie. I don't know what your life is like in L.A. but you are a known celebrity here and you have to be careful."

"Funny that is the second warning I have had…and I don't even think I have become that famous yet," Mica observed.

"You don't know yet who you've become."

"I would say you are right when it comes to the screaming…how would you say it here…poofter…over there who wants to marry me. But as far as the suave and dashing undertaker, I would be happy to have him take me under. Besides it is never going to happen. He doesn't even know where I am staying."

Nate lifted his champagne and Mica followed suit. "Like he said," Nate punctuated. "Here's to new friendships." They clinked. "Now let's get some dinner before you elope. I am simply not dressed to be the matron of honor."

4

Ted racked up some significant points with Mica, as he was able to find and contact Mica. First, with a bouquet of flowers and bottle of Bollinger champagne sent to The Coliseum hotel along with a note saying how lovely it was to meet him. And the second was by phone, a phone call Mica almost didn't pick up when the caller had no return I.D. Mica had been warned about his fame and that everyone from rabid fans to the intrusive and invasive media could go after him. So a mystery phone call was to be avoided. If it was important they would leave a message.

But Mica, against his better judgment, picked up the call. Ted had arranged for a table at the Wolseley restaurant, just walking distance, just up from The Coliseum on Piccadilly, for Friday—Mica's last social night in town. As much as Mica wanted to have dinner and get to know the mysterious but clearly efficient Ted, last name unknown, it being his last night in town meant he wouldn't be going out with Andrea or Nate or any of his other new found friends. But there is just something about him. Mica wanted to know more about this Ted. He is a gentlemen in the ways of fashion and comportment and a romantic in the ways of flowers and champagne. Mica just doesn't come across the 'old fashioned' sort in Los Angeles. He would make his excuses to all concerned and go out on his first 'date' in months—not since Chad Martin, if you could call their slinking around 'dates'.

Filled with industry suits, fashionistas and the 'see and be seen' sort, the Wolseley is a cacophonous former bank building turn haute restaurant. The paparazzi strafed Mica when he arrived and Mica thought to himself he must be more prepared with a standardized pose and smile for such moments. He was sure he looked like shit in most of those shots. Look at that, he thought, it took me getting a career six thousand miles away to 'go Hollywood'! By the time Mica arrived, Ted was already at the bar with two martinis—gin for Ted and vodka for Mica. As Mica snaked his way through the crowded tables, a few presumed fans but possible peers waved or mouthed a "hello." A few even stood and shook his hand. Again, Mica, without Nate or Andrea in tow to make the appropriate introductions, was left taken aback at his newly acquired celebrity. Despite a smattering of the crowd paying attention to Mica, when he arrived at the bar, Ted stood and lightly planted a kiss on both of his cheeks.

"Does this meet with your approval?" Ted asked.

"It's great," Mica shot back excitedly.

Ted handed Mica his cocktail, "Vodka for you."

"How did you know?"

"I do my research," Ted teased. That gave Mica pause before he sipped and approved of his drink.

Who is this man? Mica thought and then spoke. "Lovely," Mica said by way of a thank you.

"Our table is ready but I thought it would be nice to have a drink at the bar before we sit, if that is okay with you?"

"That is just fine with me," Mica returned. "You are quite detail oriented when you 'undertake' a project...or dare I say, a person."

Ted simply smiled. Mica knew instinctually there is much more to Ted than what meets the eye. But what meets the eye is particularly pleasing—suited and tied in a light wool, navy, two button, classic from Savile Row. In this light, Mica could see his light hair was thinning for his age, which made him look somewhat vulnerable. But it is his smile and the moments when he says nothing while his eyes drill into yours that has Mica's swooning. He is all man but in a traditional way, not in an L.A. manufactured way. And he seems not to be afraid of being gay. He just doesn't need for it to be on display.

"So how was your day? How was your stay?" Ted asked.

"Overwhelming and short at the same time," Mica returned in a contemplative way. Already he felt comfortable talking to Ted in real terms and not puffery. "I didn't expect the reception I have received from everyone from my co-workers, to my peers, the audience and even the people I meet on the streets. That has been overwhelming. On the other hand, my boss doesn't care that I am overwhelmed. He expects me to deliver—to do the job I was hired for—and that is a lot of work. I wish I had more time here to acclimate to it all. But accordingly, I will be back sooner than not."

"I hope so," Ted said and smiled that smile.

"It is a shame that we are finally getting together on my last night. But I have a plane to catch tomorrow and back on the air Sunday night for Monday morning. No rest for the weary."

"That is my fault I fear," Ted said. "I've had a busy week. I was at the Palace again last night for a reception and this was my only night available before you leave. I didn't want to miss the opportunity to see you before you go back."

"I am sure we can make the best of it." It was Mica's turn to smile and wink.

With that, the maître d' walked up and suggested a migration to the table for which he placed both their drinks on a silver tray and guided them off to the side. The table, a cozy round for two, is as discretely placed as it could be in the cavernous room. The large centerpiece of seasonal flowers is definitely more ornate, more over the top, than the single stems decorating the other tables throughout the room. Ted could see Mica staring at the flowers as they approached. "Too much?"

"Did you do that?" Mica asked as they arrived. The maître d' pulled out a chair for Mica and then one for Ted.

"For you," is all that Ted said and again, Mica blushed.

"You shouldn't have. I certainly can't take them with me. They will go to waste."

"They are for the now," Ted corrected and leaned in and kissed Mica squarely and forcefully on the mouth. Mica recoiled ever so slightly. "Are you okay?"

For the first time in his entire gay life, Mica Daly was embarrassed by gay affection. Perhaps, it has been the constant warnings from those around him to guard his celebrity. Perhaps, it is the lingering guilt from his time with Chad Martin when it was Chad guarding his celebrity and Mica not understanding the need for discretion. Mica paused before he answered Ted. There were no shrieks from the crowd; no lightening bolts from above and no hell nor damnation was cast upon them. It was just a kiss and damn good one at that. "I am fine. You just took me by surprise." With that, Mica leaned in and returned the favor.

"Uh hum," the waiter discretely cleared his throat just loud enough to disrupt the embrace. The interruption didn't seem to perturb or disturb Ted one bit. Mica again blushed. "I thought you might like to see the menu."

"That would be great," Mica said as he reached for the menu.

"That won't be necessary," Ted said to the waiter turning to Mica. "I took the liberty of ordering for us."

"That is correct sir," the waiter interjected. "This is a printed menu of what you have selected. This is for your guest." And as he handed the beautifully printed sheet to Mica, "And I must say, welcome to the Wolseley Mr. Daly."

Mica turned to the waiter, "thank you." And then he turned back to Ted, "And thank you."

"I was thinking meat," Ted said.

"I hope you are," Mica returned sotto voce. The waiter smiled.

ᴧ ᴧ ᴧ

A foie gras terrine, asparagus soup, filet of beef and then for dessert, a spotted dick. Mica wasn't sure if that meant to be a joke or not but it was delicious. Equally delicious was the conversation.

It seems Ted Harrelson is actually Edward Harrelson of South Africa, not English at all. His distinctive public school accent, which is very English, is the product of boarding school. His parents are divorced but his father still runs a successful business consultancy in Joburg—Johannesburg for the uninitiated— and his mother is ensconced in a lovely, if not slightly baronial, country pile just outside of Windsor. He studied political science with an emphasis on world governments with a side interest in mechanical engineering—all done at Cambridge. At 33 years old he is a PhD, a decorated war pilot and works for the Ministry of Defense. By the time four courses had been served and a life story told, Mica, who despite having a college degree in journalism, was feeling slightly inferior. Interviewing stars versus saving lives on the war front is hardly a comparison worth making. But in spite of, or perhaps because of, their differences, Ted and Mica got on handsomely. Mica for his part was completely smitten by the suave and mannered intellectual doctor, war hero, and defense something or other. All he knew is that Dr. Ted must also be interested in him as between anecdotes and laughs; they kissed—for God, the world and the rest of the restaurant to see. They were in mid-kiss when the champagne arrived, "Regards from the gentleman at the bar."

Sitting at the bar, alone, or so it appears, is Freddy, Duke of Clarence. Mica raised his glass to him and he in return to Mica.

"Should we invite him over?" Mica asked innocently enough.

"No," Ted snapped quickly.

"Oh?"

Ted quickly readjusted his tone. "He's a mess...from what I read in the tabloids. Always getting drunk and making a scene. We don't need that to interfere with our evening. As this is your last evening."

"Fair enough but I should at least go over and thank him."

Ted nodded and Mica made his way to the bar. "Thank you for your generous gesture Lord..." Mica was lost as to how to address a Duke.

"For the record it is 'Your Grace', but for God's sake call me Freddy."

"Well thank you again..."

"How long are you in town for?" Freddy interrupted.

"I leave tomorrow."

"What are you doing later? Can I meet you for a drink?"

"That might be a bit awkward as I am with somebody," Mica explained.

"Oh I see," Freddy said.

"You do have my card?" Freddy continued.   "I do," Mica assured. "You gave it too me at the premiere."

"You should have come to the palace that night as my guest. My mistake for not having invited you. I live there you know, at St. James's Palace."

"No I didn't know." Mica was beginning to feel played. "I need to get back to my guest. I don't mean to be rude but you must excuse me."

"No. No. Of course. But I do wish to speak to you. Do let me know when you are back in town."

"I think it will be soon," Mica said as he headed back to his table.

Once back at the table, Mica found that Ted had finished his champagne and paid the bill. "That was unnecessary," Mica said. "We should have at least split it."

"Nonsense."

"What now?" Mica asked innocently enough.

"Well I know you have a big day of travel tomorrow but the least I can do is walk you back to your hotel."

"That is very nice of you. But I insist on buying you a nightcap." They shared a look that suggested 'nightcap' is just a metaphor.

As they reached the door, a voice purred from behind and stopped them both, "You two look very comfortable with each other." Pamela Smythe-Lyons, in little more than a pair of heels higher than her dress is long, stepped up and draped herself between Mica and Ted. "You can't be leaving. I've just gotten here."

"Pamela, so nice to see you again," Mica said as he pulled away from her dead weight arm. "May I introduce you to my friend..."

"Alton," Ted said and he too shook her arm away and extended his hand. "Alton White."

"Alton?" she questioned, clearly having had a pre-dinner cocktail or two. "You don't look like an Alton."

"And what does an Alton look like?"

"Fat!" she declared and burst into laughter. Then she turned her attention to Mica. "You have been a naughty boy and not called me."

"It has been a busy time for me," Mica said truthfully and in his own defense.

"When do you go back to Los Angeles?"

"Tomorrow."

"Shame. Having a traditional Sunday roast at my house. Would have loved for you to have come. And you wouldn't even have to worry...I am not cooking!" She burst into laughter once again.

"Well, next time I am in town, we will have to get together. My club perhaps." Mica couldn't wait to say 'my club' in a sentence, let alone as an invitation. He felt so elitist and yet one of the 'in' set. "Until then, good to see you."

"Oh there is Freddy," she waved over to His Grace still sitting at the bar. "Gotta run." She kissed both Mica and Ted, née Alton, on the cheek and darted off.

"Alton? Alton White?" Mica quizzed as they walked out the door and on to the busy street.

"Force of habit," he said and shrugged.

ʌ ʌ ʌ

"Nice room," Ted panted, exhausted and sweaty.

"Nice cock," Mica returned.

Ted tilted his head and gave Mica yet one more kiss—gentler than the rest, more loving. They had been kissing since leaving the restaurant, down Piccadilly and into Fluid, the bar just off the lobby of The Coliseum. They had been making a bit of spectacle of themselves in Fluid, until, with a tap on the shoulder, Hillary Stewart made it clear that they should take the action upstairs. And they did.

Once inside the room, Mica had grabbed Ted by the tie and pulled him close. Ted groaned with anticipation as he forced his tongue into Mica's mouth and practically down his throat. Ted's tongue explored all parts of Mica's mouth while it danced around Mica's tongue. They intermittently sucked on each other's tongues, a preview of coming attractions.

Both kicked off their shoes and let the other start to undress each other— aggressively tearing at each other like a child does on Christmas morning with a wrapped gift. Mica, with his penchant for going commando was naked first, leaving Ted in just his boxer briefs, his socks and that tie. Still locked at the lips, they fell onto the bed and then slowed down.

Mica started to untie the Windsor knotted tie with both hands as Ted's hand rubbed up and down Mica's back and over the cheeks of his ass. Tie off, Mica reached down and slipped his hands under the elastic waistband of the boxers and slid them down, taking a moment to grip Ted's hardening cock and cup his smooth balls. They kissed again.

Mica moved first, pushing Ted on to his back with his head nestled in against the pillows. He moved his way down from Ted's mouth to his chest, firmed by military training, and began to first suck on the right and then left nipple. Clearly, Ted was wired and the nipple play only hardened his dick even more. Ted reached up and stroked Mica's head and, in turn, Mica reached down and began to stroke Ted's thick penis—the ample foreskin gliding up and over the head and back down again.

Guided by his tongue, Mica made his way down Ted's flat stomach, tickling

50

his belly button and to the waiting and throbbing cock. He couldn't help but notice that Ted's pubic hair is far more ginger in color than the hair on his head. That turned Mica on.

Mica had been once told by a friend who claimed to be an expert on such matters, that red haired men had large and very low hanging balls. He hadn't noticed earlier, but in the case of Ted, the premise seemed correct. Mica by-passed that gorgeous cock and buried his face in Ted's smooth scrotum, taking each meaty ball in his mouth one at a time and popping them out making a cork sound.

As Mica played with Ted's balls, Ted grasped the base of his cock and started slapping it against Mica's face. The weight of the slaps only told Mica that cock would eventually feel good in his ass—firm, large and strong. He would take a pounding and love every minute of it. They hadn't talked such subjects of 'top' or 'bottom'. Why would they have? They both enjoyed each other and would let nature take its course. But Mica twitched with anticipation.

As Ted's hard cock slapped against Mica's forehead and then face, Mica reached up and grabbed it from Ted and pressed it against Ted's pelvis. Mica gently licked each of Ted's balls and then led his tongue up the shaft of the hard cock, up and down, up and down and then nibbled at his foreskin. Ted moaned his appreciation and then forced Mica's head down on to its head and pushed it into Mica's mouth.

Mica went to work on Ted's cock for a few minutes but from his position laying between Ted's splayed legs his face buried in his crotch, he could only swallow so much. With one move, Ted threw his right leg over his left, rolled over and, when Mica too rolled over, Ted fed him the full length of his shaft, pushing deeper and deeper down Mica's willing throat. Highly turned on by this forced feeding, Mica began to stroke his own hard cock with one hand, leaving the other to stroke up and down between Ted's thrusting ass crack.

Ted spit in his hand and quickly used the fluid to lube up his button of a hole. First one finger, then two, Mica began to play with Ted's ass as he continued to suck hungrily on his engorged dick. Ted arched backwards, pulled his dick from Mica's mouth and slid down Mica's body and positioned his tight hole over Mica's throbbing member. Slowly he lowered himself down on the waiting cock and groaned his satisfaction.

For Mica, this was a rare reward, usually succumbing to being the bottom, at least initially. Ted road Mica's cock slowly first and then, flexing his well-developed thighs, bounced aggressively up and down. Ted leaned over and kissed Mica hard as he stroked his own cock. When he pulled back, a string of spittle joined the two from bottom lip to bottom lip much like a spider spins a web—ties that bind, Mica hoped. As charged as he was sexually, it wouldn't be long before Mica burst and he could tell Ted didn't have long to go either.

Ted bucked a few more times, threw his head back and with one almighty grunt shot his load up and over Mica's face and on to the headboard beyond. The thunderous groan brought Mica to his own climax. Careful not to shoot inside Ted, Mica thrust one more time, pulled out and shot all over Ted's smooth ass crack after which Ted reached back and rubbed the warm cum into his skin. Ted rolled over and panted exhaustedly.

A moment of quiet passed. "I can't stay," Ted whispered.

"What?"

Ted cleared his throat and spoke up, "I can't stay. In fact I shouldn't have stayed this long."

"Why not?"

"I have to be up early. My club is right around the corner near St. James's and I keep an extra suit there so I don't have to go all the way home."

"Where is home? And what is this club?" Mica sat up and was intrigued.

"Home is across the river. And the club is Boothby's."

The name meant nothing to Mica, of course, but Boothby's for those in the know is one of the oldest, most established gentleman's clubs in Great Britain. It is known for two things: the absolute exclusion of women members and its open secret of being the harbinger of clandestine members of the Ministry of Defense, Special Branch, MI5, MI6 and various notorious Members of Parliament.

As Ted stood, Mica got his first look at his taught body. Mica liked what he saw; pinky white skin, a compliment to Ted's ginger hair, belied his trained musculature. His would be described as a swimmer's build. "Are you sure you can't stay?" Mica asked as he grazed his hand along Ted's well-proportioned dick.

"No I can't. It's not that I don't want to. I just can't. And I have lunch at the Palace tomorrow. I can't show up with my colleagues doing the walk of shame in yesterday's suit and tie."

The firmness of his tone drew suspicion in Mica's mind. He has no idea who this guy really is, what he is, or whether he is, in fact, even single. Mica doesn't want to know, not now at least, not in the throws of his warm afterglow.

"You have quite a line you know," Mica began as Ted pulled up his pants.

"I do?"

"The undertaker bit. I 'under take' what you need. What does that mean?"

Ted was taken aback, stopped what he was doing and thought a moment. "Well, I told you I work for the Ministry of Defense."

"Doing what?"

"Research."

"Research? You were at the Palace for the premiere, the Palace last night and tomorrow the Palace for lunch. How does a lowly researcher end up at the Palace for lunch?" The journalist in Mica was bubbling to the surface.

"My boss has business there and I come along."

"Well that could not be more vague." Mica sat up and crossed his arms.

"It is not meant to be. But it might be a conversation for another day," Ted dismissed. "You reporter types…always thinking there is a story behind the story."

"Because there usually is." The both laughed which broke the rising tension in the room and Ted leaned in to give Mica one last kiss good night. "I have one last question."

"Oh?"

"How did you get my phone number and know that I am staying here. You had flowers delivered. I never told you where I am staying and the staff at the show would never tell."

"Research! I am good at my job," Ted said, winked at Mica and headed toward the door before the interrogation could continue.

"I will be back soon enough. Will we see each other again?"

"Of course," Ted assured.

"How do I reach you?"

Again, Ted paused, "I will get in touch. But right now I have to go." With that, Ted was out the door.

Mica reached over and picked up the card—just his initials and a phone number. Mica is both intrigued and now, again, aroused but the mystery man with the tight ass.

5

The streets glistened by the light of the streetlamps hitting the damp coating from the subtle drizzle falling. It is not enough of a rain to call for an umbrella but just enough to put a glow on the city. The streets of London were expectedly quiet at this time of night, or morning as it were, with the exception of the odd black cab puttering along Piccadilly one way or the other. Ted could have hailed one of those lonely cabs but rather enjoyed the relatively short walk from The Coliseum hotel to his club, Boothby's, tucked in on a side street in Mayfair, equidistant from St. James's Palace and the hotel.

For all its grandeur on the inside, Boothby's could easily be missed from the outside and the members like that just fine. There is no signage, just an address—a brass set of numbers on the doorway in the middle of what appear to be four adjoining townhouses nestled in the middle of a non-descript street. After all, a gentlemen's club is for just that, gentlemen—those who don't have to flaunt their wealth or position—and to keep the hoi polloi just where they need to be, at the gutter's edge on the street outside. Inside, Boothby's offered all the comforts of an in-city home for the country squire or a refuge for city dweller. Most of the activity of the club centered around and in its large lounge, which took the role of its main meeting/smoking bar. There is a separate library, five star dining room—open for breakfast, lunch, tea and late supper—a series of small offices to be used as catch can and approximately twenty hotel quality rooms which normally have to be booked ahead. It is rarely sold out as most members have places in the city already and just use the rooms to avoid domestic issues or to 'sleep it off'. For Ted, who keeps an extra suit and some toiletries in a member's locker room downstairs, Boothby's has proven to be quite convenient.

Boothby's isn't for everyone. In fact, as private clubs go, it is considered elitist. The buildings go back generations longer than the club but the club itself has a pedigree of over two hundred years. Built by the combining of four townhouses by the gregarious and quite eccentric Lord Boothby—who couldn't stand the "nattering" nor the "opinions" of women who somehow began to creep into the coffee houses of the intelligencia of inner London. He wanted a refuge, a place where men could be men. Boothby's was founded and became an instant success, so much so that a code of acceptance had to be created in order to keep the throngs out. Boothby aired on the side of the politico, as he loved political and social debate. So very soon, Boothby's became the club for politicians and those with government standing and, of course, those close enough to them.

Today Boothby's cuts a wider swath by allowing those in the various ministries as members. And Ted fits that requirement.

Ted usually thought of sex as a perfunctory act and he was careful to never get emotionally attached. He couldn't afford to. Yet this night, with Mica, had been different. He genuinely likes Mica or is at least is intrigued enough by Mica to let his guard down. He knows that if he is ever going to change his life, get out of the life he leads and into a life of normalcy—no secrets, no lies—he must let go of his tight guard and let others in. But everything about his training and his conditioning tells him to defend that wall.

Mica is unusually high profile for Ted's normal comfort level but to his credit is intellectually stimulating, a good conversationalist and curious about the world around him. Those are definitely traits Ted would look for in a partner, if, in fact, he was looking for a partner. The fact that Mica knew his way around and between the sheets didn't hurt either. But what is a plus to Ted is that Mica actually lives six thousand miles away most of the time and Ted couldn't be expected to commit to someone with all that physical distance between them. There will be no rush for Ted to break down his walls anytime too soon.

It is not like Ted to be this introspective but as of late he has caught himself thinking a lot. He relishes moments like these in no man's land—time spent in a taxi, on the tube, walking from here to there—between the assignment and the task, when he gives in to such self absorbed thoughts as to 'what if...?' And more and more, 'what if...?' is less of a fantasy and more of a plan, just on a slow burn.

He is startled out of his moment of solitude. The echo of his footsteps off the bricks of the building lining the tight streets of Mayfair suddenly became the echo of multiple footsteps. There is no one in front of him and Ted hadn't clocked passing anyone along the way. He ever so subtly speeds up. This isn't the usual neighborhood for late night muggings but you never know. Just as reaches the steps of Boothby's he spins around to confront whoever is on the street—friend or foe. His eyes meet a dark but familiar figure.

"Are you following me?" Ted asks.

Silence.

"Stupid question, I know. The question I meant to ask is: why are you following me?"

"G" stepped out from the shadow, paused for a moment and with a husky whisper said, "Mac wants to know why you haven't returned his messages."

Ted fumbled for his phone, which he inadvertently turned off and stupidly kept off, and hit the 'on' button. "Is there an issue?"

"Now that I see you, no."

Can't I have just one night off? Ted thought to himself. "Just how long have you been following me?"

"Long enough."

There is a silence long enough for Ted to assess what that may or may not mean and then turned and continued up the stairs.

"Call Mac," "G" said and then exited into the night.

6

hen Mica arrived and drove into the cul de sac in the Deepwell section of Palm Springs where Roger Keenan's sprawling mid-century modern house is nestled, he couldn't believe the number of cars. Being a cul de sac, there are generally no cars on the street unless a neighbor is having a guest or Roger is throwing a party. At two in the afternoon on a Friday, Mica wouldn't have thought Roger is throwing a party. But you never know with Roger Keenan.

Mica has really come to respect and appreciate Roger's friendship as it has grown over the years. Roger is a father figure, confessor, playmate and industry peer. And Mica truly admires Roger's naughty side—part old Hollywood, part an eighties throwback and part hedonist. Anything goes behind the gates of Roger Keenan's houses. His dinner parties are legendary among those in the know and envied by those not on the list. But moreover, Mica has come to rely on Roger's advice—both personally and professionally. He's an ex-pat from Britain, whose accent has been Americanized into oblivion except for effect, mostly when he wants to impress someone. His incredibly gregarious nature has deemed him the 'host with the most' when it comes to throwing parties—some of the most infamous in Hollywood—where A-list attendees, live sex acts and gourmet food all mix perfectly and harmoniously. Only Roger.

Roger is a character for sure—dressed in bold fashions like lime and peach colors, boldly patterned pants, an ever present Panama hat and a stylish selection of reading glasses perched precariously at the end of his nose more for effect than efficiency.

Roger has made a good deal of money in the marketing end of the movie business and then parlayed his smart investments into a reasonable fortune which has afforded him not just this Palm Springs getaway but also a historic Mediterranean styled palazzo at the base of the Hollywood hills on the Hollywood/West Hollywood border. Many a fun night has been had with Roger's retinue of industry insiders and stars and his penchant for young sinewy boyish models at the Hollywood manse. But Mica prefers coming to Palm Springs where he and Roger can spend a couple of days truly talking and not just partying.

Mica found a parking space a block or so away, grabbed his duffle and headed for the door. He didn't knock, just entered, and found himself standing the middle of a crowded living room filled with video equipment and a crew.

"Mica darling," Roger's voice rose over the din of activity. "I thought all this would be gone by the time you arrived. There is just one more scene to shoot and then they'll be off." Mica made his way through the small, by big budget standards, crew of about fifteen following Roger's fading English accent. He got a kiss on both cheeks when the two finally connected.

"What is going on?" Mica asked.

"It's porn dear. Isn't it delicious?"

"You're shooting a porn video at your house?" Mica shot back.

"Well I'm not. They are. You would be surprised by how much I can rent this place for filming. A few extra ducats in the pocket never hurt anyone and the view can't be beat. Wait until you see these boys."

"I thought this is supposed to be a quiet weekend," Mica mumbled, taking it all in. Suddenly he could see a number of beautiful naked boys by the pool, one eating at craft services and another on the couch jerking off—or as he would probably say, "prepping."

"All the greats are method actors," the kid said in a cheeky reference to having been caught by Mica.

"And it will be all ours once they leave." Roger leaned in to whisper, "I have asked the boys to stay. Do find one you like. They are all paid for."

"You never cease to amaze me," Mica chuckled as he made his way out the back door and on to a chaise. Mica, no saint in his own right, recognized a couple of faces from videos he's seen and waved a hello across the pool. Roger joined Mica on the adjacent chaise after placing two large fruity vodka concoctions on the table between them.

When they brought their glasses together to toast, Roger took off his sunglasses and Mica noticed the bandages and some slight bruising on the side of Roger's eyes. There is more bruising just under Roger's chin.

"Jesus Christ! What happened to you? Were you mugged?"

"Really?" Roger returned, slightly disappointed. "Have you lost all sense of your Hollywood instincts now that you are a big star in Great Britain. *Have I been mugged?* I have had work done."

"When did you do that?"

"While you were gone. I have come down here to recuperate. It is just a little maintenance…tightening the chin and lifting the eyes."

"Oh my God, you are such a queen," Mica chortled.

"You will be there soon enough and you will be thanking me for having done the leg work." They toasted again. "It is good to have you here darling. Now tell all."

But before Mica could utter a breath, they were both silenced with a loud and direct. "QUIET ON THE SET!"

There are six boys in this particular scene—the climax as it were. Five are already naked, engaged in an orgy of oiling and massaging, while the sixth, clothed, is peaking from around the side of the house. One of the collective five spots the peeping Tom and warns the others. A seventh man, also naked, comes up from behind, grabs the curious kid and drags him to the others. What ensues is a classic porn rape scene.

"The little guy is certainly taking it like a man," Roger whispered just loud enough for Mica to hear.

The little guy, or the 'victim' in the scene, is certainly earning his money, being bounced around, flipped and fucked, stuffed and sucked by all six of the others. But when they forced him on to all fours, shoved one dick in his mouth and double penetrated him from the rear, Mica began to squirm.

"Hot isn't it?" Roger whispered again.

Mica is feeling a stirring in his groin but also instinctively clenched his ass as he watched. He is never sure if double penetration is more pain than pleasure and isn't about to find out anytime soon. But the boy's got to make a buck, so pound away.

As a producer, Mica was equally interested in the action off the set. There are two cameras floating around with shirtless cameraman dressed in just board shorts, sweating under the hot Palm Springs sun. Along with the cameras, two boys—let's hope of a legal age—are hovering nearby with bounce screen reflectors to wrangle the light. Over to the side is the soundman and the director has his face pushed close to the two monitors showing the angles of each camera. "Now flip him over. Sam trade off with Cory and Todd with Bryan. Double penetrate from this angle."

The poor victim seemed to be in a state of erotic discomfort but said nothing to stop the pounding. Again a cock was forced down his throat and he took it like a trooper.

"Oh to be young again," Roger sighed.

"Oh to avoid an anal fissure," Mica snapped back.

Within a few minutes the dance between cast and crew was coming to it's natural end. One star grunted he was ready to cum and the rest, followed suit holding back just long enough for the two cameras to capture the 'shot' from a close up and a medium to long shot. Once drained, no one moved—the sign of true professionals. "We need to record your cum faces," the director shouted from his place over by the monitors.

Standing in the position in which they came. Each, in turn, had a camera pushed close to their face as they simulated the last moments of moans and groans just before climax. The process intrigued Mica. Yes sex had occurred but there was very little that is sexy about putting it on video.

"That's a wrap. Thank you everyone."

With that the crew scurried around dismantling lights, moving furniture back to its original spots and generally cleaning up. The boys on the other hand all jumped into the pool for a much needed cool down. Fucking that hard in the Palm Springs heat surely took it out of them. The young victim, who should have been the most worn of the cast, walked over to Mica and Roger.

"Thank you for letting us use your place," he said, not sure which one to direct himself towards. "It was a pleasure."

"Are you sure?" Mica asked. "It looked painful from here."

"Fuck no," the kid dismissed. "If you want you could have a turn."

Mica wasn't sure if the kid was offering to fuck or be fucked but he didn't have a chance to respond when Roger jumped in. "Well I would say the pleasure was ours. I do hope you will stay with your friends here and have a drink and relax...do whatever comes naturally."

The kid sort of giggled having gotten the joke. He was particularly cute, distractingly so. Mica hadn't noticed the director walk up. "I was wondering if you two would like some pictures with the boys? We have our still photographer here..."

"NO!" Mica snapped at the same time Roger shouted, "Absolutely."

"I can't," Mica said apologetically. "My agents in London have suggested I not find myself in any compromised situations."

"Now where have I heard that before?" Roger questioned sarcastically. "Oh that's right from Chad Martin at one of my parties, no less. And you thought he was being ridiculous."

The note of hypocrisy hung there for the length of a symphony. That was the very issue Mica had with Chad when Chad didn't want to be seen in public with Mica or go to any place that could connect him to the gay community. His rational was that it would be bad for his career. And here was Mica playing the same card. Was he being a hypocrite or could Mica finally empathize? That would be an introspection for another day but right now, Mica tried to deflect. "I don't want you to stop from having fun. Take your pictures, do your thing, I just don't want to screw anything up."

The boys gathered round a very happy Roger and Mica slipped out of his shirt, dropped his jeans and dove into the pool buck naked like the rest of them. The water felt great. And as soon as the photo session was over, the boys were quick to join Mica in the pool.

"What is your name?" the kid asked as he rose to the surface just in front of Mica at the far end of the pool. The rest of the boys, except one lying on a floater, were busy splashing and frolicking on the other end.

"Mica."

"I am Andrew...well, Kai is my on-camera name so I answer to both. But I was raised as Andrew."

For as small in stature as Andrew is, he has a substantial dick and Mica could understand how he would want to turn that into an income. Andrew had one hand on the coping of the pool to keep himself buoyant while the other hand brushed lightly against Mica's thigh and cock.

"Aren't you tired?" Mica asked innocently enough.

"That was work. Now, it's all about pleasure." Andrew spoke in a soft voice. "I can go all day. And if not, there is a large bag of blue pills that can keep us all going for as long as anyone wants." Andrew placed a firm grip on Mica's cock, which had already begun to grow. "Have you ever fucked a porn star?"

"Can't say that I have."

Before the words had a chance to settle, Andrew wrapped his legs around Mica and inserted Mica's hard cock into his waiting hole. Mica instinctually pushed and was well inside Andrew's welcoming ass causing him to momentarily gasp and then smile. "Now you can say you have."

Andrew bounced a few times, riding Mica's cock, and Mica too got into the rhythm thrusting in syncopation with Andrew. Andrew clenched his cheeks and tightened around Mica's rod and continued the rhythm. It didn't take long before Mica threw his head back, thrust hard and released deep into Andrew.

"Do you want it?" Andrew asked and he continued to clench and keep Mica's still hard cock deep inside him.

"Want what?"

"Your cum."

Mica wasn't sure where Andrew was going with this, when Andrew released Mica, climbed up on to the side of the pool and pushed his smooth little ass towards Mica's face. With that Andrew relaxed himself and let Mica's warm juices trickle down his scrotum and into the pool where they made cloudy droplets. If there is ever a visual that reminding Mica how different his life is to that of a porn star, this is it.

"Thanks for the fun but I need to get back to my friend and you to yours," Mica said politely.

Roger was waiting at the other end of the pool with a towel and refreshed drink by the time Mica swam back. "That looked like fun 'Mr. Camera Shy'."

"Of course…but weird in that porn star way," Mica clarified.

"Gotcha," Roger fully understood, having surrounded himself with porn stars and their friends for years.

They lay on their respective chaise lounges to soak up the sun and finally talk.

"So, how were my old stomping grounds of London?" Roger asked as he took a long and well-needed swig from his drink. It is hot.

"Fantastic." It had been a couple of weeks since he'd gotten home from London and had hit the ground running. His stint on the sofa made him more popular than ever with the audience and the powers that be wanted to exploit this newfound popularity to the hilt. So they piled on the assignments and Mica has been working day and night—reporting by day and presenting by night. He is exhausted but thrilled with the ride he is riding.

"You met someone already, haven't you?" Roger prodded, already knowing he was right.

"Kinda. But more interestingly how could you tell? I've barely had time to think of him with all that has been going on over the last couple of weeks. So don't tell me you are reading my mind."

"Let's just say I assumed you would have. But what the hell does 'kinda' mean?"

"Well first," Mica began, "let me just say work is great, the people are an interesting and diverse lot and I have made a couple of great friends."

"Blah, blah, blah and you are a star on the rise," Roger interrupted. "I know all that from my people over there. And congratulations. Now who is this man?"

"Funny you should ask that. I don't really know. He is dashingly handsome and works in the government in some capacity or other. I think."

"You think?"

"He claims works for the Ministry of Defense in some capacity."

"Is he a spook?"

"A spook?"

"A spy!"

"Don't be ridiculous! He is probably some mid-level bureaucrat. The funny thing is, he told me he works for the ministry. But if you were to talk to him in public he is very enigmatic about what he does…"

"Typical spook," Roger chuckled. "I've known a few in my day. Careful who you are playing with. None of them can be trusted."

"Either he is a lying sack of shit or has a really dry sense of humor. But I am interested in finding out."

∧ ∧ ∧

Now that Mica is a full-fledged member of his London club, he is determined to frequent the annex on Sunset Boulevard at the edge of Beverly Hills as much as possible. Not that he doesn't still enjoy his gay watering hole The Cathedral just down the hill on Robertson in West Hollywood, but the club has a more sophisticated industry clientele and sometimes Mica prefers rubbing elbows with peers over queers.

The place is large, the top two stories atop a rather undistinguished high rise office building—the former apartment of a Los Angeles industrialist who quite literally lived above his empire. Once off the elevator, you are faced with a massive staircase that takes you above the private screening rooms and dining rooms and on to where the real action is—the bar and adjoining restaurant. The surprising and sprawling square footage of the place sharply contrasts the cramped warren of rooms, which make up the London mother ship of the club's home base. Still the bar décor, with it's overstuffed drawing room sensibility and the restaurant's bijou atrium feel, give the place a comfortable atmosphere high above the cityscape below.

"Darling how dare you not come and sit by me and share all the news of London," spoke the familiar voice of Marilyn Lassiter, the society doyenne with an impressive Rolodex and little actual influence, who introduced Mica to Hillary Stewart of The Coliseum Hotel in London. Mica likes Marilyn in the way one enjoys a cartoon character but he could never figure out how Marilyn and he became friends—certainly not in the traditional way, as she is wont to glom on to people she feels can feed her social climbing ambitions. They met sometime during his days working as a reporter for *Drop Zone* when she would accompany some star down a charity red carpet or similar event and hope to see herself on the air in one of Mica's segments on the show. Now a 'celebrity' in his own right on Britain's *Rise 'N Shine*, he just may be feeding the beast as one to whom she wishes to see and be seen with. At the very least, by the nature of his job, he can keep her in the know by collecting celebrity information, news and gossip. And is that so bad? He likes the way she collects people, mostly has-been celebrities who may have stepped out of the spotlight but not the hearts of Hollywood nostalgia lovers. A party at Marilyn's is like playing a game of 'dead or alive' where every guest, although alive, is an obituary waiting to be written.

Mica turned from his barstool facing the spectacular view of Beverly Hills to face Marilyn, "Good to see you Marilyn." He kissed her on both cheeks. She is dressed impeccably in Chanel, perfect for a ladies lunch, but far overdressed for the hip, casually chic, young Hollywood who are dotting the room "I would never have ignored you if I had known you were here," he said apologetically. "Where are you sitting?"

She led him to a small table in the corner just offset of the fireplace. The waiter followed behind with his drink. They settled in their chairs with a café table between them.

"What brings you out all by yourself this evening?" Mica asked as Marilyn signaled for two more cocktails.

"Who said I am by myself?" she joked and waved her hand across the room.

The room was fairly crowded with a mix of British accents and Hollywood faces. Mica recognized Sterling Lowe, the über agent with International Management Cooperative who handles Chad Martin among others of Hollywood's A-List. Across the room, making a spectacle of herself by draping her rather endowed cleavage on to the bar for the salivating pleasure of a substantially older man is Suzy Chambers whose reality television fifteen minutes garnered her a more 'shit' than 'IT' status in the industry. How the hell did she get in here? Mica thought. Just down from Suzy are supermodel Francie Johansson and her football player husband. Not much of a sports enthusiast, Mica couldn't remember his name but would remember to Google him when he got home. He's hot! Rounding out the room are a couple of soap studs, a former Spice Girl, the director Drew Peters, and Gina Hamilton, the former star of the television soap dramady *Divas* who coincidently caught Mica's eye and gave him a wave. Funny how forgiving Hollywood can be when in the right setting. The last time Mica ran into Gina Hamilton he was also with Marilyn Lassiter, at a lunch, and Mica and Gina nearly broke into a catfight over Chad Martin. Here, all these floors up, perhaps the altitude has caused Gina to forget. Or perhaps she is just trying not to be forgotten.

"I could ask the same of you, Mica." Marilyn returned. "What are you doing all by yourself at the bar?"

"Me?" Mica returned. "I am just trying to get the most out of my newly minted membership card."

They chuckled.

"So, tell me all about London. Did Hillary treat you well?"

"I must thank you for that introduction," Mica began. "She is lovely and I can tell why you two are the best of friends. She is your European doppelganger, at least in terms of social connections."

"Good. I am glad you two made friends. I have got to get over there soon myself. I heard Ivana should be going over on some sort of book tour. Or is it the cosmetics she's hawking? In either case she is always fun to travel with."

"Well, I must say," Mica continued shifting the focus back to him, "my cohorts at *Rise 'N Shine* all seem an interesting group. Some of us will be great friends and others footnote colleagues for my memoires." She shrugged her shoulders in agreement. "But I did meet the most intriguing man. Says he works for the Ministry of Defense but always finds himself invited to and attending these very chic parties at places like St. James's Palace."

"One of them is he?"

"Them?" Mica asked.

"I call them the 'indistinguishables'. They are always filling out the room at the Palace." Mica was shocked to hear that Marilyn Lassiter, of all people, has been to the Palace. She could read his surprise on his face. "Darling, if you donate enough money to the Royal's causes, you get such invitations."

"Of course you do," he acknowledged and began on the newly arrived second cocktail. "So what are they like?"

"Well, it is all very formal, as you would imagine. But a party never seems like a party."

"How so?"

"Well, there are always a good deal of celebrities—mostly British, so I really don't know most of them—and, of course, the smattering of politicians, whom, other than the Prime Minister, I couldn't pick out of a police line up. And there are plenty of the 'indistinguishables'."

"And who are they?"

"Well, you can assume some of them are just old money who have contributed to the cause. But there are a lot of business types. And you have to wonder if you are at the palace or at an office party for the Fortune 500."

"Well I could imagine corporate money is just as good as private donations," Mica dismissed.

"Well yes," she agreed. "But there always seems to be a lot of what I observe to be clandestine conversations and hand shake deals going down. You can just tell from the body language and the 'over in the corner' meetings that something is going down. I initially passed it off as a cultural difference. Now I think those nights at the Palace are just a ruse for on-going business dealings." She paused for a moment and then just shrugged her shoulders again. "But it is the Palace darling and who doesn't love that?"

Mica too paused to absorb what she said. Is Ted one of the indistinguishable? And, if so, what is he doing there on behalf of the Ministry of Defense?

˄ ˄ ˄

The doorbell rang and Mica caught himself in the mirror just before opening the door. He looked good—good hair and just enough of a dusting of makeup to look natural for the photo shoot. He opened the door and the smile on his face deflated, a moment not lost on the first arrival.

"And fuck you too," Anthony White mumbled and pushed his way inside.

"No," Mica apologized. "I was just expecting the crew and I was trying out my movie star moment smile."

"Well it is too much," Anthony snapped. "That is, if you're looking for just anyone's opinion."

Anthony White is hardly 'just anyone' in Mica's life. If it weren't for Anthony, Mica's career would surely have been a footnote in the Chad Martin story. Anthony, as Mica's agent, turned all that trash into treasure and both were succeeding nicely because of it—Mica, of course, finding success across the pond and Anthony with a thriving boutique talent agency.

"The place looks great," Anthony said.

"Thanks," Mica acknowledged looking around his modest Hancock Park adjacent apartment—a rent controlled, 1920's jewel adorned with hardwood floors and ornate moldings—that Mica has lived in since before his days on *Drop Zone*. "I have been thinking of giving this place up."

"Why?"

"I don't know," Mica mumbled. "It might be time for a change. Maybe it is time to buy something. I would love a place in Palm Springs."

"That's convenient," Anthony pointed out sarcastically. "You work one hundred and twenty miles away in Hollywood. That is a hell of a commute."

"That is when I am not working six thousand miles away. Hey, maybe I need a place in London?"

"That might be a bit premature."

"Why? You got something better for me?" Mica questioned coyly. He likes to tease Anthony by pitting him against his British agents to see who is coming up with what. The Owens gals in London seemed to be aggressive in terms of lining up guest appearances and shoots like this one for *Gotcha!* magazine that provides a lucrative secondary income.

Although Anthony didn't set up this AT HOME WITH... photo shoot with *Gotcha!* magazine, nor will he get a percentage of the ten thousand dollar fee, Mica wants Anthony to be a part of, or at least aware of, everything that happens in Los Angeles. Anthony is a shrewd strategist and Mica knows the more Anthony

66

is involved, the more he can make new things happen on the back of existing opportunities.

The doorbell rang again. And again, Mica glanced in the mirror before he answered the door. The moment isn't lost on Anthony who suppressed a chuckle.

Ian Shepard is the newly ensconced west coast editor of *Gotcha!* and comes with some pedigree. He worked his way through several celebrity magazines but still has the nose for hard journalism having begun his career as a political researcher for a news daily, then parliamentary reporter, followed by 'royal watcher' for the *Daily Mail.* He prides himself on being part of the team turning *Gotcha!* from a simple pictorial magazine focusing on 'IT' girls and fashion faux pas to an insightful interview magazine. A spread in *Gotcha!* is now considered a coup and a validation of your career rather than a relay of gossip.

"Hello Mica." Ian greeted the smiling Mica with his hand extended. "We tried to keep the crew tight to respect the fact that we are shooting in your house."

"I appreciate that," Mica returned.

"Don't need too many feet trampling through your home, do we?"

With that, Ian walked in followed by the unexpected makeup person, floral deliveryman, lighting man and the photographer, Joey Chase. Mica is well aware of just who Joey Chase is and wasn't sure he was comfortable having him in his home, or even knowing where he lives for that matter.

Joey Chase lives in the dual worlds of being a paparazzo and a legitimate reportage photographer. But if you ask him, he is nothing but legitimate. Yeah, right. He is the photographer responsible the invasive over the wall shots of Chad Martin and an unidentified 'friend' lounging naked by the side of the pool at Chad's Hollywood Hills mansion. Those pictures began a scandal surrounding Martin's career and led to Mica's downfall. To this day, Mica has never admitted that his is the face obscured behind the palm frond but both he and Joey know better—resulting in a professional détente.

"Bet you're surprised to see me here," Joey chortled as he walked past Mica and into the apartment. "Nice place you've got here. It's no house in the hills but what the hey? That's all water under the bridge. You seem to be doing just fine now."

Anthony stepped between the two. And almost as quickly, Ian called from across the room, "Joey, I think we can start here in the living room." And then Ian turned to Mica, "By the way. Sorry nothing came of the Hollywood diary segments for the magazine but it seems you are spending too much time in London. But I really like your voice and I am sure that we can do something together real soon. So I am keeping an open mind."

"Great. Let's see what comes along."

For the next twenty minutes, while the makeup artist touched up Mica and Anthony and Ian confabbed about other opportunities, Joey went to work redesigning Mica's living room, dining room, kitchen and bedroom to look even better than they do in real life. Moving an ottoman from one position to another in the middle of the room, in reality looks disproportionate and random. But through the lens, the perspective changes and the room suddenly seems grandiose and, as Mica put it, "excusing the pun, it all looks picture perfect. " With every move, Joey politely and professionally had both Mica and Anthony look through the lens for their approval. Joey was quickly moving from invasive paparazzi to becoming an impressive artist.

Mica changed clothes between shots and was moved from room to room, posed in various areas including lying under the dining room table in a picture that proved to be Mica's favorite. It was a different world for Mica being the star and the focus as opposed to being the journalist on such a shoot covering the star. And he liked the experience.

Two hours flew by and then it was a wrap. The makeup artist, who was clever enough to leave her card, was the first out the door. The lighting assistant and then Joey were next. Mica was enthusiastic in his thanking Joey for the effort he put in and was cautiously optimistic that they could now be, at least, professional friends. Mica poured some champagne that was originally bought as a prop to the three who remained: Anthony, Ian and himself.

"So how are you enjoying the show," Ian asked more for conversation than interview purposes.

"Great! Surprising actually."

"Surprising? In what way?" Ian asked and then took out a notepad to start capturing nuggets.

Mica continued to talk about his fascination with all things British, his love for all things Hollywood and his curiosity for all things celebrity for the better part of half an hour at which point Ian called an end to the interview. "I think we have more than enough. For a man who has spent his career asking questions, you certainly are a wordsmith with the answers," Ian complimented.

"Thank you," Mica returned. "I think that comes from seeing more and knowing more than you can actually tell. Someday, who knows, a book?"

With that Mica pulled out a second bottle of champagne. Anthony declined. Feeling confident that Mica was in no danger of any sort of an ambush, he felt he could excuse himself dutifully. "We will talk soon Ian. I have plenty of clients who would love a spread in *Gotcha!*," Anthony threw out to Ian before his exit.

"It is true you know."

"What?" Ian questioned as he gulped the last of the champagne from his glass and offered the empty up for a refill from the newly opened bottle.

"Anthony has created quite a roster of talent considering how the big agencies swoop down and gobble up so much of the new hopefuls these days. You could do some business with Anthony," Mica reiterated to Ian.

"I will certainly keep that in mind," Ian returned noncommittally.

"I have to thank you," Mica began.

"For?"

"Not bringing up the Chad Martin stuff...again."

"I have been watching you for some time. At least ever since all that went down. And you have been very good about not saying much and yet answering questions perfectly. I figured it was a non-starter. But moreover, it is old news. Let's face it, I am not looking for a lawsuit from him and you apparently have said all you are going to say, so what is in it for me to stir that pot? Besides you are far more interesting than that...or so you seem."

"Thank you. I was told to be wary of the British press and you have only been professional."

"I will take that as a compliment but beg you not to tell my peers," Ian laughed. "You could ruin a reputation it has taken years to form. But in all honesty, I have softened now that I cover celebrities. When I was on the political beat, I really had to throw some knives to get any sort of respect."

"I had forgotten you come from the world of hard news," Mica said. "Especially politics." He paused for a moment to collect his thoughts. "I wonder if you could give me some background on something."

"Shoot."

"I have a friend in London who is a member of Boothby's. It's a gentleman's club in Mayfair..."

"I know Boothby's," Ian interrupted. "Just how old is your friend. Most of the members of Boothby's are either dead and don't know it or are close enough."

"Actually my friend is fairly young."

"Works for the government I can assume," Ian interrupted again.

"As a matter of fact..."

"An up and coming Member of Parliament? Military background? Something in Defense?"

"Two out of three actually. But how did you know that?"

"Boothby's is well known as an elitist club where only the inner circle are members," Ian explained.

"Inner circle of what?"

"The government," Ian continued and indicated the need for a refill.

"I googled Boothby's and all it stated was where it is and how it came about. The way you talk about it, it is riddled with intrigue."

"Because it is. It is like an open secret. Everyone knows the members are part of the spy set but you couldn't find a soul to talk about it. Like Yale's Skull and Bones or the Freemasons. In fact, I am amazed that you met someone who would even *admit* to being a member. That, in itself, is a confession."

"You have to be kidding me," Mica mumbled somewhat awestruck.

"Let me put it this way. It is as if the CIA had their own gentleman's club. Only it is MI5, or 6 for that matter, who control Boothby's. Just who is your friend?"

"I am not sure," Mica said, honestly.

"I could do some checking," Ian offered, hungry to get back in the old game and genuinely intrigued by what Mica is hinting at.

"That might be a bit of an overreaction," Mica dismissed, deflecting really. "He is just an acquaintance I met with a number of others over drinks. I am... was...just curious. That's all."

"Well if you change your mind, I know people...who know people."

"I will keep that in mind," Mica returned and filled their two glasses.

7

Ted has a desk at the Ministry of Defense, which as of late, has been empty. His Lieutenant status in her Majesty's navy has been out-ranked by former General and now knighted, Sir David Mackenzie, Ted's boss at MI5. Mackenzie, "Mac" to those close enough and "Sir" to everyone else, has been relying on Ted quite heavily these days. So a world away from Whitehall but just up the road on the north bank, Ted sits in his small office at Thames House, the storied home of the intelligence community. He stares at the clock on the wall in the outer office bullpen and watches the seconds tick by as he waits to go into an eleven o'clock meeting with Mac.

At eleven o'clock on the dot, Ted knocks on the door. Since his military days, Mackenzie is a stickler for time, "precision" as he calls it, and counts on the twenty-four hour clock.

"Come in." Mac has a gruff voice that commands authority.

The inside of Mackenzie's office is much like the library at Boothby's—worn leathers and aged wood, a throwback really, in a building with as much sophisticated and state of the art technology as Thames House has.

Mac is a lifer at '5'—a career man in Foreign Service who was brought back to the special branch during the height of the cold war when Britain's best and brightest were, for the most part, anti-establishment. He never left. He is highly respected and by the book, with exceptions on a case-by-case basis. He's one of those "I've forgotten more than you'll ever know" kind of guys but would never throw it in anyone's face, his encyclopedia like brain over their lack of experience. A gentleman would never do that and he is, above all else, a gentleman.

Despite his devotion to the service, he has carved out a private life if you can call it that. He has a wife, Helen, of some thirty-five years who asks no questions and to whom he offers no tales. His only son was brought up in boarding school and is now happily married himself and lives in the country. They rarely visit, Christmas and such, and pretend to know each other better than they do. Because, after all, neither the wife nor the son really knows what Mac does.

Knighted at the behest of the Prime Minister for services to his country, much of which can't be discussed publically, his new title of 'Sir' is both a blessing and a curse. His newfound notoriety means his life has gone from covert to the cocktail circuit. He is, for all intents and purposes, now a figurehead and puts a face to the cloak and dagger secrecy assumed in the spy game. But that doesn't mean he doesn't still have his fingers in the pot. He is the chess master, always moving pieces and manipulating the game.

"Edward," he began before Ted had a chance to sit and settle himself, "let me introduce you to Graham Nothrup."

"You can call me Ted," he said as he extended his hand to the stranger sitting next to him.

"Okay, I will," Graham returned.

"You two share a similar past," Mac continued. "Both alumni of the same college etc., etc. But I've wanted you two to meet for some time as Graham has shown exceptional promise even in these early days here with the organization. Reminds me of the beginning years of your tenure here Edward."

There was a pause but nothing was said. There is a compliment in there but no reason for 'thanks'

"We've had an episode," Mac began rather dramatically.

"An episode, Sir?" Ted questioned. An 'episode' in Mac-speak could mean anything from a breach of security, to a mission gone awry, to a personal infraction.

Ted knew he had been off his game of late—beginning the night at The Coliseum when he was out of communications for the better part of twelve hours—twelve hours during which Mac was trying to reach him. That too was an 'episode'. So, he quickly scoured his brain as to whether he had dropped the ball as of late and was about to get his hand slapped or worse.

"Our work at the Palace has been fruitful. Operatives are getting the correct face time with their respective notables. But tonight there is an issue. We are scheduled for a do at St. James's during which our man in the Middle East and our guy in South Africa have both requested a word with our Right Honorable operative in Parliament. Fair enough. But neither can know that the other has had a conversation with him. Now, Edward, you have worked with both separately. Again, tonight neither of them can know you've known or worked with the other. I will handle our Middle East associate and young Graham here can hand hold our man from South Africa."

"Are you sure you're not too...shall we say 'high profile' to blend very easily into the situation?" Ted asked.

"The Prince..."

"Our Middle East contact," Ted whispered to Graham while Mac's back was turned. "Not *our* Prince."

"...And I go back far enough that ours can look like a convivial conversation." Mac concluded.

"And what does that leave me to do?" Ted quizzed.

"Nothing," Mac shot back. "And that is the point. I want you to be seen by both men as being present to calm their jitters but do not engage either. If you do, you will be compromised."

Mac paused to let that settle in.

"Now, I want you to debrief Graham on what has been going on and what is expected this evening." With that, Mac waved his hand and sent them on their way.

Λ Λ Λ

By stark contrast to that of Sir David Mackenzie's ornate office, Ted's had been decorated out of the same catalogue as most in the building. Two chairs, a desk, requisite lighting, a set of shelves and some file cabinets. There are no personal items, no framed pictures on the desk, no certificates of merit, and no art on the walls. It is an office and nothing more. It is not that Ted would not appreciate a more cozy atmosphere, it is just that he has moved up the ranks so far, so fast, he has never really put down professional roots anywhere. And as of late, Ted has gotten that itch that tells him change is coming yet again. So why bother?

"Arms trading," Ted explained as the both sat in the stiff, but comfortable enough, set of chairs. "It is as simple as that. Our guy in the Middle East wants them. Our guy in South Africa wants them, too. But neither wants them for a higher good. Our Right Honorable MP knows how to broker them through the Americans without the Americas looking like they are aiding and abetting. Ugly stuff really. That is what tonight is all about."

"But why are we brokering a clearly illegal arms deal with either of them?" Graham asked with all the naïve wonderment one would expect from a newbie.

"There is a bigger picture, a bigger infrastructure and a bigger fish. All which are above your pay grade to know about at this stage. Your job is to simply facilitate alone time between your man and our man during tonight's event."

"But why is this happening at the Palace?"

"Because that is why we have a Royal family," Ted quipped. "Or I should say one of the reason's we have a Royal family."

Graham couldn't help being unable to mask his curiosity.

"I will explain," Ted began. "The average person thinks the Royals are good for tourism or opening the occasional hospital and shaking the hand of the odd pensioner. And they do, brilliantly. But the government has another use for them. Smoke and mirrors. All these receptions and teas and parties and drinks are all smoke and mirrors. They allow for the more covert aspects of government to hide in plain sight. In other words, neither of these characters tonight would be allowed to walk into Parliament or 10 Downing Street with the kind of agenda they have. In fact, they should not be seen at all and certainly not with a Member of Parliament tied to the military infrastructure. So tonight, while the media believes we are all gathering to raise money for some good cause or another; among the celebrities—who, by the way, always throw off the media—and the politicians present are a certain amount of invitees either known as civilians or businessmen. During the normal mingling of a cocktail party setting, the operative businessman meets the desired politician and small talk is made that can change the dynamic of world equilibrium. Voila! Covert operations have happened in front of everyone. You have to think about it like a magician. The trick is always in the hand that you aren't watching but the hand is always in plain sight."

"Fascinating," was all young Graham could mutter.

"This is the big leagues now. This dance in which you are going to participate tonight has to go down with acute precision as to not compromise any of the subjects. We will practice how this is going to go down and it will go like clockwork." Ted could sense that Graham was beginning to tense at the idea of what he was about to face. "Don't worry. It will go off without a hitch. You'll see."

Graham wiped his brow but he was clammy all over. "How did I get chosen for this? This seems like something that should be handled by someone with much more field experience."

"I was thrown into the deep end," Ted explained. "And I too inevitably took over for the person who did this before me."

"I am not trying to take your job," Graham shot back and reached for a bottle of water from the tray between the chairs. The ominous nature of the conversation hung in the air like humidity—palpable.

"Don't worry, it is not about that. These are assignments and nothing more personal than that. But what happens here, and with these mid-level assignments, is that Mac likes to rotate the manpower so none of us get too deeply entrenched In that way, the subject matter or operatives don't become too dependent on a familiar face. We are meant to be anonymous as well as available and there is a fine line between the two. It wouldn't surprise me if Mac has something else up his sleeve for me and is rotating you in in my place...eventually." Ted smiled at the more calmed Graham. "Now what is all this about us being alumnus?"

"Cambridge?" Graham asked.

"Yes, in deed."

"That's where they found me," Graham continued.

"I was told they stopped all that poaching on the university campuses," Ted chuckled. "I guess the more appropriate word is recruiting. But nonetheless, it was all supposed to stop."

As if he needed to exorcise some hidden demon, Graham just spewed his story.

"I took the diplomat exam on a lark and then one day I was sitting on a bench cramming for my next class when a man tapped me on the shoulder and said he wanted to talk. The next few years are a blur really. I graduated, was put in military training—boots on the ground in Afghanistan—decorated for my service and marched right in to the halls of the Ministry of Defense and now here." He spoke with such speed and purpose. Ted understood completely. When one enters the world they have, there is no one to confide in, no one to share with. It is very isolating. Ted just let Graham vent.

"My story is virtually the same," Ted said when Graham took a pause for some water. "With the exception that I went into the Royal Navy, everything from bouncing Harriers to helicopters off of aircraft carriers the world over. I felt as if my feet never touched the ground for two years." And then in an uncharacteristic moment of introspection he declared, "Ironically, I still feel that way."

They both paused.

"And now you're here," Ted spoke up. "GD4 ranking. That is always impressive. I was GD4 myself."

"GD is just general detail," Graham corrected. "That can't be all that special."

"It isn't," Ted corrected. "It's the '4' designation. That fast tracks you. Which is probably why you are here talking to Mac and me about your assignment. Someone, somewhere, has put you on a fairly heady trajectory here at 5. You've impressed someone."

"Now, I suppose I just have to impress you."

"Not me...Mac. But call him Sir. He is both the brains and your lifeline around here. Most of what you do for the foreseeable future will be done in a vacuum...all on a very need-to-know basis. Eventually you will be allowed inside and it will all make sense."

⋀ ⋀ ⋀

Freddy isn't used to being turned away at the door of what he considers his own home. But the Palace isn't his home. He may live in a grace and favor apartment on the grounds of St. James's Palace but the Palace itself is no one's home.

He'd become used to the comings and goings throughout the Palace and considers every reception, ball, party or otherwise an open invitation for him to attend. No one seemed to mind up until now.

"I am very sorry sir," a well-spoken gentleman at the door explained yet again. "But your name is not on the list. And as a result I can't let you in."

"Do you know who I am?"

"Yes sir, you have explained. Several times."

"I am the God damned Duke of Clarence. I live here for fuck sake!"

And as Freddy's voice began to rise, the gentleman gatekeeper's seemed to lower in direct proportion, trying to keep a lid on what is fast becoming a very combustible situation.

"But you are not on the list," he nearly whispered.

Another gentleman with an equally rigid clipboard arrived to handle the growing, and not flowing, line behind Freddy while Freddy and the first gentlemen stepped to the side at the behest of the now diligent security team.

"I will not step to the side, not at my own home."

"You will sir," the uniformed officer spoke directly and sternly. "Other people have arrived and must be allowed in."

Down the row and several people back, Sir David Mackenzie and Ted joined the line. Graham was to come separately per protocol. "What on earth is the hold up?" Mac muttered. He is a man of punctuality and precision and doesn't much care for the foibles of circumstance.

"Right this way, Sir." The gentleman with the clipboard guided Mac and Ted past the commotion and toward the stairs. "There is a gentleman at your left to take your coats."

"I KNOW YOU!" came the shout over the din of the crowd. And then to the gentleman and security office, "I know him." Everyone turned to see Freddy clearly pointing to Ted. "I KNOW YOU. We met at the Wolseley. I KNOW YOU."

"What's this all about?" an agitated Mac whispered to Ted. "Are you in some sort of compromised situation here?"

"No sir," Ted stammered. "You go along and I will catch up with you in a moment. I will handle whatever this is."

Mac squinted at Ted, shook his head and made his way up the stairs to the reception. He doesn't like surprises and this clearly has surprised both of them. Ted composed himself and walked over to Freddy.

"I am sorry but I don't believe we know each other," Ted stated rather officially to the clear understanding of both the greeter and the security officer.

"Yes, we met at the Wolseley the night you were out with Mica Daly from *Rise 'N Shine*. I am Freddy, Duke of Clarence..."

"I know who you are. I do remember meeting you briefly but I wouldn't consider it to be that we know each other." Ted was not used to being recognized publically. It had never happened before. And surely he'd never been publically associated with a celebrity. This is unchartered water for Ted and he is paddling delicately.

"And I have seen you here before," Freddy persisted. "You've been here dozens of times for various functions. I have seen you."

"I am not sure what you are trying to get at," Ted pried.

"What I am getting at is that you can vouch for me. You have surely seen me here on many occasions and tonight should be no exception. But there seems to be some clerical error with the guest list. I want you to tell these gentlemen that it is okay to let me in."

Ted looked at them and they to him and then Ted shifted to Freddy. "I am just a guest here this evening. I have no influence over who is and who isn't allowed in. In fact, I have nothing to do with the guest list. I assume that is made up by, and is at the discretion of, the Palace. So I am sorry, I can not vouch for you."

With that, Ted nodded to the two gentlemen, turned on his heels and proceeded to the stairs.

"Damn you. I will find out just who you are and make sure you never see the inside of this Palace ever again!" Freddy shouted. "Do you know who the fuck I am?"

Yeah I know who the fuck you are, Ted thought. And it appears you don't even have enough clout to get through your own front door.

Still, the moment unnerved the normally unflappable Ted. His whole professional life was to be lived in the shadows. But one night of personal pleasure—a date—and he has been publically linked to a famous face. Thank God Mica lives six thousand miles away. Ted knows that Freddy is little more than a mouth that roars and consistently proves an embarrassment rather than a voice to be heard. But he has to take Freddy's threat with some sort of validity. He is a loose cannon who knows what he is likely to stir up. Being linked in any sort of way to the happenings at the Palace or any other events like this could be career ending.

As he reached the top of the stairs, Ted found himself face to face with Mac who had kept a keen eye over the banister and had been watching the happenings below. He didn't like what he saw. "You know Edward, we will have to have a conversation about this."

"I am aware Sir."

"I have to ask," Mac whispered with a certain hint of solemnity. "Are you on top of your game? We have work to do. And there can't be any distractions."

Ted knew the question was rhetorical but chose to answer anyway. "I am, Sir."

∧ ∧ ∧

Red is the new black, at least in the world of clubs. Red, tucked away behind Liberty department store in a no-man's land of a street, has become the hottest club in central London. It has a ten thousand square food main party room with several bars, ample booth seating and a dance floor. Surprisingly, despite its vast area space, the room is more intimate than overwhelming. The red walls, shockingly red, close in the space. When it first opened some critics said it was nothing but a cheap knock off of the Buddha Bar in Paris—with the only fair comparison being the color red and the fact that the main room is actually downstairs from the entrance. In the case of Red, the main room sits just fifteen stairs below the double door entrance. It only took a couple of the right 'celebutants' to fall down drunk and stars dodging the paparazzi outside to put Red on the radar of every "IT" flavor of the moment —including the young Royals. Before you knew it, Red had a man at the door with a list in his hand and not just anyone was allowed in. The velvet rope is mightier than the moat.

When Freddy pulled up in the cab he was ready for a fight. That embarrassment at the Palace had set him off and he wasn't going to be disrespected like that again. He'd had it from the 'family' all his life and he wasn't about to take it from perfect strangers who had no idea that in a different time, in a different world, he would be the toast of society and envy of the world—heir to the throne of England and parts afar, his rightful destiny. His second rate status with a less than title is perhaps a settlement but, by no means, left the matter settled. To his mind, he deserves better. That is his birthright.

Red is a logical place for Freddy to blow off some steam. But again he is not on the list. But this is not the night to take him on. He is not about to defend his status or his celebrity for that matter. He is going to get out of the car and walk through the door like he is meant to be there.

As the cab pulled up, Freddy saw the throng of thirty or so wannabe entrants behind a large man with a list. A second larger man stood rope-side ready to allow the chosen few in. And there are a couple of paparazzi standing on each side, just in case. The car pulled up, Freddy threw a crisp ten pound note at the cabbie and opened the door. "Freddy, look this way." The camera flashes temporarily blinded the Duke but he didn't break stride as he headed for the door.

The larger of the two men, the gatekeeper of the rope, discretely eyed the other man with the list. The man with the list simply shrugged and nodded and the man dropped the rope for Freddy to enter.

"Thank you my man," Freddy acknowledged with a tone of condescension unique to Freddy and stuffed a slightly insulting fiver in the jacket pockets of both of the men. Sometimes you have to listen closely to hear it and to others it rings out like the clang of a bell. This was one of the bell ringing moments and not lost on the two at the door.

Inside is hardly teeming and they could have easily let the thirty or so at the door in without filling the place. But having people wait outside looks more attractive to the average Joe than no one waiting to get in. Freddy made his way down the stairs, slowly and deliberately, hoping to be noticed on his way to the bar. "Hendricks and tonic...please."

Freddy perused the scene. He spotted Andrea Lyttle from *Rise 'N Shine* in a booth close to the bar. She didn't strike him as the 'club' sort, being older and more refined. Although he wasn't fond of her, as she, like most real journalists, wasn't a particular fan of Freddy or any of the 'family' on the grace and favor lists. The prevailing thought is that most of the lesser Royals were hangers-on who should get off the handouts and into real jobs like everyone else. Even Freddy believed that to be true in *some* cases but certainly not his. Still, Andrea Lyttle is one person closer to Mica Daly, who is on his radar as a man to meet. And after the humiliation of this night, he was determined to tell his story to Mica and let the world know who he really is and moreover the dirty dealings they didn't even know he understood that go on behind those very palace gates from which he'd just been banned. He made note to stop by Ms. Lyttle's table later after sending over a drink.

Freddy stood tapping his foot, getting just a little agitated that no one had noticed his presence let alone come up to acknowledge him. It had been a night of this kind of treatment and he was getting tired of the cold shoulder. He was never comfortable standing alone. He needed to feed off others. The minutes passed and Freddy downed his cocktail, turned to the bar to order a second—and one for Ms. Lyttle—when he heard a familiar voice.

"I would like to buy that drink for the good Duke," Pamela Smythe-Lyons purred to the bartender.

"That would be lovely but not fitting. A gentleman buys for the lady," Freddy returned and then gave her a big hug. "What the fuck are you doing here?"

"I should ask the same of you. I thought there was a big event at the Palace this evening. My parents are there. Why aren't you there?"

"Sometimes those evenings simply bore me," he dismissed. "I needed a change of atmosphere."

"So who have you come with?" she asked innocently enough.

"No one actually," Freddy cringed. "This was a spontaneous thought and I didn't think to call anyone. I figured that surely I would meet someone here. And look, so I have."

"You could have called me."

"But here you are anyway. Kismet."

She took Freddy by the hand and led him to a small gathering of mostly men. Freddy recognized Mick Styles, the son of a high profile industrialist who plunged a fortune into buying a historic old pile of a home out in Sussex from a poor but well titled Earl. Now Mick, with his new money and public school upbringing , struts the streets of London like landed gentry. Second generation middle class money always annoyed Freddy, the hypocrisy of his own situation notwithstanding.

Freddy reluctantly shook hands with Mick and was introduced all around. The other four men are friends of Mick and the only other woman, who Freddy recognized from the pages of *Gotcha!* was another of Pamela's "IT" girl cronies. Freddy felt slightly uncomfortable in the mix and simply sniffed an acknowledgement of each—a snub not lost on Mick.

"How is the house coming along," Freddy began with the only subject he could relate to. "The renovation of those old relics must be a beast to take on."

"We are changing the name of the place to *High Styles.*"

The gals giggled their approval and the guys high fived. Freddy rolled his eyes. Again, Mick took note of Freddy's rudeness.

"Come on Freddy," Mick began as he put an arm around Freddy's shoulder. "Did you roll your eyes when Posh and Becks named their country spread *Beckingham Palace?*"

"They didn't. The media did."

"Whatever," Mick dismissed. "Surely you, of all people, understand the concept of social climbing?"

Pamela playfully slapped Mick on the hand. But before Freddy could respond, Mick continued. "By the way. I could use your help finding staff. I gather you have quite an accommodating staff."

"What do you mean?" Freddy asked, completely thrown.

"Oh come on. You know that good help is hard to find. But *hard* help is good to find." Mick winked.

"I have no idea what you are talking about," Freddy seethed.

"Fellatio Freddy, word is out that there is service and then there is getting serviced."

"Mick, what on earth are you saying?" Pamela questioned.

Freddy's mind raced. He knew Ben would never say a word about their special arrangement. Had another on the staff found out? Walked in unnoticed? Had Freddy himself, during some drunken rant, told the tale? And, moreover, why is Mick Styles attacking him?

Before Freddy could make heads or tails of the situation, one of the other 'friends' spoke up. "Wait I know you. Aren't you the one with the story about being heir to the throne or some sort of bullshit like that?"

"Johnny, please," Pamela interceded.

"So the heir is a queer," one of the others jibed.

"Ladies and Gentlemen, let me introduce Fredrick, Duke of Clarence," Mick began. "The Queen who would be King."

That was enough. Freddy hauled off and with all his might punched Mick squarely in the jaw, knocking him back just a couple of steps. The girls squealed and guys roared with laughter. All of which got the room's attention.

"Now, that was more 'bitch' than 'butch,'" Mick chided as he landed his fist into Freddy's face.

Within moments, the two were rolling on the floor, tables being knocked into and drinks smashing to the ground. If it weren't actually happening, the scene looked to be choreographed right out of an old Western movie saloon brawl. Security pulled the two apart and the moment was over in what seemed like seconds after it began. Freddy, being lead out the door first with Pamela close behind, was clearly the casualty with a bloodied nose and a cut lip, both of which look worse than they actually are. It would make for great copy once the paparazzi got a few snaps off.

∧ ∧ ∧

With the reemergence of the operative from South Africa and the Right Honorable MP from a side vestibule, shaking hands and looking chummy, Ted figured his night was very close to wrapping up.

Everything seemed to go smoothly. Mac had an appropriate interface with the Middle Eastern and Graham moved expertly with the South African. And both had acknowledged Ted's presence with a very discrete nod. All was well in the covert community. Time for a last cocktail and then Ted would retire to gather his thoughts for the debrief in the morning.

"Sir?" Ben, Freddy's valet who had been charged with double duty as a server for this event, approached Ted. "Sir, please pardon my intrusion. But I have a message for you."

"For me?" Ted seemed startled and glanced around the room for any subtle signs of trouble.

"Yes sir. I am a valet to the Duke of Clarence and he wanted me to hand you this note."

Ted took the envelope and opened the note inside. He couldn't help but notice the fine Smythson stationary and for a moment lamented the lost art of note writing. It's all emailing and texting. He couldn't remember the last time someone sent him a note. There is something almost romantic about it.

We need to meet. They're trying to shut me up! The note was short but to the point and included a cell phone number. Not even a signature, just a fanciful script written "F". Ted took a moment to digest the note and then slid the card into his pocket.

"Tell the Duke that won't be necessary but thank him for the suggestion," Ted instructed the obviously nervous Ben. Ben nodded and backed away. The one thing Ted didn't need is the Royal pain, Freddy, Duke of Clarence looking for an ally in him.

∧ ∧ ∧

By Monday, the swelling had turned to bruising and Freddy refused to leave his rooms. He'd confronted Ben who actually had tears in his eyes at the thought of being implicated as disloyal. He assured Freddy that he hadn't and would never say a word. All of this set Freddy on a witch hunt to find the person on staff that may have spoken. That went nowhere fast and it was settled in Freddy's mind that the whole thing, although damaging, was the result of downstairs gossip and jealousies. Freddy didn't like it but there was little he could do.

Freddy had bigger issues to deal with. Bad press. The tabloids exploded with the shots of Freddy staggering out of Red, bloodied and beaten, with Pamela Smythe-Lyons on his heels. She too had her own embarrassment to deal with as one unflattering shot caught her with a nip slip with one of her breasts seemingly to falling out of her dress as she was racing to the car. The two of them were instantly branded the poster children for excess among the spoiled class and the hoi polloi were calling for their heads.

Andrea Lyttle had reported on it just the next morning on *Rise 'N Shine* with the added validity of her being an eye witness to the very goings on which and led to the unseemly paparazzi shots. And worse yet, Mica was propped up in L.A. to comment on the epidemic of 'celebrities gone wild', which only inflated the story from and incident to a full blown scandal.

And surely none of this had gone down well with the 'family' but he had yet to hear from anyone of them. Sometimes silence is worse than confrontation.

The one person who wasn't seeing 'red' is Ian Shepard from *Gotcha!* He loves a good scandal and always thinks a hearty mea culpa and pictorial spread is a great way to sell magazines. And he is right. Needless to say, a good scandal always leads to a good idea.

As Freddy lay on the sofa, his robe opened and naked otherwise, with a three day beard and an ego as bruised as his face, Ben walked in to the sitting area with a large bouquet of flowers—a gift from the equally distraught Pamela. Ben placed the flowers in water and put the arrangement on the table in front of Freddy and then Ben knelt down and the two kissed. Without saying anything, Freddy gently pushed Ben's head down between his legs and for the first time Freddy felt Ben's hesitancy.

"Sir..." Ben stammered. Since the accusations of disloyalty, Ben was simply uncomfortable. Freddy uncharacteristically understood the awkwardness and winked at Freddy in that way that said nothing needed to be said. The moment, tender in its way, was broken by the phone ringing.

"Pamela darling, I just got them. They're beautiful and completely unnecessary."

"It is the least I can do after what Mick did to you. I am so sorry. I didn't see it coming."

"But darling, tell me why did he attack me. We barely know each other and he went at me like we were long feuding cousins."

"He is a bully. And let's face it; you have had a bit to say about him in the past. All that talk of new money etcetera. You have to think about what you say and who is listening."

"But he is new money..."

"It doesn't matter." There was a pause to let Pamela muster some courage. "And...all this talk about your position. It doesn't sit well. People are saying that you are no different than the new money you so detest."

"You are talking about my birthright!"

"Freddy, you know I love you. But I just fear that your mouth is going to get you into real trouble one of these days." He could hear her sigh. He knew it took courage for her to say that even though he didn't like what she had to say.

"Noted darling," he conceded with a lighthearted lilt in his voice that clearly indicated he was through with the topic. "And as soon as my face returns to something able to be seen in public, let's get together for drinks and some real fun." Not waiting for her to answer, he blew a kiss into the phone and hung up. My mouth is going to get me in trouble! His mind raced. Well, they haven't heard anything yet.

The latest issue of *Gotcha!* with the spread on Mica's home came to the offices of Owens & Owens even before Mica got his copy. It was just a matter of the time difference really. A messenger would deliver Mica's copy about eight hours from now. Both Angela and Elizabeth were ecstatic with what they saw—all five pages worth—turning Mica's modest digs into a grand home worthy of any interior designer's bragging rights. They were itchy to call Mica but it was 1 a.m. L.A. time and they didn't want to wake him.

"Wait a minute," Elizabeth calculated while reaching for the television remote on the edge of the desk. "Isn't he on the air this morning? That means he is in the studio and wide awake."

The television flickered on, an old box of a set with a VCR built in—the Owens were not much for change—and Elizabeth turned on *Rise 'N Shine* just in time to see Mica sign off with Corrine.

"How long before we can call him?" Angela questioned.

"Ten minutes. He should be in the car by then."

They both crowded around one copy and giggled as they picked out details of his apartment. "Chaps!" Elizabeth called out the assistants in the outer offices. "Can one of you run out to the newsstand and gather up a bunch of copies of *Gotcha!?*"

"Has the check arrived?" Angela thought out loud. And then to Elizabeth, "Remind me to chase that up today."

The check was for a tidy ten thousand dollar, payment for Mica's spread. It never ceased to amaze Mica that magazines and talk shows in Great Britain pay you for your appearances and interviews. In the U.S. that would be considered publicity and you'd be lucky not to have to pay *them* for the exposure. Ten thousand dollars it seems is a modest pay off compared to some, but neither Mica nor the Owens duo are complaining.

As they waited to call Mica, the ladies fingered through the rest of the magazine. In a spread less glamorous were the now often printed pictures of Freddy, Duke of Clarence, staggering out of Red along with Pamela Smythe-Lyons and her well-exposed breasts.

"What on earth is she doing with him?" Angela asked.

"Remember we almost signed her," Elizabeth said. "Dodged a bullet there."

The story—more of a paragraph blurb—was really focused on the nip slip incident than Freddy but you couldn't show one mess without the other. "They say there is no such thing as bad publicity," Elizabeth lamented. "But this is about as bad as it gets."

"I've got Mica Daly on the line," one of the 'chaps' from the outer office shouted.

Elizabeth pushed the speakerphone button and spoke first. "We have been waiting to call you. Your ears must be burning."

"Have you seen *Gotcha!* yet?" Mica practically squealed.

"Yes," Angela answered. "But how have you seen it."

"I haven't gotten a copy yet. But they used the pictures on *Rise 'N Shine* so they sent copies of them over the satellite so I could comment on what they were looking at. They look great."

"They certainly do. We didn't realize you live in such a palatial place."

"Hardly. I mean, I saw the pictures the day of but simply looking through the camera didn't do them justice. I mean I am ready to throw out some of that furniture. Now it all looks designer new."

"We are glad you are pleased," Elizabeth gushed. She loves when new clients get their first real taste of celebrity. And this is Mica's moment.

"By the way, have either of you seen the pictures of the Duke of Clarence covered in blood coming out of some club over there?" Mica asked.

"Have we?" they chimed in together.

"They have been everywhere," Angela explained, "including, again, in your issue of *Gotcha!*"

"Great!"

"Why is that great?" Elizabeth asked.

"Well Ian Shepard from *Gotcha!* wants to do a spread on him. I don't know if it's some sort of redemption article or one of those "Who is this mess with a title?" piece. But either way, he wants me to be the interviewer."

"That is fantastic," Elizabeth squealed.

"This could be a first of many," Angela followed.

"That seems to be where Ian is going with this. He sees me as the man who interviews Hollywood Royalty and thinks mine would be an interesting perspective on interviewing real Royalty," Mica explained.

"If you can call the Duke of Clarence royalty!" Angela mumbled. "He is not exactly well thought of," she explained to Mica.

"Please! I live in Hollywood. It's the land of those least deserving getting the most reward."

"Since you put it that way, you might be the perfect person for this assignment," Angela giggled.

"There will be a fee?" the always monetarily diligent Elizabeth questioned.

"I didn't discuss that..."

"Well don't. That is why you have us."

"No problem," Mica sighed. He hates talking about money, especially when it comes to his own worth.

"We will call you after we have spoken to Ian. And for that matter, after you've had a night's sleep. But well done and congratulations on the magazine spread."

Goodbyes all around and they all hung up.

ᴧ ᴧ ᴧ

"This is so much more civilized. Don't you think?"

Mac Mackenzie's question was more rhetorical than literal. He wasn't looking for answer. He and Ted settled into two wingback leather chairs at the window looking over the back garden, which looks decidedly gray today. The drinks arrived, a scotch for Mac—the good stuff—and a usual gin and tonic for Ted. Ted wouldn't normally drink in the middle of the day but when the boss summons you to Boothby's for a mid afternoon meeting and orders a round, you drink it.

Ted is surprised at the number of people present in the middle of the day. And Mac could read his mind. "A lot of important business goes down in the this room at this time of the day. It's not as if any of these men are ditching school."

"Is that why we are here? Important business?"

"Yes...of a sort."

Ted deliberately sipped his drink to avoid asking or saying anything. He had been off his game as of late and presumably Mac knows it. Could he be getting the sack and Mac is being nice enough to handle it off campus? And would that be so terrible a situation, moving into the private sector in some capacity or other. Ted has been at a crossroads, wondering how much longer he can do this—living in the shadows, lying to his friends and family about who he is and what he does. Most people would consider Ted's situation a job for life. There is too much of an investment in the training. And, the truth is, you know too much. You are too much of a liability to simply cut bait and let you swim off. Still, those who have left have segued nicely into the world of the ordinary—been set up with resumes and references for jobs they've never had in order to smoothly transition into middle management at some multi-national corporation. After all, it is hard to walk into a job interview with 'spy' on you c.v. and expect to be taken seriously.

"Ted, I like you," Mac began. "I see a lot of myself in you. And I believe you have a bright future with us. If you want it."

Ted paused for a moment and measured his thoughts. "I am one hundred percent in the game."

"That is what I wanted to hear. But I know you have been hesitant lately.

And I just want you to know, we all, from time to time, question this life, this career. If you don't occasionally question your resolve, you wouldn't be human. But we need you and want you at, what you say is one hundred percent."

"I am there for you Sir," Ted reiterated.

"I will just ask you if you need some time off? Young Graham seems to have moved in nicely and that should take the pressure off for a while."

"No Sir. I am fine."

"Glad to here that. Because I would like to shift things around a bit."

"Oh?" Ted looked puzzled.

"I have been thinking about what happened the other night at the Palace with that damn Duke of Clarence. I don't understand how people like that can't simply accept what has been given to them and live their privileged life with the class they have been anointed to. It reminds me of Diana all over again. She should have shut up and accepted the life she had been given."

Ted always cringes when the late Princess of Wales is mentioned. There are two schools of thought among people who would know: either that Diana was a loose cannon or that she was a victim. Clearly Sir David Mackenzie shared the loose cannon opinion.

"And we all know how that ended up," Mac mumbled as he took a large swig from his crystal tumbler, downing the rest of the drink. "Loose lips, my boy, loose lips."

"What are you saying?"

"The 'family' is not happy. His recent antics are just another example of his potentially being a loose cannon. The 'family' is happy with the trajectory of the Royals these days, their acceptance with the people and the bright future. They don't need or want the Duke stirring the pot with accusations and innuendo," Mac explained.

"And?"

"We need someone to watch him."

"And that someone is me," Ted concluded.

"Well, the other evening at the Palace when he confronted you. He said and I quote "I know you..." I thought you had been compromised but now I think it may work to our advantage."

Ted interrupted. "I can assure you he doesn't know me at all."

"But he does recognize you. And that may be enough."

"Enough for what?"

"That should it come to that, he is warned to back off." The second round of drinks arrived and Ted was bemused, as he didn't even notice Mac indicate an order. "What we need you to do is just to keep an eye on him. Travel in his circles. See to whom he is talking and, better yet, find out what he is talking about. Is he just a rogue Royal or is he really playing with fire?"

"And if he is...playing with fire...what then?"

"We will cross that bridge, as they say, when we come to it. We have dealt with the loose cannon in the past."

"But no one knows what he wants."

"That is just it," Mac returned. "And no one knows what he is capable of. At this point, he may just be looking to get his name in the papers. As abhorrent to me as that is. In my day, you fought like hell to keep your name out of the papers and now, for this generation, all they want is publicity for doing nothing, achieving nothing, and becoming nothing. And it is the case of the Duke. He is an embarrassment without having to say a word. The way he came to his title alone is too much of a story to tell for some and she, in particular, does not want to see the details of that rehashed in the headlines over her morning tea and toast. But the bottom line is, he needs to be silenced. He is, if nothing else, the disposable Duke."

Ted cringed again. He didn't like the implication.

"One more thing," Mac said sotto voce. "There is the belief that the Duke is a poof."

"Oh?" Ted shifted in his chair. Homosexuality is not an open topic at MI5 and up until the recent past you could be fired for being gay. Times may have changed but Ted isn't about to test the waters and has chosen to remain safely in the closet at the office. This too is one of the reasons for Ted being uneasy about his future. His reckless public displays of affection with Mica, if continued—and Ted certainly hopes they will—are the very thing that could put an end to a bright future.

"We don't want you to be uncomfortable but you may travel in circles where homosexuality is the taste of the crowd, shall we say."

Ted nearly laughed at how delicately Mac was trying to say he might have to follow Freddy into a gay bar. God forbid. "I will be just fine," Ted assured him.

ᴧ ᴧ ᴧ

Andrea Lyttle, second only to being a competitive journalist, is also a voracious social butterfly. Shedding the conservative daytime suits, raising her hemline and slipping into higher heels for the evening, she takes at least a decade off her appearance. And for those who only know her staccato, news reader speech cadence, they are usually surprised to find a smooth talking, highly intellectual, sharp tongued, opinionated, quick-witted woman who is quite the entertaining conversationalist. To accomplish this yin to her yang, she's learned to sleep in shifts—an afternoon power nap from four to six allows her to go to bed as late as midnight and still be up at 4 a.m. She's out most evenings—mostly for social obligations and the charity circuit—but tonight she's on a date with the always-entertaining Nate Griffin. Of course it is nothing romantic, just a couple of work pals getting together for a long overdue night on the town. Although they both have to be up and in the office in the wee hours of the morning, Nate has yet to master the split shift sleeping arrangement that keeps Andrea fresh. He knew he would be paying for this evening the next day. But a night out with Andrea is always worth it.

The plan is for dinner somewhere in Soho—they're thinking Quo Vadis but neither had bothered to make reservations and they would hope for the best. But before dinner it's cocktails. They'd already stopped at the entertainment industry mecca, Groucho club, but it was rather slow and both were looking for more of a laugh.

"I've got an idea," Nate piped up when it was suggested they move on.

Andrea knew the 'idea' meant a gay bar and she was neither excited by nor adverse to the notion. She prides herself for being 'a go with the flow' kind of gal but she could see Nate was itching to migrate to familiar territory.

"Do I look okay?" Andrea began to question her wardrobe. "You queens can be vicious."

"You are the envy of any drag queen," Nate soothed.

"High praise indeed," Andrea snapped.

Within a few minutes and a several block walk, they found themselves in Nate's favorite haunt, the glass fishbowl of a place around the corner from Old Compton Street.

The place is teeming to overflow with drinkers spilling out on to the corner. There is a buzz when they entered. Upon entering, Andrea Lyttle, the face of morning news, became a bona fide iconic fag hag and the boys couldn't wait to praise her very presence. Andrea never shies away from attention and busied herself shaking hands and saying hellos while Nate made his way to the bar.

"Nice gams, Andrea," one shouted over the din. "We never see your legs behind that news desk you sit at and now we can practically see your vajayjay. You're hot." These are Andrea's people for sure.

"Not bad for a broad of nearly fifty," she commented to the boys but more for herself.

He no sooner placed his order, two G&T's, Nate heard something familiar.

"I'm an undertaker," the voice explained. "Whatever you need, I undertake."

Nate thought for a moment before he turned and standing head and shoulders above his conversation mate is that guy he met with Mica. His name escapes Nate and he wracked his brain to remember it as he made his way back to Andrea.

"I have to introduce you to somebody," Nate said as he handed one of the drinks to Andrea. "It's the guy that Mica and I met here and Mica subsequently went out with."

"Our Mica Daly?" Andrea questioned. "He pulled someone from here? Good for him."

"Well it didn't exactly go down like that. He is a bit of an enigma. Come on, let's go say hi."

They made their way back through the crowd but Ted wasn't where Nate had left him and they found themselves on the far side of the bar before he was spotted again. Nate nodded to Andrea and tilted his head to indicate the tall man before them is Ted. Andrea couldn't help but to be slightly stunned by how handsome he is. Ted smiled when he saw Nate—one of those smiles that said the face looked familiar but he couldn't place how.

"Hello again," Nate said as he and Andrea sidled up to the side of the bar.

"Hello," Ted half questioned.

"I'm Nate Griffin. We met here some weeks ago. I was with Mica Daly. We work together."

"Of course. How are you?"

"Fine. Let me introduce you to another of our colleagues, Andrea Lyttle."

Andrea and Ted shook hands. "Pleasure to meet you," Ted said politely.

"And your name is?"

"Ted," he returned.

"That's it!" Nate exclaimed taking both Andrea and Ted aback. "Ted! You're Ted."

"Yes I am," he laughed.

"And I gather you are a friend of Mica Daly?" Andrea asked.

"Yes," Ted responded with trepidation. "He's a great guy. But I haven't seen him for a while."

"Well, he's back in Los Angeles," Nate offered. "But I gather before he left you two had quite a lovely dinner."

Ted blushed. He isn't sure just how much they know, how much Mica may have told them. "Like I said, Mica is a great guy."

Andrea could sense some discomfort and shifted the conversation. "So what is it you do?"

"I am in banking," Ted answered.

"Oh that must be interesting," Andrea began but was cut off by Nate.

"I thought you said you were in business of some sort," Nate quizzed.

"Isn't banking a business?" Ted returned.

"Yes but what about your undertaker line. Whatever you need, you undertake?" Nate pushed further.

Ted through his hands in the air, "Caught me!" There is an old trick in the news business. If there is a pause in the conversation, people tend to get nervous and begin speaking to fill in the void. If you simply shut up, the other person, usually being interviewed, will start to speak to end the awkwardness and inevitably they will tell you something they didn't intend to. Instinctually, Nate and Andrea simply shut up and within a few seconds Ted spoke up. This is not like Ted. He too is a trained interrogator, which is just another word for interviewer.

"I am part of a consultancy business. Nothing as glamorous as a television, mind you. So I tend to not talk about it."

There was something slightly off about the whole moment and for the sake of Mica, both Nate and Andrea didn't push. "Well, it is certainly great to run into you again," Nate said.

"Likewise but I am afraid I am meeting friends for dinner and can't stay," Ted returned. "Great meeting you Andrea but I must be off."

They didn't speak until he was safely out of earshot.

"That was weird," Andrea began.

"He was like that the first time we met, very elusive," Nate explained. "And yet, Mica said he was extremely interesting. Just who is this guy?"

"Well, we know he is not in banking, certainly not a consultant and I can make a fairly good bet he is not an undertaker. I wonder what he does do? Do we have his full name? I know people who can find people. Maybe we could do a little background check...you know, so that Mica isn't mixing with the wrong people."

"Yeah," Nate and Andrea clinking glasses. "For Mica."

⋀ ⋀ ⋀

The elevator doors opened and as Mica stepped out he ran right into and almost knocked over Lance Novak, the lawyer to the stars at Dunning, Baker and Astin. Mica blushed, as they hadn't seen each other in months—not since that harmless business dinner turned into a one-night stand.

"Mica?"

"I am so sorry," Mica apologized.

"Don't be. It is good to see you."

Mica had practically forgotten just how good looking Lance is—East Coast chic in his tailored suits and defined jawline. Why hadn't he stayed in touch? One night may just have led to a lifetime.

"How have you been?" Mica questioned politely.

"Oh you know me. It's always the same. Keeping clients out of hot water."

"Do tell," Mica quizzed playfully. "Any stories I can run with?"

"Not this time." It was Lance's turn to blush. Lance had been a valuable source sometime ago with one of Mica's more explosive scoops. And, as such, Mica liked to keep a better than professional relationship alive with Lance.

Mica discretely took Lance by the arm and walked him to the far side of the club's entrance, away from the well-honed, radar-like ears of the hostess. This may be a private club and, or because of that, members tend to let their guard down and speak as if they are immune to the help picking up a few dollars by leaking information to the tabloids. He may be paranoid but better safe than sorry. "There may be something you can help me with."

"Be careful," Lance smiled. "I bill at four hundred and fifty dollars an hour and at fifteen minute increments."

Mica laughed. "You whore!"

"So you do remember me! " Lance shot back. "What can I help you with?"

"I am doing an interview with one of what you could consider the lesser Royals in London. And I gather he has a penchant for saying rather explosive things. If something comes out of his mouth that I use in the article and it proves to be liable, slanderous or just irritating; am I accountable?"

"Are you anticipating something like that to happen?"

"You never know with this one," Mica sighed.

"I think your editor will have a say in what passes the litmus test. I wouldn't worry. Now I really have to get back to the office."

Mica leaned in instinctively to give him a kiss but Lance backed away and winked at Mica instead. Mica got it.

As he walked past the bar, he noticed the crowd is rather light. What did he expect for four in the afternoon? Some people actually *do* work in Los Angeles. Give it an hour and the place will be hopping.

"Mica!" he heard from over his shoulder coming from the particularly excited Michelle Bianco.

"Michelle!" They kissed on both cheeks. "What gets you out of the office in the middle of the day."

"Lunch turned to drinks. What can I say?"

He could now attribute her giddiness to a couple of chardonnays and something fizzy at the bar. And clearly her schizophrenia has kicked in because suddenly she and Mica are BFF's again. Mica is always cautious when dealing with rabid publicists and she is the alpha-dog when it comes to that pack. He is no fool; clearly she wants something.

"You know Sean?" she declared more than asked as she dragged Mica by the arm to the corner stool at the bar. "Sean Jones this is Mica Daly."

"Hi there," Mica said as he reluctantly stuck out his hand.

"Congratulations on the *Rise 'N Shine* gig," he said surprisingly, taking Mica aback.

"You've seen it."

"My mum watches all the time back in Wales. In fact, she thinks I should stop playing around with this acting thing and get a proper job like you have."

"Well, you should tell her if it wasn't for people like you, I wouldn't have a job."

"She loves you" Sean sighed. "Can I get you a drink?"

Mica blushed. "No, thank you, I don't mean to disturb your meeting."

"Don't be ridiculous," Michelle chirped. "This is fortuitous."

"It is?" Both Mica and Sean chimed in simultaneously.

"Sean is filming a movie back in London," Michelle began to explain with a lilt in her voice as if she was about to give out a prize. "And I think it would be great if Mica went on the set for a behind-the-scenes and perhaps a profile interview with you Sean."

"What is the movie about?" Mica asked.

"Well you know me," Sean joked. "I get to beat up a lot of people." Michelle laughed out loud, somewhat disingenuously. "It is an action flick. You know, I have twenty-four hours to kill or be killed. There are *a lot* of stunts, good visuals for a set visit."

"Well, coincidentally, I am also doing some work for *Gotcha!* magazine. I wonder if they would be interested in a spread as well?"

"Yes!" Michelle snapped.

"Needless to say. I have to run it by everyone concerned." Mica turned to the Michelle. "I will call your office and we can maybe talk about some dates and when I am going to be in London next." Mica stuck out his hand to Sean. "Great seeing you again. And I hate to leave you but I have some friends I am meeting and I am already late." The two shook hands and again Michelle leaned in for a kiss on the cheek.

"This is going to be great," she whispered in Mica's ear. "Just like old times."

Mica wasn't sure how to take that and simply smiled and walked off and spied the waving arms of Roger Keenan who was already ensconced with Marilyn Lassiter on the leather couch by the fireplace.

"Aren't you the popular one?" Marilyn teased.

"I am just trying to get my money's worth out of the club dues," Mica joked back. "Who knew this place was so expensive to be a member. I had to pay for the international membership because of London."

"Couldn't you get the show to pay for it?" Roger suggested.

Mica rolled his eyes and shook his head no.

"Look at it this way," Marilyn interjected. "It's a tax write off. Just like my parties. All business expenses. All courtesy of Uncle Sam."

"Michelle Bianco?" Roger questioned—fishing really. "Isn't that swimming with the sharks?"

"Kinda. Except today we are the best of friends," Mica answered.

"Go figure. She must be off her meds," Roger shot back.

"Don't worry, this new found friendship won't last. I will fuck it up again one of these days."   "Work talk. Work talk. Work talk," Marilyn snapped. "Gimme gossip and not talk."

"First a drink," Roger snapped for a waiter. Rude but effective.

"I'll have a tea," Marilyn spoke delicately. Both Mica and Roger simply stared at her. "Oh what the hell. I'll have a champagne instead."

"Vodka martini for me."

"Make it two," Roger seconded. And as the waiter backed away, Roger turned back to Mica. "So what is going on that you summoned us two?"

"Besides the fact that I *love* your respective company…"

"Yeah, yeah, fuck you! What are you getting at?"

"Roger!" Marilyn snapped.

"What I want is some insight," Mica began. "I have a special assignment from *Gotcha!* magazine to do an interview with the Duke of Clarence who is a bit of a playboy…a bit of a mess really, is what I have been told."

"I'd say," Roger harrumphed. "He's been all over the tabloids lately."

"That's why the magazine wants to do a profile. You know one of those 'who is the man behind the reputation.' That kind of thing," Mica explained.

"So what do you want to know from us?" Marilyn asked.

"Both of you have had dealings with the Royals—either from events you have created, Roger, which they have attended or on the charity circuit with you Marilyn. Hell, Roger, you are a Brit. I am just trying to get a feel for the kind of people they are."

"They're Royal. Their trained not to speak," Roger summated. "They're not like the stars you chase. They don't need the publicity."

"This one does," Mica corrected. "At least some good publicity."

"Well for one thing," Marilyn began, "The Duke may be titled but he is hardly Royal. The last time I was at the Palace, attending a function with any one or the other of them...something to do with the Prince's Trust...I forget why we were there...but the Duke turned up and there were audible groans. They didn't even acknowledge his presence and the snub was obvious. So who the hell he is? Where did he come from?"

"Maybe that's the story right there," Mica exclaimed with an ah-ha moment.

"Be careful though," Roger cautioned. "There is always a fine line between being a journalist and a shill. That might not be what you want the story to be about. It maybe all about what he wants to say. You may be nothing more than a stenographer."

"Especially when it comes to the Royals," Marilyn added. "Even if he says something topical, or incendiary, or politically incorrect, or insightful for that matter; you may not be able to print it."

"Well the piece, as I understand it, is designed to mend his playboy reputation. To that end, he'll have to say something about his wicked ways in order just to explain himself."

"We'll see," Roger smirked. "You will be able to count the syllables at the end of your interview and I bet they don't add up to a sentence."

The drinks arrived as if on cue. As they each took hold of their respective glasses, Mica raised his. "To the Royals."

"Off with their heads," Roger trumpeted.

"I say let them eat cake," Marilyn joked.

"Enough with the puns." Mica sipped his drink and stood up. "If you will excuse me. I am off to the restroom for a Royal wee."

"I suggest you don't use that line during the interview," Roger jokingly cautioned.

"I suggest you don't use that line ever!" Marilyn punctuated.

⋀ ⋀ ⋀

The phone rang and Mica fumbled for it, half asleep. He caught the time on the clock as 11:00 p.m. The television is still on as are the lights, Mica must have crashed. The phone rang again and the caller I.D. read a British number. Mica is used to the show calling him at all hours of the day and night, as the support staff can never do the math and realizes he is eight hours before them. He answered.

"Hello?"

"Mica?"

"Yes."

"It's Ted."

Mica sprang up and came to life. "Oh my. I didn't recognize your voice."

"I am not calling you too late am I?"

"No…oh please, don't worry about it. I am glad to hear from you."

"I would have called sooner," Ted began, "but it has been awfully busy. And then I ran into a couple of your colleagues and it reminded me that we haven't spoken in ages." Mica couldn't tell because of the poor connection, but it did seem that Ted's words were ever so slurred.

"Whom did you run into?"

"Now you can't hold me to their names," Ted strained. "But I believe she is the news woman and he is the director. Something like that."

"Andrea and Nate…interesting they didn't tell me that they ran into you."

"Oh it was quick. They may have forgotten."

"I would have called you," Mica countered, "if I had any contact information on you!"

"Ah right, sorry about that. Anyway, how are you?"

"Good. Busy. But it looks as if I will be over there sooner than later."

"Fantastic. Why for?"

"Interviews," Mica explained. "A Sean Jones set visit and one in particular I think will be interesting. I am supposed to interview Freddy, Duke of Clarence for a spread in *Gotcha!* magazine."

There was a noticeable pause.

"Ted? Are you there?"

"Yes I am here."

"Did you hear me? I am going to interview the Duke of Clarence."

"Are you sure you should be doing that?" Ted asked with a certain caution in his voice.

"Why wouldn't I?"

"Well what do you know about him? What is the story?" Ted had an urgency in his voice and it wasn't lost on Mica.

"That is being worked out. Why do you ask?"

"Well, he is a bit of a volatile personality at the moment and not well liked."

"All the more reason to tell his story."

Again there was a pause and then Ted collected himself. "Is your trip contingent on this interview happening?"

"No. Why?"

"The Royals. They are not always agreeable to the media and well...well we'll see. But it is great news that you are coming over. We must have dinner."

"As soon as I know the details of my trip, I will let you know. But enough about me. How are things with you?"

"Fine...yeah...fine."

"That doesn't sound so fine."

"I am just thinking about a lot of things at the moment and what the future holds, that sort of thing. Nothing you have to worry yourself over. But I would like your input when you are here."

"Can do."

"Well I must let you go. It is getting late your time."

"Ted...?"

"Yes."

"Nothing. Just...I had a great time with you the last time I was in town. And...well...I am just looking forward to seeing you again."

"Me too. Now get some sleep."

Before he could say another word, Mica's phone went dead. And again, Ted slipped away without providing a way for Mica to contact him. He instinctually pushed the redial button.

"Thank you for calling Boothby's," the voice said at the other end.

9

Ted simply showed up, unannounced and unexpected. The knock at the door startled Mica. He had gotten back to the hotel relatively early, 9:00 p.m., knowing he had to be up for the show the next day. Mica opened the door and gasped. He'd forgotten how handsome Ted is, in that dashy bespoke way.

"What are you doing here?" Mica stammered

"Can I come in?" Ted stood waiting.

"Of course. But what are you doing here?"

"I could leave if this is a bad time," Ted teased.

"No…oh, shut up…seriously, what are you doing here?"

"I was in the neighborhood, sort of, and I thought I would drop in."

As much as he is happy to see him, Ted continues to confound Mica with his mysterious—if not romantic—ways. Mica hadn't heard from Ted since that late night phone call almost two weeks ago. Mica, needless to say, hadn't told Ted he was in town. And yet, Ted managed to know that Mica was there and staying at The Coliseum. He even got the room number right. They kissed, deep and hard.

"Pardon my confusion, but how did you know I am here?"

"I saw you on the air today. You were in the studio and the studio just so happens to be in London. I put two and two together," Ted joked.

"And how did you know where I am staying?"

"You always stay here. So lucky guess."

"And how did you get my room number?"

"I have been walking down the halls for hours now, knocking on each door until I found you."

"Cute," Mica sighed. He knew he wasn't going to get a straight answer out of Ted. That is part of Ted's charm, but also part of his enigmatic persona.

"It doesn't matter how I got here or what it took to get here, I am here now."

"True."

Not much was said as drinks were poured but barely touched and clothes were peeled away. Mica with only a t-shirt and jeans on was quickly naked but he took a long and sensuous time with Ted, slowing untying his tie, unbuttoning each shirt button, the belt and the zipper. The whole striptease had left Ted with a raging hard-on, which Mica squeezed through Ted's boxer briefs. They kissed passionately as they made their way to the bed.

Ted pushed Mica backwards on to the bed, pulled down his restraining boxers, climbed on top and began to grind himself against Mica—their cocks doing a kind of snake dance with each other. Mica moaned appreciatively.

Ted pulled back, looked deep into Mica's eyes but said nothing. Mica melted under the stare, nothing needed to be said. Ted kissed Mica gently and then, with his tongue, traced over his chin, down his neck, flicking his nipples, down his torso and to his cock. Mica's cock jumped with anticipation. Ted licked gently around the head, up and down the shaft and back to the head again. And with one smooth move slid Mica's engorged member down his throat. Mica could have cum right then but relaxed and let Ted go to work.

An hour later, after both had been sucked and fucked, strained and drained, Ted, now sweaty and spent, rolled over with a sigh, grabbed his drink and took a large gulp. "I *have* missed you!"

A moment passed. Afterglow. And then Mica spoke up, "What do you do when I am gone?"

"Work."

"All work and no play makes for a dull boy," Mica recited back.

"Well I am kind of dull when you think about it."

"Hardly. You have a very interesting life with the Ministry of Defense. A life you have yet to explain completely. But I have to assume it is interesting if you keep ending up at Royal receptions and such."

Diverting where the conversation is heading, Ted sat up and looked at Mica hard. "And what do you do back in L.A. when I am not around?"

"Fuck like a bunny!"

"Nice." Ted slid back down.

"No, no. I think of you and touch myself...mostly."

With one quick swoop, Ted hit Mica in the head with his pillow and they both started to laugh—a laugh that ended with a deep, long kiss."

"So what are your plans while you are in town?" Ted asked.

"Some time in the studio. I don't know what my people have planned for me. But I have an interview with Sean Jones on the set of his new movie. And then there is the Duke of Clarence."

"So sorry to hear about that," Ted began. "I know you were looking forward to that."

"What do you mean?" Mica quizzed.

"It's not happening, right?"

"I don't know anything about it being canceled. What are you talking about? And how would *you* know if it was canceled."

Ted was caught off guard. He shouldn't know but he does. "Oh, I thought you said it was off. Maybe I misheard you. Sorry, misunderstanding." It is not like Ted to miscue like that. It seemed to be happening quite a bit lately and he wasn't sure if he was letting his guard down purposely or simply self-sabotaging.

"No. It is on as far as I know."

Ted's answer to any awkward moment with Ted was a deep and passionate kiss. They continued to kiss as Mica reached for the light switch and plunged them in to blackness. Both, exhausted were asleep in minutes.

It wasn't long though before Mica rolled over to find Ted's side of the bed empty. He could see by the glow of the clock that only forty-five minutes had passed. His eyes quickly adjusted to the dark and he could just make out the shadow of Ted pulling up his pants. Mica chose to lie there and say nothing. Ted finished dressing and as stealthy as he arrived, he was gone. But to where, or to whom?

∧ ∧ ∧

The interview on the sofa with Sean Jones could not have gone any better. His hard assed, strong man persona seemed to melt away and he was glib, playful and almost flirtatious with Mica.

Mica had spent a full day on the set of Sean's movie *Cover's Blown* filming just outside of London. As promised, it is action packed and stunt heavy. These days are a director's dream as they really get to see their vision come to life. So the fact that Mica was there was less of a distraction and more of a chance to peacock his storytelling prowess. So it was carte blanche for Mica and the crew. They, the producers and Sean, had orchestrated a day's visit that would be particularly visual with a building being blown up and Sean's character to be blown out of the third floor in the process. Sean, being the he-man that he is, had decided he would do his own stunts for this movie. So the day promised to be even more dramatic and provide spectacular footage. They had even set up a mini-stunt for Mica to try—being blown out of the first floor and landing on the very large, very safe, air bag. The entire day was intermittently playful, with Sean mugging to the camera, the director and producers providing color commentary on the goings-on and including Mica in on explaining everything that was to happen. And on the serious side—there was a actually a movie being filmed, after all. Mica had been on many movie sets over the years and mostly the experience was a big 'hurry up and wait' for something to happen. This visit was non-stop and exhausting in all the best ways.

By the time they had reached the sofa on the set of *Rise 'N Shine* for the live interview, Sean Jones and Mica Daly were best buds. Even Michelle Bianco, who needless to say was omnipresent, thought this was one of the best set visits and subsequent interviews Sean had ever done. They'd played the five minute long taped segment of Mica's set visit followed by another five minutes of live interview on the sofa. Ten minutes of morning television is almost unprecedented. Michelle could not have been more pleased and promised more access to more clients, sets and events. Mica is officially back in her good graces.

As Mica said his "good-byes" and walked off the set, Andrea was waiting for him in the green room.

"Coffee?" she asked.

"Sure," Mica said.

"Do you have a moment?" Andrea asked as she handed Mica a cup of espresso.

Mica fumbled through the baked goods and fruit on the side table and thought otherwise and put down the muffin. "Sure, what's up?"

"Let's go to my office."

"Ooh, this sounds official," Mica teased.

"Not really, just a curiosity."

They started down the hallway and toward the elevator and ran into Nate coming out of the control room. "Great show."

"Thanks," they responded but didn't really connect with Nate.

"Anything wrong?" Nate asked.

Mica shrugged.

"Well then I will leave you two alone." Nate knew enough to step aside. "Lunch?"

"I'm in!" Mica said.

"Can't," Andrea added. "Out in the field today."

As the elevator opened and Andrea and Mica stepped in, Mica turned to Nate. "I will find you." And as the doors closed, he then turned to Andrea. "So?"

"It is your friend, Ted."

"Oh?"

"Did Nate tell you we ran into him one evening?" Mica shook his head, no. Of course he had but Mica thought he would get more information out of their side of the story if he just played dumb. "Well we did. I had never met him and Nate introduced us. And, well, in my opinion he was acting particularly strange."

"Okay..."

The door opened and they walked silently and directly to Andrea's office, shut the door and sat.

"What are you getting at?" Mica probed, somewhat irritated.

"First of all, when you were out with Nate and you first met Ted, he said he was in business. When I asked him what he does, he said he was in banking. You're a journalist, Mica. You know when something doesn't seem right. It is a gut thing. Anyway, it got me to thinking just who is this man. So I did a little investigating."

"You what?" Mica had to suppress raising his voice.

"I know. I know. It all seems creepy. But I know people who know about people and I was just curious," she defended. "Don't you want to know what I found? Nothing!"

"That's good right. There is nothing to be found."

"No," she said, clearly excited by this phenomenon. "I mean nothing as in no driver's license, no address, no records of any kind. I mean if my people look up anyone in this room, you will find something, anything. But with your friend Ted, there is nothing. Don't you find that odd?" Mica didn't know what to say. "Do you know anything about him?"

"Well, I do know that he is not a banker and does work for the Ministry of Defense in some capacity or other." Mica paused to think. "I don't know much about him at all. Oh, but I do know that he his a member of a club called Boothby's."

"Boothby's?" Andrea nearly squealed. "Do you know what that means?"

"No."

"That of course we can't find anything about him. He is classified."

"Classified?" Mica questioned.

"Are you sure he works for the Ministry? People who are members of Boothby's have very covert connections. This guy could be really interesting."

"He is really interesting," Mica snapped back at Andrea. "Look, no one asked you to investigate my friend in the first place. This is making me really uneasy. All I know is he is a nice guy who seems to like me for me, not me for being on television, and that is quite an aphrodisiac these days."

"All I am saying is that if you are not concerned, you should at least be curious."

"I don't know that much about you Andrea but I like you too. There is a line here and you are dangerously close to crossing it."

"Enough said." Andrea backed down.

Just as the tension piqued, there was a knock on the door and Stuart Brewster stuck his head. "If you gals are finished gabbing, could I see you, Mica, in my office?"

Mica turned to Andrea, "Can he get away with calling me a gal?"

"I can get away with just about anything. I am the boss." Stuart shut the door behind him but stood in the window for a second mouthing "now".

Mica stood. "It looks like it's a day for interrogations."

"Mica, I am not interrogating anyone but I was simply curious. Now, to be honest, I am more curious."

"To be perfectly honest," Mica conceded, "so am I."

ᴧ ᴧ ᴧ

Mica likes Stuart's office—a corner with two walls of glass that overlook the Thames with a picture postcard view of Tower Bridge. Stuart's desk is positioned diagonally in the apex of the two windows, with his back to the spectacular view, facing out to the bullpen of workers. Mica has grown to like Stuart even though they barely interact and he has a reputation for being a hard assed taskmaster. But Mica appreciates an executive with a vision and the means to get there. That, and the fact that Mica is a darling of the show at the moment and therefore treated with respect and professionalism, only heightens his respect for Stuart.

"What are you doing?" Stuart fired at Mica.

Stuart has the ability to strafe a person with words. When fired up, he speaks with a staccato speediness that nearly stings the ear. It's effective when he wants to intimidate the conversation. Mica felt a strafing coming on.

"What do you mean?" Mica asked back.

"What are you doing in London?"

"Well as you know, I am doing a set visit with Sean Jones..."

"Yes. And..."

"Well I have an interview with the Duke of Clarence for *Gotcha!* magazine, which I believe we can piggy back on with our cameras."

"That is not going to happen." Stuart clearly had made this decision long before this conversation and had simply lured Mica into a verbal trap. Mica is smart enough in moments like this to say nothing and show no emotion. "First, we are not interested in that subject. Second, you need to run your assignments by me."

"But I did."

"No I mean your freelance work. I am not going to stop you from working for *Gotcha!* magazine. But I need to know what you are doing for them...for any-one for that matter. What you do outside of these walls reflects back on what you represent for those of us on the inside of these walls."

"I can and do appreciate that." Mica isn't sure whether he is being chastised or simply warned but is going to take it on the chin no matter what.

Stuart leaned back in his chair and folded his arms. "Besides, I don't think that interview is going to happen."

"Why do you say that? We have a contract."

"He is currently an embarrassment to the Royals and that is never a position of power. They don't want him talking. The Palace has to approve all interviews and I would bet a week's salary that it is not going to happen. I know. We have tried to talk to him before. And believe me the ramifications were too great."

"Ramifications?"

"Oh things like the show being banned from any Royal events. That sort of thing."

"I see." Mica paused to digest the situation. "But we talked about him the other night. Andrea did the story on how he was part of that bar brawl at Red and then I talked about celebrities in scandals. Isn't that coverage?"

"We covered an event that everyone ran with. That is far different than giving him a voice."

"Gotcha!" Mica said. "Excuse the pun."

Stuart got up and walked around the desk. Clearly the conversation was over. Mica stood and Stuart gave him a hug. Mica had forgotten how short Stuart is—a Napoleon complex would explain a lot. "You're doing a great job for us. Keep it up and don't fuck it up!"

"Gotcha!"

"You've used that joke. Do you have lunch plans?"

"I do actually," Mica confessed but didn't dare tell him it was just with Nate. Stuart squinted. "But I could cancel."

"Don't be ridiculous. But we will have some time together while you are here." That sounded both ominous and definitive.

"Definitely."

∧ ∧ ∧

Back at The Coliseum, Mica was ready for a relatively early night but the perpetual night owl Hilary Stewart caught him at the door. "You have a guest. He is waiting for you in Fluid and I have already ordered you a martini." She has a mind like a steel trap when it comes to the minutia of people's connections to other people and the appropriate drink to go with such a rendezvous.

Mica handed his briefcase containing his computer to the bellman and requested that it be brought to his room. He was flush with anticipation, knowing the only visitor he could possibly expect would be Ted. Although he had an early morning ahead, a little late night fun is not out of order.

It takes a minute for Mica's eyes to adjust in the darkened bar. The dark wood panels and dim wattage simply ate up the available light. The glow from the bar is the only spray of real light. As Mica walked in, he saw a couple at the far corner, two business types at the small table and a backlit figure sitting at the bar. Ted?

"Hello Mica," the voice is familiar but not Ted.

"Ian?" Mica guessed.

"How are you doing?"

Mica took a stool next to him at the bar and the bartender dutifully handed Mica his well-deserved martini. "This is a pleasant surprise. First, let me thank you in person for that fantastic spread in the magazine. The pictures were beautiful."

"Yes we thought they were great too," Ian clinked glasses with Mica. His drink of choice is a scotch.

"So you've come over, presumably, to watch over me during the interview with Freddy?" Mica asked.

"Well that was the plan," Ian began. "But now the interview has been canceled."

"What?" Mica is shocked but shouldn't have been. He'd been warned.

"Let's just say the Palace is being less than cooperative."

"I've heard they could have been. And clearly they are. Well that is a shame. How has the Duke taken the news?"

"He is not happy." Ian rolled his eyes. "And of course, he wants us to honor the contract."

"Meaning?"

"He still wants to be paid."

"Ah." Mica paused for a moment to take in the news. It is interesting how Stuart knew, or at the very least assumed correctly, that the interview would never happen. But more interestingly, was how Ted seemed to know as fact it wasn't happening. "I am just curious. Does anyone else have a say in the decision about a story being dropped?"

"Anyone else?"

"Does anyone else have a say besides the Palace?"

"Plenty of people can intercede. The government for instance can point out that a story is not in their best interest. But this is *Gotcha!* magazine—hardly the news of record. These are for the most part fluff, exploitive pieces. Why do you ask?"

"I don't know," Mica dismissed. "Just a gut feeling."

"My guess is the whole thing is a slap on the hand because of his antics that night in Red. The Palace may have found that embarrassing," Ian concluded.

"But wouldn't they have made that point from the start and not waited until the night before the interview to pull the plug?"

"One would have assumed. It would have saved me a lot of time and money."

"Perhaps they weren't embarrassed at all…yet. What if he has something to say, they don't want heard?" Mica's mind is overdrive at the moment.

"Listen to you," Ian chuckled. "You sound like a proper journalist."

Mica smiled and took the compliment and then ordered a second round of drinks. It seems he didn't have to be up early in the morning after all.

ᴧ ᴧ ᴧ

Freddy had summoned Ben up to his rooms and to bring up a bottle of gin. Freddy had gone through the remainder of the bottle he had and was looking to tie one on. When Ben arrived, he found the front reception room scattered with the dismantled remnants of the large and beautiful flower arrangement he had just delivered that afternoon, the one which was to be the center piece for the photo shoot with *Gotcha!* magazine. This didn't bode well.

"Sir?"

"In here Ben," Freddy snapped from the sitting room. Cautiously, Ben enters the room to find Freddy in an open robe and nothing else, downing the last of his existent drink. "Could you pour me another and make a fire. I am a little cold."

"Certainly, Sir."

"That's right. I am your master and you will do as I say!" Freddy snapped and startled Ben. He'd never spoken that way before—not to or about Ben directly. "You will give me the respect I deserve even if the rest of them won't."

"Of course, Sir."

Ben wisely handed over a lightly poured gin and tonic to his clearly inebriated boss and went over to tend to the fireplace. He got down on all fours to place the wood and Freddy came up behind him, reached between his legs and fondled Ben's crotch. "Are you wearing it?"

"Yes, Sir."

"Very good." Freddy reached around and unzipped Ben's zipper, letting his soft but still impressive cock, balls and golden cock ring fall out into Freddy's cupped hand. "Very good, indeed."

"Shall I stop with the fire, Sir?"

"NO!"

Ben nervously continued stacking wood, placing kindling and getting ready to strike a match, all the while Freddy tugged Ben's pants down to his bended

106

knees and buried his face between Ben's smooth, white, cheeks. It is hard for Ben to concentrate; the feeling is so sensual. He couldn't help but relax, push his ass forward and let out a subtle moan.

"You know what your master wants?"

"Yes, sir!"

As if choreographed, at the exact moment Ben struck his match, Freddy rammed his stiff pole into Ben's wet hole. The force of which almost sent Ben into the fireplace. Ben let out a squeal of both pain and pleasure.

Freddy pounded Ben, harder and more aggressive than he had ever before. The sound of Freddy's balls slapping Ben's ass was almost rhythmic applause. "YOU WILL FUCKING TAKE MY COCK!"

The fucking went on for several minutes as the fire grew in the fireplace, putting Ben in actual danger. "Could we move to the sofa? The fire, sir."

Freddy, silently grabbed Ben by the tie and led him like a dog to the sofa, pushed him back into the corner and lifted his legs in the air. Again the force of Freddy's thrusts is almost too much for Ben to take. But still, Ben was being turned on by Freddy's aggression and he began to stroke his own hard cock in sync with the Freddy's pounding.

"You like it don't you?"

"Yes sir," Ben moaned.

"You will take it! Just like they will take it!" Freddy shouted. "They think they can shut me up. Well they haven't heard anything yet! I will fuck them harder than I am fucking you!"

With one final thrust, both Freddy and Ben came together.

10

An invite to Sir Daniel Wynn-Thomas' garden party is something akin to going to the Oscars on someone's front lawn. Only the cream of society, politics, theater, television, the movies and music are invited. And no one says no.

Wynn-Thomas is a septuagenarian television icon whose claim to fame is as a noted hard-hitting interviewer on his *Hot Seat* talk show. Over the years he has managed to parlay this one-trick gab fest into a cottage industry with top dollar lectures, best selling books, highly paid radio and television appearances and a well respected philanthropic foundation—for which he was knighted by the Queen. And along the way were four, very busty, very blond wives; the fourth of which, Caroline, Lady Wynn-Thomas, seems to be a keeper.

The magnitude of the invite was lost on Mica, who was aware of the work of Sir Daniel but not the extent of his iconic status. The invite arrived at the office of Owens & Owens, his agents, along with one for Andrea Lyttle. Mica caused a little faux pas in the studio rattling his anchor team after the invite arrived and he blurted out that he would be attending *the* party of the season, if not the year. Clearly neither Euan nor Corrine had been invited, again, and the fact that the up-start American had been, caused Euan to storm off the set and not speak to Mica unless on the air. Mica was sure he had caused some sort of irreparable harm but Andrea assured him that Euan was simply being a spoiled child who didn't get the toy he wanted and was pouting. She went on to say that this provided gravitas to Mica and would keep Euan in his place. Corrine for her part, although beloved by the morning audience, is barely a blip on the radar of the kinds of people seen at a Sir Daniel Wynn-Thomas event.

As stated on the invitation, both Mica and Andrea could invite an escort—a 'plus one' to the party. It was decided that both would take an Owen, Mica with Elizabeth and Andrea with Angela. The Owens had organized a car and driver on the day, Saturday, which turned out to be sunny and glorious. The party, in a gated garden in Chelsea, wouldn't need the foul weather tent at all.

Security was tight as the car pulled up. Before the car was allowed into the square, guests were expected to show both their invitations and some sort of identification despite most of the guests having obvious fame and instant recognition. Once in the square, guests were dropped off at the only gate at the end of the square where a metal detector had been installed and then were checked in against a more formal invitation list. There was a line by the time Mica and the lot arrived and they dutifully stood in the queue just behind the former Bond girl turned sitcom star, Joan Lonsdale. Lonsdale had become quite the gay icon in America for her perpetually stoned and drunk, social climber of a character. For the first time in a long time, Mica found himself star struck.

"Ms. Lonsdale," Mica stammered. "I am Mica Daly and I just wanted to say..."

The aging but attractive comedian cut him off, "I know exactly who you are. I watch your segment all the time. You are very funny."

Mica was thrown. "Thank you. But I was going to tell you that on behalf of the entire gay population of Los Angeles, I bow down."

"Oh please...and thank you...but really it's the writers who are the secret to my success. I just chain smoke and drink my way through their lines." She moved forward and through the gate. "Lovely to meet you. Have fun today."

Mica nearly screamed with excitement. "She watches *my* segments. Can you believe that?"

"Yes," Elizabeth stated as a matter-of-fact. "You are a very popular person on a very popular show. Enjoy the compliment but know that most people here will know who you are even if you don't know them."

With that, they showed their respective invites and identifications and walked through the gate and into a sea of Britain's who's who—linen on men, hats on women, the quintessential English garden party. They made their way to the bar. There is nothing as hard as a martini to be had—Pimms and champagne, mimosas, white wine, a blush wine and of course tea—all so civilized. Mica chose champagne; the ladies opted for the blush.

As they wandered around, each of the four started to break away, talking to familiar faces they met along the way. Mica, for his part, drifted in and out the crowd, finding himself at various moments face to face with everyone from the Prime Minister, to Fergie and the Princesses, a Rolling Stone, two different mystery authors, Joan Collins, the opera singing Dame, Michael Crawford, several political faces who knew Mica but left Mica bemused and several television personalities.

"Mica? Mica Daly," the familiar but slightly shrill voice of Pamela Smythe-Lyons rang out over a somewhat sedate crowd. "I just knew I would run into you one of the these days again. Naughty boy for not telling me you are in town. I must say, I loved the spread of you at home in *Gotcha!*. Simply darling place you have in Los Angeles. Now who are you here with?"

Her constant rapid-fire conversation starters are close to exhausting. "Thank you and I am here with my agents and a colleague, Andrea Lyttle."

"Oh I like her. She's on your show."

"It's more like I am on hers," Mica joked but it was lost on Pamela. "And I guess I should ask who you are here with."

"Freddy," she turned as if he was next to her and, of course, he isn't. "Now where did he get off to? Freddy!" She shouted and then leaned into Mica. "He's my guest, my 'plus one'. He'd kill me if he knew I told you that. I know he is on everyone's shit list but I think he is great fun. Freddy!"

Out of the crowd emerged a nattily dressed, if not slightly disheveled with a loosened tie and silk pocket square pouring out of his jacket pocket, Duke of Clarence with a drink in each hand.

"Well I can't believe my luck. Mica Daly." Within the few short steps it took to reach Pamela and Mica, Freddy choked down one of the champagnes and simply dropped the glass from his right hand on to the lawn and extended the same hand to shake with Mica. A diligent waiter scooped up the glass before anyone else could notice the rudeness of the gesture. "Am I happy to see you!"

"I am so sorry we were not able to do the interview for *Gotcha!* magazine. I was so looking forward to it."

"So was I," he began. "But you know there was a whole lot more to the killing of that story than meets the eye." He winked.

"I was told the Palace had said..."

"Nonsense!" Freddy snapped. "Redemption is the 'family's' favorite past time. They like nothing more that a big mea culpa in their eyes when you do something wrong. And they believe I am constantly doing something wrong. So there was some other force at play here. The 'family' simply went along with it."

Mica wasn't sure whether to laugh at all this self-importance or be piqued by the prospect of something more sinister at play.

"I have such a fascinating story to tell. And it is not one the family wants me to let out. But it is time to talk and I think you are the man to tell it to," Freddy declared.

"Well I am flattered."

"Let us have lunch at the Ivy this week. I want to be in a public place when I speak."

"Okay." Mica began to believe Freddy is a bit of a nut. But what the hell? Why shouldn't he hear his story? Mica would be the toast of a Marilyn Lassiter party with an inside story on one of the Royals.

A hand landed on Mica's shoulder. "Mica Daly. So good to see you again."

"I know you," Freddy nearly shouted. "You are the man from the Palace. I told you I knew you and I do. I demand you tell me your name."

"Alex," Ted said. "Alex Stevens."

Mica nearly dropped his drink when he turned and saw Ted. "Alex? So good to see you too."

"Now I hate to be rude," Ted began quickly before Freddy could get another word in edgewise. "But there are a few people who would like to meet Mica. Great to see you again. No doubt it will be soon." Ted took Mica by the arm and started to lead him away.

"The Ivy. THIS WEEK," Freddy shouted at the quickly departing duo. Ted took note of the plan.

Once out of sight of the Duke and Pamela, Ted stopped. "Sorry about that. But I overheard him say he has a story to tell you…"

"Wait a minute. *Wait a minute…Alex*! What the hell was that all about?" Mica isn't amused.

"I am trying to tell you…"

"And who the hell is Alex Stevens?"

"I made that up obviously. He doesn't need to know my real name."

"Why is that?" Mica quizzed. "I was beginning to think that Freddy is a fruitcake, bat shit crazy. But now I think there might be two of you here."

"Look I will explain everything. Just know that right now, you need to stay away from him."

"Why?"

"He is upsetting a lot of people with his threats of this story he wants to tell. The last thing you need is to be the person who he speaks to. Trust me on this."

"What are you doing here?"

"I was invited," Ted stated.

"No you weren't. You're here for a reason," Mica whispered. "Do you know who killed the interview for *Gotcha!* that I was supposed to conduct with Freddy."

"Yes."

"And…?"

"We can't talk about it here."

Just as they reached a standoff, Andrea approached. "Ted, how nice to see you here. Nice company you keep."

"Nice to see you again. But I was just leaving. Good to see you again, Mica. I will be in touch." Ted and Mica shook hands and in so doing Ted slipped Mica a card—his phone number. Mica discretely slid the card into his pocket. Andrea didn't need to see the card. Ted darted off.

"He must be some banker...or business man for that matter...to end up at a party like this," Andrea stated as she watched Ted disappear into the crowd.

11

amela Smythe-Lyons prides herself on being a gal of many talents. But bulimia will never be one of them as she lost her gag reflex along with her virginity at the ripe old age of fourteen, in secondary school. Simon Parker was the happiest player on the school rugby team but not the only satisfied customer. The boys referred to it as 'getting a PSL'. Today, with the frequency she gives out her famed PSL it is a wonder she has not contracted an STD. It may be common knowledge but no joke that the only job she has ever had is a blowjob. Three abortions later, it is also an amazement she has not sired a junior.

Freddy lay there rather disengaged as Pamela went down on him. His mind wandered as to whether her talents bests that of valet Ben Foster. She certainly has ability, but Ben has a certain hunger that is both exciting and highly charged. Freddy isn't really in the mood and thought for a moment of bringing Ben into the fray to move things along when the phone rang. He jumped to answer it, nearly knocking the oblivious Pamela into the coffee table.

"I have to get this," he explained.

"Really?" she huffed. "You don't even know who it is."

"At this hour, it has to be something important."

Standing naked with his back to her, Pamela couldn't help but to notice the tautness of his body and his perfectly shaped buttocks. His cock is a nice size too—not too big with plenty of girth. No wonder the boys liked him. She wondered about her chances of becoming a Duchess.

"You must cancel your lunch tomorrow," the voice on the other end of the phone spoke ominously.

"Who is this?" Freddy could almost recognize the voice but it wasn't coming to him.

"That doesn't matter."

"And why must I cancel my lunch?"

"It is not in your best interest to speak to a journalist." The voice got more specific and articulate.

"I am having lunch with a friend," Freddy countered. "And as you probably already know—not that it is any of your business. I have a story worth telling and it is time it is told."

"The 'family' and others more powerful than yourself do not believe it is in your best interest to tell that story. Keep your mouth shut, your position safe and your story to yourself."

"So I am being shut up, again, by the 'family' and mysterious others?" Freddy grew indignant. "Well I have a message that you can tell them. YOU CAN'T STOP ME. I will be going to that lunch."

"That's just it. They can and they will. It's happened before to others who wanted to speak their mind. Remember that. This is bigger than you."

"Wait a minute." Freddy suddenly had an epiphany. "I know this voice. You are the man from the Palace, the man at the garden party. Is this some sort of joke?"

"You would be best served if you paid no attention to the messenger but paid plenty of attention to the message."

The phone went dead. Freddy tried to redial but the number hadn't registered on his phone. All of a sudden, the magnitude of what just happened washed over Freddy. "I've been threatened," Freddy mumbled loud enough for Pamela to hear.

"By whom? Over what?" she questioned.

"I am not exactly sure by whom. But I know over what. My very existence scares them."

"Scares who?"

"The family...and others it seems."

"Perhaps it is not you, per se, but rather your insistence on telling people who you are. No one will believe you are the rightful heir anyway," she dismissed.

"DNA will prove everything," Freddy snapped.

"And then what? You pull down the institution of the monarchy. Is that what you want? Live your life...your privileged life and be done with it."

"But there is more to it. They are not scared of who I am but what I know. That has to be it. They are scared that I am a wild card. And that is my life insurance."

"Perhaps you just need to settle down," she purred, "and find yourself a nice Duchess."

"If that is what you are fishing for, forget it. Remember a blowjob is just a blowjob. It is not a marriage proposal. And speaking of that, crawl over here and finish what you started."

ᴧ ᴧ ᴧ

"Were you talking to me?" Mica asked as he exited the bathroom. "Because I couldn't hear a word you said." He reached for the remainder of his 'chamtini',

114

a vodka and champagne martini—a drink created a lifetime ago under similar circumstances.

The light was off on Ted's side of the bed and he had rolled over in the fetal position. Clearly the fun was over for the night. "No, I had to make a work call."

"A work call? At this hour of the night?" Mica quizzed. "One of these days we are going to have to have a long conversation about how you define 'work.'"

Mica wasn't joking but it fell on deaf ears as Ted was already breathing heavy—not quite snoring—an indication that he'd already fallen into a deep sleep. Mica had been in awe of how Ted could simply drop off, as if being exhausted to the point of needing immediate sleep.

Mica lay in bed, sipping his drink and listening to the rhythm of Ted's breathing. He had turned off the light, hoping the dark and Ted's breathing would lull him to sleep too. It seemed like hours but really was just a matter of minutes before it worked. And then just a few minutes more he was awaken again.

Ted began to thrash in the dark. "No. I can't do it! I can't do it!" he yelled into the night.

"Ted?" Mica reached over to calm him but found he was still asleep.

"I won't. This is wrong," he yelled again and then startled himself awake.

"Are you okay?" Mica asked with genuine concern.

Mica flicked on the lamp at his side of the bed. There was a pause as Ted regained his composure. Mica asked again but got nothing at first.

"I'm sorry," Ted muttered. "I should go."

"No. Don't. Let's talk about what happened. Are you okay?"

"I am fine. It is just stress." Ted dressed quickly and never looked at Mica as he headed for the door.

"But where are you going at this hour?"
"Home. My club. It doesn't matter."

"Is there someone else?" Mica asked hopelessly.

"No. There is some*thing* else," Ted said and then stepped out into hall and shut the door behind him.

Something else? Mica thought. That was the first time Ted had cracked. There is more to this man than he is letting on.

ʌ ʌ ʌ

The text was clear enough, clear enough to instill second thoughts: if you attend your luncheon, we can't guarantee your safety! This is not a warning...it is a threat!

There was no way to trace from where the text came. That in itself was a red flag for Freddy. He tried to call Mica and then text him with the idea that if they changed the location at the last minute, the warning would be moot. But he couldn't reach Mica at the office or on his personal numbers.

It was not like Freddy to take a threat like this seriously but something in his gut gave this credence. What to do? What to do? He didn't have much time.

∧ ∧ ∧

The pop was such an elegant muffled sound, it hardly registered. But the result was perfect. The tire on the speeding taxi had blown and the taxi careened off Shaftsbury Avenue and into a street lamp, narrowly missing the half dozen or so people walking on the sidewalk. The impact was fairly intense considering that a taxi speeding isn't all that fast by the standards of the average car. But the impact sent Ben flying from his seat, smacking his head against the Plexiglas partition between the driver and the passenger. He was knocked cold and bleeding.

Freddy had sent Ben on a mission—to deliver champagne and flowers to Mica at the Ivy. Freddy had woken up in the cold sobering daylight, thought about the phone call from last night and rethought the notion of lunch. It is not that he didn't want to tell his story anymore; he just thought better of the timing. Until he could wrap his head around why someone would call late at night and threaten him, he figured he could always reschedule a lunch. The problem was he only had one way to reach Mica—at the studio. And by the time he left a message, Mica had left the building. Freddy hastily put together an act of contrition and sent for some flowers from the Palace, a bottle of rare champagne and jotted a hand written note of apology.

The police arrived first and noted Ben's uniform—instantly recognizing he was in livery at the Palace. But which Palace? If it was determined that he was on an assignment for anyone with the title H.R.H., this little fender bender could be assumed an act of terrorism. If nothing else, Ben was considered to be a V.I.P. A groggy Ben was grilled before the ambulance arrived and he managed to spell out that he was on an errand for the Duke of Clarence and the police collectively exhaled.

Ben looked worse than he was. When the ambulance arrived it was determined that Ben most probably had a concussion and needed several stiches. The driver got off easily with a speeding ticket.

Ben put up a bit of woozy struggle when laid on the gurney. He insisted the flowers and wine needed to be delivered. And one sympathetic cop read the name on the card and assured the agitated Ben that it would be taken care of.

A crowd had formed across the street. And as the gurney rolled into the back of the ambulance, the crowd began to disperse—all but one. A tall man dressed in black motorcycle leathers with a black helmet and smoked out windscreen, simply stood there. No one really noticed. After all this was a simply a tire blow out. The man, "G", wasn't about to leave until the subject was securely taken away and the job was done.

ʌ ʌ ʌ

Mica wasn't pleased that he had been stood up. He could have stayed at the studio, done his editing and been out of there by now. Now he has to make his way back across the river and back to work for conceivably the rest of the afternoon. He was even less pleased that he is caught in horrendous traffic as the taximeter is ticking up a sizable fare. "Do you know what has caused all this traffic?"

"An accident," the driver explained. "Must have been a good one because there are a lot of police."

By the time he'd made it back to the studio the fare was near twenty pounds. And again Mica wasn't pleased. He was so distracted by the fare; he didn't even notice Andrea coming out of the building as he was walking in.

"Well aren't you the man of the moment," Andrea announced.

"What?"

"An interesting story came across the police scanners," she began. "It seems a valet from St. James's Palace was in a bit of a taxi accident while trying to deliver flowers and champagne to *you!*"

"What are you talking about?"

"Were you supposed to have lunch with the Duke of Clarence?" she quizzed.

"Yes. But how did you know that?"

"The police stopped by with the flowers and champagne. Seems you have a fan on the force. The valet, it seems, explained how the gifts were from the Duke because he had to cancel his lunch appointment."

"That explains it," Mica mumbled to himself.

"Your goodies are up stairs in my office," Andrea said. "But just a word of caution. There was a reason your interview was canceled. Don't become fast friends or even acquaintances. I would stay away from the Duke. He is bad press and you don't need that."

"He wants to tell me his story."

"He *has* a story?" Her sarcasm was noted. "Don't get enamored with a title. He is bad news."

ʌ ʌ ʌ

Mac Mackenzie rarely loses his British cool. But when he does, he is a force to be reckoned with. "What the bloody hell happened?" he screamed into the phone with a tone just above a growl and below a screech. His face reddened as he spoke. "How on earth did we hit the wrong man?" Ted just heard the tail end of that question as Mac waved him in the door.

"What do you mean we hit the wrong man?" Ted asked as he sat by the desk.

Mac put his finger to his lips to shush Ted and pointed to the phone on the desk.

"We didn't have a clear view of the passenger," the voice came through the speaker. Ted recognized the voice as that of the mysterious 'G'.

"Then you should never have taken the bloody shot! This is not a shooting gallery. In broad daylight, on a busy street no less." Mac shouted. "This is not supposed have escalated into another Diana scenario…yet."

'Yet?' Ted thought. Just what had he walked in on.

"Do nothing until you hear from me again," Mac instructed and then slammed the receiver down on the phone, cutting off the speaker. "God damn trigger happy son of a bitch!"

"Okay. What am I missing?" Ted asked immediately.

"The taxi cab we hit today didn't contain the Duke," Mac huffed.

"What taxi cab? I thought the Duke was under my watch. What am I hearing and why am I hearing it last?"

"Calm down, Ted. This whole operation was on a need-to-know basis. The less people involved, the better. I wanted to keep your neutrality. You are going to have to talk with the Duke and I didn't want your finger prints on what was going down."

"What did you mean this was not to be a Diana scenario yet?" Ted folded his arms and waited for an answer.

Mac measured his words. "She was supposed to be scared silent."

"But instead she was killed."

Mac pounded his fist on the desk. "The problem was solved," he spat coldly.

"And the Duke?"

"You are dangerously close to surpassing your pay grade," Mac cautioned. "Right now all you need to do is convince him to shut his mouth."

12

lthough the staff works downstairs, the living quarters for such people as Ben Foster are upstairs—way upstairs—in the attic-like dormitory. Freddy had never been there. Why should he? Ironically, in the life Freddy was actually born to, Freddy could have found himself in rooms just like this—making his way in the world, searching out a career. But that was lost on Fredrick, Duke of Clarence.

Walking down the long corridor, Freddy spotted a familiar face—Violet, Rose…some flower name—who cleans for him. "Hello there. I was wondering if you could direct me to Ben's rooms. Ben Foster?"

"Certainly, your Lordship." She walked nervously down the beige—a job lot paint color if there ever was one—and dimly lit hallway and around the corner and then dutifully pointed at the door.

"Thank you."

Freddy knocked and, without waiting for an answer, walked in. Bandaged on the forehead with a neck brace and a shiner of a black eye, Ben is fast asleep. Freddy took a moment to take in Ben's pathetic look. He seems so much smaller and particularly vulnerable lying there. Then Freddy took in his surroundings.

Ben's rooms were *a* room with a bed area, dresser and small closet along with two chairs, a side table and television set sitting area. There is one window with not much of a view—a tile roof to be exact. Not much at all. But what do they expect? They live rent free, Freddy thought to himself, ignoring his own freeloading status. On the bright side, the room is painted a familiar robin's egg blue—a color adorning the corridor walls of Buckingham Palace. Trust the 'family' to never let a can of paint go to waste. Oh the frugality of the Royals! Freddy sat in the more plump of the two chairs and began to drift off as well.

"Freddy?" Time had passed as the light from the window had faded and Freddy had fallen into a deep sleep. "Sir? Is that you?"

"Yes!" Freddy shot to attention. "Did I wake you?"

"I believe it is more like the opposite," Ben smiled. "What are you doing up here? This isn't a place for you."

"I feel my place is right here, beside you."

"Nonsense. I let you down. I am afraid I didn't get to the restaurant.

"I am aware of that. Don't worry about that. Now, how do you feel?" Freddy has genuine concern in his voice. He might just be falling for young Ben!

"Sore...but I will be back to duty as soon as..."

"And I don't want you to worry about that either. The others can take care of your duties until you are fully fit."

"I am sorry, Sir."

"Do not be sorry in the least," Freddy began as he moved from the chair to the bedside. "It is I who should be sorry because I feel this was all my fault."

"First. I should have gone to the lunch in first place and not stayed home like a coward. Second, I should not have sent you to deliver the wine and flowers. That only made you a target."

"A target?" Ben questioned, coming out of his drowsiness. "For what?"

"For me. I don't think this was an accident. I think this was a message, a warning."

Ben attempted to sit up but Freddy waved him back down. "What does that mean?" he questioned nervously.

"We have to take care of each other." Freddy had already said too much.

13

ica had come to accept that Ted was mysterious, erratic and unavailable as boyfriend material. And yet, those are some of the very things that attracted Mica to him—he was an effort and when they are together, that effort is more than worth it. Ted is intelligent, engaging, quick-witted and genuinely interested in Mica's world. On the flip side, Ted's work schedule precludes any sort of long-term plans, leaving just a series of spontaneous moments. But Mica, took it all in stride. After all, Mica is not in town on a permanent basis and has an unreliable schedule as well. Theirs is a match not made by a calendar but on a whim. And for the moment, that is just fine with Mica.

But last night was different. He not only didn't show up, he didn't call or text. Mica, for his part, finally has gotten a contact number for Ted—a big step for sure—but he neither answered nor did the phone transfer to voice mail. Mica was up to his ass in 'chamtinis' and lube with no one to share. So he chose to drink himself in to a blur and turn in earlier than expected. It wasn't until this morning when he got a text stating: "Coffee? I can explain!" that Ted made contact.

They met at Café Nero on Piccadilly, just up from The Coliseum and around the corner from Boothby's and, ironically, not far from St. James's Palace. And true to tradition, Ted had no explanation for his actions besides the ubiquitous "work".

"You can make it up to me by coming to dinner tonight. Hillary at the hotel has fixed the whole thing. And you will get to meet some of my friends from Los Angeles."

"I don't know." Ted is his usual non-committal self. "It all depends on work."

"It always does," Mica sniped. "It is not just any dinner. Friends are in town for our work and it will be fun."

"I will try."

Before the conversation could turn into a fight, Ted's phone went off. A text. Work. "I have to get going. Like I said I will try to be there tonight."

Both Mica and Ted headed for the busy curb and were able to hail simultaneous taxis. When Mica got into his, he had an idea. "Follow that cab, please."

"Like in the movies," the cabbie joked—even laughing at his own joke. "Hey aren't you that guy from television?"

"Yes I am," Mica acknowledged.

"My missus loves you," he said.

"Thank her for me."

"I never watch."

Of course you don't. That's how you were able to recognize me through a Plexiglas partition in the back of your cab within moments, Mica thought. But he gets that a lot—men like him are always nervous to admit they watch the gay guy on the tele and, worse yet, enjoy him.

"Wait until I tell my missus I've had you in my rear," he said.

"You tell her that!"

By the time this banter had subsided and a few silent minutes had passed, the first cab pulled up just on the edge of Lambeth Bridge to a yellowed brick building of non descript features.

"Is this the Ministry of Defense?" Mica asked.

"No way. If that's where you wanted to go, it is the other way along Whitehall. I thought you wanted me to follow that cab."

"I did." Mica watched as Ted got out and walked right in the front door.

"What is this place?" Mica asked.

"This is Thames house."

"Of course, thank you." That meant nothing to Mica but that didn't mean it meant nothing.

"Do you want to be dropped here?"

"No, take me back to the West End."

On the way back, Mica texted Ted: About tonight, I know you said you would try...try hard!

Almost immediately a text came back. I WILL.

Are you at the M.O.D.? Mica quizzed.

Yes. Why?

Just curious why you had to run off so fast.

Duty calls.

Mica leaned it to the window in the partition. "I have changed my mind. I would like to go to the Ministry of Defense."

^ ^ ^

There used to be a Joe Allen in Los Angeles, a hot writers and entertainers restaurant on Third Street—for those who could differentiate between a power lunch and a creative think tank. It became Orso, under the Joe Allen ownership but without the gritty, artsy, atmosphere nor the hearty fare. There is still a Joe Allen in New York, appropriately ensconced in Midtown, nestled within and among the theater folk. Joe Allen in London is haven,for the home away from home set and a theater haunt for sure, nestled behind Covent Garden and just over the river from the *Rise 'N Shine* studio. It is the perfect place to meet for lunch.

"This feels like home. Well, home and days gone by," Mica said as they sat in the corner between a poster of "Hello Dolly" and "Phantom of the Opera"—the original with Michael Crawford. "I don't want anything too large as I have a dinner tonight back at The Coliseum."

"Posh," Nate quipped.

"Can anyone come?" Andrea questioned playfully.

"Actually that is a great idea. Why don't you both come?" Mica said enthusiastically. "Of course that maybe a lot of me for one day!"

"Ha, hardly," Nate said. "Lunch is enough of you for one day."

"Cute. You're off the list!" Mica joked.

"Well I will be there for sure," Andrea declared.

"Let me think," Nate returned. "I will have to squeeze in a nap. Put me down for a probably."

"Perfect. I'll let Hillary know there will be two more. You will get to meet some of my old cronies and friends from Los Angeles. It is the convergence of two worlds...can't wait. So what is everyone eating?"

"Bar steak with Béarnaise sauce," Nate announced.

"And I am going to have the eggs Joe Allen," Andrea chimed in.

"Me too," Mica concluded. "That's settled. Wine?" There was a collective roll of the eyes as if the question even needed to be asked. "I gather no one has to go back to the office."

"As if that would have mattered," Nate murmured in one those dramatic stage asides. They laughed.

Andrea, although adept at small talk, is always quick to get down to business. "So why the impromptu lunch?"

"Can't friends get together for a fun lunch with out there being an agenda?" Mica teased.

"Bullshit," Andrea snapped.

"You were fairly emphatic that we get together," Nate reminded him.

"I know. I know. It's about Ted."

"I knew it," Andrea squealed.

Mica relayed the events of the morning. How they had met for coffee and Ted was ambivalent about attending the dinner this evening. And how when they left the coffee place, Mica followed him to work and it turned out not to be the Ministry of Defense. He went on to explain that stopped at the Ministry and was told that no one by the name of Edward or Ted Harrelson worked out of that office anymore. "Can anyone tell me what Thames House is?"

Both Nate and Andrea looked at each other—Nate surprised and Andrea self-assured.

"I can tell you exactly what that is. Spooks house," she reveled.

"MI5," Nate added. "The headquarters of our equivalent of your CIA."

"Your man is a spy," declared Andrea as she slapped the table triumphantly. "I knew it."

"That is ridiculous. Who dates a spy? Who even *knows* a spy? And how would you know if you did? You can't prove it."

The wine arrived and it was a perfect moment to sit in silence as the waiter poured. Mica could see that Andrea was dying to speak. As soon as the wine was poured, each took a large gulp.

"What do you mean you can't prove it?" she jumped right back in. "It speaks for itself."

"Maybe the Ministry has work for him at MI5?" Mica defended.

"Maybe the Ministry is a cover."

Again they collectively paused and gulped.

"Well he is invited this evening. If he shows, ask him yourself."

"That's it. I am in," Nate announced. "I wouldn't miss this for the world."

"What do you mean *if* he shows?" Andrea, always the journalist, misses nothing.

"He is rather elusive and non-committal. He's more prone to surprising me than making defined plans."

"You mean like a spy would be?" Nate interjected.

As the food arrived, Andrea tapped on the bottle of wine indicating they would need another. "This is a two bottle lunch for sure. We have plenty to talk about."

^ ^ ^

Ted sat as his desk and stared at the text: About tonight, I know you said you would try...try hard! Try hard, he thought. He pondered for more time than his day should allow. He has things to do, a subject to follow—a subject that, as the agency defines, is agitated.

The intercom system on Ted's desk phone is loud and tinny—an irritant really—designed to make him take notice. So when the Scottish accent coming through what sounds like a tin can rang out through his office, Ted sat up. "My office," it said and Ted knew who it is and where to go.

Mac Mackenzie was not, as of late, a happy man. He had his ass handed to him on a platter over the botched accident involving the Duke of Clarence's valet by higher ups that were even madder than he. Attempting something daring in the daylight is one thing. Attempting it on a crowded street is quite another. But having the wrong intelligence and it all going horribly wrong is simply unacceptable. And although, as the saying goes, the fish smells from the head down, in this case, the blame trickles down. Mac had become mildly obsessed with the irritant known as the Duke.

Ted walked in to the office to find Mac pacing around his desk. This was never a good sign. "I don't like it. I don't like it at all."

"What would that be, Sir?"

"Don't be naïve with me, Edward," he said with just enough sarcasm to let Ted know this was one of *those* moments. "The damned Duke. He has fast become a boil on the ass of this department. And I want it finished."

"What are we to finish?"

"We no sooner let him know that we need him to shut up, then we hand him publicity. That damn accident made every paper and the ten o'clock news. We're literally handing him publicity. Not to mention ammunition."

"Ammunition, Sir?"

"Do you not think he suspects that someone was behind that accident? Even if we weren't, he would assume we were because he is becoming paranoid. Or, if he isn't, than he is simply an idiot. And no one believes he is an idiot. So tonight..."

"I can't," Ted interrupted.

"I beg your pardon."

"Whatever you are about to suggest, I can't. I have a personal issue and I can't be trailing, following, interacting, making contact or whatever you have in mind for the Duke and me."

Mac is taken aback. No one in his command had ever refused an assignment, let alone one that hadn't been officially assigned. "Is everything alright with you?"

"Yes Sir. Or it will be Sir. But I am simply not available tonight."

"We are not playing a game Mr. Harrelson. This is a life devotion we ask of each other. Personal lives come second in our world. You are aware of that?"

"Yes."

"But, given that this is not an issue that has come up in the past, I am willing to grant this pass. I appreciate that in the rarity certain personal obligations are unavoidable. Do you truly believe this 'personal issue' is worth the compromise of an assignment?" Mac questioned.

"I do," Ted returned unwaveringly.

"Enough said," Mac said. "But be prepared. It all begins all over again tomorrow."

Ted said nothing as he left the room.

∧ ∧ ∧

The table was set in the middle of the room—not the best idea for a group that could be conversationally loud. As proprietress of both the hotel and the namesake restaurant, Stewart's, Hillary had no problem accommodating Mica's last minute request to add two to the table. Everyone met first for a cocktail in Fluid. 6:30 p.m.

Hillary is an amazing hostess. Not only is she able take care of her seven guests but also manage the needs of the other patrons in Fluid, spending just enough time with each to make them feel special and welcome.

Present, accounted for and on time were Roger Keenan, who is in town for the preliminary promotional work on *Cover's Blown,* the Sean Jones movie for which, Mica had a great set visit; Marilyn Lassiter who is in town because she is simply bored with L.A. and thought a visit with her old pal Hillary would be a good diversion; B.J. the senior supervising producer of *Drop Zone*—Mica's former colleague and friend during his previous incarnation as a reporter for the nationally syndicated entertainment series—who is in town for her own set visit with Sean Jones; Nate; Andrea and, of course, Mica. Although, the most anticipated guest, Ted, is still M.I.A. But that was not going to stop Hillary from proceeding.

"I see you all have a drink but I have ordered some champagne," she announced. "I'd like to propose a toast." Everyone grabbed a glass, leaving the eighth behind on the bar. "I just want to say how great it is to meet new friends both from near and far and I want you to know that you can always find a home...or home away from home...here at The Coliseum."

"Here, here." They raised their glasses and sipped appropriately.

"I too have a toast," said Roger with his glass still raised. Somehow Mica knew he was going to pull out an old chestnut he'd heard many times over dinner at Roger's house. "As we say in Los Angeles. Here's to old friends. And here's to new faces. And here's to old friends who *have* new faces."

With a chuckle they again raised their glasses.

"Marilyn?" he teased.

"You bastard," Marilyn spat all in good humor.

"Marilyn, dear, fear not. You know I believe the most desired accessory in Hollywood are scars behind the ears," he continued.

"I heard that and I take umbrage," Ted announced as he walked into the

126

lounge. "So sorry I am late. I'm Ted. And all of you must be friends with Mica."

Mica grabbed the remaining champagne off the bar and handed it to Ted. "Better late than never. I seriously didn't think you would be here," he whispered.

"It wasn't easy. But I took your earlier text rather seriously," Ted returned.

Mica made his way around the circle, making new introductions with Ted and B.J., Roger and Marilyn.

"We've certainly heard a lot about you," Roger said.

"I certainly hope not," Ted shot back and then looked at Mica who simply shrugged.

Andrea piped in. "Well I would like to hear more!" She shook his hand.

"It is nice to see you again," Ted responded.

"I do hope we are table mates this evening," Andrea continued. "There is so much I would like to ask you."

As it was, Hillary had set the circular table in the dining room with place cards. Andrea got her wish. Circling from Ted and moving clockwise is Andrea, B.J., Nate, Mica at the six o'clock seat, Roger, Hillary and, finally, Marilyn who'd be seated to Ted's right. Dinner was to be a set menu of an appetizer of terrine of fois gras, a mixed salad, a main course of grilled salmon and a steamed pudding dessert. Drinks or wine would be of choice.

Finished at the bar and appropriately escorted to the table, each found their seat. Andrea wasted no time in diving in. "Ted, I would love to get your opinion on something. I was just interviewing the Chancellor of the Exchequer and he was talking about our dependency on the dollar. You being in banking, I would be interested in your thoughts." Nate would have, but mercifully couldn't kick her under the table.

Before he could answer or at least attempt an answer, he dodged a bullet as Marilyn chimed in. "Oh you are in banking. How delicious to meet someone who doesn't do what we all do."

"And that is?" Ted questioned.

"We're all in the entertainment business." To say that Marilyn Lassiter is in the entertainment business is a stretch at best. But how else would she describe herself? Social climber?

"I thought you were in the defense industry?"

"Not exactly," Ted squirmed and looked at Mica, which, in turn, made Mica squirm.

"Well which is it?" Roger pushed.

"Banking or defense?" Andrea pushed harder.

Always an astute hostess, Hillary jumped in. "Now, now, all this business talk. I know that poor Ted here is the new attraction at the table but let the man have a drink before you attack."

"Yes, a drink." Ted turned to the waiter, "Gin and Tonic please. No, better yet, make it a gin martini. Up. Very dry."

"Very good," the waiter acknowledged. "Anyone else?"

"I will have another martini...vodka." Mica said. "And please don't mix mine up with his. I detest gin."

"How very anti-British of you. The Brits love their gin," Roger pointed out. "Don't insult your hosts."

"That's right we Brits went to war with you Yanks over tea. We can again over gin," Nate declared to everyone's amusement.

"So," Andrea began again turning to Ted but was cut off quickly.

"Now, enough about me. How do you all know each other?" Ted asked as the perfect diversion.

Conversation then flowed around the table as each told how they know Mica followed by talking about their relationship with each other. It is all very pleasant dinner conversation. And then, as these things do, the conversation began to splinter off into individual twosomes around the table. Roger asked Mica if he would mind sharing his set visit footage for his electronic publicity campaign. Nate in turn quizzed B.J. on working with Mica in the early days. Marilyn and Hillary caught up on mutual friends. And Andrea was left to grill Ted.

She leaned in as to make sure the others couldn't hear. "What is it you actually do?"

"Why does that matter to you so much?" Ted fired back.

"Curiosity I guess. I am a journalist after all. It is my job to ask questions."

"Ironically, it is my job not to answer them," he laughed.

"So that rules out banking," she laughed back.

"Yes it does."

"I confess," she began after a sip of wine. "Mica told me that you do something with the Ministry of Defense."

"Did he now?"

She simply stared with that look that says: we don't need to play games.

"Let's just say I am in middle management and leave it at that."

She took the hint and backed down. Ted, slightly annoyed, shot Mica a look and mouthed: we have to talk.

∧ ∧ ∧

"What are you doing telling your colleagues that I work for the Ministry of Defense. That is something I entrusted you with." Ted's voice was not raised, just firm.

Dinner had gone remarkably uneventfully. Andrea pushed as much as she could with Ted but inevitably Ted was rescued from embarrassment or incrimination by a tidal shift in the conversation around the table. Still, there was an undercurrent of tension across the table between Ted and Mica. Now, back up in Mica's suite, and a few drinks into the evening, Ted was free to lash out.

"I trusted you."

"No you haven't," Mica said indignantly while pouring yet one more martini.

"If you trusted me, you wouldn't have told me you work at the Ministry at all."

"But I do."

"Really? Where were you today?"

Ted sensed that he was being boxed into a corner. "What does that mean?"

"Where were you?" They paused and then Mica spoke again. "Don't bother making up something else. I followed you after coffee this morning and I know you went to Thames House...or as I was to find out, Spooks House."

"You followed me," Ted snarled.

"That is not the point. The point is that when I called you to ask where you are, you said the Ministry and not Thames House, which I had just seen you walk into. Secondarily, I went to the Ministry to see 'where you work' and they said a Ted Harrelson no longer worked out of that building. The point, Ted, is that you've been lying to me and I want to know why."

Ted sat at the end of the bed, head down, and sighed. "I knew you would figure this out. I think that I wanted you to figure this out."

"And what does that mean?"

"I am tired. I don't know if I can do this anymore." Ted was talking more to himself than to Mica, a sort of confessional. "I had to literally put my job on the line just to be here tonight. I had to put my job on the line just to have dinner with you and your friends."

"Do you know how ludicrous that sounds? That you had to put your job on the line to be here tonight? What could have been that important?'

"That is just it," Ted explained, or attempted to, "you don't know what I do day in and day out. It is a matter of national and sometimes international security."

"Who or what are you really?"

"I work for MI5."

"So you're a spy?" Mica quizzed hardly believing he was asking that question.

"That's a way of putting it," Ted conceded.

Mica sat and took a very long sip of his cocktail. "Should you be telling me this?"

"No but you asked for the truth. If I tell you the truth I compromise my career, my very existence. If I make up a cover story, I would be lying. And you don't want me to lie," Ted sighed again. "I take that back. I don't want to lie. Not anymore."

"Are you in danger by telling me this?"

"I don't know. How well can you keep *this* secret?"

They both paused again.

"I have been wondering how long I could keep this up ever since I met you. I have been living in one deception after another. I now know how much my life has been compromised by this cloak and dagger existence and I don't think I want it any more. When I met you in the bar that evening, I knew in my heart of hearts you would end up pulling me out of this clandestine closet," Ted confessed.

"So you used me to do what you couldn't or wouldn't do on your own."

"I don't see it that way."

"Of course you don't. You're not equipped to see things the way they really are. You tell lies. That is what you do. How can I trust a man who tells lies for a living?"

"I should go," Ted said as he got up and reached for Mica.

Mica pulled away. "You're right. You should go."

14

Curiosity had simply gotten the better of Mica. He had heard versions of "No!" and "don't do it" too many times. He'd received notes and flowers and invites all from Freddy asking, nearly begging, to get together to talk. Friends, colleagues and Ted had all warned Mica not to do so. All of which had led Mica to the bigger question of "why?" Why was everyone so concerned about them meeting? Sure co-workers such as Andrea and Nate believed Freddy would be just using Mica as a sounding board for his rants and it would simply be a waste of Mica's time. Still others such as Ted believed there is real danger in colluding with Freddy. But what kind of danger could there be? So rather than consulting the crowd, Mica took it upon his self to contact Freddy and set something up.

"I chose the Wolseley because I could walk here. The last time we were supposed to meet, my valet was almost killed in a mysterious taxi accident," Freddy stated as a matter of fact somewhat breathless from his brisk walk.

"I thought it was something like a tire blowout," Mica returned. "Couldn't that have happened to anyone at anytime."

"Too much of a coincidence for my liking."

"Coincidence?"

"To Diana! Car accident. Do the math!"

"That is a stretch at best." Mica took what Freddy was saying with a grain of salt. Perhaps everyone was right and Freddy is the blowhard Mica was told to expect.

"I brought you something," Freddy said as he handed the deeply colored Mulberry shopping bag to Mica. "It's a bit of a gift."

"But there is no need for this," Mica blushed.

"Ah but there is as you will see."

Inside, within it's own soft carrier bag, is a classic printed calf single briefcase in grey. Stunning, and at over one thousand pounds in cost, far too extravagant. "I can't accept this. This too much."

"But you must. Look inside." Mica pulled out the bag and started to unlatch the polished silver key lock. "Discretely," Freddy warned. Inside is a set of papers, a manuscript of sorts. Mica didn't take it out. "This is the cleverest way I could think of to get this to you without anyone seeing me hand off papers to you."

Freddy may have been overly dramatic about the hand off but he was inadvertently correct in assuming people are watching. "G" is sitting at the end of the bar, dressed in a black leather blazer, black tee shirt and black jeans, with a direct sightline to Mica and Freddy's table. He has no chance of being spotted, as Mica has never seen him. Ted, on the other hand, is across the room blending into the crowd.

Mica and Freddy ordered a bottle of wine. Freddy told the waiter that they would need a moment before they order their food as they had plenty to talk about. The wine came, and with its pouring, out poured Freddy's story.

"I get that you are the product of an affair. And I get with whom," Mica spoke cautiously as Freddy was fired up and clearly emotional as he talked. "But what I don't get is why you don't think you have been legitimized. I mean you have been given the title, an apartment and presumably some income."

"But you don't see me being invited for Christmas or to Scotland in the summer. They ignore me, talk as if I am not family. I should be H.R.H.—His Royal Highness—a title only given to blood."

"But to do that, they have to admit the truth and you know they are not ever going to say that you are heir to the throne. So what more is there?"

"They just may have to admit the truth."

"How so?" Mica quizzed.

"DNA. I have been quietly collecting silverware, napkins and glassware—anything his lips touch—for analysis one day. It is sort of my collection of smoking guns."

"But what will that do?"

"Prove they are liars and have disavowed the rightful line of succession." Freddy sighed, almost exhausted as his emotions had piqued, and signaled for another bottle of wine. "And what about my mother. They've never done anything for her."

"But did you really think they would parade her out in public? She is the other woman."

"He married the other, *other* woman didn't he?"

"Ah, point taken." Mica had to give him that one. But the whole story sounded more like a mixture of buyer's remorse and spoiled rich kid more than just a cry for recognition. "But what if it doesn't work? Let's say the smoking guns don't provide enough evidence. You will be portrayed as a ranting idiot and may lose what you've been given."

"I can take them down," Freddy said with an almost sinister lilt to his voice.

The journalist in Mica kicked in. This is where the story gets interesting in his mind. "How so?"

"I know what they do. How they work. I know that the government uses the royal receptions for a cover to covert actions. Shady people meeting high profile people, closed door handshakes and dirty dealings. I know how it is all done. I can tell that story. And if the British public ever knew that side of the Royal family, it could be an off-with-their-heads moment. Imagine people knowing that they are being paid millions a year to be the puppets for MI5 and MI6. Disgraceful."

"Ironically you are asking to be legitimized by the very family you want to take down," Mica countered. "Seems more than a little hypocritical."

"I don't want to take them down. I also understand that they are doing a service to their country and the world government in total by allowing and participating in such activities. It is all in the way you look at it. It is not that I want to take them down. It is that I can take them down."

"Dangerous talk."

"I know. Look what happened to Diana when she started to find her voice," Freddy said. "And that is why I have written it down and given it to you. If anything happens to me, you will have a copy of the story in my own hand."

"Why me?" Mica began to get uncomfortable with his new insider status.

"The British press think I am a wanker," Freddy admitted.

"And me?"

"I think you could do a fair and balanced interview on the subject, break the story and give it journalistic integrity."

"I do entertainment. This is some heavy stuff."

Freddy reached over and put his hand on Mica's arm. "Think about it.

Mica saw the sincerity in his eyes—almost a vulnerability. "I will read it on the plane. I am heading back to Los Angeles the day after tomorrow. It'll give me something to do. Something to think about, as you put it."

"I will be back in a moment." Freddy was off to the restroom and that gave Mica the break he needed to digest all that was thrown at him.

Across the room Ted gave "G" a nod and "G" followed Freddy into the men's room while Ted made his way to Mica. "What's in the bag?"

"A briefcase," said a stunned Mica.

"May I see it?" Mica pulls it out ever so slightly providing more of a flash than a gaze. "I am looking for a new briefcase. But that is a little out of my price range. Expensive gift for a first date. Could I take a closer look?"

"This is not a date. And No." Mica slid the case back into the bag and tucked it under his seat.

"Is there something you're hiding?"

"That is rich coming from you. What are you doing here anyway?"

"My job."

"Trailing me is now your job?" Mica questioned.

"No trailing him." Ted sits next to Mica and leans in to talk quietly. "Look, I have told you he is on the radar with important people and you shouldn't take anything that he says very seriously."

"But isn't that exactly what you are doing...taking what he could be saying *very* seriously."

"I need to know what you have been talking about." Ted spoke directly and with purpose. "Can we get together for dinner and discuss this? And perhaps discuss us?"

"I have to think about it...both requests. I am going back to L.A. the day after tomorrow and that does not leave much time."

"How about later tonight? I will be in touch," Ted said and retreated back to his table.

∧ ∧ ∧

Inside the restroom, Freddy stood where men do and proceeded with what came naturally. "G" just following behind, walked in, shut the door, leaned against the sink and waited. When Freddy finished and made his way to the sink, "G" blocked him.

"Excuse me," Freddy said politely, "but I would like to use the sink."

With one swift move, "G" shoved Freddy back against the far wall, placed a gloved hand over Freddy's mouth and spoke. "You will get a chance after we have a chat."

Freddy simply nodded. The fear in his eyes said it all.

"What are you doing with your friend out there?" He released his hand just far enough for Freddy to speak.

"Lunch..."

"And a little chat? About what?"

"Things..."

"Like?"

"His job. I find broadcasting very interesting."

"And are you broadcasting anything else?" "G" asked.

"Such as?"

Again, "G" shoved Freddy against the wall with enough force as to knock some wind out of him. "Don't get cute with me you little shit. We know you are itching to play storyteller. And I am telling you that it is in your best interests to not be opening your mouth to anyone. Let this be a direct warning." He let Freddy go but Freddy was too stunned to move.

"G" walked over to the sink, took a look in the mirror and buttoned his blazer. As he turned to walk out, the now buttoned blazer stretched tightly across the man's back and Freddy could see the clear outline of what appeared to be a gun attached to his back belt. Message received.

Λ Λ Λ

Back at Thames house, Ted sat with Mac Mackenzie for a standard debriefing. Mac is pacing again which is not a good sign. Something is agitating him.

"I don't like where this is heading," he announced as if there were more than just the two of them in the room.

"A friendly lunch is not necessarily a red flag," Ted suggested.

"Bullshit," Mac snapped. "Where there is smoke there is fire. I will give you that he can have a 'friendly' lunch until it is with a journalist. And then I begin to think there is more to it."

"I see."

"Do you?"

"Of course, Sir."

"Let's recap where we stand," Mac began, slightly indignantly. "Every time the wayward Duke drunkenly falls out of some trendy club—which is more often than not—he shouts to the waiting paparazzi that he has a story to tell. We know his lineage links but is that all he has to say? That would cause enough of an uproar. But what else does he know? We know he made you at the Palace that evening some time ago. If he knows who you are but not what you are, so be it. But if he has been able to put two and two together, we have a problem. And then there is the question of the valet. Does he know that was not an accident? He should be scared silent by now...and yet he is not."

Ted simply nodded and took in the analysis.

"Our little backdoor liaisons are necessary. In the coming weeks we have the Middle East, Africa and that whole Syrian mess all wanting time with the Home Secretary. And that is not going to happen on campus. I shouldn't have to tell you that these are behind-the-scenes talks that can literally change the fates of nations."

"I am well aware, Sir, of the importance of our mission."

"This is not like when the Americans come over and we can parade them through the streets and into the doorway of 10 Downing Street for all the world to see and everyone knows damn well what they are here for. These are covert, classified and, again, a necessity."

Again, there is little for Ted to say. He simply nods in agreement.

"There is a function again at the Palace, a concert of some sort. Our man is a businessman representing Emirates oil looking to make a deal now that Syria is so unstable. Nothing earth shattering. Barely covert. I think you should be there, just in case the Duke makes an appearance and see what he does when he sees you."

Marching orders stated, Ted stood to leave but was waved back into his seat by Mac. "And what is the Duke doing with your friend?"

"My friend?"

"C'mon. Do you really think we haven't known about your friendship with the journalist? What is his name?"

"Mica Daly."

"That's him. Morning television I believe. My wife watches him," Mac mumbled.

"You had *me* followed?"

"Everyone is followed. You should know that by now. In my day you would have gotten the sack just for having a friendship such as yours. Sleeping with the enemy and that sort of thing. We have come a long way here at '5' but I just need to know where your discretion begins and ends. What have you been talking about?"

"None of this, I assure you," Ted shot back.

"Perhaps you are too close to this—now that your friend has been approached and the asset has been warned."

"Except I have both their, well certainly Mica's, confidence. If he is going to tell anyone what is going on, it would to me."

"You may have a point there," Mac conceded. "But...and this is a strong *but*... we need to know what he knows sooner rather than later and whether he agrees to work with the Duke on telling his story. And just what that story is going to be."

15

ica had only been gone a couple of weeks and already had forgotten what it was like to be stuck in L.A. traffic. The ride from his home to the law firm of Dunning, Baker and Astin—a less than five mile trek through West Hollywood and Beverly Hills—should take a few minutes. But on this and just about every other day it is forty-five minutes to an hour. At least it is sunny, something Mica *had* missed.

Lance Novak had recently been made partner, which did not mean he had to move from his corner office but rather was given a substantial budget to redecorate. Mica hardly recognized the place—having gone from airliner chic modernist to a comfortable eclectic mix of modern basics, Japanese antiques and a few designer one-offs. Mica wondered if his apartment had also had a similar upgrade in styling. He liked Lance's comfortable West Hollywood condo with the fabulous view.

Caroline, Lance's assistant, let Mica into the office and asked if he needed something to drink. "No thank you."

"Nice briefcase," Lance began as he bounded out from behind his desk.

"Thanks, it's new. It was a present. A very unexpected present."

"Please sit." Lance moved them to the sitting area. "Are you sure that Caroline can't get you something."

"A coffee, I guess." Mica was never going to touch the coffee as he was on his third cup of the morning already, but he felt bad that she was simply standing there like a waitress waiting for him to order.

"Two please," Lance signaled to Caroline.

Mica had also forgotten how good Lance looked in his suits. This one Gucci with an Hermes tie and Cole Haan pumps. Mica couldn't help but stare at the one who got away.

"Is everything okay?" Lance asked breaking Mica's stare.

"Yes. Of course. I was just thinking how well partnership looks on you."

Lance blushed. "It is just a job."

"Hardly."

There was an awkward pause, as neither knew where to go from there.

"How is London treating you?" Lance asked.

"Great...which is why I am here really."

"Oh?" Mica reached into the briefcase and pulled out Freddy's manuscript, which he had devoured on the plane. It could be all gossip and conjecture but Mica loved it. "What's that?" Lance asked.

"It is a poorly but hand written story by the Fredrick Charles Arthur Henry, a.k.a. Freddy, the Duke of Clarence."

"And that means what?"

"Well he has an interesting story to tell. He says he is the rightful heir to the British throne, having been a product of an affair between his common mother and his rightful heir father."

"Now that *is* interesting," Lance conceded.

"When he started to get a little too loud for comfort, he was granted the title of Duke of Clarence, given a grace and favor apartment at St. James's Palace and some sort of stipend to live on."

"How do we get that deal?" Lance joked.

"Isn't that what you've been granted here? A decent title, nice digs and a healthy stipend your Lordship?" Mica fired back.

"Shut up!"

"That's just it. He no longer feels that is enough. He wants legitimacy."

"They are not going to give him the throne."

"No. I think he just wants to be recognized. This is a cry for recognition more than anything."

"So why doesn't he go public?" Lance is starting to play lawyer.

"He has been warned in a number of ways to keep his mouth shut. That it is a matter of national security etcetera. That has only infuriated him more. He has counter threatened with going public with a number of secrets of the ways of the Royals such as they're being used as puppets for covert actions of the government. It is all told in the manuscript."

"So what are you doing with it? What is your involvement? And what are you doing in my office?"

"I will answer the last part first," Mica said, changing his mind and taking a sip of his black coffee. "I want you to hold the original manuscript for safe keeping. I have made copies but I want the original in a place of both safety and witnessed as given."

"I can do that," Lance said. "And...?"

"He wants me to be the journalist in whom he confides to tell his story. Or should I say, I would tell his story for him."

"Now, as a lawyer...as your lawyer in this...I don't think that is a good idea."

"Why?" Mica quizzed wondering if he should start taking notes.

"Well as you mentioned he has already been threatened. By whom or what is not important. If it is a viable threat, that should warn you off. But also, they are the Royal family you are talking about. I can't imagine you can take them on and it end well. I say walk away."

"But it is a great story," Mica stated, almost pleading for permission to follow through.

"You have had other great stories that haven't turned out best for you."

"Thanks to you," Mica shot back. "You are his lawyer!"

"Exactly my point. Can you imagine the number of people like me the Royal family has on retainer to stop people like you moving forward with stories they don't want out there? You can't take on the Royal family."

"And I can't take on Hollywood Royalty either."

"How did that end for you? You took on Chad Martin, the highest paid star in town and no matter whether you were telling the truth or not, you got shit on. And where did that get you? Bounced off American television and nearly, or literally, out of the country."

Mica paused to take it all in.

"It is the Royal family. They head the United Kingdom and several protectorates. If you piss them off and you could be running out of places you can go."

"But what if it is true?"

"Then you are sitting on one hell of a story!"

"Are you saying you don't want me to tell the story?" Mica asked.

"I am advising you not to tell the story."

"And if I don't take your advice, will you stand in my corner?"

"Absolutely."

Λ Λ Λ

Anthony White has done well for himself since his days as an assistant to former child star turned agent Albert Switzer. Today he represents a dozen or so young actors, all of whom are working on lots from Disney to DreamWorks, even in these tough economic times when names get parts, not struggling new artists. But his biggest claims to fame are Mica Daly, who, ironically is not even seen by American audiences at the moment and his recreation of Suzy Chambers from the once reality television star/joke to a bona fide talk show panelist on a daytime series called *Chat* and a recurring role on a web phenom of a sitcom called *Girl Crazy*.

Part of Anthony's success is that he has kept his organization lean and mean, creating a live work office space in a loft condo building in West Hollywood that went bust and turned all the units into rentals. He took a two-bedroom place for which, de facto, the clients pay. For what equates to a home office, he has done it right—polished concrete floors, white leather, mid-century classic furnishings, glass desk and industrial chic storage. Besides the pictures of his clients with take away tear sheets that line one wall of his office, the art is silver framed etchings on paper and black and white photography. It is all very tasteful and looks like it is supposed to—like he's an established boutique agency with some clout behind it.

He wanted to meet Ian Shepard in his own office rather than to schlepp across to the Miracle Mile to the offices of *Gotcha!* magazine for two reasons. First, he wanted the upper hand. If Ian comes to Anthony, the negotiations are already skewed in Anthony's favor. And secondly, the matter is too sensitive for Anthony to potentially be overheard in an office that large. Even Anthony had let his assistant go home early rather than having another set of ears in the room.

Ian is late, but that is not surprising to Anthony. Parking is a nightmare in West Hollywood and the building, as it was built for residential use, has no guest parking. Anthony poured himself a drink, sat behind his desk and waited. Ten more minutes and half that drink later, the buzzer rang.

Compared to Anthony in his slim fitting Calvin Klein dress pants and tight turtleneck pullover shirt, Ian looked a bit of a slob in that rumpled British journalist sort of way. "Drink?" Anthony offered after the obligatory hellos.

"I wouldn't say no," Ian grumbled. "Been a long day."

Anthony poured what he is having, vodka on the rocks, and handed the hefty drink over to Ian and the two moved into Anthony's office.

"Nice set up you have here," Ian said, genuinely impressed, and took a big gulp from his glass then choked loudly. "Is this straight vodka?"

"I assumed a Brit could hold handle hard liquor," Anthony said calmly.

"Handle it yes. But I almost drown from it."

"I could get you something else," Anthony continued.

"No I am fine."

"Than shall we begin."

"Sure." He took a more conservative swig.

"First, I want you to know I represent both Mica Daly *and* the Duke of Clarence in this matter."

"Impressive but what matter."

With one quick move, Anthony reached into a drawer, pull out and dropped with a thud on to his desk, the Duke's dense manuscript—a copy of the one Freddy had given Mica.

"And that is?" Ian questioned.

"The Duke's story in his own hand."

Ian is intrigued. "The last time I tried to have the Duke tell his story we were shut down by the Palace."

"You don't have to tell me. We all lost out on that deal," Anthony huffed.

"So how do I know this is real? And what are you trying to do with it?"

"You will know that it is real because it is hand written and it is easy enough to prove it is the Duke's handwriting," Anthony began. "As for what we want to do with it…publish it."

"I would have to read it," Ian said slightly hungrily.

"No you won't. It is poorly written which is where Mica comes in. He will be co-writing it with the Duke. Better yet, writing it for the Duke with full author credit. But I have done a five-page synopsis of the contents. That you can read and take with you. You will have to trust that the story stands up." With that, Anthony tossed his typed print out of a synopsis across the desk and at Ian.

Ian scanned quickly and lines, phases and words like 'illegitimate', 'heir to the throne', 'compensation with Dukedom', 'Palace intrigue' and 'backdoor meetings' jumped off the page and got Ian thinking. "This will take a lot of trusting," Ian said, trying to regain the power position.

"You were already going to do a story on him for the magazine. So you already know he has something to say. Just think of this as a longer version. And as your magazine is owned by a publisher, you are not even taking the deal out of house."

"I would have to be the editor," Ian said.

"Naturally. That is why we are talking."

"And the Palace approves?"

"I don't know."

"Ah, now there is a twist. You know if they found this book or even parts to be scandalous or salacious, they would have the legal power to have it pulped—literally pulled off the shelves and destroyed."

"Not if it were published in America first."

Ian leaned back in his chair and took a slow deliberate sip of his drink. "I like the way you are thinking."

∧ ∧ ∧

If there is one person Mica misses from his previous job back on *Drop Zone* it is B.J.—a smart, dynamic, producer who is as beautiful and stylish as she is savvy and intellectual. Mica knew she would be as interested in the Duke's story as he is and would be salivating for a piece of the action. So, of course, he couldn't wait to talk to her about all the goings on. But moreover, he simply missed her quick wit, good gossip and ability to cut through life's bullshit. Being as prompt and business like as B.J. is, it didn't surprise Mica that she arrived first, had settled at just the right place at the bar where there was an excellent view and enough discretion as to not be overheard and had taken the liberty of ordering two over-sized martinis. She's quite the producer.

Mica hadn't been to The Cathedral in weeks. His once stomping ground of a bar has been usurped by travel and his more upscale visits to his club. But seeing B.J. in London made him think about times gone by and when he got back to L.A. she was one of his first calls. They made a date and made The Cathedral one of his first stops. And after the meeting with Lance Novak, Mica could use one of The Cathedral's signature oversized martinis.

"I can't believe you were in London, even for a short time, and we were only able to see each other during that dinner," Mica said as they climbed on to their respective bar stools in the open air of the central courtyard.

"It's been too long, period," B.J. reiterated.

When Mica was a reporter for *Drop Zone*, B.J. and he were the best of friends. On many occasions he and she, hid out in her office escaping the tantrums and general craziness of the executive producer, Lydia Gray—the very woman who would go on to fire Mica but grow to depend heavily on B.J.

"She's still nuts," B.J. pointed out. "But I have heard her say, and more than once, that she wished you were still there."

"Empty words," Mica dismissed. "But I wouldn't want to be back into that grind again anyway."

"Not with your cushy new life of as a celebrity," B.J. joked. "I saw how people reacted to you there. It was crazy. I mean even if you still were reporting for *Drop Zone* you still would not have that measure of celebrity. Not by a long shot. No wonder you are having so much fun. Of course, you have become everything we used to loathe."

"I will admit it is a bit schizophrenic to call home somewhere that is almost six thousand miles from your celebrity. Look around. No one knows me here and yet over there it is all autographs, paparazzi and great invites. I am not bitching about it. But it is strange."

"So tell me about your handsome date at dinner that evening," she coaxed and for the next forty minutes and a martini and a half Mica explained the weird and wonderful experience known as Ted. She sat mouth agape, like a small child being read to—some fabulous fantasy that could not be real.

"And yet I still don't even know the complete story," he punctuated.

"All this makes me feel like my life is so boring and routine," she pouted.

"Nonsense. You are the senior supervising producer of a hit nightly entertainment series. You should be proud."

"But look at the world your are traveling in and the people you are meeting," she moaned in a self-pitying sort of way. "It is fantastical. Almost as fantastical as the circumstance that got you there." She paused. "Not to bring up a sore subject. But have you ever heard from Chad since?"

"No, not really..."

"What does that mean?"

"Well professionally we have run into each other and he is always friendly... and clutching Ashley Beckwith."

"That is all in the past anyway," she dismissed. "You have Mr. Mystery now."

"Not really." And again, he went on to explain how on the night she met him; they broke up—if there was anything there to break up in the first place.

By the third martini, Mica had made his way to the Duke of Clarence and the somewhat intriguing situation he found himself in. B.J. was, again, all ears and from an American prospective thought this might be the biggest story he could land. "You have to run with it," she encouraged. "When do you ever get a chance to break a story about the Royals?"

He pointed out that she was looking at things as if he were still working for *Drop Zone* and that such a story would be a coup. But in far off England, where the Royals are sacred, he posed the question that maybe he would be biting the hand that feeds him. She was forced to agree. "But, if this is true, this is a great story. If you don't run with it, I would like to," she pleaded in a friendly competitive way.

"Will do," he joked. "But I was just looking for a second opinion, not for someone to steal the biggest story of my career."

"What do you mean second opinion?"

"Actually," Mica spoke with all seriousness. "I'm looking for less of a second opinion and more for someone to agree with me that this is a big story. I am getting a lot of blowback from those I have talked to, and there aren't many, who don't think I am poking a sleeping lion with a stick."

"Well you know my opinion. I think it is certainly worth checking into. Seriously, keep me posted." She reached for the check and they had a friendly give and take before she pulled out her company credit card.

"If these are on Lydia Gray then the bill is all yours!"

Just as she was paying a familiar voice came from behind the two of them. "Mica?

"Lance? What are you doing here?"

"When you left my office, you mentioned you were coming here. I thought I would catch you here on my way home and see if you wanted to catch something to eat, but I see you have a friend…"

"Oh please, if you knew the hours I keep," B.J. interrupted, "you'd know I should be in bed already. I was just paying the bill. You two go and have a great time."

Before Mica could protest, she jumped from her chair, gave Mica a peck on the cheek and shook Lance's hand. "Mr. Novak, perhaps another time."

"It's Lance…"

"And you, Mica, keep me posted."

∧ ∧ ∧

They lay in bed, panting now that it is over and glistening with the slightest sheen of sweat. Mica still loves the view from this apartment—the city lights twinkling from downtown to the ocean. So romantic.

"So how is he?" Mica asked.

"Who?" Lance knew damn well about whom Mica is asking.

Mica sat up and looked squarely at Lance as if to say: don't make me say his name. But he did anyway. "Chad."

"Chad is a client. He is off limits."

"I am not asking about the details of his last will and testament or the perks he is demanding in his latest contract. It's just that his name came up when I was talking with B.J. and I just want to know if he is happy and okay."

"He is the biggest star in the world. He is happy," Lance said, noncommittally.

"Spoken like a true lawyer," Mica sighed.

"Hey don't get shitty with me. We just had sex…"

"Made love," Mica corrected.

"Worse yet, if that is the way you look at it. We made love and prior to that you tell me all about this spy you have been dating. And, after we finish you want to know about the man you claim to have been fucking, who just so happens to be a client of mine. I guess that would classify me as just a hole and a pole."

"I am sorry," Mica is genuinely contrite. "I didn't think you were reading anything into this…this, with us, I mean."

"I didn't, and I certainly won't now, but I don't need to be reminded that this is just a fuck."

Mica didn't say anything, just got up and started to dress.

"You don't have to go," Lance said.

"Clearly, I do. But for the record, I thought you would be interested in the spy because he was a spy and not a fuck. And we've broken up. Because of all things, he is a SPY! And, you and I both know that Chad and I were not a myth. I recognize you have a fiduciary responsibility not to acknowledge it happened. But it happened. And you know it. I just want to know how he is. And don't tell me happy because he is living a lie and that can't make him happy."

"And for the record," Lance stood up and headed to give Mica a hug, "I don't just sleep around." Mica loved the sight of Lance's naked swimmer's build. "And for the record, again, Chad and I don't discuss his past. I am there if there is indiscretion of any sort. But that is attorney client privilege. Don't ask anything else."

Mica didn't have to. The fact that Lance mentioned "indiscretions of any sort" gave it away. Chad Martin is still at it. Mica somehow felt both vindicated and violated at the same time.

"Look, don't go. I don't want you to walk out like this. We have stuff to talk about."

"Stuff? Like?"

"Freddy."

"Oh?"

"I read the manuscript. I think we should talk about your options with the story and see where it goes. Could be a minefield. But..."

"It wouldn't be the first time something has blown up in my face!"

16

The Chuck Corman studio on Beverly Boulevard is abuzz with activity. His assistant Dan is tweaking the lens, makeup is being applied, hair styled and clothes stylist Bobbi Friedman is pulling 'looks'—the usual for a fashion photo shoot. But Chuck Corman doesn't shoot *just* fashion and he doesn't shoot *just* anybody. This is a fashion shoot for *Gotcha!* and the subject is the Duke of Clarence.

Freddy sat in the chair, lapping up the attention, playing equal parts aristocrat and spoiled brat. Chuck had a vision to push the limit. So for every different fashion look there would be a different symbol of royalty. In one picture, for instance, there would be an ermine cape and in another he will be holding a crown and still another twirling a scepter—all in good fun but making a point. Bobbi put together a number of looks from seven different cutting edge British designers: Agi & Sam, Christopher Shannon, William Richard Green, Baartmans and Seigel, James Long, Oliver Spencer and Matthew Miller—not your usual noble knock-abouts. Freddy was like a kid in a candy store when he first saw the clothes and wanted them all. As part of his compensation for this shoot, he insisted on keeping the wardrobe. But Ian settled on two outfits. Freddy said he would make his decision on just which two after he saw the proofs and could see which looked the best on him. Fair enough.

Mica stood in the corner as they teased Freddy's hair and darkened around his eyes in a very Goth/Johnny Depp look that changed Freddy's persona completely. It was strangely sexy. "It always amazes me how makeup can change a look so dramatically," Mica said to Ian.

"Do you like it?" Ian asked.

"Yes, I do actually," Mica returned.

"Good. I want the readers to see him in a totally different light. And with your excerpts, I think it will be a great couple of issues."

Silence fell over the room when Chuck walked out of his private office and peeked into the lens for the first time. Mica hadn't worked with Chuck since a photo shoot with Chad Martin where Chad was shot completely drenched in water for the clothed part and naked for the behind the scenes shots. What was brilliant about that day's shoot was because his clothes were drenched you could see the outline of Chad's substantial endowment. But in the naked pictures he was strategically covered. It was like reverse pornography. Mica knew right then that there is no one better than Chuck Corman—not just a photographer but also a visionary artist.

Freddy stood in the center of the backdrop and was thrown a pair of shoes. They didn't want Freddy to scuff the backdrop flooring so the shoes would be put on when he is in place. "Do you think...?" Freddy began.

"I think all the time," Chuck fired back, cutting him off. "But it is not your job to think. It is your job today, to stand, look pretty, follow my directions and shut up."

Freddy looked over to Mica and Ian. Ian simply shrugged his shoulders. "You heard the guy. It is his studio, his vision and his genius. I'd advise you to shut up."

Two camera clicks into the session, late and loud, Michelle Bianco all but fell through the studio door much to the distain of Chuck and company. "So sorry I am late. Parking is a bitch. Have you started?"

"Yes!" Chuck snapped which sent Michelle slinking over to Mica and Ian on the far side of the set.

She pointed to the look—Goth with a Baartmans and Siegel suit and a draped ermine—and mouthed: I love that!

"What is she doing here," Mica whispered to Ian.

"I asked her," Ian said. "I thought she might help with promoting the book."

"Ah...wish I had been in on that conversation."

"Is there a problem with you two?"

"Not at the moment but you never know with her."

Dan the assistant turned to Mica and Ian. "Shhhhhh!"

By then, Michelle had tip toed her way across the studio and over to the guys, kissed both on the cheeks and the three sat to watch magic in the making.

Three looks later, Chuck mercifully called for a break and everyone in the room exhaled. Everyone, crowded around as Chuck showed Freddy some of the images on the computer screen as they were instantly downloaded digitally. Chuck is a master at immediately ruling some out and putting others into a special file to be examined later. The end results were nothing short of amazing and Freddy, who is attractive in his own way, comes across as a super model.

"I think we can do a lot with these," Michelle said.

"This is a *Gotcha!* shoot, paid for with *Gotcha!* money," Ian pointed out. "I control these pictures."

"Of course," she backed down. "But they will create a great amount of buzz and we should talk about having three that don't make the magazine available for other press. And later we can talk about what we would like for a book cover look."

"Are we jumping ahead here?" Mica intervened. "Can I be brought up to speed?"

"I have brought Michelle on to work on the publicity of the book," Ian explained. "As it will be launched in America first, I want a hot American campaign for the launch."

"Don't worry Mica. You will be an important part of everything I…we…do," she added.

Mica thought for a moment and pulled Michelle aside. "This book is important to me and to Freddy. I need to know that we, you and I, are standing on solid ground."

"I am always on solid ground with my clients," Michelle said. "Mica, the past is the past."

"That is what I needed to hear. Thank you."

Despite that little interchange, Mica is not quickly going to be letting his guard down when it comes to Michelle Bianco. Keep your enemies closer.

Before long, Freddy donned another look, somewhat hip hop—not Mica's favorite—and posed using a scepter as a baseball bat, then a cane, then twirled it in the air. The scepter took on a life of it's own and suddenly the choice of least favorite outfit was eclipsed by the action of the shot. That, again, is why Chuck Corman is worth every penny of his substantial fee.

Mica made a mental note to talk to Ian about doing a shoot with Freddy and himself for the back cover of the book. But before he could say a word out loud, Ian suggested a shot with both Freddy and Mica to put in the articles for the magazine. Fine with Mica, and he climbed into the makeup chair for a touch up. Mica happened to be wearing blue jeans, a white tee shirt and black blazer—perfectly neutral. Bobbi suggested throwing a scarf around Mica's neck for a punch of color and everyone was happy.

As Chuck snapped the two of them, first smiling to the camera and then the two pretending to preen each other—Freddy adjusting Mica's scarf and Mica tying Freddy's tie, that sort of thing—Michelle and Ian stepped back and to the side.

"Is everything okay?" Ian asked.

"With?"

"You and Mica. I saw you talking. And I want to make sure this is a holy alliance."

"You have nothing to be worried about. In fact, I think Mica is a good asset for you to be using with the book and with the magazine. He is actually very good at what he does. Despite our rocky past, I respect his work."

"Great. Then we have a deal. When this shoot is over, why don't the four of us go up to Sunset and have a drink at the club to celebrate."

"Fantastic."

Chuck, Dan and Bobbi were discretely asked if they wanted to join the post shoot festivities but each declined. Ian knew they would have work to do when we left but wanted to, at least, extend and invitation. "Please send me some proofs as soon as you can," he said to Chuck who simply sniffed. "We go to press on the nineteenth for this issue," Ian pointed out.

When the shoot was over, Freddy wanted to stay in the clothes he had chosen but Bobbi insisted on wrapping them up and sending them to Freddy, after a few tailoring tweaks. Freddy slipped back into the suit he was wearing, so over dressed for L.A. and enthusiastically looked forward to seeing the Los Angeles version of his club in London. For the first time in a long time, Freddy felt that he was being treated like the Royal he is meant to be.

17

When Ian met with Mica, he knew he had the potential of a best seller on his hands. The fact that the book would not be released in Great Britain, at least until public demand insists; only fueled the fire. American's would eat up the British Royal scandal which would offset all potential British sales. But what they could publish in Great Britain were excerpts in magazines and newspapers—feeding the beast without ever having to produce the end result. To that end, *Gotcha!* magazine, paid Mica a small fortune to create two excerpts of the book—the first sympathetic and the second scandalous.

"Remember," Ian cautioned. "This is a magazine and not the book itself. These excerpts need to be short and punchy...a tease."

Excerpt One:

My fashion photo shoot in Los Angeles with the genius Chuck Corman was something out of a fantasy—all the attention, the pampering and the feeling of stardom was simply overwhelming for a boy from a small village and modest means.

I grew up just outside of the village of Lacock, which in turn is just outside the city of Bath. We would travel into Bath quite often, to do big shopping excursions of a Saturday or to have a special treat meal, and I would look at all the fabulous buildings and think they were castles. Of course I did, I was just a boy and compared to our very tiny but sufficient cottage they were castles. I pointed to the Cathedral often and thought that is where I would live if I were king. Little did I know. My mother, a single woman of common decent but polite breeding, would laugh at me and take me for ice cream—the food of kings.

My mother didn't approve of my kingly aspirations—for reasons I would eventually figure out. When she felt I was getting too big for my britches, she loaded me in the car, drove me over the Severn Bridge from Bristol and into Wales. I loved that bridge. As I child I thought it must be the biggest bridge in the world which, ironically, took me from my world to a whole other world. We didn't stop the car until we were up and over the hillside and into the fading coal mining valleys in places such as Merthyr Tydfil. Such valleys, at the time, were in the process of shutting down their generations-old coal industry. She would tell me that just a few years back these valleys would be grey with soot and coal dust and the prospects for coming out of these valleys to work in another industry were equally as bleak. We would travel down the long roads of two up, two down row houses, some still with the shed for the outdoor plumbing in the back yards. It was dank back then for sure and as foreign as the native tongue was Welsh not English. We would stop for traditional pasties—miner's food—and tea at the local café and I would think the lilt of the shopkeeper's accent was something out of a storybook—so thick and barely understandable. They called me "boy O" when I was used to "lad".

These little excursions to Wales were all part of my mother constantly reminding me that there are those who are less fortunate than I and there are those much more privileged than I, but neither should define them, just shape them just as I should never be defined by my circumstances. It is my character, she would say, and not the coins in my pocket that will make me the man I should be. It was something she was hoping I would take into my adulthood,

My mother was perfectly well educated—never went to university but took her O and A levels to graduate. She was, at times, a bank clerk, a secretary and worked for the tourist board for the surrounding areas. The latter was how she met him. A Royal stop on the way to Wales brought him to Bath. As luck would have it, she was the woman chosen to present the flowers. They were declined, as flowers to a male Royal seemed too feminine a gesture. He felt bad and took the flowers from her and then presented them back to her in a rather grand gesture that made the front page of the local paper. She's had the flowers dried and they have been under glass in our parlor ever since. The newspaper clipping still hangs above them.

I am an only child and that suits me just fine. But as such, rather than being a wallflower, I demanded attention. My mother, determined neither to spoil the only child nor ignore me, worked hard to stay neutral. I would be dutifully punished for being too obnoxious in school yet encouraged to join in when it came to standing and being seen, such as in school pageants or plays.

I didn't know who my father is until my mid-teens. Up until then, I hadn't really cared. He had never been there through good or bad. I had never needed more than my mother's guidance and care and she never referred to him. All I knew was that we lived a fairly comfortable life thanks to a monthly check. But from whom and where it came, I had no idea. But one day when I was about to turn fifteen years old and I was hunting around the house for hidden birthday presents, I came across a box I had never seen. It was a sturdy box, something in which you would store a keepsake, and fairly large. There was a good-sized ribbon tying it shut. By then, I had become quite the Christmas snoop and was able to slide the ribbon off a wrapped box without disturbing the tied bow.

Inside was a virtual treasure trove of letters and small trinkets, pins and jewelry that he had given her over the years. Knowing she was out of the house for several hours, I sat down and began to read. My lineage and legacy spelled out in front of me.

"Perfect," Ian declared as he read the first short missive. "He comes across sympathetic and not whiney, a man in need as well as want. Perfect."

"Thank you," Mica said as they sat in Ian's cramped office. It is not that the office is small, just crowded. Past issues of *Gotcha!* are piled high as well as older tabloid newspapers, as you never know where a story may come from. The shelves are lined with published biographies and autobiographies of everyone from Hollywood stars to British politicians. And the furniture itself is just too big for the room. But, in the true spirit of the British journalist, there is a corner bar with plenty of choices and a nice set of crystal from which to drink.

"Shall we have a toast," Ian suggested. "You know what we say? At four we pour and we fuck with time zones."

"Meaning it is four o'clock somewhere in the world," Mica chuckled.

"That is correct. But as it is, it is four o'clock right here in Los Angeles. What can I get you?" Ian asked as he poured himself a generous glass of scotch.

"Vodka will do me just fine."

"We are going to organize a fashion shoot with the Duke for the first excerpt. And, as we are not allowed in the apartment, for the second excerpt I was thinking of putting him outside Buck House, St. James's, places like that, that show him on the outside looking in. Subliminal."

"That sounds great," Mica agreed. "Very clever."

"Not to mention a nice by-line with your name in bold letters and a nice picture of you. We want everyone to know who is writing this."

"Thanks."

Now let's talk about the second excerpt," Ian began as he settled back behind his desk. "I was originally thinking scandalous but, if you could hint that a scandal is brewing I think that would be great. I can see Brits flying over here on holiday just to read the book and go back!"

Excerpt Two:

The Dukedom came in the form of a simple letter. No great proclamation, no ceremony, not even a welcome to the family. No brunch, no lunch, no hats, no gloves, not even a sip of champagne. But I was suddenly Fredrick Charles Arthur Henry, Duke of Clarence—a long lost title that hasn't been used in earnest for six hundred years. So be it, the title is mine. It didn't come without a fight though and my mother was not happy.

I told my mother that there should be some recompense for the years of illegitimacy. She took the let-sleeping-dogs-lie defense and tried to thwart my efforts for some sort of acceptance of my birthright. I persisted. Letters to my father went unanswered. All the while, letters from my mother and to my mother were sent on a semi-regular basis—letters I can guarantee concerned me. That only infuriated me more. How dare he ignore his progeny and accept his lover?

The final straw for the 'family', but not for me, was that I threatened to go public. What did I have to lose? I threatened to tell the story of a young girl from just outside of Bath who was presented flowers—flowers that still exist mind you—and then was courted on the side for weeks and months and eventually impregnated with a bastard child—a child that was cared for but never recognized. So a Duke I am and have been given what some call a privileged life after all.

I live a life, probably envied by many, but modest by Royal standards. My apartment has the requisite parlor, drawing room, dining room, bedrooms and kitchen—functional but not flamboyant—with a rather posh address, St. James's Palace. But my life has become more silence and sorrow in a home that has become a gilded cage. You see, I am still not acknowledged and barely tolerated. I may show up at the occasional function but that is from my doing and not by invite. And as I get louder again, they circle the wagons...or should I say carriages.

What are they afraid of?

Are they afraid of pathetic little me who was raised solidly but not regally; me who wanted recognition but got restitution: me who lives a privileged life, poorly? (I am aware of my reputation for scandal and embarrassment.) No. They are afraid of the truth. It is not what we see. It is what we don't see that has them both running from me and now towards me.

What we do see is arcane prestige without power, performing in a public forum for fundamental good. Hundreds of appearances a year—the openings of hospitals, libraries, senior centers, leisure centers...you name it, they're there. That's good for the people. It allows the government to govern while the monarchy puts on a show. There are the tourist dollars flowing from across the great pond as those without Royalty crave even the slightest peak behind the heavy drapery. That's fine for the economy. And then there are the causes of ecology and charity and the encouragement to give back. That's good for the future, the less privileged and the common good. The monarchy is fundamentally good.

What we don't see is the puppetry behind the pageantry. The Royals are not just figureheads and tourist attractions but also rubes for the government. They are, in fact, the magician's hand. When you watch a magician perform, you are fully aware that a trick is happening, an optical illusion. The trick inevitably happens in the hand to which you are not paying attention. And viola, magic! The Royals too are a band of merry magicians, providing necessary smoke and mirrors for a government that needs such cloak and dagger to exist and perform routinely. I have seen first hand how this works. But, like being a member of a very exclusive club, I am not supposed to tell the secrets of the magician's tricks. But that is a story yet to be told.

What am I seeking?

I am seeking simple acknowledgement—in its many and varied forms. And if not, I have a story to be told. And as such, they are running scared.

The two issues of *Gotcha!* featuring the excerpted memoir sold out in hours and at a record printing. That may be good for book sales but as the Duke said, it also means that certain people are circling the carriages.

18

When the phone rang, Mica thought for a moment before picking it up. Since the magazine excerpts ran, he'd been getting a lot of calls for comments from other magazines and newspapers looking to run their own story on Fantastic Freddy, the Duke that almost wasn't. But this number he knew and that is what made it all the more difficult to pick up.

"Hello?"

"Hello," said the voice at the other end and Mica felt a flush of excitement.

"Ted, to what do I owe this…"

"I was thinking of you. I have been reading your work in *Gotcha!* and also watching your segments. It just reminded me how much I miss our time together."

Mica wasn't sure what to say. He hadn't quite gotten past the fact that Ted is fundamentally a liar, a professional liar at that. But he is also the man who makes him weak at the knees.

"Mica, are you there?"

"I'm here…just digesting. I miss you too. But I miss the man I thought you were not necessarily the man you really are. Because I don't know if I ever met him."

"Maybe you should get to know him," Ted suggested.

"Right at the moment I am in Los Angeles, so that might be a little difficult."

Just then there was a knock at the door. " Can you hang on a moment, someone is at my door."

"Sure."

Mica opened the door to find Ted standing there. His knees nearly buckled in one of those only-in-the-movies moments. Mica couldn't believe how much he missed Ted until he was standing right there in the flesh. Without a second thought, he just leaned in and kissed Ted hard and passionately. "What are you doing here?"

"I had some time coming to me and the office is getting tense. So I decided I needed a break. Do you think I could come in?"

"Oh, of course. Come in."

They settled in with a couple of drinks. And made the requisite small talk about how nice Mica's place is, that sort of thing.

"So how long are you in town for?" Mica asked.

"Don't really know. Until I feel like I can go back."

"Have you been fired?" Mica asked with genuine concern.

"No, I have just racked up a lot of leave time."

"Where are you staying while you're here?"

"I hadn't really planned that out..."

"Of course you can stay here if you'd like. If you feel comfortable." Not that Mica was particularly comfortable with the offer as the words were falling out his mouth.

"I was sort of hoping you would say that."

"I figured," Mica said, smiling. "But before you unpack your baggage, both literal or emotional, we have to clear the air of some things. "

Ted put his drink down and sat back. "What do you want to know?"

"I know I have gone through some of this before over various conversations. But again, I just don't know if you have been lying or what?"

"So? How do I prove my truth?"

"You can't. I am just hoping I can feel the truth."

"Okay. Shoot."

"First do you work for the Ministry of Defense?"

"Technically yes."

"Are you a spy?"

"Yes. My cover is the M.O.D. working in mid level management covering logistics. And it comes in handy with the other work as it gives me access to Ministry intelligence."

"And as a spy? What do you do?"

"Most of that is classified. I was observing, cultivating and conversely stopping international arms dealing. But I can't go into many details about that."

"And now?"

"Currently, I watch your friend the Duke."

"Watch?" Mica quizzed. "For what?"

"You tell me. You are writing the book."

"And are you watching me?"

"Maybe," Ted jibed.

"What does that mean?" Mica shot back.

"Personally yes. Professionally, not yet."

Mica blushed. "How do I know that what you are telling me is true?"

"Faith," Ted said quickly. "You have to believe I am telling the truth."

"But as a journalist, I like things verifiable. I want proof," Mica countered.

"Well it is not like I can call my boss and have him talk to you. In fact if I called my boss he would deny my existence as a matter of protocol."

"This is frustrating," Mica declared and got up to make them a drink.

"Perhaps we should go out for a drink?" Ted suggested. "That way we are on neutral ground."

"Oh we will. I am going to take you to a place called The Cathedral. But I am not quite done with my interrogation yet. Why are you telling me this now."

"It is like going to AA for the first time. You have to come clean eventually or it will just eat you up. At least that is my scenario. I want to come clean. And I want to come clean to you. It is the first step to the rest of my life. Look, I know this seems like it is fantastical and made up but, so far everything I have told you has come to pass. So, you know I am not lying. In fact is it just the opposite, I am trying to climb out of the lies. Believe me, this is very cathartic for me but I am taking a big risk. If you went public with any of this, I could go to jail for a long time for treason. So I have a lot on the line in trusting you. So, now, what else do you want to know?"

Mica sat and thought for a minute. That beat led to another and another. And then he spoke, "how did Princess Diana really die?"

"Ah," he said. "Well first, I have to say that she wasn't supposed to die that night, just be scared silent."

"Silent?"

"She had announced a week before she died that she was coming back to England and had something important to say. People automatically thought that she was going to say she was engaged or pregnant. Neither was the case."

"What was she going to announce?" Mica sat closer, thoroughly intrigued.

"We are never going to know now are we? But the intelligence community thought she was going to talk about much the same things that they feel your Duke is so eager to spill...about the inner workings and relationship between the intelligence community and the Royal family."

"So is someone planning to scare him silent?"

"Nothing is off the table, Mica," he said directly and authoritatively. "That is why I have been trying to tell you that you are playing with fire. This book is a bigger deal than you can possibly know."

"Is that why you are here now? To scare me silent?"

"No."

"But?"

"But a sincere and friendly warning is not out of the question."

Mica took a large gulp of his drink, looked Ted right in the eyes and neither blinked. Mica considered himself warned…sort of. "But there are so many swing variables in the death of Diana, how can you say it was orchestrated?"

"Think about what you already know. The drunken chauffeur. He worked for a powerful family. In no way would he be drunk on duty. Could there have been a drug put in his drink that accelerated the process? Also, why were Diana and her boyfriend in the Ritz in the first place? They were specifically told to stay at the mansion. The only two people who know why they went to the Ritz that night are now dead. But, it was the only opportunity for the driver to get drunk. Coincidence? And just before they left the Ritz, the cars were swapped out. We know that as fact. Why would the cars be swapped out unless one happened to be necessary for them to travel in? That leads us to the paparazzi following them. Were they following them or leading them down a trail? Now we know some of them were paparazzi. But were all of them? Did someone in the car see a gun that caused them to speed up? Now the accident…or supposed accident. We know they switched cars. Could the car they had gotten into have been booby trapped with exploding tires, for instance? Now what do you think?"

Mica sat with his mouth agape. "Of course she was killed."

"Now I did not say that. I simply proposed a set of questions with no answers. You came to that conclusion. The beauty, if there is art in what I do, is to leave a scenario with plausible deniability. None of those questions can be answered or refuted. They simply paint a picture that says, *what if?* And that is what I do for a living."

"You killed Diana?"

"Not me personally. And in fact MI5 had nothing to do with the scenario at all. We called in friends—international types like us. One can't trace our fingerprints on any of it. Plausible deniability. But you said she was killed. And I say that was not the goal, just the outcome. For some it was a problem solved and, for others, collateral damage. We can drag this out in court cases and sympathetic tribunals and books by learned people and there will never be an answer, just an outcome."

Mica paused for what seemed like a very long time. It is one thing to hear this scenario from just anyone and it is altogether quite another to hear it from someone who creates scenarios for a living. "You said that this was all predicated on Diana having something important to say. But no one knows what that was. The Duke is shouting that he has something to say. Could something possibly happen to him?"

"If he doesn't stop, something could very well happen to him. I just can't tell you what," Ted said.

"Can't or won't?

"Can't because I don't know what might happen. It is on a need-to-know basis and currently, that need-to-know is slightly above my pay grade. I am just telling you, with this book, you too are getting in deep. I don't want anything to happen to you."

"Is that a threat?" Mica questioned with genuine concern.

"No. Just a warning again. You are playing with fire."

"I need a real drink, not this pussy wine we've been drinking," Mica snapped, "and some fresh air. Come on; let's go to The Cathedral where, just in case any thing happens to me, we are in a crowd. By the way we are taking my car. At least I know there are not exploding tires on it."

Ted leaned over and kissed Mica. "Don't worry, I have your back."

"You've had my back," Mica joked as he kissed back. "Let's go before I become agoraphobic. But one more question."

"Yes."

"If you are trained to lie and never divulge the secrets, why are you telling me all this?"

"That is too long a story. Meeting you was the final straw. I now know there is life beyond the lies. I am thinking of getting out of the business," Ted confided.

Λ Λ Λ

Brunch at Roger Keenan's is it's usual happening. It was told it was to be 'boys only' today, much to the dismay of Marilyn Lassiter and the relief of everyone else. Marilyn was eager to see Ted again as she hadn't seen him since that evening in London. But Mica promised an afternoon at the 'club' with her to join to make up for the brunch faux pas. But 'boys only' was just a ruse to keep Marilyn from crashing. There would be Diandra, Mrs. Barry Stegman—the owner and CEO of Spectrum Studios; Ashley Beckwith, Mrs. Chad Martin; Suzy Chambers—along with her and Mica's agent Anthony White; and Simone, the French girlfriend of Sean Jones all along with their respective dates. Ashley would be there alone as Chad had previous obligations—meaning he'd been to several of Roger's events and had been dutifully scared off.

Roger's Los Angeles house at the base of the Hollywood Hills, just a few houses shy of Laurel Canyon is legendary for its elegance and debauchery, the two of which Roger can mix beautifully. As usual, this being no exception, one could expect a smattering of gay male porn stars walking around naked and entertaining each other in the pool—a sight that caused Sean Jones to reiterate to anyone who cared that he is "not gay".

"Okay," Roger huffed.

The brunch was served buffet style, nontraditional at a Roger Keenan event, but added a casualness to the morning/afternoon that said there was no time limit on the day. Nice.

Mica walked Ted around introducing him to the various guests. And when the inevitable L.A. first question: what do you do? popped up, Mica deflected by saying Ted was in the government—a topic that can shut any Hollywood event down with a single statement unless it begins with the word 'Democrat'.

Ted is mesmerized by the porn stars who, rightfully so, had no reason to be shy. So too was Sean Jones, who only knew Roger through the publicity campaign on his latest movie but, was intrigued by the way he chose to 'decorate'.

"How are you mate?" Sean enthusiastically shook Mica's hand. "I love the piece in *Gotcha!* as well as the segment on *Rise 'N Shine.* My mother caught it."

"No, thank you for your openness and willingness to talk. Not everyone is like that these days. And we, the media, are considered the enemy."

"No worries, we are mates."

"Good to know," Mica mumbled.

Mica made his way over to the Stegmans, who had many times been guests of Rogers and knew what to expect.

"I have been hearing good things about you, Mica," Barry bellowed as he is likely to do. "We should talk."

"About?"

"That's funny Mica," he roared. "Most people couldn't give a shit about what I have to say, just that I am the one saying it. With you it is just the opposite. I will have my girl call you and we will set up lunch."

"I am wearing Dolce and Gabbana," Diandra whispered as if she was on a red carpet and Mica was to report on her "who are you wearing?" moment.

Bless her heart, Mica thought. There has to be more to her than meets the eye.   Roger took Ted by the arm and walked him around the pool, on the far side of where the action was taking place. Ted, seemingly adroit in any circumstance, was understandably taken aback by the action in the pool. "I know what you are thinking." Roger said.

"And that would be?"

"That we are a crazy lot here in Hollywood. The truth is, I am the only crazy one left and I have a reputation to uphold. This," he said waving to the porn stars, "is just what I do."

"I see," Ted acknowledged. "It is very entertaining."

"So how did you get into the spy business?" Roger asked with no filter.

Ted stood, somewhat stunned, and didn't know whether he should engage in this conversation.

"Mica told me enough of your story and I filled in the blanks," he dismissed. "I know. I know. But, you see, it is you who is in the business of keeping secrets and Mica is in the business of telling them," Roger admitted. "Don't blame him unless you are ready to blame yourself. It is just the other side of the coin."

"I see," Ted said.

"You have to understand, that you unloaded a great deal of information on Mica the other day. Yes, he told me about that too. He processes with his friends. I am probably the most discrete person he could have chosen to unload upon. Consider yourself lucky."

"Let's hope he's been discrete about some things," Ted said, somewhat jokingly and then thought for a moment, realizing if he were going to get out of the business, questions like this would persist. "I was recruited in college," he began.

"You know," Mica interrupted, "you should really think about a job in Hollywood. There are plenty of positions for a person with your 'unique' qualifications."

19

amela Smythe-Lyons had reached her breaking point. Freddy's head had swelled immeasurably since the photo shoot and the subsequent magazine excerpts. There are only so many clubs and, further to the point, there are only so many clubs you can fall out of drunk, entitled and belligerent. But Freddy seemed to have found them all. And therefore, there are only so many clubs left that will let them in. Red seemed to be the last.

Fortunately for the two of them, the paparazzi hadn't gathered by the time they had arrived, which for her was considered a social faux pas. No paparazzi meant no publicity. And no publicity meant why bother? But these days Freddy was poison and no publicity might actually be better than the publicity they'd get.

Once inside, Freddy, a few drinks ahead of the night, pushed his way to the front of the main bar and demanded service. "I would like a Hendricks martini and she would like a champagne," he shouted belligerently.

"Hello, I'm Simon. Is there a problem?" Simon is the very slick manager of Red. With his model good looks and his silky voice, he is the very personification of calm. Just don't cross him. The band of burly security men littering the place can be at you and on you in moments.

"Just ordering a drink," Pamela diffused. "I'm..."

"I am aware who you are Ms. Smythe-Lyons. I know who both of you are. I just want to make sure that everything is in order and we don't have a recurrence of the last visit here." The warning fell on deaf ears with Freddy.

The place is hopping and large enough to hold a thousand people and not feel crowded. It is easy for Freddy and Pamela to blend into the fray and easier still for Freddy to sneak more drinks than necessary to be having fun.

Simon escorted them to a booth, more for safety than status. They're easier to control confined to a booth.

"I have determined you need something to do," Pamela announced to Freddy as they sat in a corner seat just vacated by Viscount Headley and that kid from the long defunct boy band who'd, against the odds, reinvented himself as a panelist on a talent reality show.

"Headley, buddy," Freddy shouted but either wasn't heard over the din of the crowd or was ignored. He chose to believe the former. "I am looking forward to a visit to his country place. We're meant for a weekend away," Freddy said. Turning back to Pamela, "And so might you, my little Duchess in waiting." He found it perversely amusing to tease her about her not-so-veiled aspirations.

"Seriously, you need something to do...to get you out of your own head."

"What are you talking about?" he questioned in a snotty tone. "I am currently writing a book."

"Mica Daly is currently writing a book about your story," Pamela corrected.

"Well, what the fuck do you do with your days except lunch and shop? Ah, the life of the rich bitches who run the streets in this town."

"I do charity work. I model. I am not running the streets. AND I am not a bitch!"

"Oh Pamela you wreak from the stench of ambition and then mask it with the sickeningly sweet smell of desperation. And right now the stink is overwhelming."

She got up, grabbed her purse and turned to leave but then turned back. "You know you are very unappealing when you get like this."

"Like what?

"Drunk!" With that, she turned on her heals and left, leaving Freddy heading back to the bar for a refresher. This would make four, here, not counting the two he downed before he left the Palace. As he reached for his next martini he overshot the glass, knocking it and its contents all over the poor woman sitting next to where he is standing. Freddy is, once again, drunk and, as pattern would have it, is continuing to be served. He reached for his replacement martini not noticing Simon signaling to the bartender that this, spilt or drank, would be his last.

What did she mean I need something to do? This is what I do. Besides, when the book comes out I will be the toast of this town, he thought. They will know the real me and applaud my honesty. I will be the King of the people, even if I can't be the people's King.

Once again, Freddy stumbled out of the club too many drinks too late and grabbed the doorman to stabilize himself—more paparazzi gold. He reached in his pocket and pulled out his cell phone and punched number nine, the quick dial number for his valet Ben. "Sir?"

"Get a car and pick me up at Red," he slurred.

Ben was confused as to why Freddy couldn't get in a taxi on his own. But duty calls.

As the paparazzi snapped pictures of the sway and braying Duke, he spewed announcements like proclamations. "You do know I will be having a book come out. Explosive is all I can say about it at this point. But be ready for some bombshells."

The doorman had the good common sense to pull Freddy back into the doorway of the club in order to stop him from making an even bigger fool of himself.

Within minutes, Ben arrived dressed in civvies—this is, after all, his night off—and whisked Freddy into the barely stopped car and sped off. "Shoreditch my good driver," Freddy barked.

"Where are we going?" Ben asked.

"I have a treat for you."

Neither noticed the darkened car following them.

∧ ∧ ∧

"We shouldn't be here sir," Ben appealed to any sort of common sense not pickled in Freddy's mind and continued to wrap a towel around his own naked body.

"This will be great fun. But remember, I am the only one who gets to fuck you," Freddy spoke stiltedly.

They had made their way to London's largest and most popular sauna—a gay sauna set up for sexcapades rather than healthy rejuvenation. It is a remarkably clean place with a gym, wet and dry saunas, a pool, Jacuzzi, locker room and several dozen cubical-like rooms for more intimate encounters. It smells of damp—either from the pool, Jacuzzi or steam room—and the arid stench of the sexual stimulant poppers, amyl nitrate. It smells of sex. They wandered the corridors, peaked behind doors and occasionally Freddy reached out to grope the random stander-by. Ben just dipped his head and followed dutifully behind him.

"Sir, Freddy, what if someone recognizes you?" Ben whispered.

Freddy, who had taken a near fatal dip in the expansive pool, was standing naked with the Royal jewels out for all to see, drying his hair just outside the cubical he hired for the night. "Who gives a shit?"

"I do and you should," Ben mumbled.

"Come here." Freddy wrapped his cold arms around Ben and kissed him hard pushing his semi-erection against Ben's leg. "I want to fuck you. And fuck you hard."

Ben shut the door of the tiny room and kissed him back, his own cock responding to the moment. Freddy pushed him back, nearly slamming him against the door. "I am glad you wore your cock ring. It gets me hard knowing you like it."

Freddy gets aggressive when he is drunk and pushed Ben face down on to the slab of a single bed. With the other hand, Freddy reached below and spread Ben's legs. Freddy spit into his hand and began to stroke his dick until it ultimately hardened. He bent down, licked a quick lick between Ben's cheeks and shove his hard dick quickly and brutally into Ben's ass. If Ben's face had not been muzzled in the pillow, the whole place would have heard his scream. Freddy, uncaringly, pumped away as Ben was forced to loosen his clenched cheeks and let the pounding happen. A few very aggressive minutes later, Freddy let out a loud grunt and thrust forward one more time. Ben could feel the explosion within.

As Ben stood up and wiped himself he noticed blood. "I am going to take a shower," he told Freddy. But it fell on deaf ears as Freddy had passed out.

∧ ∧ ∧

By the time Freddy opened his eyes, his head was pounding and he was trying to understand the surroundings of this tragic little cubicle. Ben's body had already been taken away. Despite his clothes being gone from the cubical, his body was found in an alley just behind the bathhouse—naked, beaten brutally and thought to have been raped.

With blood streaming down his legs, the presumption of rape was an easy observation, although premature until the coroner's report. His face was battered and bruised and it appeared that he might have some broken ribs—again a presumption, but based on having been punched and stomped. The presence of semen suggests that DNA might point the finger at an attacker. Could this have been simply a brutal robbery? The gold and diamond cock ring, the present from Freddy, is also gone. Of course with no identification present, the real question is who is this man?

"G", the only man on the scene who knew the truth, who knows what really happened, had sped away in that darkened car long before the authorities arrived.

∧ ∧ ∧

As soon as the media connected the dots between Freddy and Ben, the headlines splashed across every newspaper—tabloid and legitimate: FAST FREDDY'S VALET FOUND RAPED AND KILLED OUTSIDE ONE OF LONDON'S MOST NOTORIOUS SEX DENS. There is such a thing as bad publicity.

Freddy hadn't come out of the Palace in days—distraught over the loss, guilty over having brought Ben there and suspicious for his own safety. And moreover, he is simply avoiding the police who have yet to know that Freddy was there, passed out on the inside while Ben was being murdered outside.

The news hadn't come to L.A. per se, but Mica consistently checked in on line with a couple of his favorite British papers, to keep up when he is away. Before he caught the worst of the details, Nate had emailed Mica to warn him what was

165

being said. "I know you are close to the Duke," Nate said over the phone. "How is he taking it?"

"I don't actually know," Mica confessed. "I have yet to get ahold of him."

"Well the story has everything we love here: a brutal crime, sex and it all being tied to a messy, titled aristocrat. This story will not be going away anytime soon. They're going to want you on the air to comment about it as you have that book going."

"I don't know that this has any relationship to the book," Mica said.

"That is not the point. You are the closest person we have to the Duke and this is a big story. Just think of it as a game of six degrees of separation."

"It's hardly a game."

When he got off the phone, Mica pondered the notion of just what might the book or even the threat of a book have to do with this crime. Surely, it is just random violence with coincidental connective tissue. The media, as they are wont to do, is simply making a bigger deal out of a gruesome tragedy. After half an hour of letting all these thoughts percolate in his mind, he decided he was doing himself no favors. He had to get back to the book and not let this incident cloud his objectivity.

Sitting behind his desk at home, he opened his laptop, ready to begin a few hours of writing. But an email alert was flashing in his in box. CHECK INTO THIS read the title across the subject line. The body of the message was from Ted:

The death of the valet was no accident. Find out where Freddy was at the time. There is more to this story. Scared silent? T.

Mica reached for the phone immediately and calculated the time difference to be 8 p.m. in London. Perfect. Presumably Ted would not be working.

"Hello?" There is noise in the background so it is clear Ted is out somewhere.

"It's Mica. I got your email. Can you talk?"

"Yes, let me step outside."

"Where are you?"

"In the bar where we met," he spoke loudly.

"Finding someone else?" Mica teased. "You've only been back a week and already on the prowl?"

"There is no one else," he assured in a much quieter tone having moved out on to the sidewalk.

"Until there is," Mica pushed for no reason.

"So you got my email." Ted turned the conversation back to the matter at hand.

"Yes, just now."

"Well as you can imagine, I can't talk. Just take my advice and instruction and go from there. Think about the book. You might not be doing yourself any favors either. We will talk soon." With that, the line went dead.

∧ ∧ ∧

A plain box arrived at the Palace, simply addressed to the Duke of Clarence. Since Ben's death, security has been tightened as a matter of course. So the box was x-rayed before it was sent upstairs. A simple ring is nothing to be concerned with.

Knowing security had gone over the box beforehand, Freddy accepted the package without any hesitation. He was alone when he opened it and was relieved for that. Inside is the gold and diamond cock ring he had given Ben all those months ago. A simple note was folded neatly inside the box: YOU HAVE BEEN WARNED!

∧ ∧ ∧

Mica listened to Andrea's report in his ear from his Los Angeles studio:

"Here's what we know. The security cameras on the street clearly show Ben Foster stepping from the taxi with an unidentified friend and the two make their way inside the gay bathhouse. Sometime later, we see a staggering Ben come out alone. Preliminary autopsy results say he had either taken drugs or had been drugged.

He walks out of the place followed by another man just a few seconds later. This is where it gets interesting from an investigative point of you. The two walk to a spot where there is no security camera coverage. Either the camera is pointed in the wrong direction or it wasn't working that night. Whatever happened in those shadows left Ben Foster naked and dead. And although we see a number of people leave the bathhouse over the next few hours, we have no idea which one or if anyone of those men is the man Ben entered with."

"Has anyone talked with friends or co-workers to find out if he visited these sorts of places on a regular basis or if he indulged in recreational drugs or, perhaps, had a drug problem?"

"That is a good question Euan. The Palace has not given journalists access to any co-workers. And we have yet to track down close friends. According to his family, Ben was a bit of a loner who was overwhelmed by the city. As far as interviews with the workers at the bathhouse, they say they don't recall him ever

167

being there before. And, needless to say, no one has come forward to say they were a customer of the place that night."

"And what of the DNA evidence?"

"According to police sources, they have the DNA but finding a match will be like looking for a needle in a haystack."

"Thank you Andrea. Now we go to Los Angeles for a unique perspective on this growing story from Mica Daly. Mica, it seems strange to be talking to the American on the staff for insight on a story that touches, even peripherally, the Royals. But you know the Duke of Clarence. You are working on a book—a book I must say that does not have permission to be published in Great Britain yet—about the life and travails of the Duke. I have to presume you have talked to him since this incident. What is his reaction?"

"Well, Euan, as you can imagine his is a reaction of shock. Officially he has said that Ben was a loyal and hard worker and by all accounts was well liked by the rest of the staff. And, of course, they had the roles of employer and employee, which in a Royal household can create a great gulf in knowing very much personally about the staff. But he did say that the allegations that Ben was even a recreational user of drugs would be hard to believe. The staff at the Palace work long hours and the Duke feels drug use would have showed in his work."

"Does he think this was a random attack, even a hate crime, as some have speculated?"

"A hate crime is the only conclusion he can come to at this stage."

"And what of the book on which you are collaborating with the Duke. There has been a lot of talk that people in the right places don't want it published and in fact it may never get published."

"Then I am wasting a lot of time," Mica joked.

"But seriously, could someone be angry enough about the book to send a brutal warning."

"Neither the Duke nor I can image that to be the case. Nor can we assume or presume this senseless act of brutality was anything more than random and tragic."

But the truth is neither.

20

"You're a mess," Mica blurted out as Freddy opened the door. Freddy hadn't shaved in days and Mica wondered if he'd even showered. He is wearing a monogramed silk robe, loosely tied and clearly nothing else. "I didn't mean that the way it sounded."

"It's fine and you're right," Freddy returned as he stepped away and let Mica enter.

"Is Pamela here?" Mica asked cautiously as it didn't seem like anyone had been here, except Freddy in days. The place seemed so dank and Freddy...well...a mess. "I thought you mentioned Pamela would be joining us."

"Pamela and I have had a bit of a falling out. And that is just fine with me. Besides, I only use her to get into the papers. It seems she's the one who seems to have aspirations for being the next Duchess. But that is never going to happen."

Even with the drapes drawn and a musty feel of being sealed inside for several days, Freddy's 'rooms' as he likes to call them are far more elegant than he let on to Mica. It is hard for Mica to mask being impressed. It is quiet, unnervingly so, except the steady tonging of a grandfather clock that has long outlived it's grandfather status.

"You like my little hovel?"

"Hardly a hovel...more like the Palace it is meant to be."

"Thank you, I make do," Freddy sighed dramatically. "Would you like a drink? Tea? Something stronger perhaps?"

"It's a little early for a cocktail. It is not even noon. Coffee would be great."

"Ah yes, you yanks love your coffee. I will be having a scotch." That settled, Freddy made his way into the kitchen.

Mica took a moment to look around. The sitting room is cozy, he decided, despite being ornate. "I think this is my favorite piece," Mica said loud enough for Freddy to hear.

Freddy poked his head out, "Which?"

"The Chinese porcelain vase next to the fireplace."

"It's Ming or Ching...something like that."

Freddy fumbled around a bit and returned with a large tumbler of scotch and no coffee. "It seems I'm out."

"That's fine. I'm okay, actually. But you don't seem to be."

He swirled his drink in his hand, the ice circling the glass with the whooshing sound of impatience and frustration. "No I am not fucking fine." Freddy slumped on to the couch across from Mica and didn't seem to mind that his robe had opened and exposed himself to his guest. Mica didn't flinch. "I am not fine at all. They killed my fucking valet."

"They who?"

"The 'family', the government, the nebulous 'they' who want me to shut up and go away. Well I won't!"

"Is that why you asked me here?"

"I need you to be my mouthpiece with this book. I need you to tell all."

Mica shifted in his seat. "You have to understand I can't just write accusations that are just that and can't be proved."

"What can't be proved?" Freddy questioned. "That Ben was murdered?"

"I understood it to be a hate crime," Mica said.

"A FUCKING hate crime against me. They hate me and Ben was killed as a message."

"How are you supposed to prove that?" Mica quizzed.

Freddy reached over on the table in front of him and tossed a small box across to Mica. In it is the prized cock ring and message sent with it. "I had that made for Ben. He was wearing it the night he was killed. And the message is fairly clear."

Mica got a chill. He too had been warned that there was something more to Ben's death than was reported but had no way to corroborate or investigate. Now, he is staring at proof. "Have you gone to the police?"

"How do I know they are not in on it? They came here and questioned me. Took a swab from inside my cheek for DNA testing as if I had something to do with it. I mean really! Besides I do not want to give up the only piece of evidence that I know to exist that says that there is more to this death than meets the eye."

"So what am I supposed to do?"

"You are the journalist..."

"Entertainment journalist. This is a little deeper than I usually step."

"But you know people and have resources," Freddy snapped.

"But again, what do you want me to do?"

"Tell my story."

"I can't go on the air with a bejeweled cock ring and say this is the smoking gun," Mica pointed out the obvious as the ridiculous.

"There is the message that came with it," Freddy pleaded. "You could interview me. I'll tell the story."

"I am not sure..."

"Well I will be telling my story whether it is to you or somebody else. They can't shut me up."

"What do you plan to say?" Mica asked.

"My whole story. I want it out there and I want to demand my H.R.H. status. And, as predicted, if they don't acknowledge me, I will blow the lid off all the dirty dealings they are responsible for...take the skeletons out of some very deep closets. Let's not forget they killed Ben."

"Perhaps that is the point of the message. As someone in a position to know told me, sometimes what they want you to be is scared silent."

"Not me. I won't be silent. Not anymore."

"Well don't do anything rash until I talk with my boss and see what he thinks."

ʌ ʌ ʌ

"What do you mean you were at the palace just yesterday!" When Stuart Brewster shouts, he means to be heard. "Look when I fly you over here, it is for the business of this show. Anything else comes second and a distant second at that. This trip is NOT a social call." He tapped his pen on the side of his desk like the rhythm of a metronome. Clearly he is pacing his thoughts and words.

"What is this trip about?" Elizabeth Owens asked.

Mica's agents, the Owens ladies—Angela and Elizabeth—were also summoned to this rare chat with the *Rise 'N Shine* boss Stuart Brewster.

"Well, as you know, we started Mica on a six month contract with three month renewals, which we've renewed. We are very pleased with his work and even more pleased with the audience reaction. I think it is time to throw out the old and start fresh with a new contract."

Mica and the Owens breathed a sigh of relief.

"At least that was what I was thinking until I was blindsided." The tap, tap, tap of the pen is subtle yet obvious.

"I beg your pardon," Mica blanched. "Blindsided by what?"

"First the public announcement that you are writing a book. Not that anyone asked me if that would be okay. Then the excerpts in *Gotcha!* magazine, that could be seen and have been seen as incendiary..."

"By whom?" Angela asked.

"The Palace for one. They don't like the idea of this book and neither do I."

"Why not?" Mica pressed knowing damn well why not?

"It doesn't matter *why* the Palace doesn't like it. But suffice it to say they don't like it enough to potentially have us banned from Royal premieres, events, etcetera, and that is certainly the threat that is looming. And just yesterday, while you just so happened to be cavorting with your friend at St. James's, I got a message from the Home Secretary of all people, wondering if the book needed to go forward with the strong hint that it shouldn't. The God damned Home Secretary! It doesn't get higher than that...unless, of course, you would like the Prime Minister himself to call. And that is why I don't like the idea of this book either."

Mica is transfixed by the BAFTA award sitting on Stuart's desk. He wondered how heavy it is and how much it will hurt when Stuart inevitably hurls it at him.

"Well canceling the book is like shutting the barn door now that the horse has run away," Angela said.

"How so?" Stuart shot back sarcastically.

"For one thing, contracts have been signed," Elizabeth pointed out. "He'd be in breach."

"He may be in breach of his contract with us," Stuart spat.

"How can he be in breach? The book does not even have a publisher in Great Britain. This is just a U.S. distribution," Elizabeth pointed out.

"Look, the Duke's story is riveting," Mica jumped in. "I found out some interesting information just yesterday that we, as a news organization, should be running with."

"Oh?" Stuart questioned. "Such as?"

"Well I can't go into much detail at the moment but there is evidence that Freddy's valet may have been murdered as a warning for Freddy to not tell his story, to scare him silent. And that is just what happened to Diana..."

"You are not going to marginalize what happened to Princess Diana by equating that tragedy to a hate crime outside of a gay bath house." Tap. Tap.

"I just so happen to be in a position to know certain things about both incidents and there is a parallel."

"Mica, you do the entertainment segment. You need to stick with what you know best rather than embarrassing the show with crazy accusations," Stuart spat as he tapped.

"I could give the information to Andrea and she could run with it," Mica suggested.

"This story is a non-starter and I strongly suggest you find a way to extricate yourself from your friend the Duke."

ʌ ʌ ʌ

By the time they had gotten over to the pub across the road, it was packed. Fortunately, a corner table was just leaving and there was just enough room for the Owens ladies and Mica to squeeze in. The noise melded into one cacophonous rumble.

"I think after that talking to, wine should be in our future," Angela said to cut the tension.

"I have never seen him angry," Elizabeth added.

Mica simply sat there and took it all in. "I can't tell," he finally mumbled, "if my job was being threatened or not."

"I think there was a warning if nothing else," Elizabeth clarified. "But that is about as close as we ever want to come to finding out. I don't think the Diana reference was the smartest contribution to the conversation."

"Could I really be in breach of contract with the show?" Mica asked truly concerned about his position.

"I don't think so," Elizabeth pondered out loud. "If you were, we would not have been just hearing about it. This conversation would have happened some time ago. I think that was a scare tactic."

"Oh," Angela jumped from her seat. "I need to call the Angus McFarland show and cancel your booking." She was out the door before he could even ask: why? "They wanted you to talk about the book and crazy Freddy," Elizabeth explained. "But I think that would be rubbing it Stuart's face if you went on that show, certainly during this visit. There will be other opportunities."

"Freddy is not crazy. He actually has an interesting story to tell and there is more to that valet killing than people know."

"And it is going to stay a secret, at least for now. And you are going to keep your job."

In the close quarters of the pub at lunch, Mica couldn't help but notice the table next to theirs had quieted down and was eavesdropping. Mica looked at Elizabeth and then indicated with his eyes for her to notice the quietness to her right. She understood. "It's a hot story," Mica whispered.

"But you're not the one to tell it. Not at the moment."

Mica already knew his book would start with the death of the valet and work backward—a best seller for sure.

⋏ ⋏ ⋏

Ted agreed to meet Mica for a late afternoon drink at Mica's club in the West End. Mica was there when Ted arrived. They settled in on the second floor in a window seat overlooking the street.

"It's been an interesting couple of days," Mica began as Ted put down two cocktails on the table between them.

"How so?" Ted asked innocently enough.

"You're the spook, you tell me."

"Well I know you went to the Palace yesterday," he said.

"How do you know that?"

"As you said, I'm the spook."

"Are you following me now?" Ted said nothing and just looked squarely at Mica. "You are! Are you on the clock right now?"

"You have ruffled some feathers and I want to make sure you're okay."

"Look, the Duke has evidence that the valet may have been murdered."

"What evidence?"

Mica thought for a moment and then decided not to show that much of his hand. "Something that would indicate that he too is being threatened and meant to be scared silent."

"Whatever it is, you should let him know it worked and he can keep that evidence to himself," Ted said. "You might just be playing with fire."

The more Mica heard everyone warn him off this story, the more interesting the story becomes. He gazed out of the window and noted the rushing of people and the car and how interesting it is to see them and not hear them. "It's awfully warm out today for all that black leather," Mica observed apropos of nothing.

"What?"

"There is a man out there looking up here in a head to toe black leather motorcycle suit and helmet. It just looks like it would be hot in all that gear."

Ted took a sip and glanced out of the window and wondered to himself, Why would "G" be following them?

21

he woke with a start in the middle of the night. Something was wrong. He registered the time on the clock by the bed at 4:20 a.m.

"Mother?"

And as fast as he woke, waves of warmth washed over him and he settled back into a deep, deep, sleep. The next day he got the call from her friend, Gloria—a woman from the village—who stopped by to see if she was available for lunch. She hadn't answered the phone or the door but her car was still in the driveway. Gloria, who knew where she hid the keys, let herself in. She had died in her sleep, a heart attack presumably. And he found solace in knowing she didn't suffer.

Freddy didn't say much in the car on the way down to the village a few days later for the funeral. On the instructions from Freddy, Gloria had it all arranged rather quickly—flowers bought, church booked, a notification in the local paper, even her clothes had been packed away ready to be given to the local charity shop. She was to be cremated, as was her wish. By the time he arrived there was little left to do but sit, mourn and say goodbye.

Freddy took Pamela, who by now was back in his good graces with him—at least for this moment. He didn't want to drive up and back alone and he would presumably have a drink, which would mean staying the night. And he certainly didn't want to do that alone—the haughty Duke back among the common people is a recipe for disaster.

The drive down was effortless and the service decidedly simple. Before the service, Freddy noticed a rather elaborate bouquet next to the casket. The card inside was still sealed. Having been distracted by friends paying their respects, he slipped the envelope inside his jacket before he could open it. Halfway through the service he pulled it out, opened it and saw *his* coat of arms—no words, just the coat of arms. So he did know. He made a note to pull several of the roses from the arrangement and place them inside the casket. She'd have liked that.

The actual cremation, although routine, never ceases to be somewhat morbid—a short conveyor ride into a furnace and that is that. He selected a simple urn that he would take back to London and then transfer her ashes into something more suitable—a Meissen box that would make the 'family' cringe over its use. And, as if planned, when the urn was presented to Freddy the church bells peeled. And for the first time all day, Freddy showed emotion with a single tear rolling down his cheek.

"We must go to the house," Freddy whispered to Pamela.

"But everyone is gathering down the street at the pub for lunch and a drink," Pamela pointed out. "You're the host. You have to be there."

Freddy thought for a moment and realized the house could wait. It could all wait really; he just wanted things done. "Fine. You're right. But we will go to the house straight after."

∧ ∧ ∧

"What a charming cottage," Pamela declared as they pulled up. "You are going to keep it aren't you?"

"I wasn't particularly thinking about keeping it," Freddy sighed. "And then I thought why should I?"

"It would be a lovely place for the weekends or time out of the city. And this village is adorable."

As he put the key in the lock, he turned to Pamela. "I have an appointment with a estate agent this afternoon. I guess I'd better decide quickly."

Inside is as charming as the outside with small-scale furniture set comfortably and without the pretense of Freddy's 'rooms'. It had been sometime since Freddy had been back here and the finality of it all caused a surge of emotion. Freddy wept.

"What will you do with all of her things…all of these things?" Pamela asked.

"Sell them. Give them away. Let them go with the house. I don't need or want any of it."

"So why are we here?"

"There are some pictures I want from my childhood, her jewelry and some papers. I know where everything is, so it shouldn't take long. You can make yourself a cup of tea while you are waiting if you'd like."

"Do you have anything stronger?"

"I don't know, look around."

Freddy had no sooner gone upstairs then there was a knock at the door and, as promised, the realtor showed up promptly on time. Pamela sat the lady in the parlor, offered tea, and darted upstairs to get Freddy. Freddy would be a few lingering minutes. The offer of tea was a nice distraction as neither Pamela nor the realtor had anything to say to each other. The ticking of the clock on the mantelpiece became cacophonous after a very short time.

Finally, Freddy, with a small duffle full of prized possessions in hand, came bounding down the stairs. "Can you take a look around," he said to the realtor. "Let

176

me know what it can be sold for and if it can be sold furnished. Here is my card and you can let me know what you think in a couple of days."

ʌ ʌ ʌ

They arrived back in London in time for a late dinner. Neither had eaten much all day and were ravenous. They'd called ahead to the Ivy and booked a table for two with the post-theater crowd. They had raced the final few miles into town and then, after navigating the city streets, were well ready for a cocktail.

They pulled up to the door and Freddy stepped out, bounced around the car and opened the door for Pamela. The half dozen or so paparazzi began a retinue of snaps. But it is clear that, for once, Freddy isn't in to the attention. And then one spoke up. "Sorry for your loss, Sir."

"Thank you," Freddy responded dramatically choking back emotion.

Another turned to the man who spoke and with a sotto voce that could still be heard, whispered, "Are you talking about the valet?"

"NO!" Freddy spit. "He is talking about my sainted mother who passed away this week. The funeral was today."

"That would be two people in your life over a short period of time," still another said, groping for a reaction.

"My valet was not in my life. He was in my service. But unlike my mother who passed peacefully in her sleep, my valet was murdered. And the person or persons behind it will be found and brought to justice. I am talking to the 'legitarati'—a legitimate journalist *AND* it won't be long before my whole story will come out. And finally, the truth will be known and many people won't be happy—from the murder of my valet to those who have denied me my rightful place. My story will be told!"

Freddy's speech is bordering on a rant and Pamela could see by the faces of the photographers, he had lost his audience. Before drink one, he was already becoming an embarrassment. "Freddy, we should go in," she suggested.

"Very well."

ʌ ʌ ʌ

Thanks to his off-the-cuff remarks, the morning papers ran competing stories of the Dukes' two losses with the headlines emblazoned with such ditties as: A DUKE IN DISPAIR and MURDER, HE'LL WRITE. Both touched on the loss of Freddy's mother. The second, more salacious, explored the accusations that Freddy knows more than he's saying about the death of his valet and that the details will come out in a book that hasn't found a publisher in the U.K. as of yet.

The second of the two articles got the attention of Mac Mackenzie over at MI5, which, in turn, got the attention of Ted who had been called in to an early meeting.

"Did you read this?" Mac asked.

"Yes," Ted answered but wondered where this was going. "Unfortunate about the mother."

"But it is one less variable we have to think about."

"We didn't...?"

"No, just a coincidence." Ted had never heard Mac talk so cavalierly. "She is one less link to the truth if his story goes wide."

"I can see that," Ted agreed nervously.

"As for the other, I want all traces of our fingerprints off the valet," Mac said calmly.

"What do you mean our fingerprints? Do we have something to hide?"

"We are '5'...we hide as an institution."

"Just how deep are we in on that issue?"

"Deep enough to be a need-to-know situation. All you need to know is that it hasn't worked. We thought it was going to be Pont de l'Alma all over again. Scared silent. All that seems to have happened is the hornet's nest was poked."

Ted had that uneasy feeling that worse is on its way.

"We have to go to plan 'B'—operation: de l'Alma. I don't think it needs explanation...just follow through."

"Sir," Mica mumbled.

"I have ordered the DNA test on the Duke's swab and the samples taken from the valet during the autopsy. I will bet you a week's wages they're a match. We pin the rape on him and people will assume murder went hand in hand."

"But we know he didn't do it," Ted groped.

"That is for a court of law to figure out."

The telephone ring pierced the silence—the old fashion kind heard from a rotary phone—and jarred Ted out of the tension of the moment. Surely, Mac is not looking to set up Freddy to shut him up. Or is he? The telephone continued to ring but Mac didn't pick up. It seemed to get louder with each ring and then nothing. Silence. A silence more disturbing than the phone.

"What are you suggesting?" Ted asked through a dry throat.

"I am just saying there are options. But the first thing is we have to know what is going into that book. We need the Duke to speak to us. Get him to confess."

"But he didn't kill the valet."

"I didn't say he did. Confess to sex, that will connect him to rape and then a trial of his peers can decide if that led to murder. You're assignment is to get him to speak on the record."

22

Roger Keenan snapped the pages aggressively, like the crack of a whip. Like most Hollywood producers, no matter what product or format, he is used to reading very quickly. And this missive was no exception. With each snap of a page, Mica was sure he was ripping his manuscript. It is just a first draft with no name yet but Roger seems engrossed.

Mica wants Roger's opinion first as he knows the players on the pages; or at least if he doesn't know them personally, Mica has filled him in on plenty of the details. Mica wanted to know if the story holds up, the content is fleshed out and, probably most importantly, that it is believable. And, although long since Americanized, Roger is British and Mica wanted to make sure he had captured the sensibilities known only to those in the know.

Roger has had the book for a week and has invited Mica down to Palm Springs to discuss it. Mica had gotten in late the night before and rather than having a heavy meal, they'd decided to hit the gay bar scene on Arenas Road. It didn't take much for Mica, with an empty stomach, to feel the effects and they were home and in their respective beds relatively quickly. "What happened to you?" Roger teased. "You used to be able to keep up." But that fell on deaf ears as Mica has already fallen asleep.

Roger was determined to finish the book before Mica got up. And it would seem that he had a bit of time to do so. He had heard Mica's cell phone alarm clock go off at a respectable 9 a.m. and it promptly being turned off. Now, just shy of eleven, Mica has staggered out to the pool, coffee in hand, where Roger is dutifully snapping through the last of the manuscript's pages.

Mica was relieved that for once the pool was not filled with hookers or wayward porn stars. It was just the two of them, just what Mica was hoping for.

"So? Is it shit?"

"Quite the contrary," Roger said. "It reads like a great pulp mystery."

"Pulp?"

"Pulp is a compliment dear."

"While there are certain parts that stretch the imagination and not every reader may buy into the accusations, it is a damn good read."

That is what Mica wanted and needed to hear.

"Thank you," Mica sighed. "There has been such blowback about me doing this at all. I just needed to know that despite putting my reputation on the line as a journalist, I was not making a fool of myself by writing a bunch of crap."

"Well, that would be my concern. Are you going to piss so many people off with this book that you are going to sully your reputation no matter what?"

"As you know, Roger, the basis of the book is based on the Duke's own writings…"

"And we know that he has an axe to grind. I just want to make sure that you are not being used as a pawn."

"I have a reliable second source but he can't go on the record or even identify himself. Suffice it to say, I know what I am saying is true. But is that enough?"

"The only one who could really confirm it is the mother and you say she's passed away."

"Ironically, just the other day."

"That is not a new twist in this conspiracy?" Roger asked but rolled his eyes.

"What was that for?" Mica snapped back.

"What was what for?"

"You rolled your eyes. You don't believe this do you?"

"Yes I do because I know you. I am way too close to the players not to believe you. But if he started saying that the government next killed his mother, I don't think there would be a shred of believability in the man."

"Well," Mica sighed. "That did cross my mind. But he seems genuinely at a loss over his mother and has never said that the government had anything to do with her death. In fact, he is being decidedly low key about the whole thing and there have been no histrionics, no public displays, nothing. She died of a heart attack but the Duke believes she died of a broken heart—a sweet thought really."

"Very sentimental. Maybe that should be an addendum to the book…an epilogue perhaps."

"I will give it some thought."

An alarm went off, this time on Roger's phone—a piercing sound you couldn't miss. High noon.

"What's that for?" Mica asked.

"Bloody Mary's," Roger chirped as he walked around the pool to the outdoor refrigerator. "It's noon already."

"Of course. What was I thinking?" Mica laughed.

"On a different note," Roger began. "You are my guest or plus one or whatever you want to call it for the *Cover's Blown* premiere on Monday."

"But I will already be on the red carpet."

"I am talking about the screening and the party. Shari Somerset from Mighty Oak Productions has put together another extraordinary after party and you should be there."

"Okay, that doesn't sound like a hardship."

"We can leave from here Monday morning."

ʌ ʌ ʌ

A Shari Somerset party is an event—many times eclipsing the movie or charity or award show you'd originally come to honor. And this seemed to be no exception. *Cover's Blown* the movie, is one of those boilerplate Hollywood shoot 'em up spy thrillers with few surprises and trite dialogue. But through it all Sean Jones held his own and, with a crook of his eye or dramatic pause, brought both punctuation and, in many cases, comic relief. As they strayed into the party, more than one guest murmured that Sean Jones is the next Bruce Willis. But, the movie itself was no Oscar winner.

The party, though, would certainly make the night's entertainment. Held in a tent that stretched across a closed section of Hollywood Boulevard, right in front of the Chinese theater where the movie was screened, Shari had recreated a small scale cityscape with shot up cars and blown out buildings as if the guests were walking right in to the movie itself. Table décor consisted of centerpieces that were funeral wreaths and ticking time bombs—another recurring theme in the movie. And somehow it all seemed as elegant as a thematic wedding. Mica made note to find the very effervescent Shari and compliment her on her craftsmanship. That would be easier said than done as on a night like this Shari Somerset bounced around like a bee in a sunflower field.

Mica and Roger found a seat and decided early on to hit the buffet before the crowd. Hell hath no fury like the Hollywood elite acting as if they were starving artists all needing a free meal. On the way to the buffet, Mica was stopped by Gina Hamilton—a star from the long-canceled *Divas* and one of Chad Martin's earliest co-stars. "Why Mica Daly," she purred as only her cougar persona could, "it has been ages."

"Yes it has. How are you Gina?"

"Fine. Why? What have you heard?"

"Nothing Gina. Good to see you." He gave her a peck on the cheek.

"Wait," she grabbed his arm to stop him. "I hear you are writing an absolutely delicious book about the Royals. Can't wait to read it."

"Thank you," Mica returned. "But it is actually about one Royal in particular, the Duke of Clarence. It is his story."

"Any chance of the movie rights being sold. Is there a part in it for me? I almost played a young Princess Margaret once for a cable movie but the project never went anywhere. Hate to think six months with a dialogue coach working on a British accent couldn't eventually be used for your project."

"We'll see where it goes, Gina."

Before she could utter another word, a savvy Roger Keenan grabbed Mica by the arm and loudly proclaimed, "Mica there is someone I want you to meet." And they both scurried off like naughty school children only to run into Barry and Diandra Stegman, of Spectrum Studio fame.

"Now there's someone who's opinion I trust," Barry said, grabbing on to Mica as he was passing. "Mica Daly. What did you think of the movie?"

"I think Sean Jones could easily be the next Bruce Willis," he spewed, carefully skirting the question.

"Exactly what we think. We are thinking of a multi-picture deal with him… sequels and such. What do you think?"

"I think I would see what the opening weekend does at the box office and what the critics think. But it sounds good on paper."

"I love the way you think, Daly," Barry said and gave him a big hug. "How is that British thing you've got going?"

"Which?"

"I was talking about the show you do. Is there something else?" Barry quizzed.

"Well I am also just finishing up a book about a Duke and his claim to the throne. It is getting a lot of buzz."

"Movie potential?"

"Possibly, but that would be in your purview."

"Get me the galleys, quick. I don't want some fucking bidding war. We go back, you and me. I want first crack."

Roger who was listening to the whole thing from over Barry's shoulder lifted a thumb in the air. This is good news for sure.

"Get in touch with my office. We should have lunch and talk about your future. I have ideas too you know." Barry said, slapping Mica on the back. "But right now, I want to say hello to the stars and get the fuck out of here. These cartoon parties kill me."

"I suggest you don't say that to Shari Somerset," Mica chortled.

"Who?"

"Never mind. Great to see you and I will be in touch…soon! I promise."

Mica shook Barry's hand and leaned in to give Diandra the obligatory air kiss. "I am wearing Carolina Herrera," she whispered, again assuming Mica is going to put that nugget in his report.

"You look lovely," he said and darted off.

"Well that went well," Roger whispered into Mica's ear as they reached the buffet. "Very well indeed. A movie? Remember your good friend for the marketing won't you?"

"Of course, you Hollywood shyster. Already glomming on!

With food in hand they made their way to the bar where "Big Eddie" Fielding is standing with Michelle Bianco and the star of the night Sean Jones. You know it means something to the studio and the star when Eddie Fielding—Michelle's boss and a managing partner at Regis & Canning—stays this late into an event.

"Mica," Michelle announced in her affected P.R. speak. "You remember Sean."

"Of course…"

"Great to see you, mate," Sean said, simply glowing. "What do you think?"

"Fantastic party."

"No, about the movie," Sean pressed.

"You were fantastic. Everyone is saying so," Mica praised, but skirted the real question yet again. "Barry Stegman is talking about multiple pictures."

"Shit! Really?"

"Well you didn't hear that from me," Mica whispered. "Let good news come your way through the right channels."

"Speaking of good news," Michelle leaned over and whispered in Mica's ear. "I hear good things about the book. I have an extensive book tour lining up."

"Well here is one better," Mica shot back. "Barry Stegman wants to read it as soon as possible and is thinking it could be a movie."

"Fantastic!" Michelle planted a big kiss on Mica's cheek.

"What's going on here?" Sean questioned playfully with a lilt and roll that only that Welsh accent could produce. "Is there something going on between you two I should know about."

"Nothing," Mica snapped almost defensively.

"Mica's gay. *Really Gay*," Michelle shot back.

"How can you be *really* gay?" Sean asked appropriately.

"You know what I mean," Michelle huffed. No one really did though.

"You are going to be in London for the Royal premiere?" Sean asked Mica. "It's Friday."

"As a matter of fact I am. I am doing a compare and contrast on what a premiere is like in Hollywood versus a Royal premiere…should be a fun piece."

"Well while you are in town, we should have a drink," Sean said.

"I will set it up," Michelle interceded but Sean was quick to dismiss her.

"It's just a drink Michelle. I think we can work it out together," Sean sniffed and turned to Mica. "Let me give you my numbers and we will be in touch."

Knowing Michelle had just been snubbed and that never leads to anything pretty, Eddie Fielding took Sean by the arm and mentioned there were other people he would like Sean to talk to. Crisis averted.

Roger and Mica returned to their seats, which had been long ago taken over by a gaggle of twenty-something wannabe actresses. So the two sat themselves at a used table, still littered with the refuse of partiers past and ate their now cold food.

As they laid their forks down, to Mica's surprise up walked Ian Shepard. "What are you doing here?"

"What the fuck do you think? I am trailing Sean Jones for the evening. We're doing a pictorial on 'Sean's Big Hollywood Night.'"

"Ian, I want you to meet my friend Roger Keenan. He did the marketing on this film." Mica began. "And Roger, Ian Shepard is the editor of *Gotcha!* magazine and the brains behind my book on Freddy."

They shake hands but, in that very clipped British way, Ian gets right to the point. "The mother's dead. Do you think we needed any comments from her?"

"It's too late now anyway. But I don't think she was ever going to talk—especially on the record and for a book."

"How's he doing? No flying off the handle, accusing the MI5 of killing his mother...any of that?"

"No nothing. Surprisingly, it has hit him hard and all the shenanigans have stopped, like he is in a period of mourning."

"Good...well you know what I mean."

"Roger had a good idea for the epilogue that she died of a broken heart..."

"Let me think about that," Ian mused.

"How did you like the draft?" Mica asked nervously.

"Loved it! Needs some work, as every editor would say, but that is what we do. But I loved it."

"Great!" Mica sighed with relief.

"On that note," Roger broke in, "one of us is exhausted and the other one of us is the driver."

"I get it," Mica sighed again. "Party's over."

"A few more snaps and I am out of here myself," Ian conceded. "Nice meeting you."

With that, the night came to an abrupt but well timed end.

ᴧ ᴧ ᴧ

"Incendiary," was the first word Lance Novak uttered.

"I hope you mean that in a good way," Mica joked.

"Mica, you are taking on the Royals with this book, talking about the death of Princess Diana and making accusations of back door deals and covert meetings. I would call that incendiary and not in a good way."

They decided to meet at Ovation on Los Feliz. The restaurant owned by friends Scott and Brian has now far surpassed the popularity of their previous restaurant Michael's on La Cienega, which, in its day, was legendary. Michael's on La Cienega was where Lance and Mica were regulars. Somehow it was right to be meeting again at Ovation. Besides, the food is great, the waiters are model beautiful and the drinks are a heavy pour. What's not to like?

Mica took note of the long table in the center which was to sit twelve. The reservation is for Bart Garcia, the newly ensconced president of one of the big three television networks. The table would be for Bart and eleven 'children'— young men all under the age of twenty-five—the kind he entertains on a regular basis at his 'sleep overs'.

"It is disgusting," Mica declared once he knew who would be sitting at the table.

"Oh?"

"He is the head of a network!"

"Is it any different than the parties your friend Roger throws?" Lance querried back.

Mica was caught short. Those are private affairs. This is a public spectacle.

Lance went on to explain that 'off the record' Bart was about to be served with a lawsuit by one underage attendee of his infamous sleepovers who is claiming rape. "It could bring him down. And he says that there are other high-powered directors and producers he can name as well with similar predilections. Roger Keenan may want to make sure he isn't vulnerable."

Mica was stunned.

They sat in the back bar courtyard under the large oak tree growing in the middle of the space as only in L.A. can you guarantee temperate weather for al fresco dining any day of the week. Mica already knew he would need a second martini as the first one arrived.

"Speaking of lawsuits, are you trying to say that I am in trouble with the book?" Mica asked as he sipped generously on his drink.

Lance chose his words cautiously as if he was talking to a client. And as he spoke he ran the tip of his index finger around the rim of his newly poured martini making a slight whining sound. He spoke in rhythm to that sound. "Well, as it is not being published in Great Britain as of yet or ever, the 'family' may just ignore it. But the bigger question is can you prove any of it?"

"All of it came from Freddy and I filled in the blanks with primarily one source."

"Will that source stand by his accusations?" The finger continued around the glass edge, whining as he spoke.

"They're not accusations, they're statements. And…I think so."

"I would make sure and know so."

Mica thought for a moment. That would mean that Ted would have to come clean. And his breaking his silence is tantamount to treason. It is not so easily done. Mica knows he is not happy with the service, but would he rat them out to save Mica's ass? That's yet to be seen.

"Okay, let's say I am sued. Can't we spin that into good publicity?" There is desperation in Mica's voice.

Finally, Lance pulled his finger off the rim of the glass and smiled. "That is one thing I like about you Mica. You can always think like it is Hollywood and turn everything into a positive."

"Well?"

"Oh yes, you will sell books. But that may either piss them off more or seek an injunction. And an injunction could stop further printings and any number of things."

"Anthony should be here to hear this."

"Anthony?"

"Anthony White, my agent. He made this deal in the first place. I want him to know what the liabilities are," Mica said. "I am going to give him a call to see if he can pop over."

"I am sort of hoping it would be just you and me tonight," Lance confessed.

"Well with my ass on the line…"

"And I was sort of hoping your ass would be on the line," Lance teased.

"Well Mr. Legal Eagle do you have a court order for search and seizure?"

"I can make a call too."

Mica smiled, took a big gulp to finish his quickly downed martini and suggested there should be a second one waiting when he got back. He left the table to make the call to Anthony.

By the time he got back there was, in deed, a second martini waiting. There is something nice about the way Lance is a gentleman, well mannered and attentive. As much as Mica has feelings for Ted, Ted lives in a world of secrecy and darkness. Perhaps that is what makes their time together so erotic but you can't necessarily build from that. Lance is stable, solid.

"Well?" Lance asked.

"Well what?"

"Is Anthony coming?"

"No, he is tied up with some other client. Can you imagine that there is some *other client* that surpasses *my* needs?" Mica declared with mock indignation.

Lance fell for it. "I do hope you are joking!"

"Of course I am joking," Mica laughed. "Sometimes, Lance, you have to loosen the tie."

"I am working on that," he sighed.

"Although it is nice to see a man in a tie in this town. And I don't mean just the wannabe agents toiling in the basement mailroom at IMC getting barked at by people like Sterling Lowe. I am talking about people who can wear a tie and work the room with it. You have that."

"Thanks," Lance blushed. "I like them and I like taking them off at the end of the day. It sort of psychologically is like taking off the ties that bind you to the office. It is very cathartic."

Mica made a mental note to send Lance a tie in the morning as a gift—just because.

"There is one other thing," Mica spoke hesitantly.

"Yes?"

"The movie rights."

"Oh?"

"I was approached by Barry Stegman, from Spectrum Studios, to read the book before anyone else. He is very interested in the potential of a movie."

"First, of course I know who Barry Stegman is. We have many dealings with Spectrum," Lance began. "I think this is very interesting and potentially very lucrative. If he wants the first and potentially only look at the manuscript, he will have to pay top dollar. Perhaps we can actually negotiate a fee just to see it first and only—a sort of priority fee or holding fee. Can Anthony handle that or should I step in?"

"Both of you."

"Second, I think we need to move that forward even before the release date of the book. So, if there is some sort of injunction, this deal would have already been made and may not fall under the auspice of the lawsuit. Especially if we don't tell anyone the deal had been made."

"I like it when you play lawyer," Mica said and raised his glass in a pseudo toast. They clinked.

"And I like it when you play bottom."

"Who's playing?"

23

Neither of them had much time, but they did have enough time for a quick one downstairs at Fluid at The Coliseum hotel. Dressed in their finery as befitting a Royal premiere, both donned their tuxedoes handsomely. Both were in town for the premiere but for entirely different reasons: Roger Keenan to handle marketing for the studio and Mica as a follow up to his Hollywood premiere coverage.

"Tick, tock," Mica said as they sat for one, and only one.

"At this point everything is as complete as I can make it," Roger said. "There is really nothing left for me to do but arrive, check on who is doing what and then enjoy the evening."

"We can share a car?" Mica asked.

"Of course."

Mica likes the feel of this bar. Even in the middle of the day, it's dark décor and dim lighting belies any sense of time—much like the inside of a Las Vegas casino where there are no windows and no clocks to let you know how long you have been sitting at the tables. Hillary Stewart, the doyenne of the hotel and social hostess at the bar, is in the office but by omniscience seemed to know both Roger and Mica are sitting in Fluid and sent over a first drink.

"It is always odd to see you, or any of my L.A. friends for that matter, in town and part of this part of my life. I feel like I live in two worlds and when those worlds collide who knows what may happen," Mica said.

Roger laughed as he was checking the media attendance list he'd pulled from his pocket while Mica was speaking. "Well, here is something that may happen," he began as checked his list for a second time. "You might not be attending tonight."

"What are you talking about? I have confirmed the crew with my office just this afternoon."

"Well I can't see you on the list."

Both grabbed their cell phones. Mica was the first to get through to his office and walked out of the bar to talk. "I am sitting here with one of the marketing people for *Cover's Blown* and he says we are not on the list for tonight."

After some give and take with both Mica and Roger's calls, both got their sides of a bigger picture forming. Mica walked back into the bar and grabbed his drink. The condensation trickling down the side of the glass matched the sweat gathering on the back of Mica's neck, trickling down his back. "I can't believe it. The Royals wanted me banned."

"I know. But there is a space for you."

"At the very end of the line. This is not good. I gather my executive producer had to negotiate for two hours to get on this red carpet and he is not happy. He wants to see me after my segment tomorrow. Immediately after."

"I am sure it is just a misunderstanding on someone's part and it will all work out by night's end."

"It's that damn book. That's what it is. Freddy warned me the 'family' didn't want the story told and I was told, in turn, there may be ramifications. I just didn't think they would be happening to me."

"It could be just a move to call their bluff. They'll blink in the end and everything will be fine," Roger reassured.

"Can we just get over there and see what is going on?" Mica asked.

"Sure."

Both finished their drinks quickly and in silence while the bartender let the doorman know they needed a taxi. As they stepped out into the late afternoon air, gusts were blowing and there is a definite chill in the air—to match the chill in the atmosphere.

Traffic was it's usual self and it took more than just a few minutes to go a very short distance over to Leicester Square. When they got there, the setting was strangely low-keyed—no big props or sets, just the expected red carpet, velvet ropes and a sea of media.

"I am going to love you and leave you," Roger said and kissed Mica on the cheek. "Good luck tonight. We will speak later."

Mica found his crew situated at the wrong end of the carpet rather than in it's front and center first placement as usual and expected.

"Who did you piss off this time?" Michelle Bianco stage whispered as she approached Mica from behind. Michelle has a knack of looking particularly ghoulish at events such as this with her exceptionally thin body, pasty white skin, light makeup, dark eyes and jet-black hair. But add to that a floor length black sheath of a gown with no adornment except a long pair of black opera gloves and she looked more graveyard ready than runway chic. "God knows we've been down this road but I thought they loved you here."

"Who knows?" was all Mica could muster. "I think it is about the book. I have been getting a bit of a cold shoulder ever since those excerpts were printed, but nothing as bad as this. Make sure you bring Sean by to talk to me otherwise I have no segment and I will be...excuse the expression, 'royally fucked'."

"I'll do what I can but no one is supposed to talk to you."

"Michelle, you represent the book. Don't think we are not all in this together."

Just then a surge of a crowd scream overwhelmed their conversation. "Let me go do my job," Michelle said and darted off down the carpet to wrangle her first client of the night, Ashley Beckwith.

From Mica's perspective—he is standing where the carpet turns and the celebrities walk into the cinema—he could see all the way down the red carpet. But as bad a location as it is, it does give his cameraman, Thom, a good angle to get plenty of the stars working the carpet and the media. Right now, Ashley, flying solo tonight without Chad Martin on her arm, who has become quite the star in her own right, is posing and posturing for the still cameras—giving Michelle just enough time to catch up with her and guide her accordingly.

As Ashley made her way down the red carpet, Mica thought this might be a good time to do one of his patented standup bridges. "As the stars and the Royals make their way down the red carpet for *Cover's Blown*, I had to think was there ever a time any of them tried to do something sneaky but their cover was blown?" Mica thought about that for a moment and worried that he really wouldn't speak to anyone and he would never get an answer to that question. So he did another to cover his ass. "This is what it is like in Leicester Square...but nearly six thousand miles away in Hollywood, this is how we do a premiere." He would get a story out of this night if it killed him.

Before Ashley could get to him, Roger and he made eye contact. Both simply shrugged their shoulders at the predicament he found himself in. Just then Ashley walked between them, caught Mica's eye and blew him a very dramatic kiss. Good for the video but no interview. She continued through the door. "Michelle?"

She simply mouthed: I'm sorry.

A similar display happened time and time again, over the course of the event. The only sound bites he was able to get was a British Big Brother contestant named Miranda Something-Or-Other, a duo of hosts from children's afternoon television, a BBC DJ and Angus McFarland, who mercifully did not bring up the fact that last time Mica was in town Mica canceled an appearance on his late night talk show at the last minute.. Fortunately Angus is a comedian and given a few set up lines, he was able to riff for several minutes on the ludicrous nature of a 'Royal' premiere. At least Mica had that to run with.

Finally, and with much fanfare the star, Sean Jones, stepped out of his limo and on to the red carpet. From way down at the other end of the carpet Michelle waved thumbs up to Mica, meaning Sean would talk. The cameraman captured every second he could of Sean on the carpet. But it was taking longer than anticipated. By the time he reached Mica, Michelle interceded. "Two quick questions. The Royals are arriving and he must be in the theater before them." The camera rolled on that incident and that would make the segment.

Sean was hugs and hellos when he saw Mica but just as Mica was about to ask his first question, the crowd swelled again. Prince Andrew is the Royal presentation tonight. Quickly behind him are the two daughters, their respective dates and Andrew's ex wife, Fergie, the Duchess of York.

"Mica I have to get him inside," Michelle pleaded.

But Mica squeezed out an appropriate question that couldn't be ignored. "How surreal is this moment for you?"

"Too much," Sean said with all due humility. "I know my mum is at home crying as we speak."

By the time he answered, Andrew had made his way down the carpet, saw Sean and called him over—more hugs and hellos, not to mention kisses on the cheeks for the young Princesses. And it all happened right in front of Mica's camera. A remarkable, if not heaven sent, save for the evening.

∧ ∧ ∧

Freddy wasn't about to embarrass himself again by being turned away at the front door of St. James's Palace, so he chose to go in through the servant's entrance, up the back staircase and into the reception as one of the invitees. Once inside, he darted directly to the bar and made himself at home with a Hendricks on the rocks.

Within minutes the guests started to file in from the premiere after party for a late night breakfast with the Royals on hand. Ted, figuring Freddy would find his way into this particular party, got his name put on the invitation list. It was a gamble that clearly paid off. The smallish reception room was nearly full when Ted stepped through the door and made his way discretely through the crowd to find Freddy.

"You again," Freddy said as Ted stepped around Ashley Beckwith and approached Freddy. "What are you doing here?"

"Strange as it may seem. I am here to help you."

"I don't need any help," Freddy shot back indignantly.

"Consider me your minder," Ted explained.

"And I don't need minding!"

The chime of some ancient clock announced the stroke of midnight and the serving of a light breakfast—scrambled eggs with heavy cream, chives and caviar with toast points.

"You may not know it but you most certainly do need minding."

"And why is that?" Freddy asked.

"You are getting reckless and upsetting the wrong people."

Freddy deflected. "Eggs? Mr...?"

"You can call me Ted and no thank you."

"I do adore late night breakfast," Freddy dismissed again.

"Your Lordship, you don't seem to understand. The idea of a you publishing a book or spilling what might amount to state secrets has more than a few feathers ruffled."

"The truth always ruffles feathers."

"Look," Ted said as he took Freddy by the arm and lead him to a far off table in the corner where they would not be heard. "You and I both know that your supposed book is a long shot."

"It is not a long shot. It has been written as we speak."

"But it is never going to see the light of day in Great Britain and who knows what the status will be between now and some unknown publication date elsewhere."

"That is rubbish."

"Never the less, we know you have a story to tell," Ted soothed.

"And just who are 'we'?"

"People you will never know but know a great deal about you."

"Oh how clandestine," Freddy shot back sarcastically.

"Exactly."

"And that would make you one of the clandestine, I suppose. So what do you want? And don't say for me to shut up. If you think you know me as well as you say, you know that will never happen?"

"On the contrary. I want you to talk. I would like to set up an on-camera interview during which you can tell your whole story. No holds barred," Ted offered.

Freddy beamed. Finally someone is listening. "I insist on Mica Daly doing the interview. He is writing my book and therefore knows what to ask."

"Fair enough. I am sure we can arrange that."

"Tell me," Freddy began skeptically. "What is this interview going to be used for?"

"Archive and insurance," Ted answered.

"Archive? But I want my story told."

"No you don't. Not right at the moment."

"Is that why you mentioned insurance? Do you think something could happen to me if my story does come out?"

"I have already told you, you have ruffled some rather important feathers."

Freddy paused for a moment, put down his fork, took a big swig of his drink and asked, "Who killed my valet?"

∧ ∧ ∧

The interview was hastily put together. Mica agreed to do it on Ted's request, with the proviso that he would get a copy of the entire interview for himself and be able to air excerpts for a profile piece on the Duke. Mica secured an empty suite through Hillary at The Coliseum in which to stage the interview but Ted would provide the camera crew—a little odd to Mica, as it is Mica who is in the television business and had his pick of a number of crews.

The Duke arrived precisely on time at 2:00 p.m., dressed in a blue double-breasted blazer, white and blue striped Thomas Pink dress shirt and a pink dominating multi-colored ascot tied around his neck and tucked into the open shirt. His pants are khaki and his shoes are tasseled loafers. No socks. With his hair gelled back and just the slightest hint of a powdered face, he looked magazine chic—just as easily having been on a yacht as at a polo match.

"You look very smart," Mica said to Freddy as he was placed in a tall back chair, an old television trick to ensure he would sit upright.

"I hope you mean aristocratic," Freddy corrected.

"Of course."

Mica was skeptical of the crew. None of them are familiar faces as from the crews he would recognize from being out in the field or on a red carpet. In fact, the man behind the camera pointed at Freddy kind of freaked Mica out—a brooding tall dark man who had only been introduced as "G". He hadn't spoken the entire time they'd been there. But Ted had assured Mica they were all professionals. But why should Mica worry? It is not as if MI5 can roust a production team at the snap of a finger...or can they?

The room looked beautiful. Decorated in a shade of rose that was particularly flattering to Freddy and looked as if it could easily been one of Freddy's rooms at the Palace. When all was set—light's tweaked and microphones tested—they were ready to go.

"Cell phone's off please," Mica announced. And despite assurances that the crew was seasoned, each reached for their forgotten phone. Mica couldn't help but make note of the amateur mistake. "Now, let's start at the beginning. Tell me about your childhood."

Freddy spoke eloquently and, at times, emotionally about his upbringing,

194

his mother and the finding out about his father. He spoke strongly and assertively about his feelings about the family and what the Royals do behind closed doors. He came across both insightful and truthful.

"Why did you want to do this interview?" Mica asked in conclusion.

"I have a very good life," Freddy began. "But it is a life based on a lie. I am not asking for anymore than what I have. I am asking to be who I am."

"You seem to want to take them down if you don't get what you want."

"I see their value and I can be a valuable part of that equation. They should know that, that's all."

"And if they don't 'recognize that'?"

"There is a price for that."

"But you will pay that price as well."

"And what do I really have to lose. Let's just see who blinks first."

Mica let a dramatic pause linger in the air and then announced he had what he needed and wrapped the interview.

"Just a couple more questions," Ted interceded and handed Mica a piece of paper.

"I don't know that I can ask these," Mica whispered to Ted, having glanced quickly over the three hastily scrawled questions.

"My life is an open book," Freddy jumped in basking in the afterglow of having finally been heard. "Ask away."

The cameras fired up again and Mica began nervously. "Tell about your relationship with your valet."

Freddy paused for a moment, somewhat startled, and then spoke. "If you are asking if we were lovers? We were."

"Did you take him to the gay sauna on the night of his death?"

"Yes. The last thing I remember is that we had, shall we say, intense sex and then the next day I was told his body was found."

"Who do you think is responsible?"

Freddy looked over at Ted, stared into his eyes for a noticeable amount of time and then turned back to Mica. "I wish I knew."

Mica felt particularly uneasy about this last set of questions. They didn't seem in keeping with the reasoning behind the interview—to get an archived interview of Freddy's life story. Ted had to be fishing for something but the questions were asked and answered.

The interview had run some two and a half hours by the time all was said and done and Mica had to get back to the office for an edit session. Normally, Mica would have helped the crew break down but there was no time for that and certainly none for the promised drink downstairs with Freddy and Ted. In fact, there was little time for anything but quick "good byes". On the way out the door, Mica stopped turned and reached out to "G" who handed him his copy of the interview on memory cards and he was out the door.

"How do you think that went?" Freddy asked Ted.

"I believe we have everything we need."

24

amela Smythe-Lyons had grown tired of playing second fiddle to the dashing but dubious headline grabbing Duke of Clarence. She too believed she has something to say, a story to tell. Whether anyone cared to listen is another story all together. She had approached Mica by leaving a written packet at the front desk at The Coliseum consisting of a short synopsis of her life story and some salacious bullet points that might make better fodder for a pulp novel than a profile piece in some magazine. She wanted him to solicit *Gotcha!* magazine.

It's not like she doesn't have the pedigree for a high profile magazine spread. Being the daughter of a close friend of the 'family', her ski trips to Gstaad, playful jaunts to the Caribbean and raucous holidays in Ibiza are all the stuff of social legend. But her recent cavorting with the Duke of Clarence has her talking to the tune of a payday of ten thousand pounds for an interview with as least one tabloid, *Splash.* Perhaps, she thought, this too could lead to a book deal just like Freddy. Of course Freddy has a story to tell.

She sat with a middle aged, overweight, reporter who had a built-in distain for all things upper class. The reporter, Millicent—a name you never hear anymore—agreed to meet her at the Ivy where Pamela stacked the deck with a couple of friends she could wave to from across the room and appear relevant in the scrutinizing eyes of Millicent.

Pamela had arrived in this season's Chanel, pink skirt with a plaid jacket with frayed edges, the look of today. Her hair was pulled back in a severe ponytail and she was careful not to wear too much jewelry. She wanted to portray class not crass just in case there were photographers out front. And there were.

Millicent, on the other hand arrived in her usual uniform—a long, below the knee skirt that had seen better days; sensible shoes; a flowered blouse and a bag carrying most of what she would need for an office on the go. Covering it all is a durable trench coat—a men's Burberry of some years old.

Just on first glances, the two could not have been more opposite.

"I am supposing you have been at this a while," Pamela began, clearly insulting the aging and tired reporter.

"A while? If by a while you mean that I have held a steady job longer than you have been alive, then yes, I have been at this a while," Millicent barked back. "Which, I suppose, leads me to an obvious first question. Have *you* ever had a job?"

"I am glad you asked that. People tend to think of people like me as lazy and that is simply not the truth. I would like a job—nothing nine to five—but a job with meaning. I want my life to have meaning."

"Are you saying that nine to five workers have little or no meaning in their lives?"

"Oh now Millicent you are twisting my words."

"No I am quoting you."

Pamela ordered a bottle of white wine. This would be harder than she thought but she had to keep her eyes on the prize, the much-needed ten thousand pounds. She might be a daughter of privilege but that privilege had its credit limits and she had long since reached hers.

There was a lot of small talk, background on her upbringing, schooling, what she does for fun—those sorts of topics—before Millicent changed her tune adeptly and leaned in for some girl talk. Three glasses of wine into the existing conversation and Pamela was ready to dish. It was, after all, what Millicent was there for.

"So tell me about the Duke of Clarence," Millicent began with a false twinkle in her eye as if to say 'this is just between us to girls.'

"We have a lot of fun together," Pamela began innocently enough.

"Like?"

"We like to go out to clubs and that sort of thing."

"And that has been a bit excessive at times. Surely you want to settle down. Perhaps the Duke needs a Duchess."

"Perhaps the Duke is the Duchess!" Pamela joked, forgetting, of course, there is no joking in front of a journalist. Everything is on the record.

"Excuse me," Millicent returned.

"I didn't mean that..."

"What did you mean?"

"I just don't think the Duke is the marrying sort. That's all."

"Why would you say that? He's young. He's titled. He's attractive." Millicent prodded.

This fourth glass of wine may have been the breaking point. "He's a bender!" Pamela spat. "A poof. He's gay."

Millicent to her credit didn't flinch. "Many a the titled have been painted with that brush only to marry and sire on. Perhaps..."

"He was sleeping with his valet for God's sake."

"The murdered boy?"

"The same."

Millicent had her story and Pamela her renewed fifteen minutes of fame. But neither got what they expected.

The story broke the next day, less profile than expose. The headline read: "THE MAN WHO WOULD BE QUEEN as told by the Duchess who will never be." The article went on to say:

> Having more wine than discretion, socialite and Royal insider Pamela Smythe-Lyons sat down and talked to this reporter about her friendship and unrequited love for her constant clubbing companion Freddy, Duke of Clarence.
>
> 'I don't think he is the marrying sort. That's all,' she confessed with all the despair and heartache in her voice as anyone jilted at the altar. The reason for this lack of amour is none other than the Duke's paramour, his valet. Yes, the same valet found dead outside a gay bathhouse some months ago. 'Perhaps the Duke is the Duchess,' she coyly joked. But it's no joke to the seductive and single Smythe-Lyons.

Within days, Pamela would be showered with offers up to one hundred thousand pounds to tell her side of Freddy's story.

∧ ∧ ∧

Mica figured he would bounce the idea off his two closest allies, Nate and Andrea, first. They met for lunch at the pub across from the studio.

"This is going to be a couple of bottles of wine lunch, again," Mica began.

"Fantastic," Nate nearly giggled.

"I don't have to go back to the office at all this afternoon," Andrea added. "Let it pour."

"Is there something wrong?" Nate asked suddenly concerned.

"No," Mica began. "Quite the reverse. I think I am sitting on a great story."

"Oh?" they both chimed.

"Did both of you see the interview in *Splash* with Pamela Smythe-Lyons?"

"Yes," Nate said.

"And let's let the dust settle and see what happens with a lawsuit," Andrea added.

"Sue?"

"I would if I were Freddy," Nate said. "That was quite some admission by her on his behalf. This may fly in her face."

"We could get on top of this story," Mica began. "I have done the definitive interview with Freddy."

"We all know you are writing the book..."

"No. I did a sit down, on-camera; interview the other day at The Coliseum hotel. And it was no holds barred. He told all, including his relationship with his valet on the night he died."

"Was murdered," Andrea corrected.

"We could air this interview and be on top of the story."

Both sat silent. Then Nate spoke. "You have to understand. The Royal family, even in its periphery, is sacred in this country. To spread even the whiff of gossip is a dangerous thing."

"We are a news organization," Andrea added. "But we are nothing without our connections. You're the one writing the book and you have already seen how that compromised one of your assignments. There is no way Stuart is going to react positively to an interview with Freddy if Freddy has nothing more than a chip on his shoulder and he is going to trash the Royals."

"It's not like that."

"Do you really think you are objective at this point?"

"Yes," Mica stated emphatically. "And to that, I would like you both to look at the interview and let me know if there is anything worth airing. I am willing to step back from the process. But I would also like you, Andrea, to go to Stuart and ask him if he is interested. I am willing to be neutral."

"Where is this interview?" Nate asked.

Mica put two memory cards on the table. "There."

Just as Mica put the cards on the table he felt a hand on his shoulder. Stuart Brewster stepped up from behind him. "Well here are my stars. What are those?"

"An interview," Mica said enthusiastically. "I have asked Andrea and Nate to look at it and tell me what they think."

"An interview with who?" Stuart quizzed.

Before Mica could spill it, Andrea jumped in. "A surprise. Let us look at it before we talk about it."

Stuart squinted his eyes and thought for a moment. "Okay. But just remember, I hate surprises! Especially when they come from you Mica." He patted Mica on the shoulder. Message received. "Now can I buy you all a drink?"

"Sure," Nate said. "We're having wine.

⋀ ⋀ ⋀

The *Splash* article was just what Mac Mackenzie was looking for—independent validation of a relationship between Freddy and his valet. Things would move fast from this moment forward. Mac met Ted in the lobby as he was walking into Thames House for what should have been an ordinary day at the office.

"Let's walk," Mac said, grabbing Ted by the arm and leading him away from the building. They headed in the direction of the Houses of Parliament and toward the Thames.

Walking was Mac's way of getting serious. When things get serious or sensitive, Mac like to 'take a walk' which gets him away from the prying eyes or potential wagging tongues within the office.

"Have you seen the article?" Mac asked as they cleared the front of the building.

"Which article?" Ted asked.

"*Splash.*"

"I have," Ted returned.

"Read it again," Mac instructed and handed the tabloid over to Ted who dutifully scanned through it. "We have to act on it."

"Act on it?"

Mac frustrates easily when Ted acts naïve. "This is the final link we have been looking for."

Ted was well aware that the DNA swab had come back linking Freddy to the bodily fluid found in and on Ben Foster's body. And the taped interview had the Duke himself admitting they had 'aggressive' sex. But they were short of a motive. Now they had one—flimsy, for sure—but a motive nonetheless. Jealousy. Ted isn't naïve at all. He just doesn't like where this is heading.

"We now have to silence him," Mac declared.

"How are you suggesting we move forward?" Ted asked, presuming there is a plan in place.

The day was atypically sunny and warm. Not the kind of setting in which Ted imagined talking about 'silencing' a Duke.

"I want you to think about that very approach," Mac suggested. "This is a step into the big leagues, Ted. You know how it was handled the last time. You know the results. Some would say it was a tragedy and others would say mission accomplished. I tend to look at it as case closed. I will let you decide where you stand on that. What could we have done better or differently and incorporate it this time."

Ted simply nodded carefully as to not reveal the mortification he felt. How could this be placed in his hands?

"I want you to come up with alternatives. We have rape and murder in play. But I don't believe time is on our side. This article is going to be an irritant and he is going to want to tell his side of the story sooner than later. By the way, when is that book supposed to be released in the United States?"

"Soon."

"Well that can't happen. What happens from this point on is a career maker for you, Ted. Eyes are watching," Mac cautioned. They walked for quite some time before either spoke. "You have "G" and his team as a resource. But remember, I want plan alternatives. The execution of the plan will be a team effort."

"Interesting choice of word," Ted pointed out. "Execution."

"Is that your plan?"

"It's not my plan, Sir David," Ted stated calmly and then stopped and looked straight into the eyes of Mac. "But the bigger question is, is that the endgame?"

The sidewalk was inexplicably empty. And that was just fine with Ted who was taking a long and winding walk to clear his head. He had had a drink and then a second and half of a third at Boothby's, a club to which he wouldn't be privy much longer. He'd come to like the staid old-fashioned sensibility of Boothby's—its traditions and rules. He realized it was a throwback to an era long ago, from times of war, the cold war and spy verses spy. But nonetheless, he was proud to have been part of it. He sat in his favorite chair, a tufted leather wing back in the window facing the street. Nearly three drinks into it, he needed to walk.

The air has the smell of damp as if it is just about to rain. The bank of clouds overhead reflected back the city lights leaving an interesting glow on the streets, which at this time of night should be darkened. The day had been a long one filled with mixed emotions, second guesses and then surety of a decision that left little time for reflection. The walk is doing him good.

He can't shake the thoughts of that day back on campus, so many years ago, listening to a rather intriguing suited man talking about an exciting life in foreign and then domestic service—for Queen and country. Then there were the years in the military on missions so secretive they were never to spoken of—some of which still leave him with agonizing nightmares. There were the days at the Ministry and then '5', rubbing elbows with some of the most influential people of our time—liaising the good with the bad, the powerful with the corrupt and the movers with the shakers.

And now it is over. He resigned.

"You what?" the normally even keeled Mac Mackenzie questioned. He couldn't mask the surprise in his voice. Ted was a lifer in Mac's mind—a company man for sure. He reached for a bottle on the shelf, scotch, and instinctively looked at his watch as if this is a significant time and date of which to make note. 6:13 p.m.

"Would you like one?"

"Don't mind if I do," Ted said.

Mac poured a heavy pour for both of them and handed the leaded cut Wedgewood tumbler over to Ted. "So what is this all about?"

"I can't do it anymore," Ted began. "I am in too deep, know too much."

"Son, you don't know shit," Mac fired back. "The things I've seen, the things I've done…"

"That is my point," Ted interrupted Mac, possibly for the first time in his career. "I don't want a life of 'the shit I've done.' Especially the shit we do. I want to be able to talk to my friends like they talk to me about their lives, their work. I don't want to walk in the shadows and I don't want to scare some rogue Duke silent with the abject hope his doesn't turn into another Diana debacle."

"Is that what this is about? The Duke?" Mac asked with a snicker as if to say 'get over it.' "I can easily reassign you."

"The Duke is the tip of the iceberg. It just goes deeper and deeper. And where does it end?"

"With a knighthood from the Queen and a career full of episodes during which, you have served your country in a far greater capacity than the average citizen and all for a greater good."

"Your knighthood notwithstanding," Ted began, knowing that he was dangerously close to insulting a man for whom he only has respect. "But has it all been for a greater good?"

"Damn right! Even the worst of it was for a higher cause. There has been collateral damage…"

"A Princess…now the Duke…"

"That's not what I meant," he scowled.

"But that's what happens."

Mac downed the rest from his glass and filled it again. "I suppose you've made up your mind."

"Yes."

"We will have your office cleared out first thing in the morning. And you will need to go through the routine debrief. Right now, I will need your clearance card, service revolver and your cell phone. And I will have security walk you out. It's procedure."

Ted anticipated this and laid his I.D. gun and company issued cell phone on the desk. He took a moment to stare at the gun. He hadn't ever used it, except for target practice, but felt sure it was just a matter of time before it would be called upon. He felt relieved to hand it over.

"What do you plan to do next?" Mac asked.

"I haven't thought that much about it. Private sector for sure. I have a degree in political science and a background in mechanical engineering. I thought I might put that to work."

"You should know that '5' has a department where we can create a declassified resume complete with references for you."

"I appreciate it."

There wasn't much more to say. Ted put down his drink, shook Mac's hand and left—the end of an era. He left the building and didn't look back. He proceeded to shoo away the taxi he initially hailed and started to walk. It was a long way to Boothby's and now a shorter walk down Piccadilly towards The Coliseum where yet another drink awaits.

ʌ ʌ ʌ

As soon as Ted walked out of Mac's office, Mac sat down at his desk, picked up the phone and pushed nine. "He's resigned. I need to know he is not going rogue and not going to do anything he might regret. Better yet, I want to make sure he is not going to do something *we* are going to regret."

Across town in a darkened loft in Wapping, "G" was already on alert. Ted hadn't been himself for sometime now and "G" was expecting a call like this. Without a word in return, he hung up on Mac, grabbed his coat, his favorite Glock pistol and headed out into the night.

It's not that Ted is now the enemy. But you never know what could make an agent turn.

ʌ ʌ ʌ

"I can't believe you quit," Mica sighed. "And I can't believe it took you this long to tell me."

Ted had a slight pant to his breathing having just completed a rather aggressive love making session. "There didn't seem to be a good time."

Thinking about that, Mica had to agree. When Ted arrived at The Coliseum, they met up with Hillary down in Fluid for a drink. Hillary, as usual regaled them with the newest gossip from the lobby—who's checked in, who's sleeping with whom and the stars' comings and goings. Mica, in turn, filled her in on the latest from Hollywood. These conversations always end up raucous with too many drinks between them all.

Too many drinks, in the presence of Ted, certainly lights Mica's libido. Although Mica wanted to keep Ted at arms' distance, sex was inevitable. And there wasn't much talking there. As Mica is wont to say, "It is rude to talk with your mouth full and I fully intend to keep your mouth full." It's their little joke between them.

It was hard for Mica to process the news of Ted's resignation. "I guess the inevitable question is 'why'?"

"Two reasons. You and a certain situation."

205

Mica sat bolt upright. "Me?"

"Do you remember when you told me you couldn't trust a person who told lies for a living?"

"Yes. And I still can't. So if this is some sort of…"

"I assure you I am very serious." They both smiled at each other.

"So?" Mica prodded.

"Well, that resonated in my head. I had to self-evaluate who and what I was and moreover what I was going to be the rest of my life. And I wasn't sure I liked what I saw."

"But that was not the only reason?" Mica continued to probe. The journalist in him was coming out.

"Yeah," Ted hesitated. "That issue is particularly sensitive and I am not sure I should share. Yet I think you need to know."

"You have got to be kidding me," Mica shot back. "You're vexed about telling me something you apparently think I need to know. You can take the boy out of the spy game but you can't take the spy game out of the boy."

"That is not fair."

"Really? Than spill it."

Ted hesitated for a minute, looked at Mica and began. "They want to silence the Duke."

"Silence? What does that mean?"

"That's just it. What does that mean? I know they want him to shut up. I know they are nervous about your book. And I know that collateral damage is not a concern."

"Collateral damage?"

"It has happened before as I have explained to you. Again, they want to scare him silent. And so far nothing has worked. But this time he is in real trouble."

"How so?"

"The death of his valet," Ted continued almost in a cathartic ramble. "They have evidence that can link Freddy to his death. And they will use it to charge him with murder."

Mica shot out of bed. "I have to warn him."

"You can't. It won't change the fact that they have evidence and they will construe it to use it. And all you will do is get yourself in deeper."

"What does the valet's death have to do with me?" Mica grew concerned.

"It doesn't but your relationship with the Duke has put you on the radar."

Mica paused to take it all in. "This is a set up though. Should I be concerned?"

"I don't know."

"So why did you resign? You could have stopped this! You know the truth."

"First of all there is more to the truth. And second, I resigned because I couldn't stop it. They wanted me to make it happen. And I just couldn't do that."

They both paused. Ted basked in the afterglow of confession. Mica needed to take in what he just heard—a conspiracy to take out, or at least shut up, an actual member of the Royal family by potentially pinning a murder on him.

"You have to tell your story."

"That would be impossible," Ted sighed. "I would be arrested for treason."

"We can disguise your face and voice," Mica said.

"They would know it was me just by the type of information I could give. It is not going to work. This is why I left '5.'"

"Then I will tell the story," Mica stated.

"This is not a game. You have to be careful."

From across the street, a darkened figure stood in the shadow and stared up at light glowing from room 607. Until the light turned off.

26

Freddy woke up with a pounding headache, more than being just hung over, throbbing like no other. It didn't help that he'd spent the last eight hours face down on a metal cot in a drab, colorless room that looked more like a cell.

"Help! Where am I?" he shouted but it only hurt his head to shout. "Anybody?"

Time ticked by and Freddy wracked whatever part of his brain that didn't hurt to figure out where he is and how he got there. But he came up with nothing. After what seemed like an eternity, the big metal door opened and in walked Graham Nothrup and two decidedly ominous men—"G" and an unfamiliar colleague.

"My name is Graham, your Lordship..."

"I demand to be let out of this place immediately."

"I am afraid that is not going to happen immediately. We have to have a bit of a conversation first."

"You clearly know who I am. Is this some sort of kidnapping?" Freddy had the sensibility to ask.

"It is nothing like that. Just a conversation," Graham reassured, barely.

"Who are you two?" Freddy asked pointing out the ominous duo.

"That's not important," Graham answered.

"Where am I?"

"That is also not important."

"Well what the fuck is important?" Freddy spat.

"You are and what we are about to tell you."

"Well I have nothing to say. So you are wasting your time."

"That's fine. You need to hear what we have to say. But first, this does not have to be uncivilized. Can I get you something to drink...a coffee or tea?"

"Something for my head and a tea," Freddy mumbled.

Graham looked in the direction of the unnamed man and he headed out to retrieve tea and something for his throbbing head.

"If you are going to ask about my whereabouts for last night, I am afraid the details are foggy. I don't even know how I got here."

"Shall I tell you?" Graham asked politely.

"Please do."

"Where would you like to begin? What is your last memory?"

"I know I started out going for a drink at my club."

"That, my friend was at least twelve hours ago."

ᐱ ᐱ ᐱ

Twelve hours ago, Freddy did, indeed, go have a drink at his club. He sat in the window on the second floor overlooking the familiar corner in Soho at the end of Old Compton Street and had several drinks and a bite to eat. He waved at a few familiar faces but for the most part sat alone and became increasingly more maudlin as the drinks flowed.

"Freddy, we're off to Red if you would like to join," offered Suzy Parker Tompkins, another of those "IT" girl socialites he was beginning to despise since the betrayal of Pamela's article.

"Perhaps later," Freddy dismissed.

An hour or so went by and the scene thinned. As most people understood, 'the club' was just a starting point, not the end point. Freddy thought about it and decided that he did need to be around people and Red was just a short ride or even walking distance away. The fresh air, he thought, would do him good.

Red wasn't exactly teeming but there was a good crowd inside. Both the doorman and the manager eyed Freddy as soon as he'd walked in. He'd been trouble in the past and no one was looking for trouble tonight. Freddy headed directly to the bar and ordered his fifth drink of the night. Of course, for the unsuspecting bartender, it was just his first.

"Hi'ya Freddy..."

"I am the Duke of Clarence!" Freddy joked, sort of.

"Yeah, yeah, we know your Lordship. Here is your cocktail. By the way, Pamela Smythe-Lyons is over to your left if you came to see her."

"I did not!"

"Okay. Just thought I would warn you then."

Freddy took a sip of his new drink and glanced over to the left. And there at the table is Pamela with her coven of cronies including Suzy Parker Tompkins who waved enthusiastically for Freddy to join. Freddy squinted his eyes, downed this latest drink and ordered another.

"The boss wants me to make sure you slow down," the bartender said as he handed Freddy his second, née sixth drink.

Freddy made his way to the table and without so much as a 'hello', looked right at Pamela and declared in a very loud voice, "You are a CUNT!"

The result of which was a stinging slap across the face from Pamela, a drink thrown at him from Suzy and an ejection from Red courtesy of the management.

"Do we need to call the police?" the doorman shouted in Freddy's face.

"Yes!" he shot back. "I have been assaulted."

Just as Freddy's knee began to buckle under the weight of six drinks, a dark suited stranger flashed some sort of identification at the doorman and scooped Freddy into his arms. "I'll take care of him."

Before the doorman could register what was happening, Freddy was bundled into a blacked out Mini Cooper and driven off. Freddy was nearly out of it when "G" jabbed him with the needle, so much so, as to not even feel the sting of the needle.

That began twelve hours ago.

⋏ ⋏ ⋏

Sir David Mackenzie would never ordinarily be at the briefing of a subject like this. But this is no ordinary situation. Graham Nothrup is the new guy on the job since the sudden resignation of Ted and not completely up to speed, he wanted to make sure the message to the Duke is loud and clear. But rather than to usurp Graham's authority, Mac stayed behind the one way glass in the next room and listened intently.

"We know you did it," Graham began now that the niceties of last night's exploits had been explained.

"Did what?"

"Murdered your valet," Graham said in an even unemotional tone.

"What?" Freddy shouted. "That is absurd. I loved Ben Foster."

"Is that why you murdered him? Because he didn't love you back."

"That's even more absurd."

"You don't have to deny it," Graham explained. "We have the proof."

"What proof?"

"For one thing we have your taped confession stating on that night you had aggressive sex with the victim. Our evidence showed he was raped."

"I didn't rape my valet!" Freddy pleaded. "Our sex was always consensual. Some street thugs raped him. You should be going after them."

"You were out of it by your own admission. How do you know you didn't do it?"

"That is ridiculous." Freddy strained to remember just what he said during that interview. He would hate to believe that Mica Daly had set him up. He refused to believe it. But what he wouldn't give to speak to him now—to have someone on his side, someone to defend him. Mica knows the truth.

"Second," Graham continued in his same monotone voice. "We can match your DNA with the bodily fluids we found in Mr. Foster."

"But that makes sense. I already told you we had consensual sex."

"But there is no other DNA to be found," Graham went on.

"So?"

"Where is the DNA from the so-called rapists?"

"They must have worn condoms," Freddy grasped.

"During a random street rape. Do you really think the rapist stopped to put on a condom?"

"That is the only explanation."

"Finally, did you not take back a gold piece of jewelry from Mr. Foster?" Graham asked.

"Jewelry?"

"A sex enhancer perhaps."

"The cock ring!" Freddy blurted out loud.

"Yes, the cock ring."

"I didn't take that back. It was sent to my apartment. How would you know about that?"

"We don't believe it was sent to you but that you took it from Mr. Foster after you murdered him. We have plenty of eyewitnesses who say they saw Mr. Foster wearing the jewelry and yet it wasn't on his dead body. If we search your home, will we not find it?"

"Yes. I just told you it was sent to me."

"So you are in possession of the jewelry?" Graham pushed.

"Yes!"

"Thank you your Lordship. I think we have all we need to send you away for a long time."

"But I didn't kill him," Freddy choked, fighting to hold back tears. "I loved him." As he began to sob, he mumbled, "I want to speak to a lawyer."

"You don't need a lawyer, not yet anyway," Mac said as he walked into the room.

"Who are you?"

"That is not important. What is important is what you need to do."

"And that is?"

"To keep quiet," Mac continued as he sat in the only chair in the room. "I would like some tea please. Would you like some tea? Where is his Lordship's tea?"

Again, the unnamed man was sent off for tea.

"Keep quiet?"

"You see, we know you have a book that we are going to actively quash."

"But that isn't even being published in the U.K."

"Please, with it being published anywhere, the internet will be carrying excerpts the world over. Don't be naïve. So we will be quashing the book. But we still need you to be quiet. Your story and the things you know are nothing when compared with what you don't know. And that is where the danger lies. You have no idea what kind of Pandora's box you could be opening just by opening your mouth. And we can't have that. No, we won't have that."

"But you can't stop me."

"Oh but we can, your Lordship." Mac paused as the man brought him his cup of tea. He twirled the spoon around the cup a couple of times, took a sip and then explained. "First we are going to have you arrested for murder. We have all the proof we need as was outlined very nicely for you by Mr. Nothrup. You will be going away and your second grace and favor rooms will be in Her Majesty's prison system—I dare say a lot less glamorous—but a place you will be spending a lot more time living in. Now who do you think is going to believe a disgraced Duke? And if you continue to speak…well, we can't always guarantee one's safety. Prisons are such nasty and dangerous places."

A single tear rolled down Freddy's face. "I didn't kill Ben. I loved him."

With that, Mac rose from the seat, gave a nod to "G" who proceeded to jab Freddy once again with a mild sedative while Mac walked out of the room with Graham just behind.

27

ica was fired up by the time the door opened and the morning crew filed out of Stuart's office for their usual show post mortem and Mica stepped in. Stuart was in an exceptionally pleasant mood as the show had gone well and the ratings are up.

"What can I do for you, Mr. Hollywood?" he began. "Not that I should really call you that as you never seem to be there. When are you going back by the way?"

"Soon I would assume," Mica retuned innocently. He didn't really know as he was always at the whim of his assignments.

"I would like to see you back in Hollywood soon. I think you need to give us a little of that sizzle."

"Well I have a story that really sizzles. Freddy, the Duke of Clarence."

"No…no, no, no, NO!"

"But you haven't heard me out."

"I know you have a new book to push but you are not doing it on this show. We are not here for your personal publicity. Besides, hasn't that book been banned in this country?"

"Not banned per se. It is just that we have not found a publisher yet. For Great Britain that is."

"Nevertheless, we are not promoting it on this show. We have laws against that kind of self promotion on a news show."

"I am not promoting the book. There is a bigger story here. I know how Diana died and I think they are trying to kill of off the Duke of Clarence the same way."

"We all know how Diana died…in a car crash."

"But it is how the crash happened which is the story. She was just collateral damage in the process."

"Watch out as to what you are saying. I met Diana several times and her death was both personal and a national tragedy. I am not going to have you make a mockery of it."

"That is not my intent," Mica tried to explain. "What I am saying is that there are parallels between what happened to Diana and what is happening to the Duke. And I think MI5 are going to kill him."

"How?" Stuart sat back and folded his arms.

"Well, first they are framing him for the murder of his valet..."

"Framing him Sherlock Daly? Is that the way you see it? You know better about the valet's death than Scotland Yard."

"Actually it is MI5 doing the framing."

"Oh even better!" Stuart couldn't hold back his laugh. "You're going to take on MI5 are you?"

"Not take them on as much as expose them," Mica said confidently.

"Not on my watch you're not."

"Look I have sources that can verify this..."

"Who?"

"I am not giving up a source," Mica declared indignantly.

"And I am not giving up airtime for this bullshit."

"With all due respect and I don't think I am getting any from your end. This is NOT bullshit!"

"Don't raise your voice to me. I am still the managing editor and executive producer of this program...and need I remind you, your boss!"

"No," Mica muttered humbly. "I apologize."

They both took a deep breath.

"So what is new and interesting about this story?" Stuart asked calmly.

"Well besides the background of how the Duke became the Duke. The MI5 has gotten agitated by Freddy's want to tell the story. Why? Because he knows where all the bones are buried. He knows how the Royals work behind the scenes to aid the government in a great deal of covert activities...some, I wonder, if they are legal."

"We are not going to accuse the Royal family of breaking the law."

Ignoring that, Mica plowed on. "Now, that they know Freddy is willing to talk, the MI5 is trying to silence him in much the same way they tried to silence the Princess."

"We have gone over that." Stuart said sternly.

"But Diana was not supposed to die that night, just to be scared silent. And that is what they are doing to Freddy—trying to scare him silent. The most recent attempt is by linking him with the valet's death and potentially pin the murder on him."

Stuart began to wave his hands in the air, "Time out. Time out. How do you know this?"

"First. I have done an explosive interview with the Duke. It is all on there..."

"I would need a second source to legitimize it."

Mica thought for a moment and then spoke confidently. "I have a second source."

"Who?"

"All you need to know at this point is that he is ex-MI5."

"Your ex-MI5 man is a source that is willing to commit high treason? I don't think so."

"You have to trust me. At least watch the interview with the Duke. I guarantee you will find it enlightening."

"Look," Stuart sighed. "I am sending you back to Los Angeles. This is fogging your ability to do what you have been hired for..."

"But..."

"No buts. I need you back on red carpets, at gala's, behind the scenes and I don't mean with the MI5. I will have Andrea look at these interviews but, seriously, your relationship with the Duke has already placed this show in a precarious situation. I don't need anymore. Pack your bags and get back to the life you know best." He looked as his watch and then up to the clock on the wall as if to verify. "Now if you don't mind, I have tomorrow's show to put together. Safe trip."

Λ Λ Λ

Before he was to leave, he needed to have a face to face with his agents. As it was, the only time to see them is on the day he is leaving. He arrived with his bags in hand and sat in the cramped office of the Owens gals feeling a lot more like he'd been summoned there rather than having been asked there. There was a hub of activity going on in the outer office, none of which pertained to Mica's meeting but it was distracting. Both Elizabeth and Angela sat at their respective desks facing each other as they talked.

"We've heard from Stuart Brewster," Elizabeth began rather authoritatively.

"My Stuart? My boss? About?"

"You," Angela concluded.

"Oh?"

"Are you pushing some interview you did with the Duke of Clarence?" Elizabeth asked.

"I am not pushing it. I am suggesting it is a great story and we should be running with it."

"You know we both backed doing the book," Angela interrupted. "But obviously that has become an incendiary topic. In fact the Duke himself has become incendiary. We know we can't stop the book...and don't want to, for you. But we just think that any stories about the Duke over here are going to be off limits."

"But I have already done the interview."

"We know," Elizabeth said. "We spoke with Andrea about this as well. You know, to get her take on the situation. And she agrees with us…"

"Or we agree with her," Angela corrected.

"What did she say?" Mica questioned.

"She thinks that Stuart and others believe you are like a dog with a bone regarding the Duke. That the book is getting the better of you and that you are not paying attention to the job you were hired to do. Entertainment."

"And there is more," Elizabeth said, "Stuart pointed out that your relationship with the Duke is compromising the show's ability to have access at certain events and with certain people. *That* is very dangerous for you. It doesn't matter how popular you are. If you are compromising the show, you could find yourself on the outside looking in."

"Are you saying my job is being threatened?" Mica asked nervously.

"Not yet. But you are dangerously close to pushing the envelope in that direction."

Everyone sat quietly and let what has been said sink in. Angela then called the outer office and asked for three cups of tea—so British in times of crisis, Mica thought.

"Now the good news," Angela began. "All this buzz has other people talking. We have heard from Angus McFarland's show. They want you on, again. Also the competition is interested in poaching you."

"Poaching me?"

"You're ratings are too high to ignore," Elizabeth explained. "Both the other morning shows as well as *A.M. Live* which follows your show are talking to us about you joining their team. We think this could be a good move no matter what. Why be sitting with a noose around your neck when you could be honeymooned on a new show?"

"That sounds great!" Mica exclaimed.

"It's all in the early talking stages right now but we think this is good news."

"So there is a parachute if this plane is going down. This is not good news, it's great news."

The excitement was interrupted by a buzz from the outer office. "Andrea Lyttle is on line one." The ladies put her on speaker.

"Andrea," Elizabeth spoke loudly into the phone speaker. "We were just talking about you. I have Mica Daly in the office."

"Mica? I have been looking for you," Andrea said. "I didn't know you were there and that is not why I called but Mica we need to talk."

"What's up?"

"Do you want to do it privately?"

"Do I need to?" The always-inquisitive Owens gals both shook their heads. They never want to miss a thing—nosey some would say. "Just say it."

"There is nothing on those memory cards," Andrea said.

"What are you talking about?" Mica questioned. "I did that interview myself."

"Both Nate and I and a studio engineer looked and there is nothing on those memory cards you gave me. Are you sure you gave me the right ones."

With the scene of when he was handed the memory cards flashing back in his mind, Mica knew immediately that he had been duped. And, worse yet, Ted was the person who duped him.

28

It was one of the most pilloried stories *Gotcha!* ever ran. Mica Daly holding up an advanced copy of the book: *The Dupe of Clarence, The Authorized Story of the Heir Unapparent.* In this final excerpt from the book, Mica states Freddy's claim to the throne and then follows up with quotes from Freddy about his current predicament being framed by the highest of authorities. The people of Great Britain were outraged to think that one selfish social climber would dare to claim rights to the British throne and then claim to be framed for murder by the very people denying his claim. They bought the magazine just to complain about it. But they bought the issue by the bushel and the second and then third printings were selling out. *Gotcha!* and the parent publishing company, which is releasing the Mica's book, could not be happier. In this case, there is no such thing as bad publicity.

Editorials ran in several papers demanding the book be pulped and never released anywhere. Not only had Freddy become public enemy number one but letters were flooding in to *Rise 'N Shine* wondering why Mica would take on such a cause and write such a defamatory book.

It had reached a point where a statement had to be issued from Mica's camp. It was decided that pithy was the answer—no defense being the best offence.

FOR IMMEDIATE RELEASE

HOLLYWOOD, CA
Contact: Michelle Bianco
Regis & Canning

MICA DALY THE OBJECT OF HATE MAIL AND MISINFORMATION DUE
TO THE RELEASE OF SIZZLING NEW EXPOSÉ:
"THE DUPE OF CLARENCE, The Authorized Story of the Heir *Un*apparent"

In light of the recent spate of editorials and other comments mocking the reputation and/or personal and professional ethics of Mica Daly for writing a story as told to him. The following is the only statement that shall be officially issued at this time:

ᴧ ᴧ ᴧ

Gotcha! magazine was so pleased with the negative response to the spread announcing the arrival of the book, they decided to rub salt in the wound by sponsoring a book signing party, complete with stars and socialites and plenty of pictures to splash through the pages of the next issue. Joey Chase, who had gone from a street crawling paparazzo to becoming the go-to photographer for celebrity events like this, is on hand snapping both candid and posed pictures as people filed in.

Some sixty people were invited, somewhat of a friends and family group for cocktails and hors d'oeuvres at Roger Keenan's home. He loves a good excuse—well, really any excuse—to throw one of his infamous parties. Sans naked porn stars in the pool, this is going to be a good one.

Among those on the guest list: the magazine's and book's editor Ian Shepard; Mica's L.A. agent Anthony Wright; P.R. maven handling the book launch Michelle Bianco, the Collins sisters—Joan and Jackie; action star Sean Jones; reality star Suzy Chambers; actress Ashley Beckwith minus Chad Martin; socialite Marilyn Lassiter; photographer to the stars who snapped the picture for the back cover of the book Chuck Corman; Spectrum Studios head Barry Stegman and his wife Diandra; and Mica's lawyer and presumed date for the night Lance Novak. And, yes, it wouldn't be a Roger Keenan party without a requisite number of porn stars—clothed this time—some passing nibbles from the foremost caterers in town, Scott and Brian from Ovation.

For the evening, Roger had removed his legendary dining table to make room for those mingling and had erected a small stage where Mica was to do a reading and a desk from which he could sign copies of the book. Ian Shepard had secured ten cases of advanced-copy books for Mica and the evening's guests.

Mica, guided by Michelle Bianco who was handing out schedules of book signings throughout the U.S., made sure to greet every guest and shake every hand. Along the way, he heard the most interesting tit bits such as Marilyn Lassiter regaling anyone who would listen that she personally knows the Duke and believes every word he says while, on the other hand, Joan Collins was telling the Stegmans how she feels the Duke is more charlatan than Charlemagne.

When most of the guests had settled into their first drink and a couple of bites of food, Roger tapped the side of his glass to raise attention. "Ladies and gentleman, I want to thank you for coming tonight and supporting Mica Daly and his delicious new book, *The Dupe of Clarence.*" Roger paused for the smattering of clapping. "I say delicious, not because I am British and love all things Royal, but because when the books arrived, I picked one up to finger through it and could not put it down. I literally ate it up. I have to admit, I thought it was going to be a rather self-serving tome filled with 'I wants' and 'I should haves' and 'Gimme, gimme, gimme.' But it is not and that is the result of the hard work by the deft hand of its writer, Mica Daly. So without further adieu, the author and my friend, Mica Daly."

Amid the applause, Mica stepped forward, got a hug from Roger and stepped up on the stage.

"First of all, can we thank Roger Keenan for yet another spectacular evening?" The room exploded with applause and Roger dutifully bowed his appreciation. "I want to thank you all for coming and supporting this rather intriguing, emotional and thought provoking story. When I first met the Duke, I'll admit I wasn't sure of him. He was pushy and in your face and determined to be heard. Sort of like some of the people in this room." He paused for the laughter. "But what I found, when we sat down and we finally talked, was that his is the story of privilege and power and promises broken. When it was decided that I read a passage for you this evening, I didn't want to take up too much of the evening. So I have chosen a brief passage which I think is uniquely solitary from a man who may have been compensated handsomely but never given his due."

When my mother died, I thought I had lost the only link to my lineage. Not that she would have ever confessed in public the truth we knew between us, she was the only true validation I had. She died, mercifully, peacefully at home in her sleep. She deserved to have no pain, no suffering, as I felt she had been living a life of pain and suffering having been shunned by the man she loved. How do I know there was love? I have the proof.

When it came time to go through her things, a process I don't wish on anyone, I came across a special box. Inside were dozens of letters written over the years from him. Words like 'darling' and 'lover' were sprinkled throughout and I knew they came from a place of mutual affection. To me that was proof enough that she had, in fact, suffered in silence, pining for a man she would never have.

While I knew my mother loved me, I often wonder in retrospect if I was not a constant reminder of what could have been and the realization of how things really were. I did not grow up rich or privileged and every gift; every treat, was an effort for my single mother. And yet she never made me feel that I was a burden or trouble. When my mother had me, girls of her time were shuttled off to homes or convents to live in the shadows of their shame, lucky if they ever saw the baby after birth and left with a life of wonderment as to how the adopted family raised their young child. Not my mother. She was of an age to chose, to live with the teasing and the ridicule in order to keep her child with her. And she did. He was not a part of the process.

In later years and even after my having been bestowed the title of Duke of Clarence, there has been no recognition—barely a conversation. Never has it been said that I may have half siblings, cousins, aunts, uncles or grandparents. I am in a family but without familial ties. That isn't what my mother wanted for me but she accepted the way it was. I do not.

When Mica closed his book the applause was deafening and a few of the women were dabbing the corners of their eyes to catch the tears before ruining their makeup. Mica was genuinely surprised by the reaction and made his way over to the table to begin signing copies. With each copy signed, Joey Chase snapped a photo of Mica with each guest.

"I wish I could write a book," Suzy Chambers said to Roger as she waited her turn.

"I wish you could read a book, dear," he muttered under his breath and escorted her to the table with Mica.

"I can't wait to tear through this, knowing the people we know," Marilyn Lassiter said to Ashley Beckwith as they stood in the queue.

Across the room, Barry Stegman had cornered Lance Novak and Anthony Wright who had been standing by the bar waiting to talk about the film rights. "I want the first look on an option. I am talking high six figures against seven for writing and executive producing titles. No one in town is going to offer you that but I will put my balls on the line with this one."

"Let's set up a meeting for this week," Lance returned.

ʌ ʌ ʌ

It wasn't exactly the suffered indignation of a perp walk. He had surrendered in his lawyer's office at Grimsby and Lloyd where the police picked him up from there. Still, he was handcuffed. Someone had either monitored the police frequency or tipped off the paparazzi but either way, they were there from the moment he stepped out of the car and made his way to the station building. This wasn't the publicity Freddy was hoping for.

Thomas Hopkins, Freddy's lawyer, followed close behind and deflected questions. But, there would be plenty more where they came from—after all, the Duke of Clarence is being charged with murder.

Inside, there was a whirlwind of activity. Freddy would be staying at least one night in a cell, solitary for his own safety—which was not something he was looking forward to—before his arraignment and bail hearing. He will inevitably make bail and be out for what could be months before there is a trial. But in those months, he will be a social pariah under indictment for rape and murder. There goes the season! And that may be worse than prison altogether.

After surrendering his watch, a ring, his wallet, shoelaces and belt, he was ushered downstairs, around some corridors and into a cell—a small grey box of a place with a cot attached to a wall, sink and a toilet. Stark is an understatement. It suddenly hit him. A place like this could be his home for the rest of his life. He started to sob.

After just a few minutes of self-indulgent crying, a time that felt like a lifetime, the door opened and in walked Thomas.

"We have to act quickly," Thomas cautioned. "They want you to be off balance with all of this in order to make a decision that will affect the rest of your life."

Freddie likes Thomas. He has a reassuring way about himself that makes you feel that you will be taken care of. Of course, he hired him because he is a shark. There wasn't much left of Lord Richard Marmouth's fortune after the divorce—a divorce for which Thomas advised. Then there was the scandalous acquittal of Sir Robert "Bobby" Longacre after the drunk driving hit and run that led to that poor girl's death. Not a day in prison. Freddy would gladly take the scandal and avoid the prison.

Moments later, two policemen entered the cell and ushered both Freddy and Thomas down the hall and into a nondescript room where Graham Nothrup was already sitting. Without waiting for either to settle, Graham began. "We warned you that you would need to stay silent. But you haven't. You gave an interview. That broke our agreement."

"I am sorry. Was there some sort of agreement?" Thomas shot back. "I would like to see the written copy of any agreement in which my client agreed to remain silent on the subject of his own life."

"Mr. Lloyd," Graham sighed. "Has your client briefed you on our previous meeting?"

"Yes."

"Than you understand what I am talking about. Can we move forward?" They both nodded. "Now, we have become aware that you are about to be stripped of your grace and favor apartment..."

"I what?" Freddy asked, blindsided by this news. "If they think that is going to keep me quiet, they won't."

"Opening your mouth is what got you into this situation," Graham pointed out. Thomas put his hand on Freddy's arm to calm him down.

"We will deal with the apartment issues," Thomas said calmly.

"But, I have the right to that apartment..."

"You have no rights anymore," Graham warned. "We both understand that you are being accused of first degree murder. We have the evidence, your DNA, your taped confession of aggressive sex and motive and opportunity. It doesn't look good for you."

"Are you testifying?" Thomas asked sternly. "Or just trying to be intimidating? Either way, you can stop the grandstanding."

"We have a compromise to offer," Graham said. "Leave the country...and don't come back."

"Cute," Freddy shot back. "You want me to disappear. I am the Duke of Clarence."

"You will either disappear to another country or into the system. It is going to be your choice. You will be convicted."

"He will be tried by a jury of his peers," Thomas corrected.

"A jury of his peers. Hardly. These will be ordinary people who will see nothing but a spoiled, entitled Duke trying to squirm his way out of taking responsibility for his actions."

"So what are you offering?" Freddy asked.

"Leave the country. You can keep the title but not the apartment. You will be handsomely compensated for your troubles. Just stay silent and leave the country."

"And go where?" Freddy looked puzzled.

∧ ∧ ∧

They decided to meet in Lance Novak's office, which threw Barry Stegman off his game a bit. Barry likes to negotiate in his own office where he feels empowered. But this was hardly a negotiation and more like a deal. Whether it was the alcohol speaking or the impassioned moment, Barry had thrown out a term that was immediately acceptable to everyone concerned. The meeting today is to put a number figure on the deal.

The deal was a simple one. Mica would receive a six-figure salary to write the screenplay of the book. And if it goes into production, he would get the remaining amount adding up to the seven-figures agreed upon.

"Six hundred thousand against one million one," Barry announced as if this was his best and final offer.

"We were thinking eight against a million eight," Anthony stood his ground.

Neither blinked. Mica said nothing but he could feel the sweat beads forming above his hairline. He didn't want to embarrass himself with flop sweat.

Lance cut the ice. "You have to understand something Barry. We are not putting this into the open market for an auction. Your opening bid would have surely been topped by now if we had. We are approaching this like we are selling not just to the highest bidder but getting the fair market value for Mica's work."

"With all due respect to Mica," Barry said as if Mica weren't in the room, "he is a unknown commodity in this world of film. I have to take that into consideration."

"He is not asking to direct," Anthony pointed out. "He is just doing what he does best—write and produce."

Barry blinked. "Seven fifty against one point six."

Eyes darted around the room with Mica's nearly pleading to take the deal.

"I believe we can work with that," Anthony said stoically.

"Work with that...fuck you," Barry joked. "If my wife didn't love this book so much, you would never have gotten me this high. Fuck you."

There was a collective laugh and a deep sigh from Mica.

Barry looked at Mica. "What's the matter kid? You've never been paid over a million dollars before? Did I break your million-dollar cherry? That calls for a drink, Novak."

Already thinking, Lance buzzed his assistant, who walked in with a tray of four flutes and a bottle of Dom Perignon. Lance eased the cork out with delicacy leaving the bottle to burp out the faintest of pops. "Quiet as a nun's fart," Barry observed inappropriately. As they raised a glass for a toast, a messenger entered the office.

"Mica Daly?"

"Yes."

He handed an envelope to Mica. "You've been served." With that the messenger turned on his heels and left.

"How did he know I am here?" Mica asked to no one in particular.

"Why does it matter?" Anthony answered.

Lance took the envelope and opened it. It is an injunction against the book. A similar injunction was currently being served to Ian Shepard across the city in the offices of *Gothcha!* magazine.

"An injunction? What does that mean?" Mica asked.

"It means you may not have a book," Lance said.

"And it means we may not have a deal," Barry punctuated.

Rise 'N Shine would never have flown him back in first class. Never. But thanks to a sharp eyed purser from first class who just so happened to be British and, moreover, a fan, Mica was moved up to the last empty seat behind the envied curtain.

"Remember that time you did all those stunts with Sean Jones. Well, my stomach was in my throat," she began with a tirade of anecdotes from segments gone by. She was not just a fan, but a super fan and Mica soon realized this bounce up to first class came with a price.

Mica wasn't sure what or how much to pack, as he wasn't sure how long he'd be in London. All he knew was that this was a Stuart Brewster command performance and he was to be there when told. Despite orders from the car's driver to head straight to the offices, Mica insisted on diverting to The Coliseum to check in, shower and freshen up. He knew the show was on the air anyway and there was no time to see Stuart when the show was going out.

He got to the office about 11:00 a.m. refreshed and ready, but perhaps not as ready as he should have been.

Stuart was sitting with his back to the door, looking out at the panoramic view his office afforded him and tapped his finger loudly. "Where the fuck have you been?" Tap, tap, tap.

"On a plane," Mica joked.

Still without turning to face Mica, he continued, "I mean between now and when the plane landed. I left specific instructions to get you here immediately."

"I went to the hotel to freshen up," Mica said nervously. Something ominous is in the air and it doesn't feel good. Tap, tap, tap.

"Is this just another of Mica Daly's ways of defiance?" Stuart spewed.

"I am not sure what you mean. But the answer about defiance is no."

"What I mean is this." Stuart finally turned and held up the *Gotcha!* magazine piece about Freddy and then slammed it down on his desk. "I specifically asked you...no told you...to drop it. And now this."

Mica wasn't ready for this onslaught and therefore had no rebuttal. "I am contracted..."

"You are contracted to ME, to *Rise 'N Shine*! At least you used to be."

"What?"

"You have a few more months left on your contract and I am willing to pay them out. But as of now, you are off the show."

"That is rather severe."

"Look, we are getting calls from rather important people and the Palace saying they won't work with us. Not while you are on the payroll. I have to do what is best for the show."

"You flew me all this way...to tell me *this!*"

"I felt that you were owed at least a face to face meeting."

"I am owed a lot."

"You are owed nothing. I gave you this platform and you pissed on it."

With nothing to lose, Mica decided he would not fade away. "Who do you think you are talking to? I am not some snot nosed kid you plucked out of obscurity and gave his first job to. I am a seasoned entertainment journalist who came to you with contacts and context. I gave you better than you ever expected and delivered ratings far surpassing what you thought you could achieve. Don't tell me I haven't earned my place here." Tap, tap, tap.

After a moments pause, Stuart spoke calmly and directly. "It was a good run. I'll give you that. But now it is over. And if you think you made yourself what you are today, you are right. You made the mess you are in. I don't want or need to take credit for that. Now you can get out."

"Really? It all comes down to this."

"You defied me and I can't have that." Stuart pronounced. Tap, tap, tap.

"I can't believe after all I gave to you...to this show..."

"Gave to me, to this show? That is a laugh. You've had your own agenda from the start—to be a star! Because you were washed up in America."

"How dare you," Mica growled.

"Everyone knows you fucked the wrong guy and then got fucked over for it."

"Is that what you think happened with Freddy?"

"First Chad Martin and now Freddy. Are you fucking Freddy? Because you are the only person I know who can fuck yourself to the bottom!"

"Fuck you. Let's talk specifically about Freddy and his story. It is an intriguing and journalistically sound story. If you had any journalistic balls you would have run with it instead of caving because of the threats of the very people we would have exposed."

"You and that supposed interview. There was nothing on those memory cards. You, the big journalist, were had. And now you are a loose canon."

"You let me write that book and now you are shoving it down my throat and choking me with it. You can't have it both ways."

"I am not having it both ways. That is why you are out." Tap, tap, tap. "And before that book can become an embarrassment for us. You are not going to sit in our chair knowing that book will force people to ask questions and, de facto, publicize the story. The show will inevitably be punished for it."

"What are you going to say to everyone who asks 'Where's Mica'? Are you going to tell them, he wrote a book, just like the rest of the anchor team have, but we fired Mica for it."

"No, a very nice statement will be issued stating that you wanted to spend more time in Los Angeles and that by mutual decision we decided to end this relationship. Don't for a minute think your fan base will save you," Stuart said rather coldly. "They will forget and move on soon enough." Tap, tap, tap.

ʌ ʌ ʌ

The irony of the location wasn't lost on Mica. The Ivy restaurant is where he had his first meeting with Stuart Brewster. And now he is having a lunch after being fired by him. It is Mica, the Owens gals and Andrea Lyttle for moral support.

"I told him when I was on the phone," Elizabeth began, "that I hope this little incident would not damage our long standing professional relationship."

"Little incident?" Mica shuttered. "I was just fired."

"Yes, but there are other clients like Andrea here who still work for *Rise 'N Shine*. We have to think of them as well."

"Yes, but can we think of me after lunch," Andrea said. Turning to Mica, "How are you doing?"

"Fine, I think," Mica said honestly. "Strangely I didn't see this coming. Now, after it is all said and done, I can see the trail. I was blinded by the book and didn't realize how personally Stuart was taking my moving forward with it."

"So what is going on?" Mica asked the Owens duo.

"What do you mean?" Angela asked.

"This poaching game. Now that I am free I can go anywhere."

"Ah, here in lies the rub," Elizabeth began. "You see the reason you were being poached was to steal you from the competition. Now that you are no longer the competition, there is nothing to steal. And I must say the book has not helped your cause. It seems that most likely everyone who was interested, won't be anymore."

"Really?" Mica said. "Everyone?"

"It seems so," Angela said.

"See that man over there?" Elizabeth discretely pointed over at a pin stripe suited man with gray hair.

"That's Gareth Chambers," Andrea said. "He's the executive producer for *A.M. Live.*"

"That's right and he is one of the men who was interested in poaching you.

And he hasn't acknowledged our presence," Elizabeth said. "We can and should go over and introduce you but I would say there is nothing on the table at this moment."

"So what you are saying," Mica conceded, "is that I am officially out of work."

"I am afraid so."

"Fuck the wine. I need a martini."

Epilogue

ica left Lance Novak's office and stopped for a coffee at the big gay coffee house on Santa Monica in West Hollywood. Lance had no news, which, de facto, is bad news. "They could tie this book up in litigation for months or years," he stated. All he had to show for all that work was a stack of hard copies he can't give away, a bottomed out career, the fall of a Duke and the death of an innocent. Despite the endless parade of sweaty hard bodies from the gym across the street, the big gay coffee house isn't cutting it.

He got back in the car and put the top down. The new car is a convertible and far more impractical for the situation in which he has now found himself. He bought it on the understanding that he had a movie deal—a big fat movie deal. And that too is on hold as they weigh their options over the book deal. Although impractical, the car somehow soothes Mica—the wind blowing or the sun beating down, at night with the smell of night blooming jasmine, a Los Angeles thing. It all works.

He pulled into his garage, walked around to the front of his building and there, sitting on the front step, is Ted. Mica's knees buckled. Ted still had that kind of hold on him despite his newly cultivated feelings for Lance. "What are you doing here?"

"A visit I guess...and an interview."

"Sorry, I am not giving interviews at the moment"

"Not you, me. I have a job interview in Long Beach with a petroleum company and, well, who knows." Ted stood and gave Mica a peck on the cheek.

"So you might move here?"

"No. The interview is here. The job is based in Africa."

"You never cease to surprise me. How long have you been waiting out here?"

"Not too long."

"And where are you staying?" Mica questioned as he put his key in the door.

"Funny you should ask that..."

"Ah..."

"It is only for a couple of days," Ted pleaded. "For old time sake."

"Old time sake!" Mica spat. "You lied to me and duped me."

"You're thinking of something specific?" Ted pondered aloud.

"You bet your ass I am. You gave me blank interview memory cards. I went to my boss with them. I put my reputation on the line with them. And they were blank! Damn you!"

"I couldn't let you run with the interview. We were using it to get Freddy. "

"Why didn't you tell me?"

"Why didn't I tell you a lot of things? That's who I was. That is why I left. That's why I couldn't be that man anymore." Ted stood and picked up his duffle bag. "I will get a hotel."

Mica just can't say no to Ted. "Come inside."

Once inside, Ted dropped his bag and kissed Mica hard on the mouth. Mica melted in his arms and then pulled away. "You're not allowed to do that anymore."

Mica poured them both a drink as Ted made himself comfortable on the couch. "So what is it like to be back and…"

"Unemployed?" Mica finished his thought as he handed a mid-afternoon vodka to Ted and then settled into the armchair to the left.

"I wasn't going to say that. But since you did."

"Freeing. I can't stay this way long, financially. But in the meantime, the word is freeing. I am certainly glad that my 'fame' or 'celebrity' happened over there and not here. So I don't have to hear people asking: what happened?"

"I get it."

"I should ask you what it is like to be unemployed."

"I don't even look back. I am too busy repairing relationships. As you put it, I spent my life as a liar…at least to family and friends." Mica sighed. "What? You have a question," Ted pushed.

"It is just that," Mica paused to collect his thoughts. "How do I even know you were a spy? There is no way to prove it. And what if everything you told me was just as you say, an elaborate lie?"

"You are right. There is no way to prove it unless I simply tell the truth. Go on, ask me anything."

Mica thought for a moment. "Who killed the valet, Ben Foster?"

"We did."

"How?"

"A syringe."

Mica sat for a moment choking back the bile rising in his throat.

"You have to remember," Ted began. "The plan was always to scare the Duke silent. We had a man follow them inside the spa. He knew they had rough sex, the

Duke had left the door open just a crack. We knew we could set him up for rape. The death was collateral damage."

"And the infamous cock ring? How did that get back to Freddy?"

"I sent it," Ted said. "The idea was that we wanted him to know that we could link him to the valet. But he just wouldn't shut up."

"You are going to have to tell all this to Ian Shepard. I want my reputation vindicated. I have been deemed a liar, an anti-monarchist and have been virtually run from the country. You owe this to me. Not to mention the Duke. You have to tell them that the book is correct."

"Again, you want me to commit treason."

"Yes. If that is what you want to call it."

ʌ ʌ ʌ

They ordered three very large martinis from the buff and shirtless bartender at The Cathedral. "You have to love Los Angeles weather. In the middle of the day, the outdoor patio is teeming and the bartenders are shirtless. It's a far cry from the damp of London."

"Cheers to that," Ted said, raising his glass and the three clinked rims.

"Oh, I meant to ask you," Ian said. "Have you heard from your friend Freddy lately?"

"No. Why?" Mica turned and asked.

"He is living in Australia now. Part of a plea bargain. They allowed him to leave the country as long as he never returned and never told his story. The alternative was prison for life for the murder of the valet."

Mica and Ted simply looked at each other.

"I tracked him down and offered him a pictorial of his new digs and fifty thousand dollars to do it. And he turned me down. Go figure. I guess when they said "no talking" he is taking it seriously this time. So what did you two want to talk about?"

"Ironically the death of the valet," Mica said.

"What about it?" Ian asked.

"I know who did it," Ted said.

There was a pregnant pause and then Ian spoke up. "Who?"

"We did."

"And you can prove that?"

"I was there," Ted declared.

"That is some good shit," Ian exclaimed. "Too bad we can't use it. Have you thought about selling it somewhere else?"

"Why can't you run with it?" Mica interjected.

231

"The magazine has gone cold on the whole thing. Even when I pitched THE DUKE DOWN UNDER, it was like pulling teeth. When he said no to an interview, it rippled through the magazine. They had decided that they had already spent too much on interviews and the book and that the story had been told and retold."

"Not this new information," Mica stated.

"You're right. And I suggest you take it to *The Guardian* or *The Mail on Sunday*. Or you sit on for a year and on the year anniversary we revisit. But right now, the story is a non-starter with us."

The three took sips from their respective drinks.

"For what it is worth," Ian said. "I would love to run with the story. And if you wouldn't mind, I would like to hear the details."

Ted began from the start.

∧ ∧ ∧

For three days, Mica drilled Ted on his side of the story, writing down every word so that if the book ever got released, he would have an update and a vindication. They laughed as they discussed who would play Ted in the movie. They settled on either Cary Elwes or Paul Bettany, as both are blond and lanky-ish. And they both agreed that Robert Downey Jr. is a shoo-in for the role of Freddy. Mica wouldn't take anyone less than Ben Affleck to play himself even though they look nothing alike.

And speaking of Freddy, on the second day of Ted's stay a post card arrived from Sydney. It simply said: You must come down under...not that 'down under'! Love, F. The timing was perfect.

The interview with the oil company went well and Ted had some tough decisions to make. It would be a fresh start in Africa—first stationed in Angola with an eventual promotion taking him down to Johannesburg.

On the way to the airport, the top is down. Motown oldies are playing on the radio. Without saying a word, Ted placed his hand in Mica's. As they approached the airport and pulled into the unloading section, Ted spoke first.

"I don't think I am ever going to see you again, am I?"

"No, I don't think so," Mica said coldly and with distance hiding his emotions. "You have a new life and I am too much a part of the old. And you for me. I too need to close for my own good. I have to move on." He had already tried to shut the door but was having a hard time. He let one tear drop.

They kissed a long and passionate kiss and then Ted stepped out of the car. Without saying another word, Mica pulled away from the curb, looked in the rearview window and returned Ted's wave. And it was over.

∧ ∧ ∧

Freddy sat at a table for one, just on the edge of the sand, at Doyles in Watson's Bay in Sydney—half a world away from the Palace. He is wearing a pair of board shorts, a tank top, and Wayfarer sunglasses. He is tanned and the sun has bleached his hair that would have long since been cut into an appropriate style back in London. But this shaggy new hair style suited him and his casual new lifestyle. He lets his bare feet dig in the sand as he waits for a local delicacy, kangaroo steak.

The headlines came and went. THE DUKE DEPARTS FOR DOWN UNDER. A PLEA TO FLEE. THE DUKE OF CLARENCE LETS GO OF HIS PALACE SQUAT. Only one paper took it fairly seriously with the banner: A PERSON OF INTEREST GOES FREE. The article went on to point out that he was up for murder charges that everyone associated with the case says would stick and yet the Duke got the privilege he always sought in being allowed to plea for his freedom.

The bottom line behind closed doors with the plea bargain is that no one wanted it. They simply felt they had no choice because no one thought sending him to jail would shut him up. He would have nothing to lose siting in prison for life. If he were offered something he could lose, such as a new life in Australia, perhaps he'd finally stay silent. So far it has worked.

He lives in relative anonymity and that is new and refreshing for him. He doesn't have to carry on the pretense and he can, as he puts it, "exhale." He frequents the gay bars but not the society pages. Occasionally, he takes in the rare horse race or polo match by purchasing a ticket and goes by the name Freddy Clarence.

With his settlement from the 'family'—oh yes, there was a settlement—he was able to purchase a modest but ultra-modern condo in a high rise overlooking Darling Harbor.

As far as that infamous cock ring. The police gave it back. Freddy brought it to his favorite jeweler at Asprey and had it stretched into a bracelet. He wears it and thinks of Ben.

ʌ ʌ ʌ

Mica hadn't told anyone he was in town. He was not there to socialize. He wasn't back for meetings. He didn't even stay in The Coliseum. He arrived in town, rented a car and headed for a tiny village just outside of Plymouth. It is beautiful countryside and must have been a wondrous place to grow up.

Like most small villages in England, finding the church wasn't difficult—it was always the most commanding of buildings in the village. Finding one head-stone was going to be the difficult part. He knew it was here because during the height of the news coverage, Ben Foster's parents were pictured kneeling some-

233

where in this yard. The rows weren't uniform and the layout haphazard but Mica was determined. He ruled out the overgrown section and moved over to the more manicured, freshly turned plots. And there it was. A simple stone with his name, birthdate and, of course, death date.

Mica knelt down and said a prayer. Not that he is particularly religious; he simply felt that Ben deserved at least a prayer. And then he began to speak.

"Ben. You don't know me but I am sure if things had turned out differently we would have met eventually. I am a friend of Freddy's and I wrote his story. First, let me tell you how sorry I am that I became part of this story telling odyssey. Perhaps if I hadn't shown such interest in the first place, it would not have disturbed a political hornet's nest and you would be alive today. I have to believe that I am culpable in some way to you not being here. And again, I am sorry.

Second, I would like to say on behalf of Freddy how much he cared about you. I know he is self-centered and I doubt has been here to pay his respects but, nonetheless, he loved you in his own way and a person should never meet their end without knowing they were loved, genuinely loved, when they were here.

And last, I have something for you."

Mica reached into the satchel he had over his shoulder and pulled out one of the rare copies of the book. He laid it down on the ground, fanned open the pages and doused the book with lighter fluid. With a quick strike of a matchstick, he set the book alight and sat there and watched it burn.

"Ashes to ashes as they say," Mica stated and then apologized again. "It was all for this. And in the end this never happened. You lost your life for nothing. Ashes to ashes."

www.ingramcontent.com/pod-product-compliance
Lightning Source LLC
Chambersburg PA
CBHW032009050726
47590CB00006B/2105